Bruised Hibiscus

A Novel

Elizabeth Nunez

Seal Press

Copyright © 2000 by Elizabeth Nunez

Cover design by Trina Stahl
Cover painting by Anni Adkins / Ahha! Art
Text design by Alison Rogalsky

Excerpt from "Laventille (for V. S. Naipaul)" from *Collected Poems 1948–1984* by Derek Walcott (originally published under the title "Laventville" in *The Castaway and Other Poems).* Copyright 1986 by Derek Walcott. Reprinted with permission of Farrar, Straus and Giroux, LLC.

Excerpt from "Why Are Writers Always the Last to Know?" by Breyten Breytenbach reprinted with permission of Breyten Breytenbach.

Library of Congress Cataloging-in-Publication Data

Nunez, Elizabeth.
   Bruised hibiscus : a novel / Elizabeth Nunez
   ISBN 1-58005-036-0
      1. Women—Trinidad and Tobago—History—20th century—Fiction
      2. Friendship—Trinidad and Tobago—Fiction. I. Title

PS3564.U48 B78 2000   813'.54—dc21   99-086362

Printed in the United States of America

First printing, March 2000

10   9   8   7   6   5   4   3   2   1

Distributed to the trade by Publishers Group West
In Canada: Publishers Group West, Toronto, Ontario
In the U.K. and Europe: Airlift Book Distributors, Middlesex, England
In Australia: Banyan Tree Book Distributors, Kent Town, South Australia

For my mother, Una Magdalena Arneaud Nunez, and her other daughters: Yolande Nunez Aqui, Jacqueline Nunez Astaphan, Mary Nunez Kerry, Karen Nunez Tesheira, and Judith Nunez Viera. And for my father, Waldo Everett Nunez, who loves us all.

Acknowledgements

I thank my agent, Ivy Fischer Stone, and my editor at Seal Press, Faith Conlon, for their faith in my work; Shirley Melzer for giving me the courage to face the pain that had to be remembered; DorisJean Austin, Arthur Flowers, Anne-Marie Stewart, Beena Kamlani, Erica Mapp, and Kiana Davenport for guiding me through multiple revisions of this novel; Malaika Adero for her wisdom and courage; and, finally, these three: Mary Nunez (who could have a more loyal sister?); Francis Carling (who could better remind me of the pleasures of the past?); Jason Harrell (who could better light up a mother's life?).

We left
somewhere a life we never found,

customs and gods that are not born again,
some crib, some grill of light
clanged shut on us in bondage, and withheld

us from that world below us and beyond,
and in its swaddling cerements we're still bound.

Derek Walcott, "Laventille (for V. S. Naipaul)"

Nobody said that suffering leads to wisdom, or tolerance. But not being
able to express terror leads to new permutations of terror.

Breyten Breytenbach

Bruised Hibiscus

⋘ Chapter 1 ⋙

It didn't take long for the news to beat through the bamboo and the mangrove bush off the shore from Freeman's Bay in Otahiti, to spread like wildfire once the fisherman, his brown skin turned tar black by the sun, and leathered by the salt in the wind and sea, staggered into the Oropouche Police Station. Terror made him incontinent: When the constable stopped him, urine ran down the legs of his tattered red shorts and splashed on the concrete floor, sprinkling the constable's trousers like holy water from a priest's Benediction.

The fisherman seemed hardly aware of what he had done. He wriggled his toes, but his eyes remained glazed, his jaw dropping and closing as if he would speak but couldn't, his mind still frozen on a strange mass he had seen in the soft dawn—a brown lump—gently ebbing and flowing with the white froth on the edge of a crystal clear blue sea, buoyed by hollow clumps of pale yellow bamboo splattered with slivers of green sea reed and the gleaming wet olive of wide sea-almond leaves.

A burlap bag stuffed with the husks of dried coconuts, the fisherman thought, dragged offshore by the previous night's stormy ravage of the sea in the mangrove, until he drew near. Squinting in the pristine light of the early morning sun, he saw the rounded bulk that had spilled out from the top of the bag take shape, and he recoiled from the horror of it.

The constable, an irascible man, would have drawn his stick viciously across the fisherman's back the second his eyes fell on the urine, steaming and stinking, curling along his spotless floor, had he not caught in the fisherman's eyes the glassy glint of pure terror he had witnessed only twice before and never forgotten. As it was, he called for a chair and a glass of water for the fisherman, and waited until the words came. Then he ordered his men to tell no one what they had heard, put on his hat and went with the fisherman to Freeman's Bay.

Such was Trinidad in 1954, and is still now, that the constable's strictures were a guarantee that the world would know—Trinidad world. So that by the time the constable reached Freeman's Bay, a tight knot of bodies had already formed around the mass the fisherman had found, and the constable had to break through it before he could see what had so engaged them. When the church bells rang for the Angelus that evening, the details of the fisherman's discovery, embellished by a hundred imaginations, had already passed far out of the village of Otahiti to the capital in the north, travelling rapidly through the towns and villages between Otahiti and Port-of-Spain without the aid of telephone, television, radio or newspaper.

For though in 1954, the British colony of Trinidad had telephone, radio and newspaper (to have television also was asking too much then of the mother country), only the colonists and a favored few had telephones; nevertheless, they did not trust them, and there was only one radio station, Radio Trinidad, and one newspaper, *The Trinidad Guardian.* In the case of *The Guardian,* it would have been necessary to wait until the next day for the news because the lone morning edition was already out, but the station had no such excuse except for the interruption of middle-class dreams: "Portia Faces Life," "Second Spring"—the serialized romantic adventures of the British that took precedence over what a poor and illiterate fisherman saw in the little country village of Otahiti on the edge of Freeman's Bay. But there was an intricate network of people who could be counted on—men's women, women's men, husbands, wives, mothers, fathers, daughters, sons, brothers, sisters, aunts, uncles, friends—who passed the word from mouth to mouth as they thought they should; news too sensational, too shocking to keep to themselves, news it was their duty to share. So that two women who lived twenty miles apart would hear it—one in the stifling gloaming of a grocery shop in the heart of Port-of-Spain; the other in the bright, breezy dining room of a tiny two-story house in Tacarigua across the wide expanse of the Orange Grove sugar cane estate.

Two women who played with each other as children and had long forgotten those times or that they were ever children, would feel the sudden panic of self-discovery, a rapid quickening of their heartbeats, the moment their husbands gave motive and reason for the appearance of the unspeakable mass the fisherman had seen. Two women, who had long ago witnessed behind a hibiscus bush a scene so brutal, so dehumanizing that they lost all innocence, though at the time they were just twelve, would, a day after hearing the news, each resolve separately to make the pilgrimage up the Laventille hills to the shrine of Our Lady of Fatima. Frightened into irrational guilt by a thought insidious and sinful that had entered their consciousness without their willing it, they felt a desperate need for absolution: a miracle of Fatima to purify them, to restore them to the numb passivity they had long grown accustomed to before the seed that had been lying dormant in their souls for years was catapulted from its protective encasement by their husbands' impassioned reaction to the fisherman's discovery.

What the fisherman found that morning was gruesome enough. Gory. Not because of what it was now but what it once had been. For the shape the fisherman had recognized tangled between the bamboo and the sea reed, rolling idly with the quiet waves, was the head of a corpse, still too fresh to have begun to decompose. A woman's head, her face protruding from the brown burlap coconut bag, gnawed open perhaps by the very fish that had nibbled away her eyes, lips and tongue, before trying to make their way past the stranglehold of the cord that secured the rest of the body hidden in the bag. A sight revolting in itself, but more so for what it had been. Enough for no one to question the story that, before the fisherman became incontinent over the station floor—though they now said urine was not all he released from between his legs—he had vomited his breakfast on the bamboo-strewn sand.

People took bets on what the fisherman had eaten that morning,

5

divining meaning from the scraps of half-digested food they claimed to have found, needing to put their world in order, to give context to the relics of the senseless horror left for them to interpret. The fish bones they said they found in the vomit foretold punishment due to the fisherman for an obscenity he had committed against the sea—the dolphin he had mangled with a metal hook, or the school of baby fish he had torn to shreds with the rusty propeller of his boat engine. Not that they blamed the fisherman for the horror he had found, but, rather, that they needed to attach some cosmic significance to the one who was chosen to see it first.

He could never be the same again, they said. And they were right, for the head had been the head of no ordinary woman—which would have been horrible enough—but the head of a white woman; the kind of woman who, to the eyes of the villagers, seemed mystically protected, unaffected by the taint of poverty, sickness, or the everyday tide of calamities taken as a way of life in Otahiti; protected certainly from the vulgarity of violence. The kind of woman who seemed hardly human, or rather, more than human: the wife of an overseer, the woman glimpsed smiling in the breeze of a passing car; or a tourist, shaded under a broad-brimmed hat and dark glasses, sipping lemonade in the sun, throwing coins to children as if money did not matter. To see one now, dead, a lump of flesh, rotting, corbeaux screeching, ready to pounce from between the rusty edges of wind-torn sea-almond leaves, there must be meaning. There must be something terrible about to happen.

So Zuela thought, though she had not seen the vultures, but she saw the Chinaman spit on the ground and heard the malice in his voice when he silenced the talk in the shop that night about a white woman stuffed in a brown burlap coconut bag and dumped in the sea in Otahiti. Later, Rosa, the other of those two women who played together as children but who no longer remembered each other, or that they had ever been children, would herself be confronted with the shocking details.

Zuela was told the news as she was bending over the flour bag on the wooden floor in the rundown grocery shop in Nelson Street, scooping out the last pound of the thirty pounds of flour she had weighed that day on the rusty scale on the counter, some in parcels of a quarter-pound, some in half-pounds, her breasts pressed against her belly, which was swollen as if she were expecting her eleventh child, which she was not; twenty-nine now, she had already had ten. At least fifty times she had bent over that belly for the flour, more times for the sugar and rice, pouring carefully on the brown paper on the scale so that not a speck would escape, not a grain; weighing carefully on the scale so that not an ounce was oversold, all the time knowing that wherever he was, the Chinaman was keeping his eyes on her.

It was the woman who came to buy the flour who told her.

"Eh, Miss Zuela, you didn't hear the news? They find a white lady in a bag in the sea in Otahiti. Dead, dead so. Fish eat out she eye and half she face. They say somebody strangle she and stuff she in the bag."

Zuela, pushing back the strands of her heavy, straight, long black hair that had fallen across her face when she bent to the flour, saw the Chinaman's fingers stop in the middle of the metal pole of his counting board. Saw his fingers clutch the yellow bead in the middle of the metal pole, but he didn't look at the woman, the last of the customers that night, or at the ragged band of men who still lurked by the doorway. Always. Every night, even after he had chased them away. Yet she felt him listening, though his eyes did not leave the counting board and his lips stayed still.

"You think is Boysie?" the woman pressed.

Zuela saw the Chinaman lift an eyebrow, but that was all. His eyes remained on the counting board.

"Is not Boysie that do everything." The voice came from a man who had unhinged himself from the clump of smirking young men in old men's rags, bellies rounded from the abuse of alcohol, and eyes that had lost their capacity to express any emotion except derision, their mirthless laughter always ready to disavow the serious, to diminish the beautiful. These were men prematurely forged into cynics by deprivation and failure, or rather, by the loss of faith in the possibility of the reversal of their misfortunes; men who, having nowhere to go, sought to build colonies of their kind if only through the debasement of others.

"Well, I watching what I doing from now on. Boysie ent go get my heart." The woman took the paper package from Zuela and clutched it to her bosom. She was not much older than twenty-five, though it was difficult to tell. Desire in her eyes, a hunger for excitement that sometimes made them wide and shiny, would at times give her age away. But her body had long lost its youthful softness. Her limbs were long and wiry. Her skin was tough and dry.

"Boysie have no uses for the likes of you." The man curled his lips and sneered at her. "If is heart he want, he looking for young heart, or white woman heart."

The woman lurched to strike him, but at that moment the Chinaman coughed, a deep, raucous sound that seemed to explode in the middle of his chest and thunder up his windpipe. His body shook with the force of the cataclysmic waves. His face turned pink, then purple, and his veins stood out on his forehead like a maze of wires inside some tiny electrical machine. No one moved or said anything. In seconds, the coughing stopped and then the Chinaman cleared his throat and spat out on the ground.

"Boysie ent no damn fool. You don't know him." And looking directly at Zuela, he snarled, his voice hoarse from coughing, "That have man-woman business in it."

It was then that the germ lodged in Zuela's soul broke loose and sprouted roots.

The young men in old men's rags, frightened not by what Zuela saw in the Chinaman's eyes, but by something more immediate—the familiar way he spoke of Boysie, confirming a friendship between them they had long suspected—edged out of the doorway, the woman behind them. And a breeze blew across the Port-of-Spain harbor up Nelson Street, reeking of rotting fruit and the putrid remains of animals slaughtered there for the market, yet it was still refreshing. The breeze lifted the heat of day that lingered about the piles of stinking garbage mauled apart by starving dogs, their rib cages etched against hairless skin, thin legs infested with sores. It fanned the stench of urine and excrement rising from open canals, and swirled umbrellas of dirty newspaper and rancid-smelling wrappings of food discarded with decaying peels of fruit and vegetables all along the broken pavements. The cool and quiet of Nelson Street after a sultry market day were broken now by the footsteps of a woman running from the Chinaman's shop and the nervous laughter of three men, and then the shout of one when he was at a safe distance from the Chinaman, "You better run. Chinaman tell Boysie what you say."

When he'd gone into the rainforest in Venezuela looking for alpagats to sell in his store, the Chinaman found Zuela, too, and had taken her for himself. Some said that it was Boysie Singh who'd led him there, not just that one time to buy alpagats and to bargain for Zuela, too, but every month, ferrying him in his boat through the treacherous Bocas up the Orinoco River. They said that at night Boysie Singh used to take a boatload of Trinidadians there. Criminals like himself, except Boysie couldn't be officially called a real criminal since nobody, not even Justice Vincent-Brown, could get a really big crime to stick to him. But Boysie did favors for friends of his friends who went in too deep with the Americans. *Rum and Coca-Cola. Waiting for the Yankee dollar.* The quick dollar to be made on the black market after the war while the Yankees were partying in the base in Chaguaramas. Women selling for five dollars an hour and rum like water. Drugs, too, if that was what Americans wanted. And a killing or two over racehorses. Boysie would smuggle bandits into Venezuela without papers, making a laughingstock of the police.

They took all the cash they could carry—these outlaws—and jewels, too. Nor was there any possibility of return to Trinidad, two facts that warmed them to Boysie. Past the Dragon's Mouth—the Bocas, swirling currents between Monos, Huevos and Chacacharacare that almost swallowed the Santa Maria and made Columbus drop to his knees before the trinity of mountain peaks rising over the land in Trinidad— Boysie poured drinks. Then, when the sea was smooth and calm again, and rum had loosened tongues and chased away the fear of the dragon's teeth, he set upon his customers with his knife. Stabbed them to death, they said, and cut out their hearts for racehorses. Some said, to feed them; others said, to rub on the hooves of racehorses to make them run fast. Or so the woman who came to buy flour in the Chinaman's shop believed, and she told Zuela about the corpse of the white woman floating in the sea between the bamboo and the sea reed in Freeman's Bay in Otahiti.

The more sophisticated knew that racehorses were not the only reason why Boysie took his prey to Venezuela. There was the prize of money and jewels. Sometimes more than three thousand dollars' worth in one night's trip. Quick, safe and easy. Except if the corpse floated on shore. Except if the corpse broke loose from its anchor. Like the corpse of that white woman in Otahiti and the body of the man they said Boysie had killed, for which Justice Vincent-Brown convicted him but he couldn't get the death sentence to hold, though they kept Boysie on Death Row for weeks before they were forced to release him.

The young men in old men's rags saw the Chinaman leave the shop, go to Venezuela and come back, safe and sound, tens of times, bringing back alpagats and saltfish for his shop in Nelson Street. And once, Zuela, too. They weren't deceived by his man-woman business answer. The corpse the fisherman found was the corpse of a murdered woman, murdered like that man Justice Vincent-Brown said Boysie had butchered and tried to bury in the sea by tying it to a thick rope attached to a heavy piece of iron. Still, the body floated to the surface. Foiled one more time and in Otahiti. It had to be Boysie. The Chinaman was protecting his navigator. Money, jewels, and dead people's hearts (this time a white woman's heart) making Boysie's racehorses win races in Arima.

But they were wrong, Zuela thought. Not this time. She had heard the malice. She understood the man-woman business that could get a woman, even a white woman, stuffed into a coconut bag and dumped in Freeman's Bay in Otahiti for fish to gouge out her eyes and feast in her mouth. She understood the man-woman business that could make even a woman (provided she had the strength of a man) stuff a man into a coconut burlap bag and dump him in Freeman's Bay in Otahiti so the fish could swallow his balls and chew up his cock.

She had never thought of murder. The seed the Chinaman jarred out of its quiet place was not bred out of thoughts of murder. Of death, yes, but not of brutality. Of wishing he would no longer be there to torment her. But then, at that moment when the slits that were his eyes narrowed to a sliver of black light, and spit jettisoned from between his teeth, stained from years of tobacco smoke and much, much more, she conceived it: his murder. The Chinaman's murder. Man-woman business.

≪ Chapter 2 ≫

On the outskirts of Port-of-Spain going south, and then farther inland to the east, the cool salt wind that blew off the Gulf of Paria across the filth of Nelson Street turned fresh and took on the odor of the candy-sweet stalks of sugar cane that were planted across most of the low-lying areas in Trinidad. The wind blew past the Croisée, with its stench of rotting fish, past where sailors took prostitutes in the narrow crevices between the dilapidated buildings and warehouses bursting with bags of sugar and cocoa, stacked to the roofs, squeezed against banks with names like Barclays of London and Chase Manhattan. The wind swirled dirty paper and dried animal droppings off the pavements in Nelson Street and then raced through the La Basse, chasing after children fighting corbeaux for scraps of food in the piles of garbage on the sea side of the Churchill-Roosevelt Highway, opposite Shanty Town, that spilled out of the foothills like an infectious disease spreading sores—cardboard shacks. Eyesores, the ladies in Goodwood Park called them, with yesterday's newspaper and the bright colors of last Sunday's comics plastered like paint on their outsides, a few lengths of rusty galvanized roof on their tops to ward off the rain.

Now buffeting the Churchill-Roosevelt, through the cane fields, toward the Caroni River, the wind was beginning to lose its salt-sea smell and the mango-sweet stench of the garbage from the La Basse. It crossed the zigzag of ditches dug patiently, then frantically, by East Indians who kept believing they could lick the power of the thunderstorms—or that their gods could—the inevitable thunderstorms that each year ruptured the banks of the Caroni, flooding the rice paddies, even the meticulous rows of tomatoes, cabbage and eggplant they had planted safely (so they thought) near the edge of the highway.

Now in the rapid descent of nightfall, the sun slipping into the horizon as if it had no energy left to linger, the wind curled softly around palm-roofed mud huts, picking up the stink of manure, to be sure, but also the pungent odor of curry and dahl from black cast-iron pots and the rich, earthy smell of the land. At San Juan, it fought with the sudden flurry of cars swirling around the roundabout: to the right, then straight, or to the left, then straight, or round and round. A tiny town, no competition for Port-of-Spain, San Juan nevertheless had its markets and its shops, too, and its share of crime (Boysie Singh was reputed to have two women there, and scores of boys in training to follow in his footsteps). The wind breezed past it in minutes, rolled lazily over the wide-open plains toward Tacarigua on the edge of the Orange Grove sugar-cane estate, blew out the thin white curtains in the dining room of Rosa DesVignes' pretty house and fanned the fire on the stove in her kitchen so that she had to shut the window tight, but not before Cedric heard it bang.

"You didn't latch the window, Rosa?"

That night was a night like any other night when Rosa anxiously tasted the food still in pots on the stove, hoping the pinch of salt or pepper she added was just right. That what she cooked would please her husband, Cedric. Except that night, her anxiety turned to fear as she felt the seed loosen in her breast where it was buried, a seed like Zuela's. Because before the window banged and the fire on the stove flared and Cedric shouted, he had walked unexpectedly into the kitchen, caught her with the salt in one hand and the spoon to her lips, said not a word about her cooking, which she was braced to hear, but cool as ice water, not facing her directly, he gave her the news that had spread up north that night, news of a white woman stuffed in a burlap coconut bag in

Otahiti, her eyes and lips and tongue eaten by fish, her body dumped between the bamboo and the sea reed in Freeman's Bay, corbeaux circling to finish her off.

"Bet they all think is Boysie. But that has no signs of Boysie. Crime passionel," he said, pleased with the sounds of his words. He was studying French, ancient Greek and Latin. "A man caught his woman *in flagrante delicto*. And then CRACK . . . "

The word cut across the room. Ugly. Like the brittle sound of a centipede's back snapping.

Rosa jumped. The next moment she was grateful for the wind that had left Nelson Street and blown through the cane fields, banging shut the kitchen windows, so hard that they sprang open and struck the walls again, making their own echoes. For Cedric didn't see the blood rush from Rosa's face, and later, at dinner, when she brought his food to him in the dining room and he repeated *flagrante delicto,* knowing well enough she knew no Latin, she had time to control the color in her face again, but not the pain in her head.

Her temples throbbed; sharp pins stabbed her eyes. *Flagrante delicto.* Even if she were not certain of the words, she understood the meaning. *Caught his woman.* She had seen that smile on Cedric's face many times. She knew that smile, the wet smile he wore only on his lips, the smile that never touched his eyes. It was a camouflage she had long learned to recognize: He wanted to be considered cultured and educated, because he thought it would hide the pictures he had in his heart. But she saw them, and pain flared across her forehead when suddenly they reflected the very images that came to her in the kitchen the moment he told her of the white woman in Otahiti, a cord around her throat, her eyes, lips and tongue gouged out by fish. She saw the images as in a mirror, but in reverse, so that where he saw woman, she saw man. Now she put her hand to her forehead to push them away, feeling too late Cedric's eyes on her.

"What's the matter, Rosa? Sick again?"

"No. No." She answered him quickly.

"Headache again?" He didn't look up from his plate.

"No."

13

"Then what?"

"What you said."

"About the woman in Otahiti?" He glanced at her with feigned concern. *"That* bothers you?"

"It's so sad."

"Sad?"

"That she was murdered."

"Didn't you hear me, Rosa? In the kitchen? I said, *flagrante delicto.* In the very moment. In the act. You understand *that,* Rosa? In the very act. *In flagrante delicto.*"

"I mean, to murder her like that."

"Like what?"

"To put her in a bag and dump her in the sea."

Cedric put down his knife and fork, dug his elbows into the table, arched his hands above them, and looked steadily at her. It was a look she had seen many times, in the last year more than she could bear. The first time he had stared at her like that, he told her why. He had married a white woman, he said. Like a fool, he had married a white woman. At another time he spoke of her eyes. "Like cubes of frozen iced tea," he said. "But your skin, not your skin. It gives you away." He told her that the sun had burned it so brown, it betrayed her. Let English people know that she lived here, not there; that she belonged here, not there, though there had been ancestors there once in the blinding white.

Now he spoke slowly, looking compulsively at the white spot that had begun to form on her lower lip where she had bitten it, watching the blood drain slowly into the corners of her mouth. "When a woman forgets . . . Thinks she can go out and take it somewhere else . . . When a woman betrays . . . You understand me, Rosa? A man has no choice. And if he catches her *in flagrante delicto* . . . " He paused, still studying her lips. "Such a man cannot be held responsible. It's a *crime passionel.*" He savored the words. "A crime of passion that even the courts understand." He shifted his eyes to hers.

Rosa's lips trembled. "But it could have been Boysie," she said.

Cedric trained his eyes on her.

"He did it before. Don't you remember?" She looked away. "Don't

14

you remember the body that floated out of the sea near the Yacht Club?"

"No one could prove it was Boysie."

"Well, it was possible. Justice Vincent-Brown said . . . "

"He didn't say *that,* Rosa."

"He said . . . "

"Not *that,* Rosa."

"He convicted him."

"Yes."

"And people said Boysie took out the man's heart."

"Not true."

"They say Boysie does that all the time. Cuts out people's hearts and rubs them on the hooves of his horses. You know, to make them run faster. This woman could be another one, Cedric. Like that man in the water at the Yacht Club."

"I warn you, Rosa, that man's heart was not missing."

"The judge said . . . "

"His heart was still in his body."

"He said . . . People say . . . "

"Shut up!" Cedric brought his fist down hard on the table.

Rosa felt tears gathering in her eyes, but still she persisted, her voice shaking. "Maybe he didn't get a chance . . . Maybe someone caught Boysie before he could take out the heart."

Frowns rolled like wavelets on Cedric's forehead. They gained speed, and then as they were on the verge of crashing, they suddenly grew calm, retreated and disappeared. Cedric threw back his head and laughed: "That's what I like about you Trinidad white people. You believe in more foolishness and superstition than colored people themselves. You believe in soucouyant and la jablesse and duene. Long after black people stop believing in foolishness like that, you Trinidadian white people still holding on. So you think Boysie's using human hearts on his racehorses? It would take people like you to believe that. Boysie must think you're real fools."

Behind her eyes it ached, and Rosa pressed her thumbs against the sides of her head.

Cedric leaned forward toward her. "You can't again tonight?" he asked. "Headache?"

She shook her head. "No, no. I'll clear the kitchen."

"Because last night . . . "

"I'm fine."

"Look, just get that Boysie nonsense from your head."

"It's okay, Cedric."

He paused, and without looking at her, he asked, "Shall I go to the study now or later?" But he didn't wait for her answer. He brought his knife and fork together in the middle of his plate and stood up. Then he surprised her, saying, "The dinner was good tonight, Rosa."

When he left, she surrendered to the tears that pricked the corners of her eyes. She knew what he wanted, what he meant by his *in flagrante delicto,* looking steadily at her mouth. By his question: *You can't again, tonight?* His tone was caustic. Mordant. It seemed a lifetime but it was only three years ago when he didn't have to ask, when she couldn't wait until he came back out of the study. There, with the dishes still spread on the table, she would look across at him and he would know. He would take her then, sometimes on his chair, pulling her legs astride his lap. He would wait only for her to unbuckle his pants and slip them down his thighs. Sometimes he would screw her on the hard floor, and later she would have to pull slivers of wood out of her backside. She knew always to close the windows before dinner and draw the curtains, but when one day she stopped doing that, when one day she removed the drapes and left only the sheers, when she suddenly stopped sending him signals that her body was on fire for him, it did not seem to matter to him whether they made love before and after he went to his study, or only after, except on nights like that one, when the wind banged the window against the wall and then blew it shut again and the noise brought him early to the kitchen.

How had she reached that moment when the thought of waiting for him in their bed until he was finished with his books brought tears to her eyes? When now she took as long as she could in the kitchen, and bathing before she went to bed was painful, washing the places he would touch?

She had wanted him from the beginning. Not that she had known much about him, or had cared to. It was his body she had desired. She had wanted sex, had been desperate for sex, and he had found her out.

Twenty-eight, the last of three sisters and still unmarried, she had been living in a residential camp on the Orange Grove sugar-cane estate in the somnolent languor of a vanishing decadence. Yellow pawpaws like the swollen udders of cows hung heavy, plump and overripe in bunches from the tops of long slim trees in backyards. Avocados were left to rot in the sun, their pale yellow flesh slimy and slithery, turning black and hard in the burning heat. Mangoes were squashed about lawns, their hairy seeds and bright yellow pulp mashed into the wet green grass. Experiments with flowers were abandoned out of boredom and excess. Hibiscus forced to be roses ran rampant, the elegant simplicity of their single-layered petals curled into ruffles resembling a French petticoat. Poinsettia, once wild, tall and wiry, now tamed, short and stumpy, were threatened into extinction by the thorny grip of bougainvillea that had defied a determination to train them into fences. Now bougainvillea scaled walls like ivy, and poinsettia bloomed way before Christmas.

Years ago they had cut down the big trees on the Orange Grove estate: the wide-trunked samaan, the spreading immortelle. They had needed the space, they explained, for a clubhouse for the women to amuse themselves with bid whist and bingo, a distraction while their men fucked the natives; later, for a gathering place where the men could brag over Scotch, thin cue sticks clenched between closed fists to stab little colored balls across green-grass carpeted tables.

For in those days, when Rosa was a young girl, sugar cane was king and no one in Trinidad dreamed there could come a time when Europe would sweeten its chocolate with beet. So Orange Grove bloomed. Its future was its present, it thought, and it splurged, believing that children loved to live in shanty towns and chase vultures, and that cane cutters were happy with ten cents a day and yesterday's newspapers plastered on their walls.

But it was not long after the war when signs were everywhere that Orange Grove had miscalculated. There was talk of the English bailing out, of colonies becoming a drain on His Majesty's Exchequer: Sugar could be produced cheaper and faster in the big countries. Frantic, Orange Grove sent its children to England for mates. If nothing else, it would secure Trinidad's white blood for its progeny. But many returned. They discovered that they could not explain to their English mates why they threw salt behind their backs and crossed themselves, or why they cut loose strands of their hair from combs and brushes and threw them in the fire. Or why they couldn't stop.

Rosa's mother sent both her sisters to England to find husbands, and when their marriages failed, she found white men for them in Trinidad. But she had not sent Rosa to England; she had not searched for white men in Trinidad for her to marry. She held her behind closed doors.

"She love you too much," the black woman who cleaned their house used to say to her. "She think you too good to give away."

Another woman had said the same thing, a woman with a butterfly on her face and a name that was both a first name and a surname: Mary Christophe. She said it when Rosa's mother left for England the second time, and Rosa asked, "Will she take me away there, too?"

"No," Mary Christophe answered. "You belong here. You one of us. She knows that. She won't take you away. *You too good to give away.*"

Yet when Cedric came, his hat in one hand, his books in the other, her mother said, "Yes. Yes, you can marry her," maybe because by then she had become an embarrassment. For in an age when women were wives before they were twenty-one, she was already an old maid, one whose habit of withdrawal was causing gossip about an unnatural woman who didn't like men—one of the zamies, *les amies,* who walked arm in arm down the main streets in Trinidad, uncaring of the scandal they caused. Yet this was not reason enough to explain why, after so many years of claiming there was no one suitable for her daughter, Clara Appleton would surrender, throw out her scruples. And for a black man.

There was speculation. At long last Mr. Appleton was dead and buried. But people observed, too, that Cedric was not pure black. Not offensively black. Some other blood had loosened the curls in his hair and tempered the dark color of his skin. He was brown, *café au lait.* And he was an educated man, a schoolteacher, a headmaster. A fact, they knew, that was not lost on Clara Appleton whose education, like that of white women of her time in the Caribbean-island colonies, was below secondary-school level. For schooling was unnecessary for the daughters of the marooned when there was a plantation owner to find, an overseer or a landlord, in islands where England had abandoned their great-grandfathers for her profit. It was superfluous when there was bait they could use in England if fishing became necessary: a promise that in the colonies a white man was worth his weight in gold.

Clara Appleton must have been impressed with the high-sounding titles of the books Cedric carried: *Ars Poetica,* the *Decameron,* the *Iliad,* the *Odyssey.* She must have swooned with ecstasy when he quoted to her from the *Aeneid* in Latin. Still, she must have been surprised that Rosa did not oppose her; that Rosa seemed eager, even, to be with Cedric; that she said yes without hesitation. Yes, submissively; yes, timidly, though not once, in the sixteen years since she had become a woman, had she shown the slightest interest in men. But Clara Appleton did not know of the passion that burned in her daughter's heart, the desire that consumed her and terrified her, too, for the power it had given her since she was twelve, when she used to lie on her belly at nights rubbing her bare skin against the hardness of her stiff mattress.

Until she saw Cedric, Rosa had managed to control the lust and the feelings of power, too. Perhaps it was simply timing, she thought; so often, no matter how much a person plans, arranges and organizes, timing is the only explanation for why things, events and people that under ordinary circumstances would never come together, suddenly do. Perhaps it was simply that Cedric had accepted the job to tutor children on the Orange Grove estate at the very time that she had reached the limit of her ability to bottle the passion she had suppressed for so many years. When she saw Cedric striding past her house, she already had lost control. His long legs, the ripple of his muscles in his thighs against his thin pants, his full lips beneath his dark mustache, the sensuous flaring of his nostrils tortured her. She thought only of having sex with him. Of screwing him.

On the nights of the days when she saw him, she tossed restlessly on her bed, finding no satisfaction in the rubbing of soft flesh against her hard mattress, consumed by the thought of Cedric's legs wrapped around hers, feeling the throbbing of his heart above hers, his breath in her mouth. She woke up in a sweat and with a longing that left her panting, until she stopped him one day and asked if he would consider tutoring a new student, a woman of her age, in fact, a woman her age. Her. Rosa herself, since she had never finished secondary school. She didn't say this last directly, but saw in his eyes when he said, Yes, he would tutor her, that he understood why she wanted to be tutored.

He came the next day, and she led him to the room she had chosen for her tutoring, near the back of the house where the grass grew tall and wild and shaded the windows. She closed the door and brought his fingers to the slits between the buttons on the front of her blouse, knowing he would reach for her breasts, and when he found them, naked and trembling, her nipples hard and erect, that he would tear her dress apart and discover that not only had she not worn a bra or a slip, but nothing else either.

They were married within three months, and for six months after that, it was never enough for her when he took her twice a day, sometimes more, without asking. Then one night, suddenly, her passion died. There, on the dining room floor, without warning, when she caught the pictures behind Cedric's smile, her desire ebbed, dried up like flour.

She could not explain it. Not sensibly. If anyone were to ask, she would have to say she didn't know what he thought, how he felt, *exactly.* How could she have known what pictures were in his mind? She hardly knew him, had not bothered to know him. Sex was what she had married him for, what she was willing to give up everything for: the things that mattered, like the Church that consoled her when there was no one else; like the Body of Christ she took on her tongue every Sunday at Mass. But after Cedric, she felt her soul was not pure enough, not white enough, to receive the Host. Not with lust in her soul.

Sometimes the sacrifice became unbearable, and desperate for the grace of the Eucharist, she waited until late on Saturday to make her confession, planning to go to the first Mass the next day, at five in the morning. But even then she knew that by nightfall her soul would be black again.

But wasn't she married? Hadn't she received the sacrament that made sexual intercourse with her husband not only permissible, but sanctified?

"Marriage between a man and woman is like the marriage between Christ and the Church. It is holy, it is pure, it is blessed by God."

The priest who heard her confession found no reason to give her penance, but upon her insistence, he gave her what he gave to schoolboys who confessed to wet dreams they had at night.

"Six Hail Marys? Is that enough, Father?"

"But you've done nothing, child." The priest was puzzled by her breathlessness, the near hysteria in her voice.

"I said three times, Father. And on Friday, four. I couldn't stop."

"God's will be done, my child."

"I don't do it for children."

"In Holy Matrimony . . . "

"I don't think about children."

"You are married, my child."

"You don't understand."

"Unless you do things that do not lead to procreation . . . "

"I do, I do, Father."

Still, it was not enough for the priest. Still, she could not convince him that there was nothing she felt for Cedric but carnal desire, raw lust, the actualization of dreams that had tormented her when she used to lie on her belly rubbing her bare skin against her mattress. She was twelve then, but even then she was frightened by the passion that consumed her. She told no one of these longings, not even the girl she could no longer remember. Perhaps she had chosen not to tell her because she couldn't; because before they both saw behind that hibiscus bush the thing that had caused them to lose memory, she already knew pleasures in dreams of sexual perversities.

Why did her passion for Cedric die so suddenly? How did the pictures she saw behind his smile that night blind her to all else? (How *could* she see them? How was that possible?) Yet her mind became a tabula rasa for everything except the shadows of what she and that little girl had seen. (Her name? It had sunk so deep in her memory she wondered now if the girl had existed at all.) What was it they saw through the tangle of vines that wove the wild hibiscus bushes together like a curtain: green splashed with the bright reds and pinks of delicate petals, long, thin stamens protruding

21

provocatively from their centers? What was it the little girl—was she real?—had told her afterward that had revolted her?

Perhaps it was because she had not seen clearly what had happened behind that hibiscus bush, had not acknowledged what she had seen, but there, that night when Cedric smiled, memory threatened to surface through his words: *Beg. Beg. You like it so. Beg.* Then, as he pressed her back onto the wood boards of the dining room floor, images of what she had witnessed that day flashed in a blur and were gone before she could be certain. But the half-memory clogged her throat and she gagged. Vomit spewed from her mouth, thick, sticky, stinking across Cedric's chest at the very moment he reached orgasm, so that from top to bottom both she and he were covered in warm liquid, his, white and shiny, sliding down her legs.

The priest told her in the confessional that memory was not the source of her torment: The devil was. Those pictures she saw in a haze above Cedric's head had no basis in fact, except that Satan was envious of a soul bound to God in Holy Matrimony and was tempting her to break her vow of obedience to her husband. But she did not want to have sex with Cedric after that night, and grew to despise herself for the passion that had ruled her, and still did.

Not so Cedric. When the next day she turned away from him, he pulled open her legs. He didn't take her in the kitchen or the dining room, or in the many places in their house where a touch from him used to send her groping for his belt buckle, but in his bed. There he took her. Nightly.

Now Rosa pulled her nightgown over her head and waited for him. She had heard his footsteps on the stairs. *Flagrante delicto.* She knew he thought she had taken a lover. More than once she had caught him searching through her dirty underwear. More than once he had left her stained panties on the bed, carefully placed there so that the crotch was laid open. Later, he would ask her, with his smile and dirty pictures, about the scratch he had made on her back, about the black and blue marks on her legs where he had pinched her skin: "How'd you get that, Rosa? Who put that there, Rosa?" Smiling.

He would warn her not to answer. "Shh. You better not tell me.

Shh. You could incriminate yourself." Smiling.

Sometimes she would try. "Last night . . . You remember . . . "

"Don't tell me. I don't want to know." He would put his hand across her mouth.

So it continued: the marks on her skin and his questions, her dirty panties spread out on her bed, his refusal to hear her answers until she became her own accuser, incriminator, informer, confessing her guilt with her silence.

"No," he would whisper, his hands over his ears as if she had spoken. "No names. I want no names." Then the smile again with the pictures, wet and ugly. "White skin you say bruises easily? White skin you say shows the bruised blood vessels? If that is what you say, but no names. I want no names."

She offered him no resistance. She let him think what he wanted. Now it was that white woman in Otahiti. He would want to catch her, too, *in flagrante delicto.* But a seed had shifted in Rosa's breast. Broken through its encasement and sprouted roots. She would content herself no more with praying for his death, with hoping that God would take him quietly in his sleep, that he would get some painless illness and die quickly. That other woman, her eyes and lips and tongue gouged out by fish, her flesh rotting, beckoning vultures, had slid into the darkest part of her soul. "Murder," she whispered and then was terrified by the sound of the word lapping against her ears.

The next morning *The Trinidad Guardian* carried a small article on the front page reporting what a fisherman had discovered in the rolling surf between stumps of bamboo splashed with slivers of green sea reeds and the rusty brown olive leaves of ancient almond trees. The column was tiny, not given much significance, for the reporter who had brought in the story had himself doubted the gossip when he heard it. A white woman murdered in Otahiti? He knew that Trinidad would have done its best to protect her. Still, he was curious, and since he was in San Fernando, not far from Otahiti, he decided to take a look. He saw the body bloated and dark, he saw the straight black hair falling past her shoulders, and he mumbled his scorn under his breath: *The masses are asses.* She was an East Indian woman, not a white woman. He penned his report on the way to Port-of-Spain, between stops to let loaded bison cross the road and trains with carriages crammed with stalks of sugar cane bound for the factories of Usine Ste. Madeline pass by. In Arima, where cars swirling around the roundabout had snarled themselves to a halt, he finished his report. There, waiting for tempers to subside and a policeman to disentangle the cars, he gratuitously expressed his moral indignation: *Once again a poor, unfortunate East Indian woman has been a victim of the wave of senseless violence that is growing wild all over Trinidad. Can a woman, even a poor peasant, be safe anywhere? Isn't it time that the little men learn that they can't take out their frustrations on their women? Violence is not the answer.*

Cedric was devastated when he read the newspaper the next morning, all his theories fine-tuned to fit Rosa confounded by an insignificant, self-righteous newspaper reporter. But by dinner he had regained his confidence. When he spoke to Rosa again that night, he strung *flagrante delicto* and crime passionel around her neck like a noose, certain then that the reporter was not only wrong but stupid, and that what he had told Rosa the night before was indeed correct. The woman the fisherman had found tossed by the surf in Otahiti was in fact a white woman. Now he knew, too, who she was, who had murdered her, and why.

He first found reason to believe she was white when he had finally put in place the last piece of a jigsaw puzzle that had tormented him all that day. Ironically, the part he needed came from the mouths of the very people he despised—the uneducated masses. Scavengers, he called them. They raked the streets for gossip they substituted for the knowledge they could get from books. Yet it was that very gossip, traveling the same route north it had taken out of Otahiti to a Chinaman's shop in Nelson Street, that gave Cedric the information he needed to make sense of the riddle that had spun his head in circles all day.

Ordinarily he would not have taken notice of anything the people in the street said, but when he collided with an unruly crowd spilling out of the rum shop on the road he took from the school, where he was headmaster, to his house, he caught between their curses and shouts the pieces he needed to finish his jigsaw puzzle for Rosa that night. He did not need the answer to the why of the mass the fisherman had found in a burlap bag in Otahiti. He knew it already. Murders such as the murder of that woman in Otahiti were common enough, and understandable: a lecherous woman, a man with no other defense but to stop her and so redeem his name, such a murder was a matter of honor. But the question of *who* arrested him, the who that drove the people in the rum shop deeper into drink with the impossibility of it. *A white woman? A real, true, true white woman? And you say fish gouge out she eyes and lips and tongue?*

It was all Cedric needed. He locked the answer to who into the other piece he got from Headley Padmore, his cousin, the call he received at lunchtime that started the spinning in his head. Like him, Headley had taken flight from Cedros, terrified by nightmares of a future of ripping his hands to shreds on salt-crusted seines and gutting fish with a beachful of men with rum-red eyes and skin coarse as raw leather. They had an old resentment between them, these cousins, over the careers they had chosen: one, Teachers' Training College (choosing the mind over brute force, he told his cousin); the other, the police force (because once you knew the three Rs, you could figure out life yourself, and, more than that, he wasn't in the business of giving teachers a job).

"You wouldn't believe who came into the police station this morning, Cedric. One of your bookmen. Wanted to report his wife was missing. A doctor. He walked into my office just a few hours ago. In shirt and tie and jacket, if you please. A doctor. Said he can't find his wife since Tuesday. You know which doctor I talking about? Well, maybe you don't know, seeing as how you living in that one-horse town. The Indian man that marry that white woman. I hear she was horning him. And he come pretending in my office like he don't know where she is. I almost told him to a man where he could look for her. She sleeping with everybody. Tom, Dick *and* Harry. Dick, that's where she is. With Dick. With Dick in her." He roared with laughter. "Probably Dick got stuck on her, or stuck *in* her."

Cedric slammed down the phone in disgust but his mind raced. All that day he paced up and down, struggling to fit together the curved loops of the puzzle that were scattered in his head. His blood beat against his temples and his temper rose with the stifling heat of the early afternoon in the close quarters of his classroom. He shouted at the children and brought his cane down viciously on the open palms of boys unlucky enough to have the wrong answers to questions he barely formed. Over and over he shifted the pieces: an Indian doctor married to a white woman. One piece. He, a colored headmaster married to a Trinidadian white woman. Another piece. A doctor with horns jutting from his forehead. Another. A white woman, legs sprawled wide open on a bed for every Tom, Dick *and* Harry. Another piece. Rosa, his Rosa. Once, now no more. She could never have stopped so suddenly on her own. There had to be someone, somebody else taking his place. He would catch her *in flagrante delicto.*

Riding his bicycle home that evening, he barely saw the road in front of him. When he ran into the people from the rum shop, he couldn't tell where he was, *in flagrante delicto* humming through his brain like a buzz saw. All he needed were the parts they gave him, shouting to each other and to him. Then the picture became clear: a white woman murdered in Otahiti, dumped in Freeman's Bay. A doctor's white wife missing, a white wife who had made a cuckold of her husband. A wife, *his wife,* who no longer desired her husband. He would make a net of *flagrante delicto* and crime passionel and throw it over Rosa like a seine. (Later, he would make it a noose.)

When he made love to Rosa that night, believing he had caught her and there would be time enough to pull her out of the sea onto the beach and send her gasping and flapping like a fish, he studied her: her honey brown hair splayed above her head like a fan, her eyeballs jumping nervously beneath the pale thin covering of her eyelids, the hair of her eyebrows shaped perfectly. He bent more closely over her and inspected them. She had done them recently. He could see two tiny dry dots of blood on the corner of one eyebrow. Another piece snapped in place in his jigsaw puzzle. She had plucked out the stray hairs under her eyebrows. For whom? For whom had she set her trap with her longing, now that she no longer wanted him?

He pumped, but there was no expression on her face, no movement except the jumping of her eyeballs. Her lips were drawn in a flat line. Soft, soft. She betrayed nothing, and yet he had seen in her eyes the disgust she felt for him the day she took down the drapes, the day she stopped groping for his belt buckle, the day he reached for her and she was cold, cold, indifferent as marble until he warmed her up. He would catch her. He pumped. He would catch her *in flagrante delicto.* He pumped, and then waited for the low moan that would filter through her lips, waited for it, for while he knew she hated him, he also knew she had not yet learned to put out the fire he could stoke within her. And when it came, first the moan and then a desperate cry for more, he plunged brutally deep inside her.

The news in *The Guardian* the next morning threw him into confusion, unhinged the pieces in the picture that had formed so clearly in his mind. He had planned to show the finished puzzle to Rosa at breakfast, to let her know he was no fool, no ignorant peasant who thought that the white woman the fisherman found in Otahiti was one of the latest of Boysie's experiments on racehorses. He would be no stupid horned cuckold, like that Indian doctor. Then he read the reporter's story about an East Indian woman and the pieces of the puzzle began to slip out of their tight grooves. An East Indian woman! Not the doctor's wife? Not the white woman who opened her legs to every Tom, Dick and Harry? He left the house early that morning in a state of intense agitation, but by dinnertime he was calm again, his facts confirmed by his policeman cousin, who gloated: "Told you the doctor was lying. He knew where she was. Every Tom, Dick and Harry. Told you."

"Paula Inge." He gave her name to Rosa at dinner. Quietly. Not looking up from his plate.

"Who? What are you talking about?"

"The woman in Otahiti."

"Which woman?"

"The woman they found in the sea yesterday morning."

"The one the fisherman found?"

"Yes. Paula Inge. The doctor's wife."

"The doctor?"

"Dr. Dalip Singh's wife."

"I'm sorry," she said.

He looked up at her. "What for?"

"For the doctor," she murmured.

He frowned. "The doctor?"

She shook her head. "No. No. For the poor woman."

He smiled.

"To die like that." Her eyes became misty.

"She deserved it," he said.

She squeezed her eyes shut. When she opened them again, the mist was gone.

"She deserved it," he repeated and sawed his meat.

"No. Not like that."

"I told you. *Flagrante delicto.*"

She looked away from him. "Boysie," she said. "Boysie, that's what people are saying. He cut her throat and slit open her chest."

He held his knife still in mid-air and told her to be quiet.

"Boysie," she repeated. "He took out her heart."

He warned her to stop.

"For his racehorses. He slit her open right down her belly. For his racehorses." The words rolled off her tongue as if by a will of their own.

He warned her again.

"He took out her heart."

He slammed his fist down on the table. "Enough!"

She got up. "Boysie," she whispered.

He ordered her to sit down. "Now. Now. Sit down, Rosa!"

She backed into the chair.

"*Flagrante delicto.* Understand? *Flagrante delicto.*"

"That's not true, Cedric." She wrapped her arms around her waist.

He leaned over to her. "She left her husband's bed."

"No, Cedric."

"Her husband's bed!"

She bit her lower lip.

Now he taunted her. "You have nothing to say about that? Talk. Give me your bogus explanation about Boysie. Tell me what you have to say."

"Boysie," she began again quietly.

"Watch out, Rosa."

"She was faithful . . . "

"Careful, Rosa."

"To him."

"I don't like to wear horns, Rosa."

"And I feel sorry . . . "

He stared at her.

"For him."

The tangle of muscles at the base of his neck tightened into a ball. Pain flared up the side of his face. *For him? For him?* "It's the woman who's stinking, goddamn you! Goddamn you!"

She put her hand to her lips. "I pity him," she said.

He lunged across the table toward her. "He's alive. Alive and getting drunk in the Pelican. Having a good time. Alive!"

She pressed her fingers deeper into her lips but she did not back away.

"You better watch out, Rosa." He sat back in his chair.

Still, she murmured, "I feel sorry for him."

"You better watch out when you're with every Tom, Dick and Harry, Rosa. You better watch out."

"I feel . . . "

He lunged again. "Stinking!"

Still, she continued, "sorry for him."

"Stinking, goddamn it!" He got up.

"No, Cedric."

"Drunk as a fish in the Pelican." He walked over to her.

"You're wrong, Cedric."

"Liar!"

She stared at her hands. "She was a good wife. A decent woman."

"Liar! You think because I'm black, I'm stupid. You think because I'm black, I can't read behind that white skin of yours."

"He was wrong. You're wrong." She looked up at him. "I pity you both."

At first Cedric simply stood still as if he were waiting for her to say more, but when the shock of her impudence wore off, he brought his face close to hers so that their lips were almost touching each other's. "Who the hell do you think you are, white lady?" He breathed heavily on her. "Who the hell? You think I'm going to beg for that space between your legs?"

Tears gathered in Rosa's eyes.

"Pity yourself, white lady." His voice simmered to a hoarse whisper. "Careful. It's mine." He watched a tear trickle down her cheek and he brushed it away gently. A caress. "Shh. Quiet. Careful." A lover's solicitude. Lethal. "Don't give it away. For then it won't be me you'll feel pity for, white lady. It won't be me."

It was the feast of Our Lady of Fatima that Saturday. Rosa called a taxi to take her to the shrine at the top of the hill in Laventille. Anyone who had seen her fingering the beads of her rosary, her black mantilla fastened with a clip on the top of her head, the intricacy of the lace casting dark shadows along the sides of her face, would have thought: This is a woman in mourning, a woman praying for a soul that had recently departed. And that person would have been partially right, for Rosa was praying for a soul, but not for a soul that had left this earth, or for one she could cause to leave this earth. She was praying for *her* soul, begging Our Lady to help her to be pure, too; to push back the evil seed that flared out of the hollow of her breast where she had hidden it, to cast out of her mind the thought that had set her brain on fire. *Our Lady of the Immaculate Conception, Our Lady of Fatima who appeared to three innocent country girls.* She rolled the black beads of her rosary across the balls of her fingers and fixed her mind on the purity of Our Lady. *Our Lady of Perpetual Help, pray for me.* She begged for a miracle. She implored Our Lady to cure her, too, to wash away the sin she had not yet committed, but in her thoughts. She asked Our Lady to erase the reflection she saw in reverse in the mirror of Cedric's eyes: Where Paula Inge was she saw *him;* where Dr. Dalip Singh was, she saw herself.

≪ Chapter 3 ≫

*Z*uela, too, was frightened into thoughts of Laventille, of climbing the hill to the shrine of Our Lady of Fatima to beg Our Lady to cleanse her of the evil that had taken hold of her soul that evening in the shop in Nelson Street when she saw through the slits that were the Chinaman's eyes, deep into his mind. Man-woman business. His business. She had seen the way he had looked at her, though he was choking on the phlegm that rose to his throat. The greed that once glazed his eyes when he took her, too, with the alpagats and saltfish he had come to buy in Venezuela, had been replaced for some time now by fear and malice—fear that his coughing would never end; malice that was directed not just at her, but at his traitorous friends who he believed were waiting their turn for the pleasures he had had with her since she was eleven.

She had seen the animal fear in his eyes stalking her everywhere—the frantic desperation laid bare in the eyes of a wild dog backed against a wall snarling, its pupils glistening. In a second, fear would make the dog reckless, would eradicate all instinctual caution, the total memory of lessons learned about avoiding entrapment, about luring the quarry into its snare for the kill. In a second, it could pounce. In a second, the Chinaman could let loose his venom.

What had made the husband of that white woman so desperate, so careless? For it was her husband who had murdered her. That Zuela was certain of, though the woman who brought her the news spoke only of Boysie. But not this time. Boysie would not have taken that risk. He had walked out of death row once, but he knew the judge would have turned a blind eye to the law and had him hanged if the man he was suspected of butchering had been white. No, Boysie had not gutted that white woman for his racehorses. Not this time. This was the work of a man turned wild dog in a jealous rage.

Zuela crawled into the bed with her daughters, in the room behind the shop where she slept at night, after the Chinaman no longer needed her, and where her sons also slept, on the other mattress against the wall. The Chinaman's coughing was bad that night, and she thought, after they had closed the shop and she heard him stumble up the open planks of wooden stairs that leaned against the back of the house and led up to the attic where he slept, that he would not call for her.

Perhaps he had not meant to let her see his malice. Not yet. Perhaps it was her silence that had so surprised him that he became unnerved. He had heard her caution her girls, his daughters, many times about Boysie: *Take care where you walk, who you speak to. Boysie looking for girl hearts for his racehorses.* Yet she had not agreed with the woman in the shop that Boysie was to be blamed for the corpse that washed up on the beach in Otahiti. Perhaps it was this that had made the Chinaman snarl at her. Perhaps, too, he had noticed when the seed took root in her chest and its shoots spread to her eyes. He knew he would need time to plot through his malice before he faced her again; retreat, plan, before he struck out again. Snuggling between her youngest girl, Celia, three years old, and the baby, who was two, Zuela comforted herself with that thought. She would go to Laventille tomorrow. She would ask for Our Lady's help to erase the evil thoughts that had sprung to her mind. The Chinaman did not have long to live. Soon, she would be free.

Now his coughing rolled down from the attic in waves, each wave ending in a silence that she hoped would last forever. But in seconds, the spluttering would begin, followed by hacking and gasping, then air would fill his lungs and he would cough again. Zuela placed her arms across her ears. She was exhausted, tired of hoping, she needed sleep. Mercifully, within minutes, sleep overtook her, but not for long. Her name broke through her dreams: *Zuela, Zuela.* She parted her eyes: *Zuela, Zuela.* Her son Alan was standing next to her bed. He tugged the neck of her nightgown. *Zuela, Zuela.* But it was not Alan who was calling her.

"Zuela. Come here, Zuela."

The boy pulled frantically at the collar of her nightgown. She pushed him away.

"No, Ma." His eyes shone like jewels in the dark.

"Zuela, Zuela." The Chinaman gurgled and spat. "Zuela, come up here, Zuela."

"Don't go, Ma."

Tenderly, she removed the chubby arms of her baby daughter wrapped around her neck.

"No, Ma." Her son crowded her. He was only fourteen, the second of her ten children. She was older than that when she had given birth to him. Still, he was younger than the daughter she had sent to the nuns.

"I'll be back." She disentangled her legs from the bed sheets.

"Not tonight, Ma." He was tiny for his age, but his voice was deep like a man's. "I'll go for you."

The coughing from the attic grew worse. It fell in heavy blankets down to their room below—terrible, frightening. The boy clamped his hands over his ears. He was a boy, still. A child. Zuela felt sorry for him.

"It's okay," she whispered.

"I'll go," the boy said again.

She turned her back on him and reached for her dress hanging on the bedpost.

"He won't need you tonight. He's too sick."

She stood up and pushed her arms through the sleeves of her dress. Alan came closer to her. "Don't go, Ma." She brushed the hair off his forehead. *So young, so knowing, so much older than his years.*

The boy's eyes were wet now. "I'll go. I'm old enough." Tears ran down his cheeks. "I can do it, Ma. It doesn't bother me."

"No!" She turned away from him. "That is not all he wants."

A terrible silence came between them, and then the boy remembered a secret they shared. He looked up and grinned. "Smoke can kill

33

you," he whispered.

Zuela smiled back at him.

The attic where the Chinaman slept was dark; the ceilings were low. When she reached the top of the stairs along the side of the house, Zuela bent her head to pass through the entrance as the Chinaman always did, and as his friends did who came later at night after the Chinaman was finished with her. Not every night, but most nights, more nights now than in the earlier years when the Chinaman kept her there longer and said he didn't need his friends anymore to help him sleep. Then the dreams came back in his nights with her, too, and he woke up screaming like a madman, raising long bloody welts along his neck with his nails until she pried his fingers back. After the first night, she cut his nails, and then she called back his friends, the ones who smoked with him, and the other one, too—the one who said, "Two pipes is enough. No more."

Although she was only five feet tall, Zuela kept her head bowed by instinct, for fear of the beams that hung from the ceiling that had struck her too many times as she tried to make her way in the dark, past the two planks of wood laid out, one above the other to make bunk beds; past the low table on the floor with its stack of tissue-thin paper, its tubes and glass bottles and metal pipes; past there to the corner where the Chinaman lay on a plank wider than those that made bunk beds for his friends, wide enough to hold him and her, though it, too, was narrow. She was thin, except for her belly that was the size of a ripe watermelon. *Zuela, how long you taking to make baby this time? The popo almost two and you belly out more than a year now. Is pumpkin you growing there or what? Is watermelon you swallow whole?*

Except for that belly she was tiny, no more than two inches taller than she had been when she was eleven and the Chinaman came to her village for alpagats her father had promised him, and took her, too. No more. Her arms were the same size, her legs slim and brown, her face hardly different from the face of the little girl she had been then: small and round, her eyes big and black. But now there was an emptiness in her eyes, a hollow lifelessness that disappeared only when she was alone with her children, and a glistening that came sometimes, but only for the Chinaman when she thought he was not looking—a dark, ugly light the Chinaman must have seen that night when he caught her before she could blink, after he told her the cause of the appearance of the corpse of a white woman stuffed in a bag and dumped in the sea in Otahiti.

Her hair was thick, long and straight. When she was a child, her mother kept it cut to her shoulders, but now Zuela let it grow past her waist. She was never quite sure, when she was asked, whether she grew it that long because she had little time to groom herself, or because it marked time, kept time for her since she sent her oldest child, now fifteen, to live with the nuns, *before she turned twelve*. Zuela wore her hair simply now, caught at the nape of her neck with a strip of cloth.

The Chinaman's hair was straight as hers, and black when he had taken her from her village, already beginning then to recede from his forehead. Now it was almost completely gray. The parts that stayed black after the gray appeared along his temples turned white during the last two years when his coughing became worse and his friends sometimes had to keep him company two nights in a row on the planks that were like bunk beds. He had grown smaller, too, Zuela thought, when she saw him huddled in the darkness in the corner on the mattress she had put on his double-planked bed. Smaller in the night. In the day, when his coughing did not bend his back, he seemed as tall and slim as the trunk of a coconut tree, the way he had appeared to her that morning when he stood above her father, seated on the ground with his hands over his face, and bargained for her life.

He had the same eyes that frightened her, that forced her to look down when he looked at her. They were jet black and seemed to fill the spaces where the white should have been, his eyelids framing them as a lizard's eyes were framed. Hairless. Like a snake's, it seemed to her, at those times when the seed she had buried jostled in her chest and threatened to burst from its encasement, as it did that night when the Chinaman spat out his black light at her.

Yet in the days when he whispered his longing in her ears and told her she chased away his nightmares and he didn't need his friends to sleep with him on the planks in the attic anymore, or the glass bottle with its

35

blue smoke, or the tubes, or the pipe, or the white powder they burned, she thought: *Not like a snake's. His eyes were more like the eyes of an iguana.* Yet iguanas used to frighten her, too. Then one day, her mother gave her an iguana. It was green and shiny, and her mother made her stroke its spiked head until its eyeballs grew heavy. Soon she saw the iguana was harmless, even beautiful.

In those days when the Chinaman's screams did not cut through the night like a machete and send her children shivering to her bosom, in those days when she had not yet been forced to call back his friends to the planks and the blue smoke in the glass bottle and the pipes, Zuela saw in the Chinaman's face the goodness that her father had seen, *must have seen,* or he would not have let the Chinaman take her, too, with the alpagats and saltfish he had come to buy. That goodness had to be there in skin so smooth and flawless, skin that stretched like silk, like baby's skin, across his cheekbones, his pale cheeks, his hairless chin. And sometimes there were days when she did not see the black spread against the whites of his eyes, nor his eyelids sweep, hairless and limpid, across his eyes—a snake's eyes.

The Chinaman heard her the moment she stepped off the stairs and bent down low to pass through the entrance to his room. He waited until she drew near and then called out to her in a hoarse whisper, "Smoke, smoke." When she reached him, he stretched out his hand to her, his fingers clutching a crumpled brown paper bag. "Smoke, smoke."

She pried back his fingers and removed the bag.

"Quick, now." He leaned against the wall at the back of his bed, drew up his legs to his chest, bent his arms and his hands cupped his jaw. Folded up like that, he seemed helpless. Harmless.

"Quick. Quick."

Zuela reached for one of the tissue-thin rectangular pieces of paper stacked on the low table near his bed. Carefully, she poured the brown crushed leaves from the paper bag into it. Carefully, she licked her tongue on the two longer sides of the paper, pressed the damp edges together and rolled the stuffed paper into a thin cigarette. She reached for a match, struck it and lit the cigarette. She sucked in the smoke, not deep, not deep. She would not inhale. Not down her lungs. She sucked until smoke filled her cheeks. Then, removing the cigarette from her mouth, she pinched her lips together like a valve and bent over the Chinaman. He was waiting for her, his head thrown back against the wall, his mouth open like a fish. She released the smoke quickly across his face, blowing it into his mouth and up his nostrils. Over and over she inhaled and blew until his muscles loosened, the curve on his back slackened, his arms fell leaden to his sides and his legs dropped to the mattress, limp and lifeless. Still, his mouth gaped open, greedy for more, and she filled her cheeks again with the smoke from the burning herbs and blew until the Chinaman closed his mouth and opened his hairless eyelids. A snake. He groped for her bare legs and slid his skeletal fingers up her nightdress. It took a minute. A minute was all he needed or had energy for. All he needed to chase away the nightmares.

When she left him she could barely see, blinded by the throbbing in her head. She felt her way down the stairs to the room where she slept with her children. In a blur she saw Alan standing by her bed. Her lips moved. "Go to sleep. Sleep, Alan. Sleep, son. It's okay." Still, he stood sentinel over her bed until she fell asleep.

Before dawn, Zuela heard the Chinaman scream again. But not for her. This time he was crying in terror of the demons that chased him. When the sun came up, the cloud lifted from her brain and her mind cleared. She knew where she had to go, what she had to do. Only Our Lady in the shrine at the top of the hill in Laventille could extinguish the fire burning in her breast, only she could cool her hatred, only she could erase the sinful thoughts in her brain: man-woman business.

◄ Chapter 4 ►

*L*aventille, home of the shrine of Our Lady of Fatima, town of tears. Laventville, the poet once called it: *To go downhill / from here was to ascend.* He would not be wrong. Yet to go uphill was also to ascend, to reach such splendor it blinded the eye. For there, at the top, the sun gilded the roofs of the shrine and the tiny blue and white chapel next to it and made the blue of the blue sky bluer and the white of the white clouds whiter. And if one looked up, as always one was compelled to do, one followed the dazzling arc of the sky to a sea shimmering gold and silver on clear days, gray and still magnificent when it rained.

One saw this from the top of Laventville, though one knew there was more: after the grassy green savannah for horse racing and polo, and men in flannel trousers playing cricket, and after the gardens for ladies strolling arm in arm along pathways lined with lilies and orchids, and after the white picket-fenced bandstand for brass-buttoned police serenading young lovers, and after the governor's white house and the other mansions (the archbishop's castle, the cathedrals, the prime minister's quarters, the sprawling villas of the merchants), after those palatial homes of the rich, and the more modest, yet assertive, houses of the middle class, there would come the others—the cement hovels of the poor—

staggering up the hill like drunks stumbling over choked gutters, stray dogs and half-naked children. *Five to a room,* the poet said. Looking back, *the hot, corrugated iron sea.*

There, on the Sunday before Zuela and Rosa were to make their pilgrimages to Our Lady, on the very day a fisherman found himself the center of attention in Otahiti, the body of another woman was discovered. Black, poor, and therefore of no consequence, her disappearance had not made news in *The Guardian,* where no one expected it would, but neither did it make news in the streets nor in the rum shops, nor in the backyards where gossip was rife. Shame and envy had silenced tongues (they said two brothers had loved her and she had had them both), silenced tongues, that is, until two pigs vomited on a dirt road in Laventille, two spike-haired black pigs caked with dried mud, fattening themselves on the remains of something that had once been alive and breathing—a carcass chopped into tiny bits and mingled with the food in their troughs, with the remains of dasheen, cassava, yam and rotting potatoes.

A young girl identified her first, pointing to an eyeball gleaming between the pink chunks of undigested food. "Melda. Is Melda self."

"No body, no crime," Boysie was heard to have said months before. No body, no murder. No murder, no execution.

His henchmen laughed in the judge's face when they released Boysie from Death Row.

Then someone spotted the chewed-off finger of a woman. Weeks later, a man no longer able to contain his grief claimed the ring she wore. "Melda. Is Melda self. I self give her that ring." *Not the brothers.*

That same week, two hearts still moist with blood were found on top of the garbage dump in the La Basse. The vultures froze in midair and then dove like bombers. In the days that followed, ten more women caught the spirit and set up shop in that town of tears. People poured out of the valley on the feast day of Our Lady—Rosa and Zuela, too—for two women said they saw Our Lady come down in a circle of bright light over the shrine of Fatima near the little chapel on the top of the Laventille hill. Our Lady here to protect them! And the priest did not dispute that, nor did he chase away the hundreds who followed to light votive candles and put coins down the slit in the tiny box he had ingeniously placed at the feet of Our Lady.

Zuela and Rosa had given money, too, but not because they were terrified by two hearts for racehorses found throbbing in the La Basse, or because two pigs had vomited the remains of a black woman chopped into fodder, or because fish had eaten the eyeballs of a white woman and gouged out her lips and tongue, but because they needed Our Lady to work her miracle on them, too, to visit them, too, to push back to the darkness a thought that now tormented them, that now gave them no peace.

It was Rosa who would bring them together, Rosa who would remember and would rekindle between them a friendship that would change what was left of her life forever, though time had seemingly calcified to stone that terrible moment she had shared with Zuela behind the hibiscus bush. Yet it was mere chance that caused her to meet Zuela again. She never would have seen her were her soul not so tormented by remorse, yet uplifted by a sort of perverse satisfaction for the thing she had not yet done. Rosa would have missed her completely were she not so terrified, and yet morbidly elated, by the possibility of doing it; if, not so frightened by this wrestling of good and evil within her, she had not sought to shut out all distraction from Our Lady, who could help her; if she had not thus forced herself into deep meditation of another mystery of the rosary; if she had not drawn her black mantilla down the sides of her face, hood-like, so she did not see Our Lady's devotees part to the edges of the dirt road; she did not hear the thunder of footsteps racing behind her; she did not jump out of the way before the gaggle of uniformed schoolchildren tumbled her to the ground. Even then she might not have noticed the woman who stooped to help her out of the bramble of bushes. Jarred forcibly out of the Sorrowful mystery of the rosary, she might not have noticed if, in that instant, she had not looked up and her eyes had not caught in the eyes of the other woman, a sadness deep, penetrating, familiar, that sent her head whirling:

One little girl.

A string of pearls.

A man with a pole.

Another little girl, her eyes as sad as a woman's. A girl. A woman-child, swishing her hips and laughing. "That is nothing. I see that already. Chinaman do that to me already."

She bolted to her feet but the woman was gone. She squeezed her eyes shut and other pictures came—distorted, blurred, hazy. Terrifying. She fought to focus them but they slipped rapidly in and out of her mind, eluding her. Frantically, she searched for the woman, desperate to stop the collision of images now falling one on top of the other—two, three, five, seven at a time. Disturbing. Unnerving. A memory? A past? She shoved her way through the masses of sweaty bodies thronging up the hill, pursued by that one split second of recognition, clear, precise, and sharp. Unmistakable. She had seen those eyes before; she had known that face well once before. *Daughter. Daughter.* The sound clear as a bell resounded in her ears. *Daughter. Daughter.* Her child's voice calling.

The sharp points of the stones along the muddied dirt road penetrated the soles of her shoes and bruised the bottoms of her feet, but she took no notice of the pain, nor of the women—their heavy bosoms drooping low over their swollen bellies, their arms lost in white suds trailing down the sides of their washtubs—who looked up when she passed, a hardness around their mouths that should have stopped her, but did not, nor of the half-naked children in tattered undershirts who streamed out of one-room houses to taunt the nuns: "Hail Mary, holy white ladies. Full of grace, holy white ladies." She barely heard them. Nor did she notice the stone-still men standing before the doorway of their houses, legs apart, arms folded militantly across naked chests turned tar black in the sun. She did not see these people from that town of tears who knew already that the rush upstream left nothing but rubble in its wake when it rolled back down again; who were certain that two brothers, fighting over a ring on the decaying finger of the body of the woman that two pigs had disgorged, were not the ones who had chopped her into fodder. For the people in that town had no doubt that such diabolical barbarity could originate only from the valley below.

Everything was obscured in that tangle of photographs in Rosa's mind. Screened out, too, was the blaze that had sent her racing to Our Lady for her cooling waters: her fear of vengeance on Cedric, which was lost now in that sudden clearing to a past she had made herself forget.

Daughter. Daughter. A tiny girl with skin as brown as sand. Through the wild hibiscus they had seen . . . *Daughter.* A little girl who lived with the woman who came on Fridays to iron clothes for her mother on the Orange Grove estate. A little girl who told her, "That is nothing. I see that already. Chinaman do that to me already."

At the top of the hill she saw her, her faded yellow cotton dress tight against a belly that rose, round as a watermelon, beneath her tiny breasts, her long black hair pulled back from her copper-brown face, her eyes staring steadily in her direction, questioning, doubting. She stood on the hill, apart from the crowd, framed by a sky indigo and magnificent, which plunged headily downward to where speedboats splayed frothy long white lines like sunrays across a glistening sea.

"Daughter?"

The woman squinted against the blinding sunlight.

"Daughter!" Rosa called out to her again, certain now. But the woman frowned, stepped back, and disappeared into a new wave of bodies crashing on the crest of the hill.

Daughter. Daughter. Again she gave voice to the name and the sound came back on her ears and unlocked the memories.

They had pressed their faces into the hibiscus bush, she and the little girl. Yet long after the girl had turned away, she still remained, her cheeks bleeding where the sharp ends of the dried twigs had made welts down the sides of her face, her eyes snapping photographs: Click! Click!

The little girl tugged her dress to force her away from the bushes, but she resisted. Click, click. Each detail was meticulously captured, each image indelibly imprinted. Click, click!

The little girl tugged again. She fought her. The petals from red hibiscus fell from thin branches and turned blue in the dirt. Click, click! The little girl laughed. "That is nothing. I see that already."

Then the world went still: "Chinaman do that to me already. Chinaman done do that to me."

Memory fused to stone and was sealed off in the horror of that possibility, sealed off until the pictures returned years later with Cedric, she sprawled on the dining room floor, panties clinging to one ankle, the ends of her skirt to her throat, Cedric thrusting, the smile on his lips indistinguishable from the smirk on the mouth of the man behind the hibiscus bush, his words the same as that man's: *Beg. Beg. You like it so. You like it so. Beg.* Then a truth more horrible confronted her, one that connected the child Rosa, her face sunk into broken ends of the hibiscus bush, to the woman Rosa, dazed by an incomprehensible sense of betrayal when Cedric demanded again: "Beg. Beg for it, white lady."

In the confessional, the priest said the pictures she saw that night did not come from memory but, rather, from a sinful imagination, planted there by Satan. None of what she saw had happened—not the man with the pole, not the girl with the pearls, not her friend, swinging her hips like a woman, laughing: "Chinaman done do that to me already." And she loosened the connection in nine days of rosaries to the Blessed Mother, buried Daughter, the child now a woman called Zuela, in a righteous resentment of Cedric three years deep.

Now, near the tops of the gru-gru boeuf trees that rose from the squalor of raw cement bricks pushing up the hill to the shrine of Our Lady, Rosa saw her again. She turned when Rosa touched her shoulders and called her Daughter, her eyes calm with recognition.

"You. It's really you." But she would say no more. "Not now," she said. "Not here in Laventille."

"When?" Rosa pressed her. "I must speak to you. *Must.*" She stretched out her hand, feverish with desperation, but Zuela pulled hers away.

"Not now."

"When?"

Zuela heard the hysteria in her voice, but it did not startle her. She, too, had removed the boulder damming her memory. "After the Benediction," she said, and turned toward the steps of the chapel where the priest had just emerged from behind the acolytes holding the gilded monstrance high above his head, his hands draped by the white shawl that covered his shoulders.

"Later," she whispered.

It was not enough for Rosa. "I won't find you."

The woman she had called Daughter studied her face. No part of her moved, only her eyes boring deeper and deeper into Rosa's as she peeled away layers to the past. "Rosa." She whispered her name.

"You'll get lost." Rosa's eyes brimmed water. "I won't be able to find you again." She reached for her hand.

Zuela frowned and pursed her lips, but she did not pull away her hand. To Rosa it seemed she stayed that way for an eternity, but suddenly she sighed, a long outpouring of her breath that seemed to empty her body of air. The sound, streaming through her lips, reverberated hollow in the cavity of her chest. "Since last I see you, I live with Chinaman." She breathed in again. "In Nelson Street." Her eyes were hard but there was a softness in her voice when she spoke, the hardness directed to something or someone Rosa could not see, the softness to Rosa. "Come see me there."

The acolytes had reached close to them and were moving in the direction of the shrine nestled just a few feet to the left of where they stood. Clouds of incense wafted from their censers and thickened the air. In the torpid heat of the afternoon, made more intense by the sweet smell of ripe mango and gru-gru boeuf and the stink of human sweat and animal excrement, the pungent odor of the incense plunged into nostrils and worked its hypnotic spell. The crowd surged forward and burst into a hymn to Our Lady, pulling Zuela and Rosa in its tow. Rosa reached for the skinny branch of a bush sprouting stubbornly through a space in the gravel-stoned pathway, and anchored herself to the ground, but when she looked up, she saw Zuela drowning helplessly in the folds of that speckled sea.

She felt cheated, robbed of her chance for the answers she was frantic to find and yet not find, that she believed were there behind the screen that had begun to part on Zuela's face. Yet before the afternoon would end she would lose this frenzied urgency to talk to Zuela, and she would wait the week it took for Cedric to send her flying like a madwoman to the Chinaman's shop in Nelson Street. For out of the dark despair that enveloped her then, came an epiphany. It left her dazed, burning, smoldering in the brilliance of its searing clarity as it must have left those who had witnessed the Vision, Our Lady descending in a blaze of light: She had had her miracle. Our Lady had made one for her in Laventille. Her revelation. And at that moment she understood, in a way denied to her before, why the little girl could not pry her off the hibiscus, why she still pressed her face into its branches though its sharp ends tore her cheeks.

For then, above the silence that descended on the crowd below the drone of the priest now chanting his prayers in Latin; beyond the shouts that followed "Alleluia!" when he raised the monstrance, the Body of Christ gleaming white from the center, radiating metal rays of gold, Rosa unraveled the threads of the knot that had tied her to Cedric, Cedric to the man behind the hibiscus bush, Cedric to the man the little girl thought no different from the Chinaman: *He do that to me, too, already. He done do that.*

How could her mother have known how desperately she needed Cedric? She herself had not known. Not in the way Our Lady's miracle would make it known to her. When she said yes to Cedric after he asked her to marry him, she thought she was giving him what she was certain he craved, what the man behind the hibiscus craved, though she did not remember him then, only the feelings: awe for the power the girl held over him, and pity for the man made savage by his hunger for her. They were feelings that filled her with such shame for having them that they detached themselves from the reality she had witnessed and sank deep past her memory. Then all that remained was the awe, and, later, the pity that surfaced with Cedric.

When she was desperate for respite from the rubbing of flesh against the hardness of her mattress and Cedric walked past her house, dark and curly-haired, the fabric of his pants so cheap and old it clung to his legs, she thought: Here was a safe place for her passions. Here was the son of a woman who scaled fish on a beach with a pan full of bloody fish guts anchored between her gnarled knees. Here was a man who did not know his father, who would not acknowledge him even if he knew him, so certain she was that he was fathered by one of the toothless men, still not old, threading twine through the loops of torn seine strung between bamboo poles, swigging mouthfuls of raw cane rum to deaden the pain of twisted limbs and wounds still fresh from their fight with the sea.

No, Cedric could not have dreamed a woman like her would say *Yes,* in spite of the Latin and Greek he read. Yes, in spite of the baccalaureate degree he would get from a university in London. He was ripe for awe of her. She could relieve her passion, surrender it to him and still keep her power. So she thought.

Then he said: "Beg. Beg for it, white lady."

Though she began to despise him, she pitied him, too, because it was she, not he, who held the power. It was she who bent his knees, like the white woman in Otahiti who drove an Indian farmer's son mad with his obsession to own her, though he was a doctor and had long since left his tomato patch.

Now Zuela had broken the lock on the vault where she had sealed off her memory of the photographs. Now she saw them clearly. Not even the tremulous shouts of a crowd hopeful for the appearance of Our Lady here and now in Laventille, nor the chants of the blue-frocked acolytes too young yet to need Our Lady's miracles, could dim those pictures now vivid before her eyes. Frame by frame she retrieved them, each one impeccably preserved, each one fresh, shining, precisely detailed as if she had taken it yesterday, printed it today.

A girl.

A girl younger than either she or the girl she called Daughter, now Zuela.

A girl no more than nine years old, in a pink sleeveless dress.

A girl in a pink sleeveless dress, straight black hair hanging long past her shoulders, bangs across her forehead.

A girl.

A little girl in a pink sleeveless dress with bangs across her forehead. Big, bright eyes.

A little girl with red lipstick on her mouth and rouge on her cheeks, a string of pearls tumbling down her flat chest.

A little girl, no more than ten, younger than either she or Daughter, now called Zuela.

A child.

A child in high-heeled shoes, red lipstick on her mouth.

A man.

A man old as her father, old enough to be the girl-child's father.

A man with dark brown skin, browner than a sapodilla's, browner than the girl-child's brown skin.

A man.

A man in long black pants and a sleeveless white undershirt.

A man, his fingers on his waist.

A man with long black pants, with his fingers on the buckle of his belt on his waist.

A man old enough to be the girl-child's father.

A man with hairy hands, his fingers on the zipper of his pants.

A pole.

A man with a pole.

Say you want it. Say you want it now or I beat you. Say you want it or I beat you. Beg! Beg!

A man old enough to be the girl-child's father.

On his knees now.

Please. Please beg. Beg, please.

A man with a pole begging. A little girl in a pale pink dress, a string of white pearls.

⫷ Chapter 5 ⫸

*T*hey say in Trinidad that what you eat can change your nature. Cedric, no less than the people he despised, shared that belief. When two pigs ate the bones and flesh of a woman two brothers were reputed to have hacked into fodder because of a ring another man had given her, the people in Laventille and the surrounding areas—Cedric, too—declared that the pigs were no longer pigs. What they were now, no one was certain, except everyone was quite sure that, having eaten human flesh, the pigs had risen above the slop and swill of their porcine nature, and, quite possibly (and this truly terrified them) had now acquired an irresistible taste for meat superlatively more refined than what their kind had ever hoped for.

Cedric, conscious as always of the heavy weight of responsibility that his book knowledge placed on his shoulders, and not willing to cast shadows on his reputation as an intellectual, which was granted him, *prima facie,* on his appointment as headmaster of the secondary school in Tacarigua, launched into an explication of the Aristotelian hierarchical scale of being, and pronounced the pigs to be somewhere between beast and Homo sapiens, not quite animal but not human either, sort of in-between beasts and humans, with brains like us but not exactly the same as us, with reason but not our reason. Sort of half-and-half, he concluded.

The people were more conclusive, as secure in their conviction as they were in their belief that the man who butchered Melda and fed her to the pigs was not one of the brothers. Not the ring giver, either. They placed the pigs in the same category with the she-devil soucouyant, that seductress with her swollen breasts and fleshy hips who lured her male prey under her silk fig tree. There, locking his torso between her sweaty arms, and his naked buttocks between her burning thighs, she rolled him on the damp earth, shedding her human flesh with her convulsions until she was a skinless jelly-like blanket stretched across him from head to toe, encasing him deep, deep within her. Then, when the moment of ecstasy came for her, she ignited them both in a ball of fire.

The women declared the soucouyant beast and human, but they did not fear her as they feared La Diablesse, that she-devil in cahoots with Boysie. They heard La Diablesse walking through the streets at night, her cloven hoof clacking against the hard surface of the asphalt road, her human foot, elegant in a high-heeled satin slipper, visible between the long folds of her gown. They said she had no children, and on moonlit nights she scoured the streets for little boys and girls who stayed out too late. Her beauty was her means of seduction, but her face, half hidden under a wide-brimmed hat, could not be seen unless you came close to her. But no one who witnessed that miracle lived to tell of it. She drew them to her bosom and took them for her pleasure to her cave in the hills. They said it was the male children she desired. She gave the girls to Boysie who cut out their hearts to rub on the hooves of his racehorses, a logic the people had devised to connect this half-woman, half-horse with the human animal that terrorized them. Now they worried that Boysie would find two new beasts to hunt his prey. Now they worried about how to protect themselves from pigs that were no longer pigs.

Their first hope was Our Lady. She could protect them. They would clear a space on the slope behind her shrine for the pigs and enclose it with barbed wire. They would get the priest to bless the ground and sprinkle the pigs with holy water. After they had done just that, a school-boy had another idea, "a sort of insurance," he said, "if Our Lady's miracles do not work" (impossible as that seemed). Though he was just fifteen, he was held in high esteem by the people in his neighborhood who credited him with being as intelligent as any white man. He had earned this reputation by getting distinctions in eight subjects on his Cambridge Secondary School Certificate examination, a test designed and graded at Cambridge University for the Queen's darker subjects in her colonies. When this boy spoke, the people listened. He argued, logically, that a way out of their problem with the pigs would be to turn the denatured pigs into pigs again. He reasoned that in the same way the pigs had lost their nature by eating that which was not of their nature, they could be returned to their true nature by eating that which was of their nature.

It made sense, brilliant sense, to the people. That day they slaughtered pigs to give to the pigs that were no longer pigs, careful not to eat any part of the pigs' flesh themselves. For to them it followed that if they ate food intended for the pigs, they would become more like pigs and those pigs that were no longer pigs would have power over them. Still, they begrudged feeding the pigs those parts that could fetch big dollars in the market. Again, the schoolboy showed his genius: "Give them the knuckles and the snout. Sell the rest to the high falutin' people in St. Clair."

It was the kind of poetic justice vulture fighters living on the La Basse understood.

Pork was plentiful that year and cheap, and though the ladies in the wealthy suburbs had heard how desire for Melda had caused two men to turn into beasts, and though they, too, believed that what a person ate could change his nature, they had not paused to wonder about the intricacies of the peasant mind. They bought pork in large quantities. They stewed it, pickled it, fried it, cooked it in pineapple like the Chinese, made it fricassee like the French, and curried it like the Indians. It wasn't simply because they gave the peasants no credit for any intellectual ruminations whatsoever, but because they had bigger things to ponder—not common matters about some promiscuous lower-class black woman with power to seize all semblance of humanity from two men (virile men who wore tight jeans that made the bulge on their crotch protrude like a giant doorknob), but about a white woman, a doctor, an ophthalmologist, murdered; her husband, a physician, the murderer for sure. About that, there was no doubt. Scotland Yard had said as much.

The constable from the Oropouche station, who had seen the body soon after a fisherman found it floating among the bamboo on the edge of the sea in Otahiti, had come to the same conclusion: the doctor-husband was the murderer of the ophthalmologist-wife. Only a skilled surgeon could have made that cut so precise, so exact, straight down the woman's chest to her lower abdomen. This was not Boysie's work, he told them. Here was no crude hacking open of the chest cavity to rip out a heart for racehorses. This was the work of a professional, a man who took pride in what he did, an artist drawing his scalpel lovingly and carefully across his canvas so that only one stroke was needed, no more, to peel apart her flesh like a ripe mango. But his colonial supervisors in Port-of-Spain dismissed him, and ignored his warnings to detain the doctor. Then the Queen's governor sent for Scotland Yard.

After that, people remembered a lot. Someone said he had lent the doctor a book about some newfangled surgical procedures not more than two weeks before the discovery of the body. Another person said the constable had told him that only the intestines had been removed from Paula Inge's body. Nothing else. The heart was intact, proof positive that Boysie had had no hand in the murder. When Scotland Yard pronounced that the doctor had gutted her and collapsed her lungs to keep the body from floating to the surface of the sea, people remembered that the constable had said that, too, though he said that the murderer had thrown the body in the river, not the sea, and was foiled by a power greater than he who could crumble a man's best plans as if they were sandrock in the dry season. "You can't put your bets on these currents. When they want to, they can slide in under the riverbed and pull out all kinds of things. What fishermen find some mornings on the sand in Otahiti could curdle your blood."

For people hovering between wealth and poverty, there was much to be pitied and feared in this story of an Indian dirt farmer who had finally pulled himself up not only by his university degree (a medical degree, no less), but by his marriage to a white woman, and no ordinary white woman at that. A doctor herself. An ophthalmologist. So preoccupied were they by that tragedy, and the scandal, too, they did not stop to think why pork was so cheap that year.

Not so Cedric. He understood the logic of his mother's people. He believed. He knew that for some time no pig would be safe to eat. Fearing that two pigs that had changed their nature could change his nature, too, he forbade Rosa to cook pork. Then one evening, a few days after Rosa had returned from her pilgrimage to Our Lady in Laventille with intentions to visit Zuela as soon as she could, Cedric choked on a piece of meat at the dinner table.

He had just begun to tell Rosa about the new evidence that had turned up in the Paula Singh murder case. Affecting an air of insouciance, he watched her closely as she served his food on his plate, waiting for the slightest indication—a raised eyebrow, a tremor in her hand, a flinch of her shoulder—that would confirm her guilt, his suspicions that she and Paula Inge were sisters of the same kind.

"Damaging evidence," he said, tucking his napkin into the neck of his shirt, "but not against the doctor. Oh no." He leaned back in his chair to let Rosa spoon gravy on the stewed meat on his plate. "Not that it comes as a surprise. I mean, why would a man who has worked so hard . . . " His voice trailed off and his eyes swept Rosa's face, but her expression was placid, unmoved. He cleared his throat and began again. "Yes, sir, damaging evidence. Not against him, mind you, but against *her*. I mean, figure it out, Rosa, why would a man go through all that trouble to be a doctor and then give it all away? Can you imagine, Rosa, what it took for him to leave his warm country for that cold England?" He lifted his shoulders and shivered, glancing slyly at Rosa, but she continued to serve him in silence, her face betraying no emotion, no evidence that she had heard a word he had said. Irritated that he had not succeeded in unnerving her, he raised his voice, "Rosa! Rosa, are you listening?"

Her shoulders flinched slightly, but that barely perceptible movement was enough to convince him that she had taken his bait and was not as calm as she seemed. Slowly, with deliberate concentration, he cut off a small piece of the meat on his plate, covered it with gravy, and looking directly at Rosa, he put it in his mouth. The second the meat touched his tongue, the scenario he had tried to stage with casual indifference was shattered. Any pretensions he had to a gentlemanly elegance were lost in that instant when the meat, saturated with pepper, set his mouth on fire. He lurched for the jug on the table, and not waiting to pour the juice into a glass, he clutched the sides of the jug and drank from it directly. A stream of yellow sticky liquid trailed down his arms to his elbows. Bubbles of gas floated up and down his stomach and he belched before he could stop himself.

"Piece of pepper," he said, putting the sliver of food he had taken out of his mouth on the edge of his plate. But he did not blame Rosa for it as she was braced for him to do. He had other plans for her that night that required her full attention. He wiped his lips with his napkin. "It takes years, Rosa. Years." He brought her back to the doctors. "Nine. Ten." He filled his glass with juice. "And if you're poor, as I know Dr. Singh was . . . " He swallowed three mouthfuls of juice and continued, "the whole family had to work to send money for you. The whole lot of them—aunts, uncles, cousins, everybody."

Rosa sat down. "Now tell me, Rosa," he leaned over to her conspiratorially, "after ten, twelve years of hard study in a place where you're a stranger, you think you'd throw it all away once you're qualified and back home? You think so, Rosa?" His eyes bored into hers. She turned away and reached for the dish of rice. Before she could get it, he passed it to her. "What do you think, Rosa? You think you would blow it all away on a white woman?" He paused, frowned, and scratched his head as if trying to unravel a problem that had stumped him. "Let me see. Let me see. I'll put it this way—if you'd gone to England and qualified, you think you'd come back here to make a mess of your life for no reason at all?"

Rosa spooned rice on her plate and kept her eyes downcast.

"No. No. Look at me, Rosa. Listen to me. Help me figure this out. How many tomatoes do you think they had to sell to get one English pound to send to Dalip Singh? How much cabbage? What do you think, Rosa?" His voice was even, calm. Deadly. "Unless, unless, of course, you had grounds, good reasons. Unless, unless you had cause slapping you right in the face. Unless you had evidence so great that like Othello you'd give it all up—your position as general, your big mansion, everything."

Now he saw the muscles along the side of her face twitch.

"Everything," he repeated.

Rosa put down her knife and fork and murmured, "If you have something to say to me, Cedric, why don't you say it? I know what you think already."

"You know?" He leaned toward her again.

"You told me."

"About Paula Inge? About the new evidence? You know about the new evidence?"

"Cedric, I know what you think."

"You know what I think? You know what I think? You think it's because you're white, you know what I think. You can read my mind?"

Rosa pressed her hands on the seat of the chair and raised her hips.

"No, sit down, Rosa." His voice was sugary sweet. "Sit down and help me figure this one out." He dug his fork into a piece of meat on his plate, examined it, and satisfied that it was not covered with pepper, he put it in his mouth. Still chewing, he taunted her. "See if your white brains are smart enough to figure this one out. One week, seven days before Paula Inge turned up on the sand on Freeman's Bay, she left Trinidad, giving her husband some bogus excuse that she had to go to a conference in St. Vincent. You think it was a conference she went to?"

Rosa got up.

"Sit down, Rosa." She obeyed. He put another piece of meat and some rice in his mouth. This time it took him a little longer to chew the meat before he could speak. When finally he moved the masticated meat to one side of his jaw, his voice had lost its jeering edge, but his eyes were murderous.

"If you ever lied to me like that, Rosa . . . if you ever lied like that, what Dalip Singh did would look like child's play." He smiled, a thin, razor-thin, line across his face.

At that moment, Rosa would probably have run out of the room in spite of his command that she sit where she was, had his packed mouth not garbled his words and made them sound less threatening.

"But, you wouldn't, would you, Rosa?"

"Stop this, Cedric. Stop it." She felt an irresistible urge to urinate and crossed her legs tightly to stop the slackening of the muscles of her bladder.

"Stop what? Telling the truth?"

"You have no reason to think . . . "

"To think what? To think you'd do the same? And you said you pitied me?" Cedric sneered. "You see how you pity yourself. Because you can't help it, Rosa. It's in you. In you. And your mother knows. She gave you the name."

"Name?"

"You know what it means?"

"Rose? A flower?"

"No, your other name."

"My saint name?"

"Yes, your saint name. You know what it means?"

"Nympha?"

"Yes, Nympha."

"It's my saint name."

Cedric burst out laughing. "As long as I live, I will never get over how you people have the *arrogance,* I mean *the unmitigated arrogance* to think you can come here and rule us, to think you are superior to us, better than us, and once you get here, you don't even open a book. You don't know the slightest thing. *Nothing.* "

Just then, just as Cedric was stabbing his fork in her direction shouting *Nothing,* a spasm of pain crossed the upper part of his stomach just below his chest. It brought water to his eyes. He swallowed hard and suddenly the pain went away. Blinking away the tears, he turned again to Rosa. "Just your white skin. That's all you need. Your white skin."

"Then why, Cedric?"

The quiet in her voice surprised him. "Why what? What?" The pain rose again. He grimaced, swallowed hard and it subsided.

"Why did you marry me?"

The pain in his stomach nagged him again and he struggled to ignore it, to prevent it from disarming him at the very moment he needed to contain the lava, hot and bubbling, pushing against the surface of his consciousness—the answer to her question: Why? Why after he had had her, which was all he had intended, did he *need* to marry her?

Rosa saved him. "I know I'm not as educated as you, Cedric." She gave him the lid to extinguish the volcano. "Not as intelligent."

Still, he was merciless. "All these years you've had the name and you don't know what it means. Didn't your mother tell you?"

"My mother?"

"*Nympho* from the Latin meaning nymph. *Mania* meaning mad."

"I don't know what you're trying to say, Cedric. I don't understand." Rosa crossed and uncrossed her legs. She could feel the urine, warm and wet, spotting her panties.

"Like Paula Inge. You are all nymphs. Sly. Innocent with your siren call. Mad for black meat."

The urine flowed freely now down Rosa's legs but she did not move. She pressed the folds of her skirt between her legs and watched it collect in the edges of her shoes.

"At first it was an Indian man, but he was not enough for her. No, not for her. She wanted the real thing. A real black man. In St. Vincent she had him all right. Now the police know everything. They know about her Negro lover. Dalip Singh had good cause, all right. Not a man alive would condemn him. It was a matter of honor." Cedric hissed the words through his bared teeth. "A matter of honor." He held a piece of meat on his upturned fork in the air as if it were a trophy and pointed towards Rosa. "Black meat. That's what she wanted." The pain cut him again and he bit his lips. "Like this." He stuck his fork viciously in his mouth. "Like this." He stabbed another piece of meat and shoved it in his mouth, his anger rising with the burning on his tongue and his inability to ignore the spikes that now pierced his stomach.

"Like this." The chunks of meat ballooned his cheeks but still he kept stuffing more and more in his mouth. "Like this. Like this." He fought with the pain until his words turned to growls then grunts, until no sound came but a gaping silence that filled his mouth. The veins in his forehead strained against his skin and his eyes widened in panic. His arms flailed wildly across the table, knocking the water pitcher against his glass and across his plate. Lines of water browned by the gravy from the stew trickled out of the plate to the white linen tablecloth and dripped down to the spot where Rosa's urine coursed in a thin gilded line down the sides of her shoes.

It was then Rosa looked up and saw Cedric gasping for air. Later, she would try to remember what she thought at that moment when she saw his eyes popping out of their sockets and the veins straining on his neck stiff like miniature wood poles propping up his head. She remembered that she thought that he was dying, that she knew he was pleading with her to help him, but she couldn't remember why she sat there and looked at him and didn't move. Then she made herself believe that it was because she was witnessing an act of God that forbade her interference.

It was the only explanation bearable to her. For the other, that she could have felt then such hatred for Cedric that she would have watched him struggle for air, beg her with his eyes until tears no longer dripped down his cheeks, and do nothing, was a sin no less than murder. No sacrament, no penance, no confession could erase that guilt from her soul. As it was, she was indeed witnessing an act of God, for only an act of God could have caused Cedric to collapse over the table in such a way that he would strike his diaphragm so forcefully against its edge that the remaining air in his lungs would push a powerful stream up his windpipe and blow the meat lodged in his throat out of his open mouth.

Instinctively, Rosa knew she had to get out of the room.

The morning brought rain and the sweet smells of sugar cane, guava and soursop. The night before, Rosa had slept in her bed alone listening to the thunder grumble across the dry cane fields and the thirsty cicadas screech for water as they birthed themselves from their brittle shells. All that night, too, she had heard Cedric pacing the floor beneath her, back and forth, back and forth, until just before dawn, just before the rain shower came down, he shouted, "Bitch, it was pork. Bitch, you fed me pork." Then sleep came to her, sweet and peaceful. She felt her power restored.

Cedric left the house early without speaking to her. At the dinner table that night, he examined the meat on his plate.

"Chicken," Rosa said. It was baked, without gravy.

"Pepper?" he asked. For he knew that was how she had masked the sweetness of the pig's flesh.

She shook her head.

He ate the thigh and leg in stony silence. When he was finished, she removed his plate and took it to the kitchen. She returned minutes later with his coffee and found him slumped in his chair, his arms wrapped around his stomach like the sleeves of a straight jacket.

He raised his head and spat out at her, "Bitch, you gave me pork again. Bitch." The whites of his eyes were bloodshot.

He did not eat breakfast the next morning. That evening he came home from work, his arms loaded with three bags of groceries. A fat middle-aged woman from the village walked closely behind him. She kept her eyes downcast when he informed Rosa that her name was Ena and explained that from now on she would cook for him. They went into the kitchen and Rosa followed them in silence. Cedric opened the cupboards and motioned to the woman to help him. Then he cleared the shelves of every item of food on them—salt, sugar, flour, tea, cocoa, coffee, cans of vegetables and meat, bread, pepper sauce, bottles of oil. He threw everything in the four empty bags he had placed on the floor. Then he emptied the refrigerator, even throwing out the ice water. When he was finished, he filled the cupboards and the refrigerator with the food he had bought. Afterward he reached into his pants pockets and took out three thick silver chains with padlocks at the ends. He threaded one through the handles of the refrigerator and snapped the padlock shut. He did the same to the handles on the two cupboard doors where he had put the groceries. Then he unfastened the gold necklace around the woman's neck and slipped one of the three tiny keys through it. He put the other two keys in his pants pocket.

"What will I eat now?" Rosa's voice shook as she watched him from the entrance to the kitchen.

He pointed to the litter of bags on the floor.

That night he made love to her. When he groaned above her, "Beg, beg for it, white lady," she not only despised him, but herself also. For her body had stretched out to meet his when he pressed down on her, and the space between her thighs dripped with her desire for him. Afterward she lay awake, her eyes open in the dark, wondering about a miracle that gave her no comfort.

The next morning, the pain in Cedric's stomach was worse than it had been the day before, and yet he had eaten nothing that Rosa had cooked. He was brushing his teeth when the blue points of fire pierced the lining of his stomach like a blowtorch. This time he could not hold back the screams that mounted in his throat. He dropped to his knees and bayed like a dog. Rosa rushed to him, and defeated by the pain, he was forced to let the full weight of his body fall against her helplessly. But every cell in his brain revolted against her touch and strained to transmit his abhorrence of her. Beads of perspiration littered his forehead; fat pools of tears gathered in his eyes and blinded him in his fury at the futility of his outrage. Yet he could not lift his arms to wipe the tears away nor stop the streams of saliva that drooled down his chin.

If Rosa felt the intensity of his loathing, his abhorrence of her then, she did not show it. She looped her arms under his armpits and dragged his body along the floor until she had pulled him out of the bathroom, where he had collapsed, and down the corridor to the bedroom. There, she braced herself against the bed frame, and slid under his body in an attempt to push him off her onto the mattress. But the effort proved too strenuous and she fell to the floor.

Her powerlessness, her folly to think she had the physical strength to raise him, gave Cedric a surge of triumph over her, a rush of adrenaline that allowed him the energy, though only for a second, to roll himself off her, onto the bed.

He whispered to her to fetch him water and fought with his pain to clear his eyes and steel himself for her. He was ready when she returned. He waited until she propped up his head with her hand, and as she was trying to push the glass of water against his clenched lips, he grabbed her wrist.

"Murderer! It was pork. You poisoned me, white lady." His voice, distorted by his suffering, wheezed up his windpipe like gale winds, dark and dangerous.

Rosa pulled away from him, terrified, but he held her firmly, twisting her wrist until the water spilled across the bed and the glass crashed to the floor sending shards of crystal skimming to the far corners.

"Don't you ever, white lady, ever . . . "

Then the pain struck him again and he collapsed on the bed, screaming.

Rosa saw her advantage. Frantically, she loosened his grip on her wrist and scrambled off the bed, bolting out of the room and through the front door.

A small group of people had gathered in the street in front of the house startled by the almost inhuman screams they had just heard. When they saw Rosa racing down the front steps, they parted a corridor for her, but then Cedric bellowed, "Murderer! Murderer!" and they closed in on her. It was his pain again that saved her. When it sliced through his stomach, he bellowed for help and the circle dissolved and the people ran to him. Rosa ducked through the space that opened up and ran down the road, a madwoman, her hair flying in the wind, her instincts fixed on one safe haven: Daughter. Our Lady's miracle for her in Laventille. Daughter. She waved her hands in the air. Mercifully, a passing taxi stopped for her before anyone could catch her.

⨳ Chapter 6 ⨳

Zuela remembered Rosa and in remembering her allowed herself to remember everything. There, on the top of the hill near the shrine of Our Lady, struggling to peel away the last layers of years that had thrown her into confusion the moment she thought she recognized Rosa in the woman in a black mantilla frantically climbing up the hill, everything returned when Rosa touched her, when Rosa said, her eyes welling with tears, "You'll get lost. I won't be able to find you again." Then in the urgency of her plea and in the forgotten affection that was revived in that voice, the heaviness in her chest dissipated. The muscles that had wound themselves like rubber bands around her rib cage relaxed; so, too, the tightness that constricted her heart that morning when she permitted conscience to bury the seed that had erupted after the Chinaman said, "Yes, yes," his fingers under her dress, "yes, yes."

The night before, her conscience was defeated by the hatred she felt when the Chinaman fell back on his plank bed, his semen, thin and transparent, curling down his hairless leg. But in the bright glare of morning, when Zuela saw the full ugliness of the deed she would do, what had seemed so justified flailed her with its sinfulness, and she ran to Our Lady. Then on the hill in Laventille, Rosa returned memory and conscience to her, the self-flagellating guilt that she had learned on this

Catholic island she had been brought to, retreated again. Not even Our Lady would deny her. With the crowd at Laventille, Zuela sang to her, feeling a new freedom in the righteousness of her anger.

For two weeks she had been daughter to the Chinaman and, after that, daughter and more for twenty-two years. Two weeks after he promised her father that his woman would be mother to her, he told his woman to leave.

"She too big to need a mama," he said.

She was only eleven. Still, he called her Daughter as her father had named her.

"Daughter. *Hija.* Daughter. *Hija,*" he said, pointing at her until she understood. "Your name is Daughter. Same as *Hija.* Is Daughter now."

Two years later when he had given her a new name, Zuela, he still counted her as daughter to him, though by year's end, she would give him a daughter.

He told her he would teach her to run his shop as he had taught his woman to do, and though he stroked her face and smiled when he said, "You'll do better, you'll do better than she," she did not feel the pleasure his praise was meant to give her. She found no comfort in his fingers brushing the furrows that had gathered on her forehead, nor in his icy lips pressed against the nape of her neck. But she remembered that once she had been afraid of iguanas. Then her mother showed her that the spikes on their backs would not hurt her. The scales on their skin were soft, not hard like fish scales. Not sharp like metal. *Touch. Touch. Feel it. See?* And the iguana her mother held between her fingers drew its hairless eyelids over its eyes and made her smile.

Then her mother died and the Chinaman came to her village to buy alpagats for his store and took her, too. Once when she and Rosa were playing a child's game, Rosa asked her suddenly, "Why did he do that? Why did your father give you to the Chinaman?" She did not know that twelve-year-old Rosa was fighting nightmares, too: Didn't her mother send her two sisters to England to find husbands? Wouldn't she be next?

Zuela gave her the answer the women in the village had given her, "I was too big to live with a man who had no woman, even if he was my father," she said.

Rosa did not understand.

At first the Chinaman was patient. He taught her everything. How to measure rice. "Keep the black stones in it," he said when she tried to take them out. "They make the rice heavier."

He showed her how to measure sugar. "Keep your hand on the scale under the paper when you weigh it. If they say anything, say, 'You want sugar to spill on the ground?'"

Chinaman showed her how to cut up oxtail. "Cut off some meat from each piece. We sell it later in the minced meat."

Chinaman explained everything, and in Spanish, so she understood. But soon he told her it was time for her to learn English words for the words she had to know—flour, sugar, salt, meat, ounce, pound, quarter, half, cents, dollars. Numbers. Then after she learned them and he was satisfied his customers understood, he spoke no more to her in Spanish.

Meanwhile, in the weeks afterward, she had lived in fear of the grumble of English sounds that made no sense to her and isolated her in ways that were unbearable. In time she learned to cope, to weave a curtain against the noise that terrified her, a barrier to separate her world from his, to shield the paintings she had stored in her head of her home in Venezuela: thick-waisted trees that mounted the sky; vines, the color of emeralds, twisting around wide branches; specks of gold from a dazzling sun filtering through the slits between the leaves down on a rich black earth.

Then Chinaman insisted, and forced her lips to shape his words. Soon he had filled the space in her mind where she kept her world. Soon she barely remembered a mother who showed her that iguanas can be harmless, that the spikes on their backs would not hurt her. Soon she learned that snakes not only lived in the forest but in cities, too.

After he taught her English words, Chinaman made her pound the poppy seeds for him and fill his pipe. Then when his nightmares came, he called her to his attic. She was just eleven.

When she was twelve, she had a chance to be a girl again. That was the year Chinaman left her with Boysie's woman in Tacarigua. That was the year she met Rosa.

Tired of getting cents, not dollars, for the goods he sold in his

store, Chinaman had persuaded Boysie to go into business with him selling opium. Chinese men were pouring into the Caribbean in search of
food, bringing with them a savage hunger for opium, instigated by the
British who needed silver to buy tea. Chinaman saw profit in their addiction. He paid Boysie to take him in his boat through the treacherous
Bocas, down deep in the Orinoco, to find ganja leaves he sold for information about opium to old East Indian farmers in Trinidad who sucked
in the memory-killing fumes to blot out the anguish of an irreversible
mistake: five years for five acres of land and a promise to return home to
India that England seldom honored. They, these dream-hating ancients,
told Chinaman about the British ships from India carrying the brown
resin he hoped would make him rich. They gave him names, but he took
Boysie with him as insurance when he boarded the ships. Boysie was an
East Indian, like most of the laborers on the British ships, and Chinaman
knew he could use his face to put them at ease. Because of Boysie they
would sell him anything.

Through the Dragon's Mouth and up the Orinoco, back out fighting currents in the Bocas to the Atlantic, he and Boysie would be gone
for weeks, sometimes months, at a time. When his horses started losing
at the races, Boysie was glad he had gone with the Chinaman. Nineteen
years later, people saw signs that his reign on the Arima race track had
come to an end when the body of a white woman washed up on the sand
on Freeman's Bay. When they cut the stitches her doctor-husband had
sewn, Paula Inge's heart was still in her chest. Only her intestines were
missing. Hearts were what Boysie fed his racehorses in Arima, hearts were
what he rubbed on their hooves. Boysie openly acknowledged his debt to
the Chinaman a year later when he was making good money selling opium
to the Americans in Chaguaramas, "He have brains. He use my face like
a passport and they let us come on the ships."

It was money that motivated the Chinaman to go into the opium
business, but not long after, it became primarily his own addiction. For
he needed opium to chase away the guilt that had hounded him like a
vengeful tyrant since that night he crawled on his belly, sliding through
pools of congealed blood that trickled from the veins of the decapitated
necks of his wife and daughter. Slipped like a snake, not turning back

once, the palms of his hands, his arms, his chest, his belly, his knees, his thighs, his legs stained traitor-red. Crawled like a snake through the reeds until he reached a boy turned statue, sitting in a sampan on the banks of the Yangtze.

The nightmares had resumed soon after that day he went to the rainforest in Venezuela to buy alpagats and saltfish and took Zuela, too. A year later he needed more than two pipes a night to stop himself from digging his fingernails across his neck until it dripped blood. He went with Boysie for three months to scour the Atlantic for British ships. It was the last trip he would make, but his brief absence gave Zuela respite, and the chance to be a child again.

Boysie had persuaded him to leave Zuela with his woman, Teresa, who knew nothing about her but understood when Boysie said that the girl's name was Daughter and she *belonged to* the Chinaman, that the girl was no longer a girl, that she was a woman-child who had lost her childhood. Moved by pity for her, Teresa resolved to return innocence to her if only for three months. She persuaded Mrs. Appleton, the woman whose clothes she ironed at the Orange Grove sugar-cane estate, to let Rosa play with the woman-child. Clara Appleton was glad enough to send Rosa to Teresa's house, too, for by then she was busy negotiating the placement of two daughters with suitable husbands in England.

In those three months, Zuela was a child again. And in those borrowed days when Time held her green, she pretended she was a girl no different from Rosa, and ran with her without care (as little girls do) through the cane fields, arms stretched out wide like the wings of a bird, fingers gliding past the long green leaves of the sugar-cane plants, heedless of the burning sun, a wonder to the small, thin Indian men, sweat draining down their faces into the necks of their sleeveless undershirts, who put down their scythes and paused to stare without malice for the memories she reawakened.

Those were the days when the cane fields were a magical place for Zuela. Until they were burned down for the harvest, she and Rosa sprawled out in the dry drainage canals, often late into the afternoon, under the shade of the sugar-cane leaves. There, lulled by the heat of the sun and the intoxicating perfume of sugar, they told each other nursery stories.

Rosa's were about the fairy tales she had read: *Red Riding Hood, Cinderella, Beauty and the Beast;* Zuela's, no less fictional (for so she believed, in those spellbound days), of a little girl who planted marigolds on her mother's grave. "They shone like the sun," she said. "Even in the night."

"Even in the night?" Rosa asked her.

"Even in the night, so the mother always had light to see where the little girl was."

They never went very far into the cane fields, never beyond where they could see the tops of cars moving along the asphalt road above the rows of cane leaves. But a week before the harvest, curiosity drove them to know what was on the other side of the road, and trusting in the invincible power of their sisterly bond to shield them from harm, they took the first step out of a world which, if not protective, had offered them the security of the familiar.

It was there, on the other side, that the first beam of darkness fell across Zuela's happiness during that brief Edenic interlude. For sitting on the front steps of a house facing the cane fields was a boy who would force Zuela to face the truth that the Indian farmers marveling at the miracle of her innocence did not see: She was a woman-child, not a girl-child like Rosa.

The boy was older than both of them. He had long thin arms and legs that protruded from his tiny body like tentacles. He was holding a book in his hands. From time to time he looked up from it toward the sky, moving his lips as if in prayer.

"Learning it by heart," said Rosa.

"By heart?"

"Memorizing it."

It was a foreshadowing of that afternoon behind the hibiscus—the first of the only two times in those heady weeks in the cane fields when Zuela could not chase away the image of the Chinaman that was always there, threatening to break the spell Rosa had cast around her. *By heart. By heart.* Each time the boy spoke to the sky, she saw him holding on to his heart as she had held on to hers at night when Chinaman was sleeping and she could use her lips to shape words she was forbidden to speak after he warned her: *No more Spanish.*

Under the shade of sugar-cane leaves she and Rosa watched the boy in silence. Minutes later, the front door of the house opened and an Indian man in baggy khaki pants and a starched white, short-sleeved shirt walked toward the boy. The boy lowered his head. The man spoke to him but still the boy kept his eyes on his book. The man spoke again and pointed his hand in the direction of the incline along the unpaved road that separated the cane fields from the house. In the distance Zuela saw clouds of dirt billowing toward them. Then she heard the beat of hooves.

The man descended the steps and waited. The horse drew nearer.

"My father," said Rosa. She recognized the man astride the horse. He signaled the Indian man to climb on the horse behind him. The man mounted the horse and wrapped his arms around the Englishman's torso. The Englishman turned around and patted his hands. The emotion he expressed had the intensity of a kiss.

Zuela glanced at the boy. His eyes were still on his book.

The harvest fires came soon after, though the people said the first one was not started by the planters but by an Indian man who lived with his son and a black woman in the house where Rosa and Zuela had seen a boy talking to the sky. Perhaps it was so. Rosa's father said it was so. He knew the man. He was an ungrateful sort, he said. The most dangerous kind. He had often given him a ride on his horse to the rum factory.

Rosa and Zuela never saw the boy again, though Rosa would desire him when he became a man. But that would be a long time off and she would not know then that the man who whispered to her on the dining room floor, *Beg. Beg for it, white lady,* was the same person as the boy who talked to the sky.

After the burning of the cane field, Rosa and Zuela thought no more of the boy, lost in new games of hide-and-go-seek they devised in the backyards of makeshift houses in the village where Zuela stayed with Teresa. Yet it was in the midst of such a game that the memories the boy aroused would return to Zuela with such force that all pretense would leave her forever. For in the cathedral stillness of a Sunday afternoon, when the blistering sun had chased every reasoned adult under a roof for shelter, animals panted in the thick shade of the blossoming immortelle, and insects hid under mossy rocks or the cool of earth holes, Rosa called her to her hiding place and she saw what Rosa saw through the tangle of a hibiscus bush: a man with a pole, his trousers to his knees; a girl in a pink dress, a string of pearls, lipstick on her mouth. A girl too much like her.

It should have been easy for Zuela to pretend she had seen nothing (she wanted so much to believe she had seen nothing), but Rosa persisted, pulling her back to the hibiscus. She tried to get away, but Rosa fought her. Again and again she tugged Rosa's dress, but Rosa dug her toes deep into the dirt and anchored herself to the thin branches that scratched her cheeks until they bled. Hibiscus shuddered on the bush and fell to the ground. In seconds their flaming petals turned bruised blue in the dirt.

Frantic to escape, Zuela twisted Rosa's hair, and Rosa slapped her. In the violence of that slap, Zuela's imagination became a child's again and made the impossible possible, so that she believed that Rosa saw in that looking glass behind the hibiscus the reality she knew too well. That Rosa could see, that she *had seen* through the wood slats of the jalousies in the darkened attic of a shop in Nelson Street, a Chinaman and a girl he called Daughter. A Chinaman as old as that man behind the hibiscus, older even than that man. A girl like that girl. A girl who had learned and then learned to unlearn that the spikes on the back of an iguana would not hurt her. And hysteria mounted her throat. Only the truth shattered the world that terrified her. "Chinaman do that to me already," she said to Rosa, laughing and swaying her hips like a full-grown woman. "Chinaman done do that to me."

But Zuela felt no awe that would fill her with guilt as it would Rosa, no awe that caused her to think that that little girl quivering behind the hibiscus had power over that man with his pole, no awe that caused her to delude herself into believing that when Chinaman pushed her down on his plank bed in his attic in Nelson Street, she had power over him. She knew only the endless midnight of an abyss she wished would swallow her.

After that day behind the hibiscus, Zuela could no longer pretend she was a girl who had never left innocence, Daughter who was a father's daughter, Zuela who was not yet a wife. When the Chinaman returned from his trip with Boysie, she made herself forget those days with Rosa when she had been a girl again, for to remember them and to know at the same time that there was no escape from the Chinaman's prison was torture far worse than if she had never known such happiness. But, rediscovering Rosa on the hill in Laventille near the shrine of Our Lady, she found the courage to remember. Now she swore she would use the anger the Chinaman had unsheathed when he slid his fingers up her naked thighs. Now she spoke aloud the secret she had shared with Alan: *Smoke can kill you, smoke can kill the Chinaman.*

Fortunately for the Chinaman, the coughing that shook his chest like a baby's rattle and popped a maze of blue wires across his forehead and down his temples had become so intense that he was forced to lie in his attic for hours, and then for days, at the very time Zuela was obsessed by a will to act out of an anger and resentment that demanded no less than his life.

That first night when she returned from Laventille where she had gone to stifle the very passions that now enflamed her, Zuela waited for him to call her, but he could not call her. In the shrouded darkness of her room she listened without pity to the sounds of his suffering pressing down from the attic. She rocked her daughters on her breasts and hoped that when he sucked in his breath he would strangle on the wind rushing down his throat. In those exquisite moments when, too weak to exhale, he thrashed against the sides of his plank bed, she counted the number of thumps he made with his fists, but later she regretted she had wished for his death then, for she thought that dying that way would be too good for him. So she prayed that the pump in his chest would push out his breath again, and she would get her turn to stop it, in her own time, in her own way, and that when he called down for her to come to him, she would be ready: *Smoke, smoke can kill you.*

But the Chinaman did not call her. Not that night or any other night. Not that night because of a nightmare he had had, worse than the others. Not any other night because he feared in her silent absence the realization of all he had seen through that terrible darkness: not two necks bleeding, but one.

He never asked the children why they, not she, brought his meals to the attic. Why none of his girls came. And when his coughing was bad and he needed the smoke he had taught Zuela to breathe on him, he showed Alan how to make cigarettes with the crushed leaves of the ganja and how to inhale and blow the smoke in his mouth and up his nostrils. "Suck. Suck. I beat your mother if you tell her. Suck. Suck till it blow out your cheek like a fish. Then puff it over my face. Don't swallow. Don't let it go in your lungs. Hold it, hold it good in your mouth."

It took the boy three days to learn and Zuela two days after that to know why, when he brought back his father's dishes from the attic, the whites in his eyes had turned red as if he had been crying, and why, when she asked him, he slumped to his bed and fell asleep before he could answer. The reason came clear to her the day Rosa ran to her, fleeing the hatred Cedric had hurled on her and the unforgiving eyes of her neighbors that scorched her with their accusations.

She saw both at the same time: Rosa, when she noticed the people in the shop straining their necks to see what had caused a small crowd to gather on the pavement outside, and Alan, when she heard his words slur against the roof of his mouth, "Ma, a white lady looking for you." But now she only had time to ease Alan down on the sack of flour behind the counter, for the crowd that was struck dumb momentarily by Rosa's surprising presence at the doorway of the Chinaman's shop became alive again, causing the Chinaman's friend to get up from his stool in the corner where he was posted to watch over the money and Zuela, and to squint his eyes from Rosa to her, her to Rosa. So she left Alan on the flour and hurried to Rosa, shifting her anger to that place in her brain where other angers waited: *Tonight. Tonight when the Chinaman is alone in his attic.* Because now she did not want to raise suspicions in the Chinaman's spy.

"White lady sick," she shouted to him and led Rosa to the back of the shop, feeling his eyes on her, but knowing he would not follow her.

The people in the shop said that Zuela was lucky that at that moment an old woman distracted Tong Lee so that he let Zuela go. The old woman had long pitied Zuela. She had seen the Chinaman's friend sit on the same stool day after day hugging a steel case, a vacuous grin on his face that changed oddly to a soft smile when Zuela stretched out her hand to give him the money a customer had paid her. She knew he was the Chinaman's spy, his eyes, even when the Chinaman was drowning in his spit on his bed upstairs.

The old woman laughed in his face, "You never see a white woman yet? Watch or I go to Hong Fat to buy my sugar."

Tong Lee turned away and Zuela felt sorry for him. A spy he was for the Chinaman, but not by choice. His smile eased the embarrassment she felt in front of the customers when she was forced to hand him their money as if she were a thief, or worse, a child too stupid to count. Grateful to the old woman, she hurried Rosa to her room, troubled by the fear she saw in Rosa's eyes, more disturbing than the anxiety she had heard in her voice when Rosa pursued her on the hill saying *must. I must* speak to you.

Still, when Zuela took her behind the curtain to the room she shared with her children, she was startled by Rosa's whiteness. She had not remembered her so pale. On the hill near the shrine, her black mantilla had shaded her cheeks. Now Zuela could see there was no color there, not even on her lips. When they played together as children they had always been in the sun. Rosa's cheeks were always flushed, her eyes full of light. Now even her golden brown hair seemed dull and lifeless.

Zuela motioned to her to sit on the bed and noticed that her hands were also pale white and that they were shaking slightly, even though she had clasped them tightly together on her lap. She handed Rosa a glass of juice and brushed the backs of her fingers while she drank until, little by little, blood returned to her face and gradually Zuela saw that it was still burnt olive as it had been when they were children together.

"You feeling better?" she asked when Rosa finally put down the glass. "What frightened you so?"

Rosa pressed her lips together to stop the tears that brimmed her eyes.

"Is the people in the shop?" Zuela held Rosa's hand. "They don't mean anything. They never see a white lady come here by herself, that's all. They see white ladies come to the shop, but they bring their maids with them. They never see one come in a taxi by herself."

Rosa shook her head. "No, that's not it." Her voice was hardly audible.

"Then what? What frighten you? You come in here looking so white."

"Cedric."

"Cedric?"

"My husband."

"You frighten of your husband?"

"He thinks I'm trying to poison him."

Zuela released her hand. The coincidence was too much for her. Just hours before, she had lain on her bed counting the beats on the wall. Hoping and hoping. Plotting a more terrible revenge.

"He made the people believe that, too. When I tried to leave, they almost killed me. I didn't know what to do. I didn't know where to go. I remembered I saw you in Laventille. You were the only person I thought could hide me."

"Me?" Zuela threw out her arms. "Here?"

"I have no place else to go."

"Is more than a week now you say *must*. I think you must mean right away."

"I didn't get the chance."

"You talked like you *had* to see me."

"I was coming."

"Like you couldn't wait. What? What you couldn't wait for?"

How could Rosa tell her about the miracle? That as soon as she had lost her in the undertow of the crowd on the hill, Our Lady parted the hibiscus bush for her and she saw it all. All that had led her to Cedric. Then she didn't need Zuela to unlock the vault where she had sealed the photographs.

"You were my best friend," Rosa said.

"That was a long time ago," said Zuela.

"When I saw you on the hill, I remembered."

"We were children," said Zuela and fought with the branches of the hibiscus that were threatening to smother her.

"But you remember?"

"Tong Lee won't stay out there forever," said Zuela.

"After that we didn't talk. Before that, remember you used to say you would do anything for me? We were sisters."

"Long time." Zuela brushed her away.

"He will kill me for sure," said Rosa.

Once Zuela had seen her reflection in the mirror next to Rosa. She was wearing one of the many dresses Rosa had given her. "Like sisters," she said to Rosa.

"Best of friends, too," said Rosa.

That was what they were in the cane fields—sisters and best friends sworn to love and protect each other.

Now Rosa was pleading with her to remember. "He will kill me for sure."

Zuela broke through the hibiscus and breathed in the air of sour milk and dried urine rising from the mattress where she slept with her baby daughters. "I can't." She stood up.

"He will kill me," Rosa repeated.

Zuela looked down and saw that the trembling had returned to Rosa's hands. *Yes, before the hibiscus, like sisters.* "I tell Tong Lee you sick," she said. "I tell him to let me stay with you a while."

She put it all behind her when she returned with Alan. All behind her that it was Rosa who never came back to Teresa's house to play with her. That it was Rosa whose eyes skimmed the ground when she passed her on the Orange Grove estate.

"Alan watch them so we can talk," she said to Rosa. "But not long." She reached for the baby crouched in the corner of the bed next to two of her other daughters. They were so quiet, Rosa had not noticed them.

"Is because they know how to keep still," said Zuela.

"They were there all the time?"

"Behind you."

"But I didn't see . . . "

"I know." She gave the baby to Alan and told her two other daughters she would be back for them soon. "Don't go to your father even if he call you." She stopped Alan at the door. "You hear me?"

"I never would have thought children could be so quiet." Rosa was still wide-eyed after the children left. "Like statues."

"They learn good from the Chinaman."

"Good?"

"How not to make noise when his customers come."

"But so quiet?"

"All of them learn."

"All?"

"All ten." Zuela saw Rosa's eyes linger on her stomach. She had caught her doing the same thing in the glare of the sun on the top of the Laventille hill, first at her face, then at the swelling that lifted her dress below her waist. There was something in the way she stared at her stomach—the tenderness in her eyes—that stopped her from feeling the discomfort she always felt when the customers in the shop looked at her. So she had pretended not to notice.

"I have none," said Rosa softly.

The longing in Rosa's eyes filled Zuela with compassion for her. "None?" she asked.

"I never conceived," said Rosa.

"I'm sorry."

"No. It's better that way. I wouldn't want them with Cedric."

Zuela brushed back a strand of hair that had fallen across her eyes and ran her hand along the length of her braid down her back. "Is not a baby I having now. It just stay so after so many times. People make joke and say is pumpkin I growing. Except for these past two years, I make one every year since the Chinaman marry me. Now it can't go down." She smoothed her skirt over her stomach.

"Every year?"

"The last three, I have one every ten months."

"My God!"

"Is not God," Zuela laughed bitterly, "though He spare me these last two years. But they good. They nice children." She sat down next to Rosa. Thirty minutes. That was all Tong Lee would give her. For the sake of a past—three months of happiness when Chinaman sailed down the Bocas with Boysie—she would listen to Rosa. Out of gratitude for a time when she could believe that the marigolds she planted on her mother's grave would light the way for her mother to see her, even from beneath the earth, she would be a sister to Rosa, always.

"We don't have much time. Tell me. Tell me why your husband think you want to poison him. Tong Lee say he close the store for half-hour. Customers gone now; they can't see you. And is after lunch time. They belly full and sun hot, so they gone to sleep. Tell me."

"And Tong Lee?"

"He gone upstairs to see the Chinaman. Don't worry. So why your husband think you want to poison him?"

"He choked on his food."

"And?"

"And he had pains in his stomach."

"And that make him think you want to poison him?"

Rosa turned away from her eyes.

Zuela came closer to her. "What?"

Rosa kept her eyes averted.

"You hiding something?" Zuela held her chin and twisted it toward her. "You try to poison him?"

Rosa pulled her chin violently away from her hand. "No!"

Zuela laughed.

"No!" Rosa shouted again.

"Because I ask you to tell me how you poison him." She was smiling, but if Rosa could have read her mind she would have known she was serious just then. Dead serious.

"I didn't do anything," Rosa was insisting.

"Then why he think what he think?"

"He got sick suddenly."

"Suddenly?"

"After he choked."

"What choke him?"

"Meat."

"Meat you cook for him?"

"Yes."

"What kind of meat?"

"Everybody was buying it."

"What kind?"

"Cedric always said I spent too much money. I was trying to save. It was cheap."

"What was cheap?"

"The meat. Really cheap. I didn't think he would notice."

"Pork? Is pork you give him?"

"I didn't think anything was wrong with it."

"Chinaman can't eat anything solid. He can't chew when the coughing starts. We have to chop up his food like baby food."

"There was nothing wrong with the pork, I told you."

"Anyhow he never eat meat. He could tell if I give him meat."

"I didn't cook only for him. I cooked for us. I ate it, too."

"And we don't sell it in the shop since that man chop up that woman and feed her to the pigs." *No way to get pork even if she could grind it in his sancoche so he wouldn't notice.*

"They caught the pigs," said Rosa.

"Yes. Yes." Zuela forced herself to focus on Rosa. "Our Lady watching them. But they still say no pork good to eat till those pigs dead."

"You don't believe that?"

"What difference it make what I believe? Your husband believe?"

"He never talked to me about those pigs."

"But what he tell you about pork? He tell you you could cook pork?"

Rosa lowered her head.

"He tell you it was okay?"

"He's a teacher. He knows better."

"But what he say? What he tell you, Rosa?"

Rosa did not answer her.

"Is not only fact that can kill you, you know. Mostly is what you believe is fact. If you believe something could kill you, ten to one it kill you."

"He didn't think it would kill him," said Rosa.

"But what he tell you?"

"Not to cook it."

Zuela looked at her hard.

Rosa got up. "I thought you would help. I thought because I saw you at the shrine after so many years that it was a sign you could help me. Would."

"I not placing blame on you. I not saying you wrong. I just want to know how you did it, if you did it."

But Rosa did not understand her. She had not seen Zuela counting the beats of the Chinaman's hand. She had not heard her praying for the valves in his heart to pump again so she could stop them later, in her own time.

"I ate the pork just like him," she said again. "And I didn't get sick."

"Maybe is something else."

"I didn't do anything."

No. She didn't do anything. Zuela pushed hope behind her, extinguished one more dream of retribution she had for the Chinaman. "Maybe something get him sick," she said.

"He thinks it's me."

"But why?"

"Ever since that doctor murdered that woman."

"Dalip Singh?"

"He thinks I have a lover."

Zuela's eyes grew glassy.

"Chinaman say man-woman business, as if that woman make her husband put knife in her belly."

"But I didn't try to poison him," said Rosa.

"No, no. I know. Like I know that woman didn't make her husband kill her."

"You have to help me."

"You can't stay here." Zuela swept her arms toward the furniture in the room. There was one other bed, next to the wall, opposite the bed they sat on. "That is for the boys. This one is for the girls and me. And they not even beds. Just some coconut fiber and ticking I sew up and Chinaman put on top of a plank of wood and four cement blocks."

Rosa began to cry silently.

"Anyhow Chinaman don't let me keep you."

Tears rolled down Rosa's cheeks.

"Go to your mother," said Zuela. "She help you."

"I can't."

"Can't?"

"She can't take the shame."

"What shame? What shame is it for her to help out her child?" *Her mother would have protected her from the Chinaman if she were alive.*

"You don't understand."

"No." *Her mother would have brought her home, if she were alive. She would not have left her to the cobra's fangs.*

"I just can't go back."

For a long while, they were both silent, Rosa weeping, Zuela looking with no particular intention at the picture of the Sacred Heart over the door that led to the shop, moving her head from side to side so she could create the optical illusion that had never ceased to amaze her: a living heart sprouting drops of blood.

"Priest tell Chinaman to put it there when he bless the shop," she said. Then thinking of Rosa and her mother, of the shame Rosa said she would bring to her if she went back to her, she added, "He bleed plenty for me. I think He bleeding now for you."

"What will I do?"

Zuela smiled a grim smile. "You just like me. You have to stay."

"Stay with him?"

"What else you do? Where you go?"

"But he'll kill me for sure."

"Not if you make him well again."

Rosa stopped crying. She stared at Zuela.

"That is, if you want to make him well again," Zuela said.

Rosa frowned.

"Do you?" Zuela asked.

A scraping sound on the floor above them—like a chair being moved, a small piece of furniture, or, perhaps, a wooden box—made Zuela sit upright and put her finger to her lips. "Shh." She looked upward to the ceiling. "Chinaman."

But Rosa had barely heard that slight noise. "You think I really want to poison him, don't you?"

The attic was quiet; not a sound filtered down. Zuela listened, waiting to be sure.

"You really don't think that, do you?"

"He stop now."

"What?"

"I was thinking he trying to hear what we saying."

"Who?"

"Chinaman."

"You think?"

"No. He can't hear. We not talking loud."

"You can't believe I want to poison Cedric." Rosa was impatient for Zuela's answer.

"No," said Zuela finally. "No, but old people have a saying: Careful what you pray for. Careful you don't bother God so much He don't answer you."

"But I'm not praying for Cedric to die."

"No. You hoping in your heart."

"I don't want him sick."

Zuela looked up to the ceiling. She thought she had heard the scraping again, but she was not sure.

"I just don't want him to be mean to me," Rosa said.

Zuela sighed. It was her imagination. She turned to Rosa. "Then do what I say."

"What?"

"Make him well."

"How? I don't know."

"Remember that woman you tell me used to take care of you and your sisters? The one with the butterfly on her face? Mary Christophe? She living in Laventille. You go to see her. You ask her to give you something to help your husband. Then when he feeling better, he don't think you trying to poison him. Then maybe he change."

Before Rosa left, she called Zuela by the name she had known her: Daughter. It was then Zuela realized that Rosa had not known that she had another name.

"Zuela now," she told Rosa. "Chinaman name me. He say he can't call me Daughter no more since I making daughter for him."

Rosa persisted. "Is he good to you?"

"What you think?" And Zuela's eyes lost all light. Then Rosa saw the little girl of her childhood again, the little girl who swished her hips like a woman, and laughed. *That is nothing. Chinaman do that to me already. Chinaman done do that.*

⤜ Chapter 7 ⤛

Chinaman had a first name: Ho Sang. Zuela did not know it until the priest asked, "Do you, Ho Sang, take this woman, Zuela Simona, to be your lawfully wedded wife to have and to hold in sickness and in health from this day forward till death do you part?"

It was one year since she and Rosa had played in the cane fields.

She was thirteen. Chinaman was forty-seven. Already his daughter Agnes was growing in her.

Chinaman had a last name: Chin. He was Ho Sang Chin. After the priest blessed them and told Zuela what God had joined together let no man put asunder, Chinaman said she was Zuela Chin. She should call him Ho Sang. She never did, neither did the people in the shop. They heard her say Chinaman so they called him Chinaman. They saw her belly rise, and knowing it was Chinaman who caused it so, they called her Chinaman's wife.

Except for the one who sat with him but did not smoke the resin, the one who smiled softly at Zuela in the shop in Nelson Street, all Chinaman's Chinese friends called him Chin. It was a name Zuela had known when he came up the Orinoco to buy alpagats for his shop and wanted her, too. Her father said, "Don't forget she still a child, Chin."

The women told her she had nothing to worry about: Chin

already has a woman.

She didn't know what there was to worry about.

Your mother's dead, the women told her. And your father needs a woman. It's not right he should live alone with a girl-child. Chin and his woman will take care of you. Yankees spreading dollars all over Trinidad. "Rum and Coca-Cola," they sang, trying to put her at ease. You can come back when you get big, they told her. You can come back when you can fend for yourself.

Chin said, "I take care of her as if she is my daughter. Ernestine help me."

Two weeks later he told Ernestine to leave. Two months later Zuela was pounding the hardened juice of the poppy seed for him.

One day he said to her, "I smoke the brown ball so Englishman can drink tea." She did not know what he meant, though she thought it strange he should say it with such anger. The brown resin seemed to silence his nightmares, to give him peace. But she had not seen him crawling on his belly to reach the Yangtze. She had not known about that, or that he had been married before. Or that he had had a daughter. She did not know that when he told her father he would take care of her as if she were his own daughter, he was in the torment of a hell he had created with a memory that would not leave him in spite of the poppy seed, in spite of an ancient resentment over tea-drinking Englishmen. A daughter he hardly knew. A wife. A daughter and wife who had become so indistinguishable for him in that pool of blood he had left behind in China, that when he thought of one, he thought of the other. When he took Zuela, he wanted them both.

Still.

But Zuela did not know that. She had only the memory of a childhood gone and a confusion about womanhood: When did one end and the other begin? Was it when he named her Zuela, stroking her straight black hair down her naked back? She had no spikes like the iguana's to protect her. The hair on her back was soft and downy like a baby's, but it stood up like metal wires when the Chinaman touched it.

"Venezuela, Venezuela," he chanted. "My little Venezuela."

When he came back after those months on the open sea with Boysie,

82

the year when, for a brief time, she was a girl again with Rosa, he sang to her, "Daughter, Venezuela. Venezuela, *Hija. Hija.* Zuela." Then he settled on Zuela two months later after she woke up one morning vomiting her insides.

The priest said to him he should marry her. The priest said to her she was lucky. Not many men would have done the right thing.

The babies came—one every year, the last three ten months apart. Good children, nice children, she had told Rosa, but she had not told her that they were also her salvation, that life for her would have been unbearable if she had not had any; if, like Rosa, she had been childless. For each time she lay under the Chinaman in the suffocating darkness of his attic, they gave her reason to continue living. Each time she felt the possibility of the Chinaman's seed taking root in her womb, the thought that she would bear one more child kept her strong: if not her childhood, theirs; if not her happiness, her daughters' and her sons'. So she protected them fiercely and Chinaman did not interfere, but only after she promised she would never say no, only after she swore she would always say yes—yes, even when yes meant nine days after her bleeding stopped, five days while she menstruated; yes, even when yes meant the night before her babies were born; yes, even when yes meant feeling the bottoms of their feet kick against the top of her womb; yes, even when yes meant feeling their heads pushed back in her again when he drove himself upwards. That was the reality of her life, but it would not be the reality of her children's lives, her daughters' lives. She gave Agnes, her eldest, to the nuns *before she turned twelve.* Now there was Alan to protect.

After Rosa left the shop, Zuela called Alan to her. "Tonight," she said, "you don't go. I go for you."

The Chinaman said that because the Englishman wanted tea, he made the Chinese smoke the poppy seed. But not her sons. Her sons owed the Englishman nothing and she had paid the Chinaman for everything. She would not let him cause Alan's eyes to roll in their sockets and turn bloodshot red.

"I take his food for him tonight," she said. "You stay."

But Chinaman had other plans. His friend Tong Lee had told him that a white lady had come to the shop that afternoon and Zuela had taken her to the room behind the curtain.

"You think Zuela know her before?"

Tong Lee told him no, but still the Chinaman begged him to listen for him through the hole he had drilled in the floorboards above the room where Zuela slept with the babies after he warned her: *Too much noise. Too much crying.* Then she had to teach her children, even the babies, to cry in their pillows so the Chinaman would not hear them. Yet he made the hole because he had to be sure that that was all she taught them: *No use in complaining. This is the way it will be.*

At first Tong Lee refused him. "White lady sick. Zuela just helping."

But Chinaman reminded him of the Yangtze, of a boy turned statue on a bench in a sampan, of a headless corpse, of many headless corpses. Then Tong Lee did as he was asked and lifted the wooden box where Chinaman kept his pipe and his resin and other things, too, and listened for him.

He told the Chinaman that the white lady was planning to poison her husband, and that Zuela had sent her to a woman in Laventille. For that was what he had heard when he lifted the box from the hole after he had accidentally scraped it against the floorboard.

Laventille. The word terrified the Chinaman. "Laventille?"

Tong Lee said it was the word he had heard.

But it was not the word the Chinaman wanted to hear, not after he had sat in his attic sucking in the ganja smoke to bury *Laventille* along with the front steps of a house, two trees and the banks of a river in China.

When Zuela told him she was going to make devotions to Our Lady, he had suspected her, but not because she had left the shop early or because she was going to pray. He had made his pact years before with the priest: He would allow her to go to Mass and to Confession and to make pilgrimages to Our Lady of Fatima. In exchange, he would exercise his sacramental right to her body. He suspected her because she did not ask. She told him. There, in the middle of the afternoon, with customers clamoring for a half-pound of salt, a quarter-pound of sugar, she handed him the measuring scoop and said, "Alan, watch the children. I going to Laventille."

He could not find his voice in the face of this new hardness in her eyes.

"Laventille?"

Tong Lee said he was sure. Laventille was where Zuela sent Rosa to find a woman who knew about poison.

Ho Sang had felt Zuela's repulsion the night before she told him she was going to Laventille. He had felt it when he snapped his hand around her ankle and pulled her down to him that night, as he had done years of nights before when he knew she would never say no if he let her send his children to school, if he kept them out of his shop, if he made no complaint when she said, No, they would not learn to measure rice; they would not learn to count change—if he stayed silent, too, when she gave his daughter to the nuns. But that night when the body of the white woman rolled onto the beach in Otahiti, she had let him see the hatred in her eyes, and the next day she told him she was going to Laventille.

He knew he should not have touched her. He had seen her turn to stone when he spat out *man-woman business,* but in the delirium before the smoke she blew in his mouth mercifully snuffed out the truth, he had found the redemptive illusion again—the woman before him was the wife he had lost in China, and the girl with the long braid, his daughter. He reached for the woman's thighs. Afterward, the nightmare that always made its way back to him was unrelenting, unforgiving. It showed him a more pitiless hell: not only a wife and a daughter soaked in a pool of blood, but a woman with eyes of steel counting his breaths.

Now more than ever before, he was afraid to let Zuela come to him. He was glad that since his coughing began, she had sent only the children. After Tong Lee left and Chinaman heard the shop door lock, he called for Alan. When the boy brought his food, he would make him taste it first. He would take no chances. Perhaps Zuela had not gone to Laventille to make the pilgrimage to Our Lady of Fatima; perhaps she had gone to visit a woman who made poison—black magic. For though he had willingly let opium take him many times to the chambers of death, he had never gone there alive, in full consciousness, and he trembled before the Caribbean magic that could lead a man like a beast on a leash to that nothingness, knowing well where he went.

Zuela heard him gurgle Alan's name from his attic and she held her son fast. "No. Stay!"

Alan had already picked up the steaming bowl of sancoche she had made for the Chinaman. She snatched it away. "I take his food to him."

When Alan fought her, she put the bowl down and shook him hard. "I don't make child to turn into zombie," she said.

The boy wrestled with her again for the sancoche. She hit him. He began to cry and his crying frightened her.

"I thought you just rolled the cigarettes for him."

But she should have known.

Before she went to the Chinaman she made sure her younger children were in bed—the two boys, six and seven, who almost could be twins, and the three girls, four, three, the last one, two. When her fifth child was born, the sole bed they had was too small to hold them all, but the Chinaman told her she had to manage. It was only after she had two more boys that the Chinaman made her another bed with his cement blocks and wood and gave her enough ticking and coconut fiber to make a mattress.

She covered the girls with the thin sheet and motioned to them to be quiet, then crossed the room and made the same signs to the boys. Earlier, her three older children—Alan; Joseph, the boy after Alan; and Helen, the oldest girl with her, now ten, a daughter still young enough not to cause her heart to tremble with the memories that made her give Agnes to the nuns—helped her clear away the grains of rice and sugar and pieces of greased paper that were scattered on the shop counter. Together they had moved the scale, the rusty measuring scoops, the brown paper bags and the bottles of pretty colored candy they dared not touch. The Chinaman did not approve. "Bad for the teeth," he said. But each night Zuela stole one sweet (he could not miss *one*), so that in a cycle of nine days, now that Agnes lived with the nuns, each child got one.

After they swept the shop, they stacked four sacks of flour on the floor to make a bench for the shop counter that at night the older children used as a desk to do their homework. Before she left to go to the Chinaman, Zuela made certain they had opened their books. Her children were her hope and they knew it. Books, she told Alan who was now contrite, were their only way out, the only exit for them from the Chinaman's shop.

She climbed the wooden stairs leading to the Chinaman's attic, carefully balancing the bowl of sancoche on a tray. When she reached the entrance, she remembered the low beams and bent her head.

The Chinaman saw her, but before he saw her, he heard her, and thinking it was his son Alan when the wooden steps creaked, he drew himself upright against the wall, kicked the sheets off his legs, smoothed his wrinkled khaki pants and buttoned the top of his shirt. For he wanted to seem strong when he asked the boy to taste the food first. He wanted to mask his fear when he complained, "Last time she put too much salt. Taste it. Taste it. See if she do same thing, stupid woman." Then the door opened and he saw her long black plait against the silvered night sky. He pulled the sheets up to his neck and backed into the corner.

Zuela put the tray on the wooden box near his bed, next to his glass bottles with the long tubes and his pipes and the brown resin. She did not look at him. She walked over to the other side of the room where he had mounted the double-tiered slats his friends used when the poppy seed made them drift into a sleep that memory could not break. There, on a low table cluttered with the tools they used—the pipes, the brass plates, the bottles, the matches—was a small kerosene lamp the Chinaman had forbidden her to light. She struck a match to its wick and the flames flickered, casting shadows across the wall.

The Chinaman flinched and drew his arm across his eyes. "Turn it off. Turn it off," he whined.

She lowered the flame. Still, it cast a pool of pale yellow light around the table and uncovered the Chinaman squeezed in the corner of his bed.

"Where is Alan? I want Alan," the Chinaman's voice wailed across the room.

Zuela did not answer him. She sat on her heels and put the bowl of sancoche on the box next to his bed. Slowly, not looking at the Chinaman, she stirred the sancoche. She was conscious of a strange power growing within her. It frightened her, yet it left her indifferent to what the Chinaman said, what he demanded, what he could do to her. Her whole being was focused on saving her son.

"Tell Alan to come," he said.

She lifted a spoonful of sancoche from the bowl and moved it towards him.

"No. Alan." The Chinaman swung his head from side to side.

She did not try to help him. She waited until his head was still again and then she pushed the spoon against his clenched lips. He twisted his face away and the thick soup dribbled down his chin and stained the collar of his rumpled shirt yellow. Zuela filled the spoon again.

"Alan. Get Alan."

She brought the spoon to him.

"I want Alan."

"I feed you."

"No." The Chinaman raised his arm and knocked the spoon out of her hand. It bounced off the floor.

Zuela bent to pick it up but she did not try to force him again to eat. Quietly she used the edge of the spoon to cut the chunks of dasheen and yam in the sancoche into tiny pieces. She felt the power blossoming within her now and knew the Chinaman felt it, too, and that he was afraid of her. She knew this not because she had found out that his spy Tong Lee had pressed his ear against the floorboards and distorted her conversation with Rosa (she would learn that later), but because she herself had been frightened by the rage that inflamed her when it lay bare before her that the red in Alan's eyes had not been from crying. Yet she was frightened less by the rage than by her ability to control it, to pace herself, to wait all afternoon until the time was right for her to release it, to talk to Rosa then, as if, in the entire time she sat with her in the back room of the shop, she had not been thinking of Alan, not been plotting her revenge on Chinaman. And after Rosa left, she returned to the shop and kept her face expressionless for Tong Lee. Later she fed her children and comforted them, and only once when she snatched the sancoche away from Alan did she let a sliver of her anger escape. Chinaman had to see it, too; he had to be terrified by all that bottled rage.

"I don't say no when you do it to me," she began. "Seventeen years. I let you lift up my dress when you want to and I don't say no." Her voice was soft and steady. "Seventeen years you take me as a child and you make child with me. You call me Daughter and then you make me your woman. Seventeen years I say nothing. I never refuse you. Even when you make me do it right up till the night I making baby, I never say nothing."

The Chinaman slid forward on the bed to see her more clearly, to find some trace, some proof that the words he had heard had actually come from her mouth, so unbelievable was it to him that she would dare speak this way. But she was calm, and the hand he saw stirring the sancoche was as steady as it had been a hundred times before when she waited for his coughing to stop and for the spasms that wracked his body to dissipate.

"Seventeen years. I say nothing because you promise me."

He slid closer to her.

"I let you take your thing and jump on me like a dog."

Then he saw the sheen on her face.

"Seventeen years."

It terrified him.

"Seventeen years."

A tremor rose beneath the walls of his thin chest and he felt the oncoming of a rush of waves. He fought against it, wrapping his arms around his chest to smother it. His face turned red, then purple, but he held the cough behind his lips until he could swallow it.

"But when you make Alan . . . "

The black light from her eyes shone on him again. His head jerked back with the force of it and the memory of that night a week ago, the nightmare that followed.

"When you make Alan a zombie like you . . . " Zuela's voice remained steady. The pitch never rose. "I make a hell for you like you make for me, a hell like that hell you see in your sleep."

Now the cough erupted through his mouth and pitched the upper half of his body across his knees. His head bounced between his open legs. When his coughing ended, he groped for the plank of wood beneath his mattress to keep himself from falling.

Zuela came closer to him and curled his fingers around the edges of the board. "I don't know what you see in your sleep, what make you tear your forehead and crawl on your belly like a snake, but I take it all away—the brown stone you smoke, everything." She gestured with her arms, a sweep across the room, over the bottles and pipes and the small brass plates with the black foul-smelling ashes, but her movements were steady, not agitated. "Everything." She picked up the opium.

The Chinaman pulled at the air for oxygen, hungrily filling the caverns of his lungs. Then just as it seemed he would suffocate if he did not release it, his head fell forward and he exhaled.

"Tong Lee," he breathed, swinging his head like a ball on a chain until the weight of it threw his back upright again. "Tong Lee." He collapsed against the wall.

She understood. But it would be too late for his spy. "You'll be gone before he comes," she said.

Spittle drooled down the sides of the Chinaman's mouth, yet he gathered his strength to fight her. "And after I gone, what you do? Who take care of you?"

Zuela did not answer him.

"Who feed you? Put shelter over you?" His voice was hoarse, raspy but willful. "Who take care of your children?"

Again she did not answer and he took courage from her silence.

"Who feed your children?"

She did not answer.

"Who put roof over their head?"

Now he saw from her silence she had not penetrated the screen he had dropped between them. She had not suspected the effort behind each word he forced from his tongue. She had not guessed his desperation to hide the enormity of his fear of her: *Not only a wife and a daughter in a pool of blood, but Zuela, alive, with hate in her eyes.*

"Who put shoes on their feet?" She threatened to take his poppy seed, his one tunnel of escape into the void: He would frighten her with the future of her children.

"Who give you money to send them to school?"

He would show her *that* hole. He would force her to back away.

"Your children push broom in the street like rubbish man."

The light from the kerosene lamp flickered across the liquid that pooled in his eyes. Zuela looked up and saw the red of the flames gleaming through his hairless eyelids. The cruelty it reflected sent her hurling against her will, backwards down the soft banks of the Orinoco to a forest thick and wild, choked with fat vines, emerald green and spotted brown. Trying to break her fall, she reached for one of the vines, which was wrapped around the branches of an ancient tree bowed low by the vampire embrace of a pink-edged bromeliad. But the second her hand grazed the smooth surface of the vine, it blinked open its eyes and plunged its blistering prongs deep into her bare arm.

She dropped the opium.

The Chinaman sucked the air and renewed his attack. "I leave you nothing when I dead. You walk the street like a beggar." He saw her shoulders sag to her bosom. He saw her swallow her rage, bottle and cork it.

"Your children sell payme on the corner of Charlotte Street to feed you. The girls end up like you."

The venom from the snake's bite rushed up her arm.

"Worse than you."

It streaked red-hot through her breast and curled around her heart, squeezing, tightening, suffocating, burning her.

"Your mother dead. Who you go back to? Who take care of you?"

The poison blazed down her other arm.

"Look at you. You ugly now, not pretty like that white woman in Otahiti."

She reached for the sancoche to cool the blistering streak that was rising again.

"I do it when I want to." The Chinaman watched her tilt the bowl to her lips; minutes before she had forced it against his mouth. Her defeat increased his courage. "I pay for it like the people who come to the shop pay for rice. They eat when they feel to eat. I have you when I want you."

He brushed away the spittle from his chin. His chest heaved but he went on gathering strength from the whiteness of her knuckles clenched around the bowl. "I see the men watching you. Don't think too hard. They want it for free. But I pay." His eyes dripped the liquid that set off her retreat. "I have right. Priest say so. I have right, he say, when I want to, where I want to." His hand beat a feeble rhythm on the bed with each word. "A right."

The room closed in on Zuela. The snake's venom finished her heart. She felt nothing, neither rage nor despair, nothing but the futility of hope in a power that was merely a mirage. She had come to save Alan and it was she who needed to be rescued—she and all her children. Maybe she could take the poppy seed from him; maybe she would not blow the ganja smoke into his lungs; maybe without the life-in-death drugs he would scratch out his eyes, put out the light. But his question tortured her: What about them? Where would they go? Who would take care of her children? *Her daughters?*

"Smoke." The Chinaman was calling to her now. "Smoke."

She moved like a thing without a will powered by a force outside herself.

"Smoke."

She went to the box beside the bed and smoothed out the thin white paper.

"Smoke."

She poured the brown dried leaves onto the paper and rolled it. She licked its sides.

"Smoke."

She lit it and inhaled, deep, deep, deep. The dark fumes curled down her lungs.

"Smoke."

Her head felt weightless. She inhaled again. The smoke gushed down her windpipe.

"Smoke."

She inhaled again but this time she held the numbing cloud in her mouth, leaned over the Chinaman and pressed her fingers into his hairless chin. He parted his lips. She opened her mouth and blew.

The second of euphoria from the ganja leaves stirred the habit in the Chinaman's groin. Weakened, he was breathing with difficulty. The palms of his hands slithered up her quivering thighs.

Later he moaned, "I won't ask Alan to do it again. I promise, I promise, I promise."

His chant, weaker with each repetition, echoed in Zuela's head and collided with the pleas of another man, a man on his knees behind a hibiscus bush: *Beg, beg, please.* Then *please* merged with *promise* so that what she heard afterward, lying in the bed with her daughters below the Chinaman's room, was promise, please, promise, please, please, please, please, until *please* broke a hole through the despair that numbed her and she remembered that *please* had made a man with a pole grovel on his knees.

Please.

If it meant saving her children she would do it.

Please.

She had seen the rigid lines on the lips of the Chinaman's spy break and soften to a smile when she handed him the money.

Please.

She would get him to say it, get Tong Lee to rescue her children.

Please.

She would get him to save them.

Please.

She would get him to free her daughters.

Please.

❦ Chapter 8 ❧

*F*or one week after Rosa and Zuela made the pilgrimage to Laventille to ask Our Lady of Fatima to smother the anger that the disemboweled body of a woman had fanned in their hearts, Laventille simmered, seethed, but remained contained. Then on the day that Rosa followed Zuela's advice and went to see Mary Christophe, that town of tears boiled over, spewing hot bubbles of rage down its winding dirt roads that burst against choked gutters and sprayed the colorless walls of cement hovels—the prisons of the poor, chained to each other by electric cables that connected street pole to hovel, hovel to pole to hovel. Bounding and colliding, the bubbles cooled finally near the foot of the hill and became a trickle; a long, thin tear that gathered in a shallow tepid basin in the valley, dangerous in its stillness, dangerous in its source.

The man who set the fire to the cauldron was the one who came to the police station to claim the ring on a finger two pigs had vomited on a Laventille road. He had given the ring to Melda, the man said, tears pouring down his cheeks; put it on her finger the night she had sworn: *No more with the brothers.* Then days later she slithered from his bed and crawled to a car purring at the bottom of the hill.

He remembered the driver. He was a bigshot-looking man, a valley man from one of those brown-skinned families with money and fancy titles. He was wearing a dark suit, a buttoned-up white shirt and a striped tie. But what the ring giver remembered most was that his skin was as smooth as a baby's bottom. He had no hair at all on his face except on his eyebrows—no mustache, no sideburns.

"He was driving a Bentley," he said. "A big . . . big and black car with a lot of silver chrome on the hood and on the doors." He remembered the license plate number: PA4295. When the smooth-faced man opened the car door for Melda, he saw the insides of the car, too. The seats were covered with black leather. They shone like the floorboards in rich people's houses, he said.

His confession was proof positive for the police: The ring giver had been betrayed by his woman. That was motive sufficient to seal his guilt— he was the one who had chopped up Melda and fed her to the pigs.

But the people on the hill knew better. They were not convinced, no more than they had been when the police first accused the two brothers. They remained firm in their belief that only a man from the valley could commit such a heinous crime. Neither the ring giver nor the brothers had enough savagery in them to chop Melda into pieces and turn her into fodder for pigs. And if they had, if they had butchered her, the police would have found them washing her blood with their tears. No, in the heat of such a jealous rage, none of them was so cold-blooded that he would hatch such a calculating plan to save his neck. Only a bookman would do that, only a man who put reason above feeling would have the wit at a time like that to construct that mathematical formula: No body = No victim. No victim = No crime. No crime = No execution.

Still, until the ring giver told them about the brown-skinned man from the valley, they did not know for certain who had murdered Melda or why he had chopped her into fodder for pigs, and, not having that information, not having concrete evidence, they were susceptible to the kind of questions that came in the dead of night, in the quiet of one's sleep when one's defenses are down and the devil is alert for loopholes to enter one's soul and cause one to doubt one's best convictions. So they fought back with intricate regulations about pork and accounts of the miraculous powers of the Catholic Virgin, merging fact with fiction, fiction with superstition, superstition with customs and gods barely remembered—*clanged shut* from them, the poet bemoaned, under those grates in the hatches of ships crossing that middle passage. But now that the ring giver had come to claim the ring, the devil had no power to seduce them from the truth. They were positive now: Not only had the ring giver proven his innocence with his tears (he said life had no meaning for him now that Melda was dead), but he had given them their man. The butcher could be no one else but the driver of the Bentley, a valley man scouring the hill for prey to slake his lust.

Five women were brutally beaten in that town of tears where deprivation forged loyalty, poverty soldered love. They were made to pay for Melda's insult to the ring giver's manhood, all men's manhood, though the ring giver insisted, not his. He was still crying for her, grieving for the woman who was his reason for living. He made excuses for her: She needed the money the valley man gave her. But the men on the hill could not forgive her or the valley man. So the cauldron boiled.

The women cursed Melda, blinded by a code of loyalty that would not let them strike out against their men—the endangered species. The men blackened eyes and made bruises that blossomed into flowers over the bodies of their women, crazed by their powerlessness, the unfairness of the advantage money allowed. They would not bear the humiliation alone; their women would bear it, also. Here, in Laventille, the forts in the valley made them hostage. The generals demanded what they wanted, even their women. Then they trampled up their territory to beg forgiveness from Our Lady.

Still, they knew how to conceal their resentment behind stone faces, so in that long pilgrimage out of the valley to Our Lady that Saturday, no one detected their anger, no one, not Rosa, though she should have noticed the defiance in the arms folded militantly across bare chests, the legs spread wide apart, the eyes fixed coldly on her. But Rosa was consumed with her need to find Zuela, so she did not see the seething rage and she was shocked when it stopped her, when the people on the hill blocked her way to Mary Christophe's.

It had taken her only moments when she returned to her house from the shop in Nelson Street to realize that Zuela was right. Mary Christophe was her only hope. For Ena, the woman Cedric brought to cook for him, the one he hired to protect him from her poison, was waiting for her at the front gate, wringing her hands.

"They took Mr. Cedric to the hospital. Nobody know where you went. We couldn't find you to tell you. So I wait for you. They say you wouldn't come. They say white people run when colored people make trouble. But I say you come back. I wait." She followed Rosa up the front steps. "They say you gone back to your mother on the estate, but I know you don't go there. I know better than that."

Rosa opened the door and entered the house. The paisley-patterned cushions from the Morris chairs her mother had given her as a wedding gift were piled in a corner of the drawing room. Fruit from the bowl she had placed on the coffee table minutes before she heard Cedric crumple on the tiles in the bathroom were squashed against her polished floor.

"I thought to clean it up," the woman said, "but I say no. Best you should see yourself."

"What happened?"

"They call the ambulance but it come with no bed. Mr. Cedric bawling, and holding his belly, saying he can't walk. Neighbor bring a cot. They push the chairs back to make room when they carry Mr. Cedric downstairs." She pointed to the cushions and the empty frames of the Morris chairs stacked against the wall.

"Where?" Rosa leaned against the door.

"Colonial Hospital. They say you shouldn't come to see him just yet."

"They?" She knew before she asked the question, it was they who had closed a ring around her when Cedric yelled out, Murderer!

"It was a whole lot of people that come, Miss Rosa. They say a lot of things."

Rosa bit her lip.

"I know you come back, but if I was you, for truth I go to my mother."

Rosa ran to her bedroom, tears streaming down her eyes.

The next morning she went to see Mary Christophe. The taxi that took her stopped halfway up the hill.

"She live there," the driver said, flapping his hand out of the window in the direction of a confusion of galvanized roofs, cement, cable wires, clothes, and what seemed to Rosa like long strings of brown toffee laced with the greens, reds and yellows of fruit trees. "Down the trail behind that other house. Sorry, my car can't go there."

But when he took the dollar notes Rosa handed to him, he met her eyes and he felt pity for her. "You sure you want to go there alone, lady? I walk with you if you want to." He counted the dollar bills. Rosa had been generous. "No extra charge."

Rosa had not seen the pot simmering on the day of the feast of Our Lady when she walked blindly up the hill in Laventille pursuing Zuela, so she told him she did not need him; she could find her way by herself. Still, after he left she was desperate to call him back, for an irrational fear came over her when the last sounds of his car spluttering down the winding slopes dissolved into silence. It was irrational, she told herself, because days before she had walked this same road without fear, and because now there was nothing in front of her to frighten her, only a deathly quiet—the sudden absence of man-made sounds—though she could hear the rustle of leaves on the trees and the swish of branches swaying in the wind. Yet this was the kind of quiet she had seen reduce the wives of overseers to an atavistic fear of their black male servants on somnolent afternoons around the swimming pool at the clubhouse on the Orange Grove estate when the children were sleeping, and the wives stretched out in all their vulnerability in bathing suits on chaise lounges, and waiters let fall a napkin, a towel, a cube of ice across their bare legs, then bent to retrieve it without saying *Madam* and *Excuse me.*

In this eerie silence, the sudden thud of a breadfruit that had dropped from a tree sounded like cannon fire to Rosa. Blood rushed to her throat, her heart beat a wild drum in her chest and her eyes skated to the ground. Then she saw the tough green encasing of the fruit split open, its yellow pulp, broken into pieces like shards of plywood, scattered across the dirt. How foolish she had been to have been afraid of a breadfruit! This was the kind of childish embarrassment these women must have felt when *Madam* and *Excuse me* resumed at tea-time.

But when she looked up, the toffee had disentangled itself from the fruit trees and had lost its sweetness.

"What you want, white lady? What business you have here?"

She would not have believed eyes could be so vicious.

"What you looking for?"

They closed in on her from the side of the road where the taxi had let her out. In spite of the heat, her arms broke out in bumps like the ridges on a grater.

"Looking for man?" One of the men came up to her. She felt his hot breath on her cheeks. It stank of saltfish.

"Naw, women like she looking for Jesus," a woman shouted.

At another time Rosa would have thought her harmless. She was standing behind the man who breathed on her face, balancing a galvanized tin bucket of water on her head. Two children, a boy and a girl, clutched the ends of her flowered skirt. Their bellies were swollen from malnutrition. The boy was clad only in a dirty undershirt, the girl in pink panties so big for her that they reached up to the tiny nipples on her chest. In another time, this woman and her two children would have come to the back door of her mother's house on the Orange Grove estate. She would have brought them a plate of food and her mother would have given the woman a day's washing to do for her if she had it, or the silver to polish. The woman would have smiled and said, "Is God in truth who make you people. God Heself. We come from behind He back."

Now the woman was saying to Rosa, "You looking for white Jesus or His mother, Mary?" The children pointed their fingers at her. "Look, look red on she toes." She wished she had not worn sandals.

"No, is man she looking for. Women like dem come up the hill for man, real man." He pushed out his chest and flexed the muscles in his arms. The children burst out laughing.

Someone grabbed her arm, another man with eyes more dangerous, and her legs buckled under her.

"Let she fall. Let she fall."

These were the last words she heard before she felt an arm encircle her waist and her head strike a chest hard and unyielding as a brick wall.

"Who tell you come here alone?"

The blackening of the light had lasted only a second. Her blood flowed through her legs when the wall held her up.

"Don't you know better than that?" The woman who held her formed a barricade that blocked the boulders.

"I see you come out of the taxi but I could hardly believe."

She did not recognize her. There was nothing in her face to trigger memory.

"Clara Appleton's child," she said. "I named you."

Her body was a cord of licorice; her green cotton dress dipped and rose out of its stiff canals. The whites of her eyes were blue with age; the pupils, hard, black beads shining above rings of purple-black flesh. The skin on her face rose and fell, its texture resembling plates of bark across her cheeks. The bark was there, too, around her elbows and wrists and around her ankles.

She waved her hand—a gnarled stick—in the air. "Go, go. I know her." She clapped her hands. "Shoo!" Backs turned slowly. "Come." She grabbed Rosa's hand.

"Is real man she want." One man, resentment still eating him, couldn't let go.

"Come." The woman pulled her past the scattered breadfruit, down a dirt track slimy with rotting fruit, and past backyards darkened by the shadows of rows upon rows of clothes strung on lines. "It's not theirs alone," the woman paused to explain, dodging the sail of a white eyelet skirt. "Some of them take in washing. Bring it back the next day. Remember when I used to do that?"

Rosa remembered, but not this woman—another woman, a fat woman who used to press Rosa's face into the folds of her apron when she begged her not to leave: "You can take care of me in your house just like you take care of the clothes." Yet the voice with her now was Mary Christophe's. She would know it anywhere. She used to hold her hand just as she did right now and comfort her: "Don't be afraid. Your mammy coming back."

Inside the house Mary Christophe chided her. "You don't know better than that? You don't know better than to come here at this time? Times now not like old times, you know. And look how you dress up. You don't know better than to wear blouse that leave your arm expose so, and shoes that show your toes. You see the children laugh. Even they know better. I thought I teach you all that before I leave. I thought I tell you day will come. Be careful."

The voice was the same, not the face.

"What you looking at? You forget already?" Mary Christophe motioned her to a chair. "Sit. Sit. Yes, is me. Selfsame Mary Christophe."

Once, Rosa had asked her why she used her last name as her first name, and she answered, "Because it's my first name."

"Then what's your last name?"

"Christophe," she had said.

Her father said to her mother, "Beware of women who take on men's names."

"All this is because of the sickness I have. It drain the juice from me." Mary Christophe brought her face close to Rosa's. "That, and old age and hard times."

Beneath the bark Rosa saw the resemblance.

"Nobody want you when you get sick. Children run from you like they see soucouyant."

Under the licorice, she saw the softness.

"I run from me, too, if I could." The bark crinkled. Plates shifted, then returned to accustomed places arching across her cheeks. "You want some juice?"

But Rosa did not hear her question. Her eyes were discovering the familiar lines down the slope of Mary Christophe's neck when she bent toward her. How many times had she wrapped her arms around that very neck and begged her to stay with her forever?

"You still look peakish. They frighten you?"

Rosa was barely aware she had nodded.

"Well, you right to be frighten. They a force now you best be frighten of. You say you want juice?"

Rosa's head moved from side to side.

"No? You don't want juice?" Mary Christophe sat down. Her neck eased into shoulders also familiar to Rosa. "I frighten you, too, eh? Well, I don't have the sickness no more. Anyhow, it was never catching like your mother say it was."

Before her mother said it was catching, she had promised Mary

Christophe that she could live out her days in the servants' quarters behind the avocado tree.

"Well, you don't have to drink no juice." Mary Christophe laughed, a dry laugh. "Could always tell when you people guilty. Look at the blood rise in your face."

"What was it? What were you sick of?"

Mary Christophe's eyes grew darker. "Never did know. My fingers and wrist start swelling up and all my bones hurt. I thought it was the old arthur." She rubbed her hands over each other. "Arthritis, you know. But they kept on swelling and hurting. Then this rash come all over my face." She touched her nose and slid her fingers across her cheeks.

Rosa remembered. She had traced her fingers over the bumps on Mary Christophe's face. The rash had spread across her cheeks. "Like the wings of a butterfly," said Rosa. She told Mary Christophe that her nose was the body of the butterfly. It was beautiful.

"Like the markings of a wolf," her father had said. But it was not so to her.

Mary Christophe had left before the skin on her face and around her joints rose and folded like hot tar and then hardened, before her body became a stick of licorice.

"I surprise myself how long I live. It must be twelve, fifteen years since I saw you last." Her eyes softened. "You and that little Spanish friend of yours, try all they do, nobody could keep you two apart. Daughter. That was her name, yes?"

"Zuela, she calls herself now."

Her mother had not waited to see if Mary Christophe would return. She gave her the servant's room to use as a playroom and Rosa took Zuela there and made it their room. Then, in those weeks that transformed them both, she forgot about the woman with the butterfly on her face whom she once loved.

"Zuela?"

"It's the name her husband gave her."

"She married now?"

"Yes."

"You know who?"

"The Chinaman."

"Same Chinaman?"

"Yes."

Mary Christophe clicked her teeth but said nothing.

"She sent me to you," said Rosa.

"To me?"

"Yes."

"Me one?"

Rosa nodded.

They were sitting facing each other, Mary Christophe on a rocking chair, Rosa on one of the straight-backed chairs Mary Christophe had pulled for her from the dining room table. Except for a tiny kitchen leading out to the back yard, the room they were in was the only one in the house. It was not big, but perhaps because there was little furniture in it—a dining room table and four chairs, a rocking chair, a bed and three mattresses rolled in a corner—it appeared bigger than it was.

"She said you could help me," said Rosa.

Mary Christophe rocked her chair and followed Rosa's eyes to the mattresses on the floor. "Mind three children now," she said, "but is not a paying job like I do for your mother. I do it for love alone now. When I mind you, I also mind you for love, but you forget."

Rosa felt blood rise to her face again.

"When I see you by the road looking like you see la jablesse, I wonder why you come here after this long time." Mary Christophe stopped rocking and smoothed her skirt over her knobby knees. "But I should know better." She sighed. "Only time white woman like you stop between the valley and Our Lady is when you have man trouble." She leaned toward Rosa. "So is man trouble you have?"

Rosa's face burned.

"I know is not to see how Mary Christophe doing that you make the climb to Laventille. But I tell you, you take a chance coming by yourself. Laventille not easy no more for the likes of you. You lucky I save you from that man."

It was too late to thank her now. She should have thanked her the moment she knew Mary Christophe was the wall that was holding her up, or the moment she had felt her hand in hers whisking her away from the danger that surrounded her, or the moment she had brought her to safety in her house.

"Not that Laventille bad. That same man who try to pull you away from me is not a bad man. He work hard every day to feed his children, but is no use. See the flower carvings on the backs of those chairs, see the caning on the seats? Is he that make that. He that make all this furniture here. This rocking chair, too. And he don't use no fancy tools run with electricity. He carve everything out piece by piece by hand until he finish it. Slow work, but is good work. Yet and still it take too much time for you people, too much time. You want everything English time. Quick, quick. And the black people in the valley following you white people now, and what he make no good for them either. They want what English people have, what English people like—English things. So he have no work, just making chairs for people like me, and we can't pay."

Rosa opened her mouth to speak and Mary Christophe silenced her.

"You people take too much for granted. You think everything stay the same, but people here tired. They tired of having nothing and then looking down on you in the valley: big cars and everything." She shook her head. "Things different now. You can't just come trampling up here as usual to see Our Lady. Last time people watch you with bad eye. Next time they do something if you don't change."

"I didn't do anything."

Mary Christophe cut her off. "Not you in particular, but you in particular could feel their anger. When people tired, they don't stop to figure out if you the particular one that broke their back yesterday. They see you all as one—one enemy. Is too late then to explain you different. You get your blows just like the rest. They don't know you marry one of us."

"You know about Cedric?"

"Everybody know when your mother give you to a black man with books. Is trouble you having with him? Trouble why that Red Indian girl tell you to come to see me?"

The roof of her mouth felt like parched paper and Rosa asked her for the juice she had refused moments before.

Mary Christophe taunted her. "You not 'fraid of Mary Christophe sickness no more? You drink Mary Christophe juice. Man trouble worse than Mary Christophe face, yes?" But when she saw Rosa clasp her hand over her mouth, she hurried to the kitchen.

She returned with a pitcher of lime juice in one hand and a full glass in the other. "Here. Drink." After Rosa drained the glass, she asked, "More?"

Rosa shook her head.

"You'll feel better." Her voice was tender.

"I feel fine now, thanks."

"You can have more if you want."

"No, no, that was enough."

Mary Christophe removed the glass from Rosa's hand. "You still knowing her? The Red Indian?" she asked gently. That was the way she used to refer to Zuela, Red Indian, to distinguish her from the East Indians who planted sugar cane in the Caroni. "You and your Red Indian friend was like laglee glue you together. See one, see the other."

Rosa thought to tell her, No, no, she had not been *knowing* Zuela. In almost twenty years she had not allowed herself to enter that vault where she had sealed her memory, and yet on that day, that chance meeting, that miraculous meeting, time had contracted and closed the gap. *Yes, she had been knowing her.*

"I saw her on Saturday in Laventille," she said. "Near the Shrine."

She was feeling more relaxed now, but just as she was beginning to reach for that other time, that other place where once she was whole, she saw her world fall apart again in the bark shifting on Mary Christophe's face, in the purple wells sinking deeper beneath her eyes. Now the spaces where blue had replaced white narrowed to slits. Two beads shone through them, hard and black as onyx.

"I ent no obeahwoman, you know."

In spite of her longing for the return of a past that was rapidly vanishing again, Rosa found herself rediscovering the markings of the wolf on Mary Christophe's face. She had told her that there was a butterfly on her face, but she must have lied; she must have believed her father.

She must have seen his twisted vision.

She was lying in bed in the dark in an empty house. Her mother had gone to England with her two sisters promising their English suitors the alchemist's dream; her father, as usual, was with the workers from the cane field. "Socializing with them at night prevents strikes," he said. But the ones who had reason to despise him knew better. He did more than socializing, they said, "And not with the women."

She was feeling lonely and so she called to Mary Christophe to stay with her. The door opened; the light behind it glowed against the white wall. She saw her body first, full and rounded as it was then when she loved her—before the wolf had dug its claws in her face. She saw the fat hips that had cradled her even when she was too big to be carried. She saw the soft stomach she had laid her head on many nights, the breasts she cuddled against. Then the light crossed the face and the butterfly flew away. She screamed with terror for what remained behind.

Mary Christophe left the next day. Her mother said, when she had returned with gold from England: "You really can never trust them. You really can't rely on them. They're never dependable. They'll abandon you in a second."

Her father said to her mother, "It's obeah. I warned you. Beware of women who take on men's names."

"You come to the wrong place if you looking for obeahwoman." Mary Christophe leaned back in her chair. Her fingers brushed the shards on her face. "But your father," she said, "he say is obeah give me this. He say I frighten you. I make you cry." Her voice was bitter. "'The devil's print,' he say. I never get over you white people and your foolishness." Her head rested on the back of the rocking chair. "You believe in all this: obeah, voodoo, miracles, statues, blood in communion bread. It make no difference. So long as it leave you without blame, is a religion you want, a god you worship. Me? I have no religion. People is my religion. But I hear you good. You say you meet your Red Indian friend at the shrine like you meaning some miracle, like you thinking if is a miracle that make you meet her, is a miracle that would happen if you do what she tell you to do. Obeah, magic, Jesus, Mary—it's all the same to you people."

"I didn't say that." She wouldn't be made guilty for that—for doubting the butterfly and seeing the wolf, but not for thinking Mary Christophe was an obeahwoman. "I didn't say you worked obeah," she said.

"No, you didn't say that, but I know what you thinking when that Red Indian girl tell you to see me. I know you come here looking for obeah."

"No." Rosa crossed her legs.

"Yes, if you tell the truth." Mary Christophe sucked her teeth. "You don't come here for me. You don't come to see me. You don't come to ask about me."

"I didn't know. I never knew where you went when you left our house."

"You think I disappeared? You think black people have power to vanish?"

"I was young." Rosa uncrossed her legs and ran her fingers around the neckline of her blouse.

"Not too young to forget who take care of you."

"I thought you wanted to leave to go live with your family."

"There was times you would have went with me."

Rosa remembered and her body grew limp, fluid.

"They made you afraid of me, too," said Mary Christophe.

"I was alone. Then I forgot."

"But you remember now?"

"Zuela told me you were here."

"*You* knew I was here."

Rosa had no answer to give her.

Mary Christophe brushed her hand across her forehead. "All that pass now. Gone. Over with."

"I'm sorry."

"Yes, you sorry."

"I didn't know which house, where in Laventille."

"Is over. I forget it. You come here to tell me about man trouble, so tell me. What that Cedric man do to you?"

Yes, that was why she was here. She would tell her, get absolution and the help she needed. She had made the trip to Laventille to ask her to shield her, to protect her the way she used to protect her as a child. "He hates me," Rosa said.

"They hate all of you."

"After he married me, he started to hate me."

Mary Christophe smiled, a wry smile. "He hate you long before that."

"No, before that he wanted me."

"I mean years before that."

"At first," Rosa began slowly, "when he came to my house to tutor me, he wanted me."

"You encourage him," said Mary Christophe.

"No. He wanted to make love to me."

"And you tell him no?" Mary Christophe waited for Rosa's answer.

"No, I said yes."

"So you encourage him. That's why he hate you."

"I didn't stop him."

"You make it easy for him, easy to take what he know he should leave. He punish you for that."

"He wanted to marry me."

"He punish you more for that."

"No."

"Is hard to know you want something you should hate." Mary Christophe's voice was soft.

"Why me? Why should he hate me?"

"Like I told you, not you in particular. You people, you people that make his people suffer."

Rosa avoided Mary Christophe's eyes. "We don't do that here anymore," she said. "Slavery was over years ago."

Mary Christophe rocked on her chair. "If you say so," she said.

"He has more education than anybody I know. And I'm talking about white people. *He* teaches us now."

"He still think he less than you. Education don't make him you."

"No, that's not true. He tells me *I'm* ignorant."

"He only say that to make himself feel good. But it don't last. He still think you better than him."

"My mother practically kissed his feet when he asked me to marry him."

"That is something else."

"She let him know that she admired him, that she thought he was smart."

"She had reasons."

"What reasons?"

Mary Christophe stopped rocking. "Reasons."

"I don't understand."

"No, you don't understand."

"Why should he think he's less than me? I said yes. My mother said yes."

"But too quick," said Mary Christophe.

"That's what he wanted. He told me so. He wanted to make me Mrs. DesVignes."

"He didn't want to make you Mrs. DesVignes. He wanted to make himself Mr. Appleton and you didn't stop him."

"Appleton?"

"In a way you should feel sorry for him. That husband of yours hate himself more than he hate you. And the truth is that he hate you more for making it so easy for him to hate himself. Now he looking for a way to pay you back, to make you suffer. Yes? That's the way it is, yes? Tell me."

"Yes." *That is the way it is; that is why he said, Beg, beg for it, white lady.*

"And tell me, how this Mister Man plan to make you pay him back?" asked Mary Christophe.

"He said I poisoned him."

"Poisoned?" Mary Christophe frowned.

"He thinks I put something in his food."

"Yes." She sighed. "Yes."

"He thinks I mixed it up in the seasoning."

"And make him eat it?"

"Yes."

"And since when the Mister Man think you make him eat poison?"

"Since the body of Dalip Singh's wife washed up on the beach in Otahiti. He said I was like her."

"Yes." Mary Christophe nodded.

"He thinks she had a lover."

"What you do, what you say to make him say 'like her'?"

"Nothing."

Mary Christophe's face hardened. "No, you do something."

"Nothing."

"Nothing? Like nothing that man and wife should do? I mean in the bedroom. I mean, you don't want to make love to him no more, Rosa?"

"It's hard to do that when someone is mean to you."

"But you understand?"

"I am faithful to him."

"Is what he thinks that matters. You say he think you poisoning him? I tell you he *know* you poisoning him."

"No! I didn't put anything bad in his food."

"Not that. You yourself is the poison. You don't see? *You* is his poison."

"No."

"Worse part, he know is he who went to find the poison. Is not you who give it to him, though you make it easy for him to take it."

"No! He has real pains."

"In his head," Mary Christophe said dryly.

"In his stomach."

"Bellyache," said Mary Christophe. "The real pain is from the poison he swallow: you."

"I never intended . . . "

"Maybe. But is the way it is for woman like you who marry man who will think they less than you. Look at that selfsame Dalip Singh wife. She never intended, but he make her pay with her life."

She knew what Mary Christophe meant, knew it when Cedric said, *stinking,* and she told him she pitied him. Cedric wanted to kill her. She had said so to Zuela. "He told me that Paula Inge and I were sisters of the same kind." She would tell her the rest. "Nymphs, he said." But she was not ready for what Mary Christophe would say next.

"Nympha."

Rosa stared at her. "You know?"

"Yes. Your name."

"You know it means mad?"

"Yes."

"Mad for black meat?"

Mary Christophe reached for her hand and squeezed it, then brought it to her lips.

"What?"

She kissed Rosa's hand.

"What? Tell me."

"I'm sorry."

"Sorry for what?"

"Is my fault."

"Your fault?"

"I was the one tell your mother to call you that."

"Nympha?"

"I tell her for revenge."

"You know what it means?"

"I tell her because I was sick and tired of how she treated me. How she treated your sisters."

"You know what it means?" Rosa repeated her question, unable to believe that this woman, who was like a mother to her when she was a child, would tell her mother to call her Nympha if she knew what the name meant.

"She think your sisters good for nothing but to sell in England. I tell her, No. I tell her, Teach them to live here, teach them to make their way here. They Trinidadians now. Their people come same time with my people. True, is a big difference: They come on the deck; we come in the hold, but all of us make baby here and all the babies make babies and they, too, make babies. All of us are Trinidadians, different color, but Trinidadians now. She say never. She don't want them to be low class like me, to be nigger like me. So she teach them only English ways—how to hold knife and fork; how to say words the English way. She tell me not to talk to them, only serve. Not to talk so I don't contaminate their English. Contaminate!" She snorted, "Contaminate!" She released Rosa's hand. "Is she who contaminate and she know it. Every time she see me, she know is she who contaminate."

She closed her eyes. When she opened them again, she spoke with deliberation, choosing her words carefully. "I know she was trying to cut out the love your sisters have for black people, for black men. But it was natural in them. All the marriages break up, break up when they come back here with their English husband. They don't last, either, when the husband take them back to England." She slapped her palms against each other as if she were washing her hands, but the action was slow, measured. "Break up. When they come back and take white men in Trinidad, she sad because she know is not the same as the pure white thing. I want to tell her they come back because they not like them. They not English. But by that time is long since she fire me. I want to tell her they get it natural. England don't give them what they want, what they *need*. But she don't want to accept."

She paused and looked directly into Rosa's eyes. "I want to remind her that is from she they get the taste."

Rosa lowered her eyes, but she didn't know why, except that at the word *taste,* she felt such shame she could not face her.

"She need to watch me, your mother. Not because of this, like you hoping right now is what I mean." Mary Christophe touched her cheeks. "Long before this, she watching me to see if I know, to see if I tell that I know what she like, what she have a taste for. But I pretend. I leave her alone. I cook, I wash, I clean. I leave your sisters to her. Then her belly swell up with you."

Rosa felt her throat lose moisture again. But no juice could relieve this dryness now, this aching of her muscles.

"Long time I know she not sleeping with her husband."

Boys, Thomas? The pain in her throat rose to her jaw and Rosa fought her fear of what was to come.

"Long time. They had big quarrel. Big, big." Mary Christophe opened her hands and spread them apart. "Big. I hear it all. She say is only man he like—little men and young boys."

Rosa tried to swallow, but she could not. The muscles around her throat got tighter. *Always in the cane field, harvest time or planting time, her mother accusing, she putting her hands over her ears so she would not hear. Little boys, Thomas? Children, Thomas?*

"She don't tell me nothing I already don't know. Everybody know."

Her mother: *You bring shame on us.*

Her father: *Shame? You brought shame on us long before I brought shame.*

"She ask him what she supposed to do when he in the cane field. He say whatever, but not with a black man. But it too late for that already."

Rosa wanted to get out of the room, to fill her lungs with fresh air, but Mary Christophe was insisting, looking into her eyes, demanding her attention.

"She come crying to me. I say, maybe the baby come out white."

Rosa's heart began to race, the palms of her hands oozed with sweat, but she could not pull herself away. She had to listen; she had to know.

"I tell her they have white women with black in them who marry black men and still the baby come out white. She say, what she going to do if the baby black? I so vex, I say I take it. She so grateful she say, black or white I let you name it."

Name it. Name it. Rosa could not stop the pounding in her head.

"I name it Nympha."

"Why?" Her lips barely formed the question.

"Why? Is years now I hoping I never have to answer why. Is years now I want to forget I could be so hard."

"Why?" Rosa asked her again.

"After you born and grow up, I see you different."

"Why?"

"I loved you."

Nympha meaning nymph. Sly, innocent with your siren call. Mania meaning mad. Rosa tried to drown Cedric's voice. "Why?"

"I say to myself, Is nigger she make her children run from, so is nigger her child will love. I say she make a daughter that want black man, so she die for him. But I was wrong to say that."

113

Before *Beg,* she unbuckled the belt on Cedric's waist. She zipped down his pants. She pulled him on top of her on the dining room floor and asked for more, even when slivers of wood pierced her backside.

"I sorry. I sorry now," said Mary Christophe.

Mania: mad for black meat.

"But I don't make obeah. At least, I could give you that. I wrong, but it wasn't obeah. I find the name in a prayer book. Is a Catholic saint name, Nympha. Yet I know what it mean, and that I wrong for. I tell her give you the name for your saint name, only I say give it to you for a first name. She say the priest will say no. She say it not the saint name on the Catholic calendar for the day you born. I tell her she promise. The priest try to break her down, but he don't tell her what the name mean. She cry and cry so much to me, I feel sorry for her. I tell her use it for a middle name. She stay loyal."

"My father, too?" Rosa did not know who she meant right then— the black father who would keep his silence, perhaps out of love for her, or the white father hiding a more pernicious secret?

"The black one go to Barbados, the white one say nothing. But I stay here, and all the time you growing up, your mother looking for excuse to make me go because she 'fraid I talk. Then I get this thing." She touched the bark on her face. "And all her promise about servant house behind the avocado tree just blow in the wind, all she say before about staying there till I get old and die. Which was the other promise she make when I say if the baby come out black, I take it. She tell me that many times, but she don't keep that promise, only the name promise. When your white father say, Is obeah make my face so, she see her chance. I know when you run from me, she tell me to leave, so I don't wait till she come back from England to insult me. I leave right away, right after your father say he don't want no obeahwoman frightening his girl child. Maybe he, too, 'fraid I talk."

Yet, in the end, Mary Christophe helped Rosa. Remorse for naming her? Pity for the danger Rosa faced with Cedric? Both. For she could not deny there was a part she had played, real or imagined, in the pain now evident in Rosa's eyes. So she threw behind her her old resentments of a white woman who loved Trinidad without liking it, of a white man who neither loved nor liked the island he rode like a jackass, then whipped to its feet again when it fell.

"Not obeah," she said when she gave Rosa a potion for Cedric. "I have no uses for obeah. Is something to calm him down, to cool the pain in his belly." She hesitated. "That is, if the Mister Man let you give it to him."

"And if he doesn't?"

"Pray. Light candles and burn incense."

"Maybe that won't work."

"What you go do? Go back to your mammy?" She hadn't meant to be so cruel. When she saw the tears well in Rosa's eyes, she regretted her harshness. "She see things different from you and me. You people don't think the same way as us."

Rosa wondered if she were aware of the contradiction in her words. Mary Christophe had tossed her from Orange Grove to Laventille as easily as a cricket ball to the wicket. *You people. Us.* She had said both as if they were the same: Rosa, the same as *you people;* Rosa, the same as *us.*

"I didn't surprise you telling you your mother's husband is not your daddy, did I?" She bent low over Rosa.

Rosa shook her head.

"All the time I feel you know it already."

"She never cared for me."

"No, not so. She frighten for you. Is the way you white people show you frighten for your children."

If she had made the error unconsciously, Rosa thought, she knew what she was saying now. There was no *us,* only *you people.*

"Your mother just clam up," said Mary Christophe. "She shut up. She hide you away. Is the way she protect you. She 'fraid somebody see the black in you. Yet nobody know for sure; your skin so white. Sometimes the black blood show up, sometimes it don't. With you, it don't show."

"That's why she was glad when Cedric married me."

"She know if you marry a white man, your black blood could show up in your children. Then everybody know what they suspect already. They know what she do and that your daddy not Mr. Appleton. That your daddy is a black man, which mean you black, too. With your sisters, is okay if they marry Englishman. Their daddy white, their children bound to come out white. Not you. She had to find a black man for you so if your children come out black, everybody say is because their father black. Then you could still be white and they never know for sure."

"And all the time . . . "

"Don't think too much about her. You have enough to worry about with that Mister Man you have. Go burn candles by Our Lady. Maybe she make a miracle for you." Her tone was sarcastic, but gentle. "Here, give this to him till the whole bottle empty. Maybe it make his bellyache go away. If it don't, pray. They say she work for you people, that's why you run up here to her shrine. Light candles. Is you people obeah. Maybe Cedric leave you."

Rosa took the medicine Mary Christophe offered her and her advice, because unlike her, she did not have the strength to live in the world without hope. Yet even before she would know whether the tonic or the prayers would work, she was grateful to her, grateful because she knew now why her sisters, not she, were sent to England, why no bargain was made with an Englishman to confirm her worth. It was a name, a curse that had drawn her perversely to Cedric. It was not her fault she desired him. Her name had sealed her fate from the moment of her birth, before her birth. There was nothing she could have done. Nympha had been waiting for the right time to strike a match between her legs.

Still, she wondered if that Saint Nympha who was doomed with the name, too, had risen above her fate. If, for example, she, too, had lain on her belly, rubbing ecstasy from lips beneath her triangle of hair. If, for example, she had felt the liquid leak when virile thighs passed her, quivering with promise.

Was denial her miracle? Two, the church said, were needed for canonization. Was humility the other? Pride had cast Lucifer into hell: *I am better than the angels. I am an archangel above the archangels.* Did she, Saint Nympha, feel superior to the men she desired, and then suppress her craving for their awe? Did she, too, once love their fearful veneration, the thrill of skating on that thin line between mordant pleasure in their hunger for her and triumph in hiding hers from them?

She would have gone tumbling down if they had found her out, if they knew that it was she who was on fire for them, she who would have gone searching for them.

Once, Rosa thought she had chosen a mate well in Cedric—he was a haven for her desires, fuel for her pride. Now the ground was slipping under her feet.

Mary Christophe offered to walk with her up the track to the side of the road and wait with her until a taxi came. But she need not have done that, because on her return down the Laventille hill, Rosa did not need protection. True, the men and women who had jeered at her a little more than an hour ago were still standing there as if they had been waiting for her, but they did not bother her. They said nothing; they did nothing; they kept their faces blank. But if she could have read their minds, she would have known they had been talking about her, about going fishing, about sticking the steel ends of their hooks in the mouth of a grouper, or a goldfish, and reminding themselves, when Mary Christophe had pulled her safely down the track to her house, that after the trek up to Our Lady, one always wiggled back on the sand dunes when the tide receded. Then they would plunge their fingers through its flapping gills, and too late the fish would know it was water it needed, not air.

The woman with the mark of the wolf had held on to this one. They would let her have her this time.

"And your Red Indian friend?" Mary Christophe asked cautiously when the taxi stopped for Rosa. "She make a better marriage than you?"

Better. Better and worse. "The same," Rosa answered. "No different."

Mary Christophe sighed.

⋘ Chapter 9 ⋙

*C*edric DesVignes was told he had cancer of the stomach. The doctor who told him so was the chief surgeon at Colonial Hospital. He had not examined Cedric, but he had read the reports of the resident doctors, and, excepting the point about surgery, he felt completely satisfied with their diagnosis.

A balding Scotsman in his sixties, Philip MacIver had devoted many years of his life in the tropics to achieving the level of artistry he thought the native doctors in Trinidad had mastered. He liked to say they had done so naturally, having the good fortune to acquire the art in their island home before they were exposed to the science. When he said *exposed,* one felt the doctor was referring to the effect of some sort of debilitating phenomenon, like radioactivity. And one would have been correct in thinking so, for MacIver believed that his education in England had been destructive to him and that in spite of ten years' training in the best hospitals in London, it was only after thirty years in the hospital wards in Trinidad that he had finally honed his skills, so much so that he could diagnose ailments with pinpoint precision and predict outcomes with nearly absolute accuracy simply by observing the behavior of his patients and talking to them.

In London, he had learned about the effects of the mind on the body. In Trinidad, he discovered that what he had learned was just the beginning—a primitive understanding of the power of the spirit. For on this island colony of his British home, it became indisputably clear to him that the spirit could cure the body, or, under different circumstances, destroy it, regardless of the most potent interventions of the Western World. In those thirty years he had witnessed patients he had given up for dead become revitalized after one visit from their obeahman. On the other hand, people he thought he had saved with his science would walk out of his ward and then, the next day, die in their beds, all because of a curse someone had put on them. Or so their relatives said, begging him not to feet guilty or responsible: Not your fault. Nothing you could do. He knew others, too, who had taken roots and herbs that had no medicinal value according to his London textbooks, yet cured their illnesses while his prescriptions could not.

Now his faith in the science of medicine, which, he argued, was limited by its reliance on the seen, the tangible, was contingent upon the inclusion of the art of medicine, which rejected such boundaries. When Cedric was wheeled down the hospital corridors clutching his stomach, MacIver saw not only the obvious—pain clearly visible in the contortions on his face—but something deeper, intangible, a disease of the spirit eating away his insides. He knew, before his residents told him, that Cedric was dying, whether from cancer or not he was not prepared to confirm, but, as he later confessed confidentially to his residents, he was ninety percent sure of the former.

He told Cedric his fate bluntly, choosing his words carefully so that Cedric would know exactly what he meant: "The report here says that the tumor is big. You need surgery immediately. Without it, you have two, at most three, months to live. Go home and decide. I'll discharge you today, give you something for the pain. Give you time to put your house in order, make peace with your wife." He told him in the way he thought men in the tropics wanted to have bad news delivered to them—no frills, no sugarcoating, no 'nancy stories he used for the women.

And Cedric did not disappoint him. He did not question him. He accepted his prognosis stoically, not because he had learned to live up to some British notion of black machismo, but because he simply did not believe him. He did not think he was lying. Rather, he thought he was ignorant, and that he possessed neither the intelligence nor the knowledge to conclude that the report was accurate. First, he had not examined him, and, second, the doctors who had in fact examined him, had had other reasons for their diagnosis. Of the latter, Cedric was absolutely certain, so he saw no reason to start MacIver off on a long explanation of what he did not know or care to know.

But about that, Cedric was wrong. The Chief Surgeon did care, for he believed that there was no medicine in his hospital that could reverse the cancer sucking away Cedric's life. The art he had perfected in Trinidad had pointed him to the root that lay elsewhere, not in Cedric's stomach.

"Go home," he said. "Make love to your wife."

Perhaps there was a time in Trinidad when Colonial Hospital had been a sanctuary for the sick: for the British colonizers, local bureaucrats, favored civil servants; though, one suspected, never for the poor. In 1957, not even favored civil servants harbored the illusion that the British had their interests in mind when they built Colonial Hospital. It was the only hospital in Port-of-Spain so one had no other choice but to go there, but one went there fully aware of the dangers—the misdiagnoses, the botched surgeries, the numerous patients who never came back out alive, or who were discharged with new illnesses, newly acquired deformities. One knew also about the humiliations: newspapers used in place of linens on beds, patients forced to lie on the floor in overcrowded wards or to sit in hallways for interminable hours waiting for doctors who were so overworked they couldn't remember who they had attended and when. The British had their excuses: World War II had sapped their strength, their will and their resources. The sugar factories were not producing sufficient profit and the cocoa plantations were diseased. It was time to cut their losses and return to England.

Indeed, Cedric was acutely cognizant of the dangers of Colonial Hospital, so much so that, as often happens when one is faced with dangers more pernicious and more potentially damaging than what one has already suffered, he no longer felt the pain that had brought him there.

He had been subjected to a humiliating and public enema and abandoned in a hallway jammed with screaming patients, some sprawled on the floor, others lying on rows of gurneys, blood seeping through the crude bandages hastily put on their wounds. When the doctor called him to the examining room some eight hours later, he barely remembered the pain that had driven him to shout, "Murderer!" and to twist Rosa's wrist until the glass of water she had brought him shattered on the floor, spraying a rainbow and shards of crystal to the corners of the room.

The doctor wanted to know why he thought he had been poisoned. "Diarrhea?" he asked.

"Not before last night."

"Cold sweat?"

"No."

"Nausea?"

"No."

"Vomiting?"

"No."

"Hold out your hands. Turn them over so that the palms are up." The doctor traced the lines on Cedric's palm with his index finger. Cedric did not ask why he did that. He knew better than to question the doctors in Colonial Hospital.

"Now turn them down again."

Cedric did as he was told.

"Chills?"

"No."

He pulled down the skin below Cedric's lower eyelids and shone his pencil light in his eyes. "Hmm, hmm." He stuck a flat wooden stick in his mouth. "Tongue feel clammy?"

Cedric gagged, but answered, "No."

"Acidy?"

"No."

"Keep your mouth open." He sniffed Cedric's mouth. "No smell. Any before?"

"No."

He put his pencil light and his tongue depressor in his coat pocket.

"Then how do you know you were poisoned?"

"I had pains in my stomach."

"It hurts now?"

Cedric answered him cautiously. "Yesterday," he said.

"But now? You have pain *now?*"

"Not as bad."

The doctor reached impatiently for the clipboard the nurse handed him, but then, just as he was about to fill out the form clipped to it, he looked up at Cedric, and seemingly out of mere curiosity, perhaps thinking to salvage at least some entertainment for his colleagues, he asked, "Who do you think poisoned you?"

It was the question Cedric had been waiting for in the ten hours, forty-five minutes and seventeen seconds he had been made to endure the humiliation of Colonial Hospital. The words tumbled out of his mouth in no order that even he would have recognized were he conscious of what he was saying, or the order he had planned before the enema given to him by a female nurse in an open ward stripped him of all dignity. He began clearly enough with his name: Cedric DesVignes; his profession: headmaster of the only secondary school on the main street in Tacarigua; his wife's name: Rosa DesVignes; the source of the pain: poison; the source of the poison: pork. But then he launched into a convoluted treatise on pigs that were not pigs, pigs that had to be placed somewhere between Homo sapiens and animals on the Aristotelian hierarchical scale of being; about pork not being safe to eat until pigs that had eaten human flesh ate flesh of their own kind, and he ended triumphantly with a repetition of the poisoner's name: "Rosa DesVignes." He spat on the ground. "Not DesVignes. She's not a DesVignes. She's an Appleton. Rosa DesVignes née Appleton. Appleton."

Out of all the information Cedric rained on him, the doctor heard only that last word, *Appleton.* "Appleton? As of the Appletons on the Orange Grove estate?" he asked.

The orderly told Cedric, as he was pushing him past the operating theater, that he was lucky he was going *past* not *in.* Cedric was a man with two lives, he said—one yesterday and one today. "Nobody accuses white people of anything in Her Majesty's hospital," he explained to

Cedric. "Is like you don't appreciate all they do for you here."

So Cedric endured the x-rays. He did not protest, though he could not feel the lump the doctor said he could touch with his fingers. He kept silent, though anger blistered his tongue when two other doctors confirmed it, when they whispered among themselves, clearly enough for him to hear, about people so ignorant they believed that because two pigs had eaten a woman, no pork was safe to eat that year. He said nothing when they showed him a picture of the interior of his stomach that revealed a ball the size of an orange lodged in the upper right corner, though that evidence was more difficult to dismiss.

The chief surgeon, on the other hand, had no doubts, only a single disagreement on the point of the operation they recommended immediately—posthaste. The diagnosis? Yes, cancer conclusively. The prognosis? It was too late for surgery.

"Go home. Make love to your wife," the doctor advised Cedric. It was the only cure he could offer him. Still, he gave him pills to lessen the pain.

But making love to his wife was the last thought on Cedric's mind, for it was screwing Rosa that had brought him to his present state. He was glad she had not come to see him in the hospital. He credited her not for virtue (he was convinced she was incapable of virtue), but for the common sense to know that her guilt would have been discovered the moment she set foot in the hospital. Perhaps the doctors would not have seen her guilt or would have chosen not to see it, but the black nurses and the orderlies and the patients who knew her kind would not have read innocence in the trembling of her lips or in the limpid pools of her eyes. They would have seen her loathing in her reticence to press her lips to his cheeks, in her hesitation to touch his hand and in the clammy whiteness of her skin when she sat next to him. They would not have doubted him afterward when he told them about the pork. They would have known that no woman who had loved her man would have fed him pork when two pigs that had eaten human flesh were still alive, expelling air on that hill in a clearing behind the shrine of Our Lady of Fatima.

Why had he married her? She had asked him that question when he had cornered her with revelations of her saint name: "'Nympha,' meaning siren. 'Mania,' mad. Mad for black meat." And didn't he know this before he married her?

She thought it was she who had seduced him with her longing and her lust. "The timing was so perfect, so magical," she said. "Just as I stepped out the front door, there you were crossing the street."

Magical? There was no magic in their meeting that day, except if it were the magic of destiny set in motion years before, when, one afternoon, two prepubescent girls sprawled out in the dried drainage canals under the tall, green leaves of succulent sugarcane stalks spotted a boy sitting on the front steps of his house memorizing a book. And if that were magic, in the sense that the moment would unite them forever— one of the girls, Rosa, and the boy, Cedric—it was not the kind of magic either was aware of, neither the prepubescent girl who soon forgot the incident, nor the boy who had never seen her. So Cedric knew of no magic that had brought Rosa and him together, only his calculated intentions. He had stalked her for weeks, watched her hover in the background while her sisters sparkled, observed her on Sundays kneeling in the church pew, her head bowed, and waited for the right moment to seduce her, knowing all the time of the fire that scorched the insides of her thighs, though he had not imagined it so strong, so intense, so consuming.

He had found out she was named Nympha purely by accident. It was on the same day he had learned that her father worshiped men— small, lithe men like the East Indians who swung their scythes across the rigid stalks of sugar cane on the estate where he was overseer. He found it out when by chance he met his cousin on the very day Thomas Appleton, a man whose name he had never been able to disassociate from his own father's death, was being carried in a hearse that had finally come to a stop at the steps of the Church of the Holy Rosary.

"Your father uses to work for a man name Appleton. Dat was before he left the cane fields," his mother had told him. "Appleton. Dat uses to be the overseer."

As he had done so often since he understood the political implications of the difference between the English the missionary teachers in his school spoke, and the dialect the people in the street used, Cedric begged his mother to speak good English.

"And what you tink it will get you? What it got your father? He uses to work for Thomas Appleton, and look what happen. He end up a poortail man in Cedros."

But in those days, Anna DesVignes needed to tell her son the story about his father, so she corrected her English. "He used to cut cane but I didn't know him in the cane fields. I was working in the factory then. Usine Ste. Madeline. I used to bring the tea at tea time for the bossmen. Put the silver pot on a white linen doily on a silver tray. It was the kind of pot with the round strainer that fit right inside it with a chain. I knew just the amount of tea leaves to put in the strainer. Just the amount for Mr. Smith who liked his tea weak. Just the amount for Mr. Appleton when he came on Fridays to make his report. He liked his strong. I put a lot of tea leaves in that silver strainer for him before I drop it in the hot water and let it stay there a long time so the tea be strong."

The boy corrected her again. "Dropped it, so the tea would be strong."

"Is a long time. Sometimes I forget to talk proper like I used to."

"You must remember, Ma. You're nothing if you don't talk like them."

She sold fish in Cedros. Cedric knew Rosa had found her out, yet she married him. He overheard her sister warning her, "He is the illegitimate son of a fisherwoman, Rosa. He doesn't even know his father. Are you sure, Rosa? Are you sure? I don't care if he can read Latin and Greek, he's still common. He's still way below your class."

But Rosa didn't blink an eye, neither did her mother who was sitting next to her.

Yet they didn't know that Anna DesVignes was not always a fisherwoman. There was a time when every afternoon she poured tea and served scones in the board room of the Usine Ste. Madeline sugar factory for a dozen Englishmen. Once, with a military band playing outside, the governor himself, who had come on a mission for the queen, remarked to her, after she had asked, "How many spoons of sugar?" that her English was as good as any he heard spoken on the island. "Better than some Englishmen I know," he added.

"He had expected you to say 'much'," said her son when she told him the story years later. "How *much* spoons of sugar?'"

But two years later, when he was fourteen, Cedric wanted her to recall that time again, and then it didn't matter whether she spoke to him in the Queen's English or not.

"How did serving tea get you to meet my father?" he asked her.

"Mr. Appleton introduce him to me. As I told you, he like your father. Said he was the best worker on the cane field. And intelligent. Said he deserved a chance at bottling and when there was an opening in the factory, he give it to him. In four months he help your father move from bottling to supervising. Then one day I serving tea in the board room and what I see but a black face in the sea of white. I almost drop the tray. Tea, scones and all. I couldn't believe it. Mr. Appleton must have see the surprise on my face because he come up to me."

By habit Cedric interrupted her. "Came up to me, Ma. Came."

"Because he came up to me, hold me by the elbow . . . "

"Held me, Ma." But this time when he corrected her, Cedric was aware he was searching for a way to distract her from the answers he was afraid to hear.

"You want to hear the story or not?" She threatened to end the telling.

The boy stayed quiet.

"Held me by the elbow and introduce me to your father. After that, like they say in the storybook, Crick, crack monkey break he back on a piece of pomerac. 'Tory over. Your father like me and I like him, right away, just like that."

But the story did not have a happy ending, for in the end his father killed himself, and his mother, wanting to distance him from the shame arising from the circumstances of his father's death, changed his surname from his father's, which was Ramloop, to hers, which was DesVignes.

It was years before Cedric knew for certain why his father committed suicide. He knew the reason was connected to arson, the fire someone had intentionally set to the cane fields, and he remembered that the night of the fire, he woke to find himself in the back seat of his father's truck speeding down a winding road to the seaside village of Cedros. The next morning he could not get rid of the stench of burning cane stalks in his nostrils, nor the sting of the black smoke that watered his eyes in spite of the sea stretched out before him, glittering silver.

"No questions," his father said when he asked him why they weren't going back to the pretty house near the cane fields where they used to live.

For days after his father's sudden disappearance in the sea (suicide by drowning, the newspapers reported), his mother followed him from room to room, threatening to suffocate him with the stories she spun like a spider's web, about serving tea and scones in the board room of Usine Ste. Madeline and about the kindness of Thomas Appleton who took his father from the cane fields to a job in bottling and then helped him get a promotion to supervisor.

The Hindu priest who conducted the funeral for his father said that his father had died swimming to India. But Cedric heard the malicious whispers: He didn't swim out in the wide ocean because he loved India. Somebody broke his heart, and it was not his wife nor any other woman, either.

When he was fourteen, Cedric wanted to know the truth: "How did Pa die, Ma?"

But his mother answered him as she had always answered him, "Swimming to India."

So he fought harder for the courage to ask her the question more directly. "Why did we leave the big house so suddenly?"

But again his mother said what she had always said, "So your father could be by the sea."

This time, however, he let her know he heard the question in her answer—"Why so far from the cane fields?"

She had to sit down to answer him. "I don't know, I don't know." But she dredged up another memory. "They say his heart broke."

"Broke?" The boy's eyes shone with false hope. "A heart attack? Pa had a heart attack?"

He knew, even before she said it, *nothing like that.*

"When it first happen, it was sudden like a heart attack. Is years your father telling me Mr. Appleton coming up all the time to the factory praising him, saying he make a good recommendation to take him out of the cane fields and to introduce him to me. Then it seem is donkey years I don't hear about this Mr. Appleton no more and I don't see him. Then suddenly he come back again. Want to take your father on his horse to the factory when your father work nights."

Cedric remembered.

"Then right after that, is he who change your father schedule so your father work only in the nights."

Cedric used to wait on the front steps to say good-bye to his father. At first he merely dreaded the sound of the horse's hooves in the distance. Soon he hated it. He despised the way his father rushed down the steps as soon as he saw the clouds of dirt rising in the wake of the galloping horse, the way the white man never spoke, never acknowledged his presence, the way he patted his father's arms wrapped around his waist. For reasons he could not confront, his father's acquiescence shamed him. Always.

"And it was a month that every day he come to see your father. Even on Sunday. And your father have to jump out of his bed to go and check on something Mr. Appleton say he *must* check with him in the cane field, though is years your father have nothing to do with the cane field since he working in the factory."

As hard as he tried, Cedric had never been able to shut out the muffled whispering of two men in the hazy darkness of the Sunday dawn: one voice, not his father's, commanding; another voice, his father's, protesting.

"I don't understand why your father must go with him, but Mr. Appleton say he *need* your father experience."

It was that need that Cedric could not allow himself to question. It drove him to the safety of his books, to worlds spelled out in words which, if he memorized, would make the unreal real and the real make-believe.

"Then one night your father come home and say we move to Cedros." His mother snapped her fingers. "Like that. Just like that. A whole month and he out every day with Mr. Appleton, like all he want to do is please him. Then one night he don't care no more. He say we must move to Cedros."

The boy Rosa and Zuela had seen memorizing a book wanted to hope again. "Because of the fire he set in the cane fields?"

"They say is he who did it," she said.

"Then that was it. That was why he killed himself. He knew the police would come for him sooner or later."

She began at the end. "You remember the two years he sit on the beach staring at the sea?"

Cedric could not forget. He had longed to comfort his father, to hold him close to his chest, to protect him from whatever it was that had made him become a stranger in their house. But his father would not speak. Even then he had already left them. He was already a dead man.

"Then the day come he make up his mind to swim to India."

Now Cedric needed to end the silence. He wanted to know the beginning.

"You know why he set the fire?"

But when his mother told him, he lost the courage to ask her to tell him more.

"They say is because somebody break his heart," she said. "Somebody. But it was not me. Not me."

Not any other woman either. So went the malicious whispers.

The boy put the question out of his mind after that and would never have allowed himself to think of it again had he not, one chance afternoon, when he was a man of thirty, found himself stuck for more than fifteen minutes on the west side of Frederick Street waiting for a hearse laden with white and yellow wreaths to pass him by, and the long cortege of shiny cars that followed, headed by a black Mercedes-Benz in which he glimpsed the faces of four white women: a mother and two daughters, sitting in the back seat weeping uncontrollably into their white lace handkerchiefs; and another woman, a daughter, too, he presumed, younger than the others though well into her twenties, sitting in front with the uniformed chauffeur, her mouth on the verge of a smile, her eyes bright and clear, stone dry as if in that whole time from the moment of the dead person's demise, perhaps even before, she had not shed a single tear.

He was craning his neck to get a better look at her, puzzled by that curious half-smile, when he heard his name above the roar of the rows of police motorcycles at the rear of the cortege. He turned and saw his cousin

Headley Padmore, dressed as the other policemen were, in full uniform—navy jacket and pants, black belt and black leather boots, plumed white hard hat, white gloves and white tasseled sash—waving to him.

Later that afternoon in the restaurant where they had agreed to meet, Headley Padmore told him, as if he had already expected him to know, that Thomas Appleton, whose funeral he had escorted to the Church of the Holy Rosary and then to Laparouse Cemetery, had done a big favor that day for a lot of East Indian men in the cane fields. "They will sleep better knowing he's six feet under," he said. Then realizing from the surprise on his cousin's face that he had given information he had not already known, he took advantage of the opportunity to impress his cousin further: "Imagine a bulla man with a daughter name Nympha."

Ordinarily, Headley Padmore would not have known the etymology of the name Nympha. Unlike his cousin, he had no interest in education, far less in Latin or Greek. His schooling ended at the primary level when he left Cedros to find his fortune in Port-of-Spain. He worked as a delivery boy, then as an office clerk, became a police cadet a year later, and after that, an officer. When he returned to Cedros that year to show off his policeman's uniform, Cedric did not appear impressed. Cedric was then in his last year of secondary school and had plans to go to Teachers' Training College. He muttered to Headley something about brains and brawn, and though Headley could not make out exactly what he said, he knew in which category Cedric had placed him. So that afternoon, having quite by accident discovered the meaning of Rosa's middle name, he held it like a trophy before Cedric.

Headley knew the name because it was on the list of names from Thomas Appleton's daughters that the family's priest had given him so that he could escort their car from St. Joseph's Catholic Church to Barrow's Funeral Home for the wake the night before Thomas Appleton was to be buried. Normally he would not have paid much attention to the list, but his glance fell on a line marked across the middle name of the last of Clara Appleton's daughters and for the rest of that night and the next morning he found himself pondering why the parish priest had taken it upon himself to cross off the name Nympha. He was intrigued, first, because Nympha was a name he had never heard before, and second, because he was certain (being a police officer with ambitions for promotion to detective) that the priest had deliberately attempted to conceal it. It occurred to him that perhaps the name itself had special significance. He knew he could not ask his fellow officers if this was indeed so, for, as was usual on the island, his question would be repeated if only because it would strike them as odd that he, who rarely had an interest in anything beyond the simplest of subjects, should have asked. He realized, too, that because he was the only one who had been given the list, it was likely he would be discovered, possibly dismissed, for breaching the trust invested in him as a police officer.

He didn't know where to begin to search for an answer. Then he thought to start where his teachers always started: *The Oxford English Dictionary.* Not knowing how to use the dictionary correctly, he did not look at the top right-hand corner for the key, as his teachers had tried unsuccessfully to teach him to do, but decided to begin at the end of the N's, starting from the bottom of each page and working his way to the front. It was because of this decision, arbitrary though it was, that he came upon the word *nymphomaniac* almost immediately, and reading its meaning, did not feel disappointed later when he could not find the name Nympha. Now sitting next to his cousin who had cheated him of his pride the day he returned to Cedros a uniformed police officer, he recited triumphantly, "Nymphomaniac—a woman with an inordinate sexual desire for a man."

It was the earlier information Headley had given him that obsessed Cedric when he crossed the street to Rosa's house on the Orange Grove estate—information about a middle-aged white man beating the cane fields for lithesome Indian men. "Indian men like your father," Headley had said and winked at him. Still, Cedric stopped short of connecting his father to these lithesome Indian men, though he could not forget the afternoons when the dirt billowed to the sky and he saw, coming toward his house, a white man astride a horse. "Mr. Appleton give your father a ride to work on his horse almost every day," his mother had said to him. It was the truth; he had seen the Englishman himself. "He always praising your father like is he who do for him and not Mr. Appleton for your father." But Cedric had stopped short of making the connection between what he had seen and what Headley had told him because he feared it would answer the question he had never dared ask his mother: *If not you, Ma, who broke my father's heart?*

Not his wife. Not any other woman, either, the neighbors whispered the day the Hindu priest presided over a wake without a body.

But when he settled on Rosa, his head pounding with the confusion of half-answered questions and suspicions he barely articulated to himself, he was glad to know the other, the prize Headley had thought would stun him. It made it easier for him when he stalked Rosa, when he measured the moments to the moment he would choose to pounce on her; easier, that is, until four years later, after he thought he had cornered her, when he found himself locking and unlocking the pieces of a puzzle: Why would an Indian doctor get up one morning and draw the sharp end of his scalpel down the torso of the white woman he had married? Why would his wife Rosa, a woman whose lust had seemed unquenchable, shun him so abruptly? Why, on the dining room floor, where so often she had pulled him down on her, would she push him away, vomit spewing from her mouth? All he had said was: "Beg, beg for it, white lady."

Rosa was calm again when she returned from her visit to Mary Christophe. She was ready to face Cedric when he came back from the hospital. She had the medicine that she was sure would work, and she had begun her prayers. On the dresser in the bedroom she shared with Cedric, she had built a little altar to the Virgin Mary, with a statue of the Virgin in a white gown and a long blue veil, around which she had placed eight votive candles, which she kept lit, and a brass censer that gave off perfumed incense through the tiny holes on its cover. She began her novena to Our Lady that first day and dismissed the cook Cedric had brought to replace her.

"I wouldn't do that, Miss Rosa, if I was you. Mister Cedric get real mad at you."

"Mr. Cedric will get better," Rosa answered her.

She didn't go to the church or ask the priest to pray for her. She decided she no longer needed human intermediaries; she would go straight to Our Lady herself. It didn't occur to her, either, to go to her mother's house or to ask any of her sisters for help, but she thought a long time about mothers: about the mothers of Trinidadian white women like herself; about the mothers of poor black people like the maids who were mothers to her; about the mothers of poor people of any color like her friend Zuela; about the women who took the place of mothers for motherless children like Zuela; about the mother of God. *She* had stayed to the end trying to protect her son.

Protect. It was the word Mary Christophe used to describe her mother's love for her. From whom did Clara Appleton try to shield her? Everyone probably knew already. Trinidad was too small. You could reach the sea in hours from any point on that tiny island. In the absence of television, even a life measured in coffee spoons was enough to stir the imagination. Her father was an overseer. He held the livelihood of hundreds of men in his hands. They would have known what he did in the cane fields at night, what his wife did when he was not in her bed. They would have searched her daughter's face for confirmation.

Until now Rosa would not have used the word abandoned to describe what her mother had done to her, though sometimes she thought it. She used to believe, as Mary Christophe had told her, that her mother wanted to protect her. She was looking for a husband for her, too, when she went to England to shop for her sisters. Mothers did that—white mothers in Trinidad. Then when she sent her to her aunt's cocoa estate in Toco for five years, Rosa convinced herself that her mother was guarding her from the presumptuous eyes of native boys. Mothers did that, too—white mothers in Trinidad.

"Things are changing. Everybody here thinks he's somebody. The estate is getting too *dangerous* for Rosa," Clara Appleton explained to her husband who had not even thought of objecting when she told him her plans. But she had struck on a word that terrified Rosa. *Dangerous.* For Rosa did not know how much longer she could keep on with the rubbing before she would crave awe so desperately that she would bring shame to her family. For awe required not one of her kind, but the other—the other, who, convinced of his nothingness, would see everything in her, all that he wished he could be.

She was already beginning to search out the other from among the sons of the laborers on the Orange Grove estate when Clara Appleton said *dangerous*.

A week before, the gardener's son, a young dougla of sixteen, a boy of Indian and African parentage, his hair ringed with baby curls close to his face, his skin black and shining like a river stone, brought her a bouquet of bougainvillea. She laughed at his folly.

"Bougainvillea? You can't make bouquets out of bougainvillea, silly. See, see, too many thorns. And watch how it spreads out any which way."

The boy knelt at her feet. "It's like you, missy, but only you prettier."

Frightened by the power he granted her when he genuflected, Rosa ran to Toco when her mother said *dangerous*. By the time she returned (she was twenty-one), the Church and five years on her aunt's estate had schooled her. She had learned the art of camouflage, mastered it; that is, until Cedric.

Now, after her visit to Mary Christophe, she understood why her mother had not been eager for her to marry. She had indeed been protecting someone, but not her daughter. She had been protecting herself, Clara Appleton. So she waited until Thomas Appleton was dead before she approved of a husband for the last of her daughters, waited because she feared the surfacing of black blood—which could happen with a woman who looked as white as her daughter if that woman who looked as white as her daughter had blood the same as the blood of the black people she despised. For in spite of the color of her skin or the color of her husband's skin, such a woman could give birth to a baby as brown as the earth. Then the world would know that such a woman was not a white woman. No, Clara Appleton wanted a safe place for Rosa, a marriage to a man who would not be surprised if his baby was brown, a man who would even be grateful, a man who, nonetheless, had some standing in society.

So it was not Rosa alone who had found a haven when Cedric walked past her house, his godlike thighs rippling under the thin fabric of his pants. Her mother had, too. For an Englishman would have exposed her secret. Then the facade she had built with her precious cardigans, her interminable, futile hunting expeditions to England, her dissolute cocktail parties, would have come tumbling down like the walls of Jericho.

Rosa was thinking about this and about mothers who protect their daughters when she waited for Cedric to come home from the hospital that afternoon. She was thinking about the little girl who opened and shut her eyelids when she asked her, "What does Chinaman look like?"

"A lizard. A lizard," she guessed when the girl opened and closed her eyelids again, this time slowly and more deliberately.

"No," said the girl. "An iguana." And she got down on her hands and knees.

Later, Zuela told her that her mother had taught her that iguanas were not bad if you stroked them.

"And a snake?"

"Not a snake," the girl said. Her mother had warned her: "A snake is a snake is a snake."

Rosa had just put a fresh batch of incense in the censer when Cedric entered the bedroom. He surprised her. She had not heard the front door open or his footsteps up the staircase. She turned in time to see him stretch his arms across the dresser and sweep the statue of the Virgin Mary, the candles and the censer to the floor. Seconds later he collapsed, clutching his stomach.

Before she rushed to the bathroom to get the medicine Mary Christophe had given her, she caught a glimpse of the statue on the floor. Nothing had happened to it. In spite of a fall of more than four feet down from the top of the dresser, the blue of the veil and the white of the gown had not been chipped. Later, this was an inspiration for her, proof of Our Lady's inviolability to harm, a sign that she would answer her prayers; that if the medicine did not work, Our Lady would help her.

⪻ Chapter 10 ⪼

*I*n the dark shadows of a shop in Nelson Street, Zuela, too, was thinking of mothers, wondering whether her mother ever knew that though a snake was a snake was a snake, an iguana was not an iguana was not an iguana.

Her mother had taught her not to be afraid of iguanas. The spikes on their backs would not hurt her, she said. Their hairless eyes were harmless. So Zuela was not afraid when the Chinaman told his woman to leave and then brought her to his attic. When he covered her with his body, she stayed still under him, as she had seen female iguanas do. Afterward, when he stroked her hair and gave her a name, she blotted out the pain. But months later, with Rosa, she saw herself in that mirror behind the hibiscus bush: a girl, a child like her, a man with a pole on top of her. Then she knew she had learned too late that an iguana was a lizard was a snake, and a snake was a snake was a snake.

Her mother had lived to teach her only a part of that lesson, the part before the iguana was a snake: the magic mothers created for their young daughters, bargaining for one more day in Eden before innocence is snatched from them forever. Maybe if that little girl's mother had taught her the rest, she would have run for her life when that man came with his pole. She would have known not to let him plant his knees in the dirt over her.

But, perhaps, it was for her own protection that someone had given that little girl to the man. It was so for her. *What were those women thinking when they gave her to the Chinaman?* They had promised her she could come back. When you get big, when you can fend for yourself, they said.

Maybe it was the truth they knew behind the lie they told that made the women give her away: They had gotten big and couldn't fend for themselves. They knew she could not come back.

Maybe they hoped. There was always that chance—a husband who would be kind and generous, who would not demand her flesh because it was his flesh that he bought and paid for each day with a loaf of hops bread, a piece of saltmeat, mattress ticking, coconut fiber, then a roof over the heads of her children.

Zuela swore to herself that this would not happen to her children. Her girls would not be trapped by a man they could not leave despite his cruelty. Her boys would not be apprenticed to some white man to whom they owed their livelihood. She worshiped at the altar of the god Education. She begged Jesus, Mary and Joseph to intercede for her, too. Her children would be free. Her children would be able to fend for themselves.

The day after the Chinaman terrified her with that improbability if he should die, she swore she would make Tong Lee her ally against the Chinaman. She would speak to him when they were alone in the shop. But the Chinaman had decided to end his confinement in the attic and early that morning he had sent Alan to call Tong Lee to him.

Zuela saw the Chinaman tottering into the shop before dawn, coughing into Tong Lee's shoulders.

"How you going to sell meat to people spitting all over them?" Tong Lee was asking him.

But the Chinaman was looking at her when he answered him. "I sit and take money," he said. "You sell."

"You don't trust me?"

"Like my brother," the Chinaman said, but it was on Zuela he held his eyes. "Like my right arm. Trust you like my right arm."

A bout of coughing seized him then and Tong Lee lowered him to a sack of sugar in the corner of the shop. When the coughing passed, he let her know why he was there. "I promised priest," he said, "but no more Laventille. No more Mass on Sunday. Nothing more."

Panic almost caused Zuela to retreat, to discard the plan she had woven all night, lying awake on her bed next to her daughters. For it was clear to her that the Chinaman intended to watch her, and that with him in the shop it would be harder for her to get Tong Lee to say *please,* to get him to help her rescue her children, *please.* But Zuela did not know that the Chinaman was afraid of her, that he had made Tong Lee press his ears against the floorboards when Rosa was confessing to her, and that he was convinced that when Tong Lee repeated *poison,* he had used that word because he could not find the word in Chinese for the thing that made animals of men.

All Zuela knew was that since that white woman floated on the beach in Otahiti, the Chinaman had fastened his eyes on her and that his willfulness had grown stronger now that he thought he had broken her.

But she could not allow herself to panic, for she could not allow him to succeed. He had threatened to steal her children's future. She would save them. She would put the Chinaman at ease, make him slacken the hold of his eyes on her. She would encourage his faith in Tong Lee's loyalty to him. Then he would be willing to pass the daywatch back to him again and leave her free to take his spy to *please.*

When the Chinaman leaned against the wall, drained by the tremors rattling the bones in his chest, she unfolded her plan. She ran to him and placed her hand on his forehead.

"Fever," she said.

He flinched from her touch and curled into himself, but she was not discouraged. It was good, she thought, good he wanted to get away from her. Perhaps he was not entirely free of the fear that had gripped him when she told him she, not Alan, would feed him the sancoche, and she burned him with her eyes. She would make that fear work for her now, make him more willing, eager even, to leave her to Tong Lee.

"I get him something," she said to Tong Lee.

"Something?"

She ran to the kitchen and returned with a steaming mug of hot cocoa. Tong Lee frowned at her. "I thought you said fever," he said.

She stuck to her plan. "Hot good for hot. It steam out the fever." She reached down, loosened one of the Chinaman's arms from around his chest and wrapped his hand around the side of the mug. Still holding the handle, she placed her left hand on the back of the Chinaman's hand and brought the mug to his lips.

"No, no, no." The Chinaman swung his head violently from side to side. "No."

"Is good for you."

"No." The Chinaman backed into the corner.

Tong Lee kneeled beside them.

"It's good for him," she said. "I do it with the children, they feel better."

Tong Lee bent over the Chinaman. "She trying to help you, Ho Sang."

"See. I make the cocoa just as you like it." Zuela tilted the mug to her mouth.

The Chinaman's back stiffened. He craned his head toward her.

"See. It taste good. The way you tell me to make it." She sipped the cocoa again.

A thin light bounced off the whites of the Chinaman's eyes. "Drink more," he said.

"More?"

"Drink more."

She bent the mug to her lips again.

"More."

"Then I drink all."

"More."

Zuela swallowed.

"More."

Tong Lee whispered in the Chinaman's ear, "You make a fool of yourself in front your wife."

Zuela did not understand his full meaning. She did not know that Tong Lee was thinking that the Chinaman believed she had put poison in his cocoa, but when he chided him, she felt a ray of hope. It would be a matter of time; soon she would get Tong Lee on her side.

"I put condensed milk in it," she said.

"Drink more," said the Chinaman.

Tong Lee took the mug from her hand. "You prove enough, Ho Sang." He pushed the mug to the Chinaman's mouth. "Drink."

After the older children left for school, Zuela rushed through her housework. She smoothed the sheets over the beds, swept the floors, washed the morning dishes, started the pelau for lunch, bathed and dressed the two youngest girls, washed the clothes, hung them on a line in the backyard to dry and finished the last night's ironing. It was nine o'clock. She knew there would be a lull in the shop by then. The early customers who came at six o'clock for their breakfast hops bread would have left, and it was still too early for those who came later to buy rice, saltmeat and flour to make dumplings and bake for lunch. She put her daughters on the bed with a bundle of blank paper and coloring pencils and warned them to be quiet. "Your father in front, in the shop." Then she returned to Tong Lee.

He was sitting on a stool facing the counter, threading the soft, white insides of the hops bread through his fingers. The Chinaman was slumped in his corner on the sack of sugar, spit drooling down his chin. The neck of his shirt was stained with dark splotches of cocoa. Tong Lee had covered his legs with a yellow cotton blanket.

It was working, Zuela thought. The Chinaman's sickness, his fear of her hatred of him, Tong Lee's loyalty, all three had made the Chinaman drop his guard, shut his eyes and leave her free to work on Tong Lee. She walked over to Tong Lee. He, too, had been put at ease by her concern for the Chinaman. She brushed her body against his shoulder. He turned, his fingers still in the hops bread, and she slid her hand over his.

"I know you never like it," she said. "I make bake for you."

She saw the panic in his eyes the second she touched him. He glanced nervously in the direction of the Chinaman, but he did not pull away his hand from hers, though her fingers lingered on his longer than both of them knew was necessary for her to remove the bread from his hand.

The next morning, after the children left, she kneaded lard and water in some flour, cut the dough into small pieces, and fried them in cooking oil. When she brought the golden bakes, dripping with red salt butter, to Tong Lee, he shifted his eyes quickly from her to the Chinaman.

"What if he wake up?" he asked.

"He sleep an hour. Just like you make him do yesterday." She put her hand on his bare arm. A faint smile crossed his lips.

The third morning, Zuela did not wait for Tong Lee to bring the Chinaman down to the shop. She had brewed a mug of cocoa and was already standing with it in her hand, next to the sack of sugar where the Chinaman took his watch, when Tong Lee entered the shop with his charge on his arm. He took the mug from her hand the moment he reached her, and barely giving the Chinaman a second to stretch out his legs when he lowered his body to the sack, he pressed the mug to the Chinaman's lips. The impatience in his voice was unmistakable. It fanned the hope already stirring in Zuela's heart.

"Drink, quick, quick."

The Chinaman twisted his head, but Tong Lee spread his fingers across his chin and held it steady again. "You making yourself a woman in front of her. Stop it." He looked up at Zuela and raised his voice. "You want people talk you bad? Drink."

When the Chinaman was finished, Tong Lee handed the empty mug to Zuela, and still facing her, he said to the Chinaman, "Is a wonder she have time to do this kindness for you. With all the children she have to mind, two babies still needing her, is a wonder she still have time to sell in the shop and cook for you and them."

Zuela had no doubt after that that her seduction was working. She returned to the kitchen and this time she pressed the dough into a single round bake the size of a plate and baked it in her iron oven. The morning customers had gone when she brought it to Tong Lee. The Chinaman was asleep.

"You don't want some, too?" Tong Lee asked after she cut him a slice.

"I make only one."

"Yes, but is enough to share." He took the knife from her and cut a slice and gave it to her.

"I make sweetbread tonight," she said, and bit into the bake. "I save some for you."

The fourth morning, she brought the sweetbread. "How long you know Chinaman?" she asked, and pulled a stool next to his and sat down.

"Long time," he said.

"How long?"

Tong Lee cut two slices from the sweetbread. She shook her head. "No, I don't want it. I make it for you. You eat. Tell me if you like it."

He bit into the sweetbread. White flakes of the powdery sugar Zuela had sprinkled on top of it stuck to his mustache. "Good," he said and bit into it again.

"I put coconut in it." She reached over and dusted the sugar from the edge of his mustache. His neck turned pink. He smiled, but just as quickly, the smile disappeared.

"I taste it," he said.

"Fresh coconut. I grate it last night."

He took another bite of the sweetbread.

"So how long?" She repeated her question.

He looked across to her, puzzled.

"That you know Chinaman," she said.

He lowered his eyes. "Long time."

She drew her fingers through the crumbs in the plate in front of him, gathered them in a heap, and separated them into thin lines. He followed her movements.

"In years, how long?" she asked.

"Over forty."

"Then how your mustache so black?"

A smile formed again on his lips and then disappeared behind his hand when he wiped away the sugar that had stuck to his mustache. But the lines on his face had softened when he answered her. "No hair," he said. He touched the front of his head that was bald to his earlobes.

"Chinaman's hair is gray," she said.

"Gray better than none." His arm almost brushed hers when she slid the bread crumbs to the edge of his plate.

"I like none better than Chinaman gray." She made tiny circles

142

with the bread crumbs and the sugar on his plate.

He looked away. "Why you call him Chinaman? Why you don't call him Ho Sang?"

"He's Chinaman to me," she said.

"He let you call him Chinaman?"

"I don't call him Chinaman to his face. If I have to name him and he's there, I say, 'the children father.'"

"And before the children born?"

"I say, 'the man I live with.'"

Tong Lee reached for the bread knife. Zuela took it from his hand.

"You like it. I glad. When I make it, I know you like it." She cut off a large slice from the sweetbread and handed it to him. He packed his mouth, chewing so ferociously that his jaws moved up and down like a hammer, stretching and folding the flesh on his cheeks and temples and distorting his face. But when he stopped chewing, his skin settled back, smooth and taut.

"So why you look younger than him?" Zuela was persistent.

Tong Lee chewed and swallowed until all the bread was clear from his mouth. "Only ten years younger," he said. His voice was tense.

"He could be your father."

"Not in age."

"Yes, in age."

"No." He got up.

Zuela removed her fingers from his plate and stood up next to him. "What he do for you that make you so loyal?"

Tong Lee backed away from her.

"Why you make yourself old as him?"

Tong Lee looked over to the Chinaman.

"Why you so loyal? Always."

Tong Lee kept his eyes on the Chinaman. "I gave him the boat that brought him down the river."

Zuela squeezed her eyes forward. "The Orinoco?"

"No, the Yangtze. A river in China."

"Not the Orinoco?" The muscles on the sides of her face slackened.

"No, not the Orinoco." Tong Lee faced her again.

"That's what *you* do for him." She put her hand on his arm. "I asked you what *he* do for you."

He pushed her hand away. "No! Not me. I didn't mean me. I didn't mean I do anything for him. I mean to say *him*. He that help me ferry the boat."

"The boat you give him?"

"I tell you is he that help me. He that save my life."

"The boat he give you?"

"No!"

"Then is you who give it to him."

Tong Lee glanced over again to the Chinaman. "He wake up. Customers come."

"How you say he save you when is you give him the boat?"

"He wake up," said Tong Lee.

"How he?"

Tong Lee did not answer her.

"Why you say he?"

Tong Lee got up and walked toward the Chinaman.

"What he do?"

But Zuela knew she had already lost him to the Chinaman. He was kneeling by his side, mopping the dribble from his chin with the edge of the blanket, when she asked him the question again, and if he heard her—which she knew he did, because she had repeated it over and over—he had clearly chosen to ignore her, he had clearly chosen his friend. And later that evening when he was gone and the Chinaman was back in his attic, she sat in the shadows of her room and grieved, too, like Rosa, that she had no mother to protect her. What, she asked herself, would her mother have told her to do? What would she have taught her, had she lived, so she would know how to break the Chinaman's lock on Tong Lee's loyalty, that she would know how to save her children from their father's spite?

But Zuela should not have despaired. She should have taken hope in Tong Lee's smile before guilt had caused him to lift her hand off his arm and walk away from her. She would have found reason to hope if she knew he was fighting a memory and losing—a memory of a boy, ten years old, bathed in his father's blood, on a bench in a sampan between the reeds on the banks of the Yangtze River, the man who had saved his life sitting next to him. For remembering the boy, Tong Lee could not stop himself from remembering the young man whose heart bounded in his chest the first time he saw her—a little girl cross-legged on the floor in Ho Sang's attic, rubbing a pellet of the brown resin between her hands, her ribboned pigtails dangling over her shoulders, brushing her knees. She had looked up when Ho Sang said her name and then winked at him. "She sweet, Tong Lee. She sweeter than opium sweet." Her little-girl sad eyes broke his heart.

No, Zuela should not have despaired when Tong Lee walked past her to the Chinaman. For though Tong Lee knew she would take his actions to mean that he had made his choice between her and Ho Sang, deciding on Ho Sang, he knew, too, that he would rather have her think that than remember the day when Ho Sang told him, "You saved my life," and meant, "I saved yours." No, he did not want to remember that day nor the other day, either, when Ho Sang asked him to hold the ring. For on that day, the innocence of Zuela's eyes burned through the obligation of friendship he had welded with the memory of an arm around his waist on the Yangtze, and in the ominous silence of the church, he let the ring slip, he let it slide to the tips of his fingers. Then when the priest asked that fatal question never meant to be answered, it fell to the hard terrazzo floor and resonated with his condemnation: *Yes, there is someone here who knows why these two should not be joined together in Holy Matrimony. Yes, there is someone—I, Tong Lee.*

Yet Tong Lee did not speak. He held his peace—forever, as Ho Sang warned him with his eyes. For the look that Ho Sang gave him when he picked up the ring and pressed it into the palm of his hand had stripped his heart bare there and then and forced him to the truth; disgust alone had not caused his fingers to tremble, his muscles to lose strength and let the ring fall. It was fear, it was desire, and it was fear because of the intensity of desire. Later, Tong Lee knew it was not merely desire but love, not merely fear but terror—terror in the face of the undeniable fact that he was not much different from this man he despised, that he, too, burned with love

145

for a child, a girl barely thirteen. From then on, Tong Lee fashioned a mask over his face and kept his distance, visiting Ho Sang only when he was certain Zuela had left the attic again to go to the bed Ho Sang built for her in the room behind the shop.

"Priest make me build it. I still take her here in the attic and she do what I say."

Only once did Tong Lee open that iron gate he used to convince Ho Sang of his loyalty. When the bed buckled under Zuela and six children, the lock snapped and he pleaded with Ho Sang, "You don't think you should ease up on Zuela? Six in eight years!"

Then Ho Sang sent his icicles into Tong Lee's heart again. "You say that like it's your business."

Tong Lee shut the gate and threw away the key. "I say that because I concerned for you," he said. "Concerned you weaken her. Then you don't have no wife no more."

Ho Sang rewarded him. He doubled over with laughter. "I strong as a bull, eh? I nearing sixty and still I going like a bull. But she a good horse, Tong Lee. She last."

In time Tong Lee taught himself how not to see Zuela, how to blind himself to the beauty that had dazzled him, how to allow himself to admit only pity for her, pity for a woman whose belly never went down, whose eyes rarely smiled, who, except in the presence of her children, seemed in perpetual mourning. But that first morning when she took the loaf of bread from his hands promising him bake, none of these lessons stayed with him to rescue him from panic, and from then on he found himself counting the seconds with the clock, selling hops bread and salt butter to the customers, but calculating all the time the time it would take for them to leave, the time it would take for her to come back to the shop and to him. When she did not return the day after he took her hand off his arm, and walked away from her to the Chinaman, time stopped for him. Two days later, unable to live in the vacuum of her absence, he gave up the last shred of his defenses. Then the fire that had smoldered in the secret part of his heart for more than seventeen years blazed through the blinders over his eyes and he saw what he had always seen in spite of the mask, what he had always tried, but failed, to deny. He saw the woman he had never ceased to love, the woman whose beauty had never ceased to frighten him, and desperate to confirm her in the flesh, he rushed to the kitchen. But Zuela turned her back on him. For believing she had lost, that she had not learned enough from her mother or from the women, either, how to take him to *please,* she had abandoned all hope.

Convinced she had rejected him for good, Tong Lee braced himself against the wooden pillars of the doorway and struggled for the strength to conceal his ardor. "No more bakes?" he asked her.

She turned to answer him. When he saw her face, there was not a pillar in the world that could protect him. He revealed it all: "Was because I remembered you. Was because I remembered how beautiful you were. How beautiful you still are. Was because of that, I walk to the Chinaman."

Zuela did not go back to the shop with him that day, but the next morning she brought him bulljhol and zaboca.

"You could be with me alone," she said and bent over him.

He had to pull in his breath to stop himself from touching her. "How alone?" His voice was barely above a whisper.

"You could tell him to let you walk me to Mass."

She had tied her hair away from her face. Still, he could see the blue and black lights flickering between the strands. "He would say the children can go with you." He fought the impulse to bury his lips in her hair.

"He know I like the five o'clock Mass. And the children don't want to get up so early. They want to sleep."

He had to clasp his hands tightly together in his lap to stop himself from reaching for her. "But why he let me go with you?"

"Boysie," she said.

He did not look at her. "He don't believe about the hearts," he said.

"But he know I do. He always hearing me warning the children about Boysie."

The scent of her body was overpowering. "Why he let you go?" he asked.

"You tell him to let me go."

147

"Why he listen?"

"He listen to everything you say."

Yes, yes, he and Ho Sang were bonded in that sampan on the Yangtze, bonded in that pool of blood. "Maybe he tell me no."

"Not this time. He change. Like he 'fraid me, but still he don't 'fraid me. He won't let me go nowhere. But he let me go to Mass with you if you tell him so."

Still, Tong Lee tried to resist her. "At five in the morning?" he asked.

"He promise the priest that married us."

Tong Lee pinched the skin at the center of his top lip and raised it to his nose. Her scent was not as strong then. He relaxed, breathed in deep and smoothed his fingers down the sides of his mustache. The hair bounced back again, stiff like the bristles on a horse.

"I don't like the feel of fooling him," he said. He let out his breath.

She asked him one more time, "What he do for you that you owe him so?"

This time his heart betrayed him. This time his love for her made him admit the truth: *It was Ho Sang who was the traitor. Ho Sang.* "He was crawling on his belly like a snake when I saw him on the banks of the Yangtze," he said.

"He dream it every night," she said.

"Blood was all down his shirt and his pants."

"He try to take it out of his hair, too," she said.

"I ask him, 'Whose blood?' He tell me, 'They kill everybody. The whole village.' I ask, 'Your wife and children safe?' He say, 'They kill everybody.' I wonder why wife and children, but he don't say. He don't say either how come he don't stay to bury them. How come he could say, 'Go. Go. Jump on the boat before they find us.'"

"Wife and children?" she asked.

"A wife and a daughter. He never told you?"

"No," she said.

"It was years before you," he said.

"Wife and daughter?" He heard her merge the words together as though they were one—both persons the same being.

"Years," he repeated.

"That's why he married me?" Her voice was tremulous.

Tong Lee did not ask her what she meant, for the quivering in her voice had taken him to that other day when her lips shook, the day she stood still at the back of the church and Ho Sang fixed the collar of her dress.

"I picked out the fabric and had it made for her for the wedding," Ho Sang was saying to him, but tears were rolling down Zuela's eyes.

"Stop it! Stop the crying." Ho Sang slapped her face. He hit her once. It was a rapid stroke against her cheek, the spanking a father would give a naughty child.

"Is too big by the waist. Is not pretty. Too big across the belly."

And Tong Lee did not interfere, though his heart was breaking and his fingers were making bruises on the palm of his hand over the ring Ho Sang had given him to hold.

But now he was thinking of the wife and the daughter Ho Sang had left on the bare earth to rot. "I'll tell him," he said to Zuela. *Before they rotted, dogs mauled their flesh, chewed their bones dry.* "I take you to Mass on Sunday," he said. "I make him let me take you."

⋘ Chapter 11 ⋙

*H*o Sang was twenty when his wife and daughter were slaughtered. Before nightmares forced him to the truth that only the brown resin could obliterate, he smoked cigarettes made from ganja leaves to deceive himself into believing he bore no responsibility for their deaths.

He had followed his father since he was ten and was already skilled at riding a horse bareback. They would speed through the brush along the banks of the Yangtze, racing to the sea, the wind stinging their faces, the sabers in their sheaths flying high against their thighs. How many times? By the time his wife and daughter were murdered, a multitude of times.

At the edge of the sea they would wait for the British ship. When the signal came, they would dismount. With twenty men to help them, they would pull out the sampans they had hidden in the willows. After they boarded the ship, they would give the Englishman silver. In exchange, he would give them crates of resin bled from the poppy seed. They knew that what they were doing was illegal and immoral, but there was a fortune to be made on the black market in China.

Yet, a little more than half a century ago, there was nothing England could offer their country, a country that recorded the history of its civilization in millennia. China neither wanted nor required the wool and cheese England produced on her island, nor the sugar and tobacco she mined from her outposts in the New World. Nothing. Greedy for the silk and tea that China had in abundance, England was forced to pay with silver that she was loath to part with. Those were the times when in one day Imperial Commissioner Lin Tse-hsü, acting under a direct edict of the Ch'ing court, slashed open twenty thousand chests of opium and almost clogged a river. Six million dollars sank under the water that day in 1839. But that was the final act of arrogance Europe would tolerate. Its revenge was lethal and immediate: wars that crippled China for three years, and then a hundred more when England fanned the scarlet petals in her poppy fields in Bengal and blew the seeds eastwards without fear of censure. Then China fell to its knees to buy what she sold, and silver flowed backwards. A country nodded, England drank tea and the black market thrived.

Ho Sang's father had one rule for his sons when they trafficked in opium—never touch the poppy juice. It was not good for business, he said. The hunger the resin unleashed was never satiated. So they sold it quickly and in bulk up the river, investing in the demanding savagery of its power to delude with dreams that killed pain—pain that made nightmares that only the resin could eradicate. They never imagined there could be a fire the brown devil could not consume, a rage it could not quell. They never thought it could fan a righteousness that would ravage cities and villages, a movement that could let loose a flood of blood for a decade and more, all because of, and in spite of it. So when the People stormed their village, they were caught unprepared. For though the People's Republic of China was an idea yet to be reified, the brutality of the Opium Wars and the betrayal of leaders who allowed their country to freefall into a nightmarish sleep because England needed silver to buy tea, had already set an unremitting purge in motion. The People spared almost no one in their revenge, though sometimes the women, sometimes the children.

They surprised Ho Sang and his men one evening just as they were unloading their sampans. They slit off their necks before sound reached their lips, sending their headless bodies pirouetting like dancers backwards into the reeds.

Ho Sang was the only one spared in the bloody carnage. They wanted him alive, they said, to send a message to the other villages. They would not tolerate the sale of opium in their country, no matter that the English Queen chose to disbelieve her ambassadors: *A country put to sleep?*

Their plan was to slice off Ho Sang's head in the public square, but he bargained with them. They had already killed his father, and he was the only one left who knew where he had hidden hundreds of bags of silver. They dragged him to the place he named. In their astonishment over the abundance of the booty, far more than they had hoped for, and dazed, too, by its value for the Movement, they did not see Ho Sang slip past them like a snake and slither through the trees. After heads cleared and they discovered their mistake, they finished off his wife and his daughter in revenge. Ho Sang found their bodies at his doorway. The blood that poured from their necks down the steps of his house had already congealed. He slid on the slippery surface and tumbled downwards. When he looked up, he was bathed in blood from his neck to his toes. Two pairs of eyes locked into his at the foot of the sapling he had planted the year before for his daughter.

On the banks of the Yangtze River he saw Tong Lee—a boy, just ten, glassy-eyed, turned to stone on a bench in a sampan hidden in the reeds. The beheaded corpse of the boy's father lay across his lap, stiff and still, like a piece of wood.

"Go! Go!" Ho Sang slid on his belly over the side of the sampan. "Go." He knew, if not the People, the women would beat the brush looking for him.

The boy did not move.

"Go!"

The boy stayed still.

Ho Sang reached over him and threw out the corpse. The body hit the water with such force that it showered the boat with glistening sprays turned pink from the blood pooled at the gaping hole at the top of the neck. "Go!" Ho Sang wiped the bloodied water from his eyes and snatched the oars out of their rings.

In the open river where the blood was not visible, the boy came alive. He wanted to know how Ho Sang had survived. Only women and children were not massacred, he said.

"Fate," Ho Sang replied.

Was he married? the boy asked.

"One wife. One daughter," Ho Sang said.

Had he left them behind? the boy wanted to know.

"No, they were massacred, too."

The boy was silent; his mother was also massacred.

"Did you bury them?" the boy finally asked. His father and three brothers had been decapitated. No one had been left to bury his mother.

"What? And lose time?"

The boy was stunned by Ho Sang's callous response. He would have buried his mother if he could. He would not have left her to be eaten by dogs. *What? And lose time?* Ho Sang had said to him, as if only a fool would have risked his life to give his wife honorable passage to the other world. Yet he would have done that for his mother. For his father and brothers, too, if he had not been reduced to stone.

He swore to himself that when they reached Shanghai, he would leave this man who had lost his soul. But farther down the river Ho Sang saved his life again. A storm had capsized their sampan. As he was sinking to the muddy bottom of the river, he felt Ho Sang's arm around his waist, breaking his descent.

"Twice now," said Ho Sang.

"That means I'm your slave?"

"No, only do what I tell you to do."

They traveled together to Canton and, there, Ho Sang traded in the last piece of opium he had with him for two passages on a British ship to the West Indies.

"We make clean break. Start fresh. Best part—no Chinese women."

And in the early days after Emancipation, it was so in the British West Indies. For when the Africans refused to go back to the plantation (the memory of whips and chains was too raw for them), the British raked their colonies in China and India, knowing well that people on the brink of starvation would willingly accept their offer of indentured servitude. The Indians came with whole families; the Chinese, more wary, left their women behind. Perhaps they wanted to test the waters. There were rumors that pale-skinned people got sunstroke and died under the brutal tropical sun. In the end the Indians proved more resilient. By the time the nineteenth century reached its halfway mark, it took just two hands to count the number of Chinese cane cutters in the British Caribbean colonies.

But though they left the cane fields, the Chinese did not leave the islands. They sent for their men friends and more than doubled their numbers. "No need for Chinese women," Ho Sang said to Tong Lee. "Black women in the Caribbean sweet. Do what you tell them do. We stay because Chinese making money in the grocery business. They pushing Syrian out. Chinese count better. Faster. White and black man prefer doing business with us."

In Trinidad, Ho Sang became part-owner of a grocery shop in Nelson Street, but, later, when he did not make money selling groceries, he decided to go back to the trade he knew best. He would sell opium to Chinese immigrants and to Americans on the base at Chaguaramas. He had one condition for Boysie when he went into partnership with him. It was the rule his father had strictly enforced: "We sell. We never smoke." Soon, however, the Chinaman was not only selling, but smoking, and, within a short time, mostly smoking, barely selling.

At first the ganja leaves were enough for him, but by the time he sailed up the Orinoco for alpagats and took Zuela, too, the nightmares the ganja had calmed were beginning to break through the haze of its mesmerizing smoke, haunting him with memories even in the daytime— a daughter and a wife, a wife and a daughter locked together as one in a sea of blood.

He had not thought consciously that Zuela would redeem him. The separation that occurred in his brain happened without his awareness of it. Zuela's father had introduced him to his only daughter whom he had named Daughter.

"Hija." That was all he said.

When Ho Sang looked at him perplexed, he laughed. *"Hija es su nombre. Es mi hija. Se llama Hija."*

Ho Sang's head spun. *A child: the daughter of a father. A girl: a female named Daughter.*

In his attic that night, on his return from Venezuela, he lit his first nodule of that forbidden drug. Then in the dreams that followed for days afterward, the heads at the root of the sapling rolled back to their headless bodies at the doorway of his house in China and became one—his wife and daughter alive, but merged into one body. He told his woman to go. One year of nightmares later, he resurrected his wife and renamed the girl called Daughter. Zuela, he named her, and made her his wife. He rescued his daughter, too, and kept her in the child named Daughter.

Tong Lee told him that if he smoked more than one pipe a week, the opium would own him as it owned their Chinese friends who came almost every night to suck the smoke from the tubes of the silver and wood water pipes they had brought with them from China. Ho Sang replied that it took three pipes a week to make you an addict; he smoked only two and just ganja in-between.

"Two is still too much," Tong Lee said. He had not known of the third. "What will Zuela do if it kill you?"

That was why Ho Sang trusted Tong Lee when his hair receded, when it turned white and the flesh on his face loosened and sagged. "You the only one who don't want me to die," he said.

When Tong Lee asked his permission to take Zuela to Mass, he agreed. "You the only one I trust to walk with her so early in the morning."

Only once had Ho Sang seen disapproval on Tong Lee's face. That was on his wedding day when Tong Lee dropped the ring. Never after that. It was as if Zuela did not exist for him. And in time Ho Sang began to believe that Tong Lee was truly different from his other friends who, he suspected, were counting the grains of sand falling into his hourglass. So he had no doubt that Tong Lee could take Zuela to Mass and back and not notice that the lights in her hair had never dulled, that her smile, though she rarely smiled, lit up her eyes and they shone like the sun filtering through the tops of trees in the rainforest.

He slept well that night after smoking the ganja leaves, and though the nightmares returned at dawn, they were no more lacerating than they had been before. For he knew that the woman he had married to replace a daughter and a wife was standing beneath the street lamp waiting for his trusted friend, not for some paramour. For he never could imagine she could penetrate Tong Lee's indifference and take him to *please.* For he never could imagine Tong Lee would think, *yes,* and dream of much more.

155

⊰ Chapter 12 ⊱

$\mathcal{S}$he was waiting for him in front of the shop when he arrived. His heart raced the moment he saw her, and his glance flew upward to the attic. If Ho Sang were awake he would know it, for light easily filtered through the wooden slats of the attic jalousies. But in the somnolent haziness of the predawn, nothing broke the darkness where nine children—four boys, five girls, two of them babies—were sleeping, and an aging Chinese man traced figures with his eyes on the beams of his ceiling. Relieved, Tong Lee let out his breath and walked briskly toward her. She smiled, and he took her arm.

For the whole length of Nelson Street, they did not speak, embarrassed, perhaps, by the stench rising from the pavements and gutters. Here, in the center of the city crowded with shops owned by children of the old plantocracy or newly arrived immigrants from Syria, Portugal and China, the descendants of slaves felt disempowered again. With no sense of ownership, and, therefore, bearing no responsibility for the safety and cleanliness of the streets, they threw their refuse where they would. But not they alone; the merchants did, too, for Nelson Street was not home to them; rather, a way station where money exchanged hands. Butchers dumped offal, fishmongers emptied buckets of fish guts and scales into sluggish canals already clogged with the peelings of fruit, mango seeds, the half-shells of oranges and grapefruit, crumpled brown paper, decaying food and the droppings of the day's sales. The street sweepers came before dawn with their long-handled brooms, but on Sundays nobody worked. On those mornings the island was in church. Later, lovers would stretch out on sun-drenched beaches and dream of evenings when they would make love six times over to compensate for days when the aching in bones left them passionless.

In spite of the apathy Tong Lee had nurtured into a habit, the stench of the Sunday streets filled him with shame and he tightened his grip on Zuela's elbow hoping she had not noticed. When they turned the corner, the stink of garbage finally dissipated in the dewy morning air, and Tong Lee led her down a street perfumed with garden roses and hibiscus, overripe mango and soursop.

"I live here," he said, stopping in front of a pretty blue house.

Zuela's eyes flew open wide. "Here? You live here?"

It was a tiny house built in the colonial Victorian style popular at the time. The walkway was covered by a narrow, V-shaped, galvanized-roof awning that was supported by four tall pillars. Under the roof, aprons of intricately carved wood, reminiscent of old lace, painted white, framed the bottom of the awning and the tops of the front and sides of the house. They lent a quiet elegance to the house, along with the tall wooden jalousies fretted above and below with the same elaborate carvings. Orange and bright pink bougainvillea leaned against white latticed trellises, and bunches of flowers overflowed in pots on the front steps.

"Like a picture," Zuela said.

Tong Lee smiled, pleased with the delight on her face.

"Is here you live? Is here, all this time?" she asked.

Tong Lee led her up the front steps.

"All these years by yourself?"

"Yes, by myself." He opened the door to the drawing room.

Zuela sucked in her breath. Everything in that room shone: the brass fixtures, the polished wood floors, the mahogany furniture. She touched the top of the dining room table with the tips of her fingers and bent low over it. "I can see my whole face."

"I keep it shined."

"And the floor, too!"

"I polish it on Saturdays."

The walls were lined with paintings, each one meticulously framed. Most were scenes of the sea—men in fishing boats pulling up nets or dropping them; some, portraits of Chinese men and women in long mandarin coats. Zuela stood before one of a little Chinese boy holding the hands of a beautiful woman and a handsome man. All three were dressed in red silk gowns embroidered with gold.

"You?" she asked.

"With my parents."

"They look rich."

He laughed. "It's how I want to remember them. My father was a fisherman. Like the others." He waved toward the sea pictures.

"You made them?"

"I like to draw and paint," he said.

"I never would have thought . . ."

"You only see me in the shop," he said.

"Yes, but I see now why you don't want a woman."

An awkward silence fell between them. It was not comforting like the silence they shared moments ago, wanting to spare each other the humiliation of Nelson Street. It was tense and strained, and Zuela floundered to put it right again because Tong Lee, who had been moving his eyes from her to the paintings and back to her as if he saw in her face the same exquisite lines as those in the portraits of the women he had drawn, had stepped suddenly away from her, pursed his lips and frowned.

"I mean . . . I mean to say . . ."

Tong Lee cut across her words. "I never said I didn't want a woman."

Slowly, Zuela unpinned the black lace mantilla on the top of her head. "I didn't say you wouldn't want to be with one." On Sundays she wore the mantilla to church and had put it on when she left the house, in case the Chinaman peeped through the slats to the street, or her neighbors saw her with Tong Lee holding her elbow.

Tong Lee followed her movements. "I just never needed to keep one," he said.

She folded the mantilla and put it down on the dining room table.

"You don't have to keep me."

"I didn't mean that."

"You don't have to owe me." She searched for the buttons on her blouse. "Not *forever.*" She undid the top button.

Tong Lee looked away from her.

"I don't ask for much."

When he looked up again, she was loosening another button on her dress. "Stop." He reached for her hand. She shook him off.

"That's not why I bring you here." He held her wrist fast.

"I have big belly, but the rest of me still good. Firm."

"No. That's not why you here."

She stroked her cheeks. "Is not pretty, but is not ugly, either."

Tong Lee pulled her toward the drawing room. "Sit. Sit down."

"Why? You don't want . . . "

"Sit." He placed his hands on her shoulders and pushed her gently down on a cushioned armchair.

This time she did not resist him. If he had read through her thoughts, if he knew now why she had come, he seemed to have forgiven her, he seemed to know that she was there because of her children, he seemed to understand. She buttoned her dress.

"You think you blaspheming against the Church coming here?" He pulled another armchair next to her and sat down.

She leaned back and closed her eyes.

"You think you blaspheming?" He repeated the question.

"Because we didn't go to church?" She opened her eyes.

"Yes."

"I don't always believe."

"I see you always going to church on Sunday."

"You see me? I never see you when I walking to church."

Tong Lee brushed his mustache down the sides of his mouth and tried to mask his embarrassment. He didn't want her to know of the mornings he stood across the street from the church, hidden behind a tree, waiting for her to walk by. "Ho Sang tells me," he said. "He tells me you go to church every Sunday."

"I go and I try to pray."

"Try?"

"The prayers don't always come. The last time I prayed real hard, I prayed I don't kill the Chinaman."

She had not changed her tone when she said that, and at first Tong Lee did not understand her. "You pray Ho Sang don't kill you?" he asked.

She laughed. "No. That I don't kill him."

Tong Lee heard her this time. He leaned toward her. "Why you want to kill him?"

"I went up to Laventille on the feast day . . . "

He didn't let her finish. "He 'fraid when you went to Laventille." His voice was low and intense.

"'Fraid?"

"After you came back."

"Why?"

Tong Lee was ashamed. He had listened for Ho Sang. He was his spy against her.

"Why?"

"I heard what your friend tell you."

"Rosa?"

"Yes."

"I thought I hear something move in the attic when I was talking to Rosa."

"I hear what she say."

"Hear what?"

"I hear her say the white lady want to poison her husband."

Zuela laughed. "You hear wrong. She say her husband *think* she want to poison him."

"Think?"

"I told her to see the old nursemaid she used to have. She living now in Laventille. I told her to ask her for medicine to make her husband feel better. That way he don't think that no more."

"Better?" Tong Lee shook his head, confused.

"You thought?" Suddenly it was clear: Chinaman's head swinging from side to side when she brought him the cocoa; his insistence on calling Alan when she took the sancoche to him. "If I kill him I don't do it like that," she said. "I have more courage."

Tong Lee could not face her.

"When I prayed to Our Lady of Fatima to stop me, I had bigger plans. Something to make him suffer, like he make me suffer."

"I could have helped." Tong Lee's voice was barely audible. "All those years I was his friend. I could have helped you."

"You seeing nothing."

"I tried to see nothing."

"I pray Our Lady give me the strength to hold back because of the children. I don't want them to know their mother is a murderer." She smiled bitterly. "Now, even if I want to, I can't kill him. He tie my hands."

Tong Lee asked her how, how did Ho Sang tie her hands? But he knew the answer.

"The children. He say if he die, he leave me with nothing."

A silvery light crossed the room. Through the window, Tong Lee could see the first glimmerings of dawn between the leaves of the chataigne tree that grew at the side of his house. "It will be day soon," he said.

"You want me to leave?"

"No. Stay. I want to hear. Tell me. Tell me why you want to kill Ho Sang."

Zuela did not know where to begin. Should she begin when she was nine and was still living in her village in Venezuela? Or should she begin when life ceased for her after her mother died and began again in those brief months with Rosa, only to end again when that man behind the hibiscus said, *Beg, beg,* then, *Please.* Was that what Tong Lee wanted to know?

"Tell me everything. Everything from the beginning. I'll give Ho Sang an excuse if we get back too late."

She sighed. "You want to know from the time I know an iguana is a snake or before that?"

"An iguana?"

"From the time my mother show me it's just an iguana, or afterward when I find out it's a lizard and now when I know it's a snake? Is that what you want to know?"

Tong Lee did not understand, but he did not ask her to explain.

161

"It was a lizard when Chinaman raped me." She knew the word for it now. She had heard it on the radio enough times, though she could never figure out why sometimes the news reporters seemed to be saying that it was the women who had caused the men to rape them.

"Not once I consent," she said to Tong Lee. "Except that time I was too young to know what it was. He take me when he want me. Many times. And I never have say."

Tong Lee looked down on his hands.

"You don't want to hear that part?"

He did not look up.

"Then I'll leave out that part. I know men don't like to hear that part."

Tong Lee stayed silent.

"I don't tell you that part, then. I tell you how he keep me as if I was still a child." She swallowed hard, let out her breath and began again. "I never hold a cent. Well, I hold it when the customers give me, but I pass it on to him. Remember how he tell you to take the money from me?"

Yes, yes, that was what Ho Sang said. She too stupid to count, he said. Tong Lee felt his face grow hot.

"He give me no money for myself or for my children. Every night he leave out so much meat, so much rice, so much flour, so much peas on the shop counter. He used to tell me how to cook it, but now I 'customed. But still he think he know how much pigeon peas and rice it take to make pelau, and how much chicken it take to make stew for nine children on Sunday, and I dare not say anything if is not enough. When the children were babies, he told me, 'Breastfeed them.' Still, every night he coming to me like a lizard."

She looked up at him. "Oh, I sorry. I forgot not to say that part." She wiped her hand over her mouth. "When the breast milk dry up, he doubt me. Say, I don't know nothing and he squeeze."

Tong Lee bit the insides of his lip. The pain calmed him.

"I suppose he sorry after that because he give me powdered milk after the sixth child born."

Tong Lee groaned.

"He give me cloth, too, when the children need clothes, and he bring a woman to teach me to sew and measure. But he get vex when I measure wrong and fabric get left over. I sew the children dress and their petticoat. I make the boys' pants. When they need underwear or shoes or something like that I can't make, he tell me go to the store and fit it on them. But I can't buy. He don't give me money. Next day, he buy the size I tell him. Many times I don't know what to tell the woman in the store when she ask me if I want to buy what the children try on. I shame and I try go to another store, but Port-of-Spain has but so many stores." She leaned back in the chair.

"The children know what happening but they never tell me to my face. They shame for me, too." She sat up. Now her eyes were shining. "Agnes, she's my oldest girl. You maybe can't remember her."

"Yes," Tong Lee said. Yes, he remembered her.

"Before I give her to the nuns, she figure out a way for me. She tell me, ask him for more than I need. When he put aside flour for the next day, she say, tell him is not enough. At first I 'fraid, but then I say it. We start saving after that. A little bit at a time so if I want to change the food he set for me to cook, I could add potatoes where he plan dumpling, or rice where he had in mind macaroni. He never eat with us, so it work. I feel good after that, though I know he still think I'm a child. His child."

She fiddled with the folds of her skirt. "He never beat me, though. I could say that for him." She stopped moving her fingers and looked up at Tong Lee. "Except for that time he slap my face. You remember?"

Tong Lee avoided her eyes.

"I see you looking at him. I think that's why he hit me. He don't like the way you look at him, frowning at him on his wedding day."

Tong Lee heard no indication in the tone of her voice that she was blaming him. She was simply telling her story. Still, he winced.

"I don't know what I was thinking. I suppose I was thinking that I was getting married, really married. Like those brides Rosa and I used to see coming out of Tacarigua church, dress up in white. Lace, veil netting over their hair and everything."

"Rosa?" Tong Lee wanted to know. "Was she the one?"

"The same one that come in the shop white, white? Yes. Same

163

person. I know her in between the Chinaman. When I was still a little girl." She paused. "That was the problem. I think I was a little girl even though Chinaman already have my belly up and tell me I big for my age. But still I dreaming. I think that's how married should be. Then he give me this ugly dress to put on. Well, maybe it wasn't ugly. It had ribbons and things, but I thought it would be white with lace and veil netting and a crown for my head. But it was just a Sunday dress and it didn't fit right. Remember I say it too big at the waist?"

Tong Lee remembered.

"Chinaman say it big, so I can wear it on Sundays when my belly get real fat. I cry and he slap me. It was the first time he slap me, and he try again. That time I have five children. Let me see—Agnes, Alan, Joseph, Helen, Mary." She counted them on her fingers and then started again. "Let me see. Agnes was four, Alan was three, Joseph was two, Helen was one, Mary was six weeks. I was seventeen going on eighteen, starting to think I big. A grown woman. One day, I decide to cut the shoe he give me when we get married. It squeezing my foot and I ask him for another shoe. I tell him my foot grow, just like the children foot grow. He tell me to choose—shoe for me or shoe for Agnes. Agnes always the problem. I could give Agnes's shoes to Alan; don't mind it's a girl shoe. Chinaman buy only watchicong anyhow. It's the same for boy as it is for girl. I could give Alan, Agnes's shoe. Open up a hole in the top for his big toe if it too tight. I could give Joseph, Alan shoe. And the two other children too small to need shoe anyways, but I always have to buy new shoe for Agnes. Well, he say, 'Agnes or you?' So who you think I choose?"

Tong Lee nodded. He knew.

"Yes. Agnes. But then my feet hurt. So one day I have this idea. I take one of his sharp knives. You know the ones he use to cut meat? I take it when he sleeping and I cut off the back of the shoe. The whole back, from the middle back to the heel. Look."

She bent over the chair and traced the area with her fingers. Her toes were turned inward. Tong Lee had noticed that many times before, from the first time he saw her walking into the Chinaman's attic. "She pigeon-toed," Chinaman had said scornfully. But Tong Lee knew she was an acrobat, a graceful gymnast, who balanced a basket full of ground provisions on her head while stepping across the narrow logs that bridged the many streams that flowed incessantly in the rainforest.

"I cut it out," she said, "and I make it a slipper. Next day my foot free and I go slap, slapping in the shop. Chinaman notice the noise but he don't look down. He just tell me, 'Keep quiet. Customer talking.' He can't hear with all that slap, slapping. But I walking around feeling good. First time my toes don't hurt and the corns don't rub up against the front of the shoe. I slap, slapping around, but then Chinaman notice one of his knives missing. I forget it in the room. I don't know what to do. I get confused. Chinaman asking me questions over and over: When last I see it? Where I see it? I thinking about the shoe, hoping he don't look down. Just when I decide to lie, and tell him a story I make up in my head, Joseph come in the shop with the knife in his hand saying, 'Ma leave it on the bed by mistake.' I know is quarrel when the customers leave because Chinaman say children shouldn't tell lies.

"After he close the shop, he take me by my neck and pull me over the sink and put soap in my mouth. The children holding on my dress, crying. I keep quiet because I can't cry with them crying and watching me cry. I stay quiet and Chinaman get vex with all the noise and the children feet between him and me. He bend down to push the children away. That's when he notice the shoes."

"And when he hit you?" asked Tong Lee.

"When he try to hit me. Last time, though. As he reach for me, he trip over the baby and he hit his head on the cinder block holding up the bed. His head cut open. Pow!" She lifted her arms to her forehead and flung open her hands. "Blood pour out of him on the cement block and on the floorboards. It was all down his face and his shirt. I had to bandage him quick, quick and take him to the hospital. When he come back, Agnes tell him God punish him. I think she frighten him. I think he think God really punish him for trying to hit me. He take it like a sign. You know, like from out of the mouth of a little child. Anyhow, he say he still have to explain. He tell Agnes the exact reason he get vex is because her mother cut up her shoe. Agnes say, 'Is Ma shoe.' He say Ma was wearing it till you big enough to wear it. She say, 'What Ma wear then?' He don't answer her. She say, 'Ma foot grow like my foot grow. Ma say her foot hurting her.' He don't give me satisfaction, though he know last time he buy me a shoe I was fourteen. He just say he's a man with six children. I am the oldest and the stupidest child. But he buy me another shoe to wear for Agnes so I could go to church on Sunday. One thing: Chinaman 'fraid that promise he make to the priest to let me go to church."

One thing: Chinaman 'fraid the blood that cover the front of his shirt and soak through his pants.

Tong Lee's heart pounded furiously the moment those words crossed his mind. He had thought *Chinaman* not *Ho Sang.* He had stripped Ho Sang bare of all the defenses he had built around him, had carefully constructed over the years, to give him an acceptable identity, to make him human. Twice Ho Sang had saved his life. More than twice he had stopped him when opium seemed the only way out for a little boy who had witnessed his father's head roll to the bottom of the boat and his body, still twitching, fall like a tree trunk across his lap: *We sell. We never smoke.* Now he saw Ho Sang the way Zuela saw him: He was never human. He was a man who could say with indignation when asked why he had not buried his wife and daughter, *What? And lose time?* He was a man drenched with their blood.

"But today you broke his promise for him," he said to Zuela. At least there was this small victory.

"You glad?" she asked.

"Yes," he answered her.

"You want to know when he turn snake?" She asked the question slowly, looking at him intently.

He nodded again.

"Agnes," she said. "I catch him looking at her like he was looking at me before I crouch down for him like a female iguana."

He should have known better, but Tong Lee was not ready for her answer. He squeezed his eyes shut. "No!"

"Maybe no, but I take no chances."

She sweet, Tong Lee. She sweeter than opium sweet. Tong Lee's head was flooded with the memories.

"I tell him he couldn't rape me no more if he don't let Agnes go live with the nuns. But I don't say rape, you know. Though is rape I mean."

She sweet, Tong Lee. She sweeter than opium sweet. Zuela was eleven.

"Then he start interfering with the children."

The image was unbearable. Tong Lee clutched his head.

"No, not that way. He only a snake, not the devil. He start interfering with their future."

Tong Lee lowered his hands.

"I don't let anything get in the way of their future."

Her eyes were hard, her voice tough and determined, and Tong Lee took comfort in the strength he saw in her. For snake though she said the Chinaman was, she seemed ready to fight him. She spoke as if she could stop him from slithering between her and her children, as if she would not let him beat her there. But just as he was beginning to savor this second victory in the litany of sorrows she had recited for him, she brought him back to grief again.

"Then he start teaching Alan to smoke."

"Smoke?" *More vicious than a snake?*

"I suspect it for a long time. Sometimes when Chinaman call me and I too tired, Alan say, 'I go for you, Ma.'" She did not tell him the part where Alan said, "Smoke can kill you." She simply shook her head. "I don't know what I was thinking. Then I see Alan eyes red, red, and I smell the leaves I roll for Chinaman."

"Ganja," said Tong Lee. His back relaxed. *Not more dangerous than a snake.*

"I tell him, don't make zombies out of my children."

"It's not as bad as opium."

"I see the East Indians smoke it, but I don't want it for my children. I taste it, too, when I have to blow smoke in his face. I know it make you sleepy. I don't want my children sleeping and their life pass them by."

Tong Lee did not know about the blowing.

"I blow it on him when he don't have the strength," Zuela answered as if he had asked.

"Why?" It was impossible to imagine she could pity him. "Why you help him?"

"So he don't use my children."

The sun was a round ball now behind the bottom branches of the chataigne tree. The sky was the palest blue, almost white. Minutes before, when the sun had not risen, it had been a luminous dark blue.

"Day here," said Tong Lee. "It come."

"Yes, it's time. Chinaman looking for me by now."

"You want to leave him?"

But Zuela did not catch the hope behind his question. "I have too many children," she said.

Still, Tong Lee persisted. "And if he dies?"

"I can't hope for him to die. He say he leave me nothing if he die." Suddenly she looked around and wrinkled her forehead.

"What?" Tong Lee asked. She seemed to have drifted, to have left the room with her mind. "What?"

She bit her lip and the frown deepened. "Chinaman right."

Tong Lee touched her hand.

"Right when he say I'm a child for sure. A child who don't know better."

"No. That's not true."

"He tell me when he die, I have no place to stay. Me and the children have to sleep in the street, but he lie. I can stay in the shop. Even if he say otherwise, I know how to count, how to sell food. I can run the shop and make money to feed my children." She laughed bitterly.

Tong Lee could not leave his hand on hers and tell her the truth. He pulled it away and sat back in his chair. "No," he murmured.

She did not hear him, or she chose not to hear him. "I know how to weigh sugar."

"It don't matter." He wished there were another way to say it.

"The children help, too."

"No." He couldn't look at her and find the courage he needed.

"When they come home from school . . . "

"It make no difference."

"After their homework . . . "

"No!"

"We could sell . . . "

"No!" And then he said no a second time, but softly. "Ho Sang

168

don't own it outright."

She waited for him.

"Luck Chow own it with him. When Ho Sang die, Luck Chow own it all."

She waited a second longer.

"Own the whole thing—the shop, the back room. The whole thing. He own all."

"All?" she asked at last.

"All," he said.

Everything fell on her: her eyes, her cheeks, her mouth, her shoulders, her breasts, her stomach, her hands that dangled along the sides of the armchair. She stayed that way for minutes, then little by little, she pulled herself upright on the armchair and forced herself to remember: That was the way life had been before she made herself believe there could be hope for her through Tong Lee. That was the way she had existed before. She pushed her hair off her forehead and asked again, "All?" And Tong Lee replied again, "All."

She smoothed her skirt over her knees. Yes, she could live with this knowledge. For years she had lived with the knowledge that she and her children were trapped by the Chinaman. She had scouted the corners of their cage and discovered no exits anywhere, none, except the tunnel she swore her children would dig for themselves with their education. Yes, she could wait the years it would take for them to finish school and get jobs. She had waited before.

Tong Lee was no longer a possibility, an alternative. Now, more than ever, she could not use him to fashion her children's escape after the Chinaman tightened the screws on the bars that imprisoned them. He had become flesh and blood to her, a person with feelings who had pity for her. There was no similarity between him and that man behind the hibiscus bush begging, *please*. But she had known that from the moment she had seen the lace in the front of his house, and the orange and pink bougainvillea spread out thick against the white trellises. Though she had unbuttoned her blouse, she knew, too, when he had told her the paintings were his, memories he had painstakingly recalled with watercolors and a brush, that she could not go through with her desperate plans to

169

use him. He was not the kind of man she could use as she would use a tool and then feel no remorse. And even if she could numb herself, turn herself to stone for her children, he would say no. He had said no.

"I'll help you," said Tong Lee.

"How? You don't want me."

"You too young," he said.

"And if I wasn't, you still say no."

"I still say no because you twenty-eight."

"Twenty-nine," she corrected him, "and with a belly that carry ten babies."

"I'm fifty-four."

"Younger than Chinaman," she said.

"Old enough to be your father."

"Not old enough to be my grandfather, like Chinaman old."

"No. I don't want you that way."

She looked up at him. Tears had collected in her eyes but not enough to drip. "Which way then?" she asked. "Which way?"

"Not the way you thinking when you come here."

"So, how? What way?"

Tong Lee reached for her hand again. "The right way," he whispered. "The right way."

❧ Chapter 13 ❧

A few miles away, in a bedroom in Tacarigua, Cedric was plotting his revenge, mapping out the best way to make Rosa pay for snarling him in that spider's web that had now spun past his mother to his cousin Headley, who then wrapped it around his neck with a wink and a smile: *Indian men like your father.* For, from that day Headley called to tell him the news that the white woman who had washed up on the beach on Freeman's Bay was the wife of an Indian doctor, Cedric was certain that the suspicions he had had of Rosa had not been wrong. She had deceived him. She had taken a lover. Why else had she plucked her eyebrows? Why else did her body grow stiff under him?

Cedric began to plan her debasement days before Tong Lee thought there could be hope for him with Zuela, in fact at the very moment he woke up from the deep sleep that had overtaken him, after he picked himself up from the floor where he had collapsed from a pain in his stomach more searing than the one that had caused him to claw the cloth on the dining-room table, pulling down the water pitcher, his glass, his plate and the bowl of stewed pork, in that single cataclysmic lurch that ultimately saved his life.

For that was what he thought had happened when he opened his eyes and saw it was morning and that the sun had risen above the cane fields and turned the sky a crisp blue to the edge of the horizon. He thought he had come home from the hospital the night before, and that just as he had opened the door to his bedroom, the pain in his stomach flared up again and brought him to his knees. But he thought it had lasted only seconds and that he was able to undress, put on his pajamas and get into bed without Rosa's help. He had a vague memory of her hovering nearby, but he was certain that as he was drifting to sleep, he heard her footsteps descending the stairs.

Now he pressed his fingers into his stomach to find the place where the doctors told him they had found a tumor the size of an orange, but he could feel nothing, as he had felt nothing there before that doctor asked his question, "Appleton? As in Appleton of the Orange Grove estate?"

Cancer? Rosa had caused that diagnosis. They would have wheeled him into the operating theater had the bald-headed doctor not stopped them. How could he have allowed himself to believe, even for one minute, that his being headmaster of the only secondary school in Tacarigua was enough to stop the derisive laughter within his earshot over the tenuous thread of civilization separating those who feared pork from those who still lived in the bush?

"Make love to your wife," the chief surgeon had said, as if he were handing him a prescription. And yet it was such a prescription that had saved the life of a widower in his village who had a tumor in his scrotum so large, its contours were visible through his pants.

Better marry than burn, the women told the man, distorting the biblical injunction. For they were speaking of sexual intercourse, not the sacrament, having little regard for the authority of either religion or government to legitimize their unions. They believed it was sinful for a man to withhold sex from a woman. And dangerous, too.

It dry up when you don't use it, they told him, convinced that the tumor in the man's scrotum was caused by the accumulation of semen he had selfishly withheld. Is nothing you save like you save money in the bank, they warned him.

Give. Give it away and it return to you tenfold.

But the man was still grieving for his dead wife and rejected their advances. Then weeks later the pain made him desperate.

172

The first woman offered herself to him without his asking. She had the gift, they said, of making men reach four orgasms in one night. She never asked for money. Just thanked God for the gift and her lovers for the pleasure. Yet after three days she was ready to concede, though without acrimony, that her talent had come to an end: No juice flowed from the penis of the widower, and the rock in his scrotum remained hard as it was before. But her surrender proved premature, for, in saying her good-byes to the widower, she stroked him with her tongue again, and an eruption so powerful jetted from his penis she had to brace herself against strangling. By the time she handed him over to women less experienced in massaging and bringing the dead to life, not even the doctor could find a trace of the cancer that had been eating away his life.

"Because he gave," Cedric's mother had said to him. "Because he gave it away."

Da.

Datta: give.

Give. That was what the balding Scotsman had asked him to do when he read the sickness of his spirit on his face in the corridor of the hospital. Make peace with his wife. Make love to Rosa. But even if in some vague way Cedric connected the chief surgeon's prescription with the advice the women had given a dying widower, even if he could have made that leap of faith and believed that in giving he could cure his cancer, he would have said no to the Scotsman. No, he would not make love to Rosa. But yes, he would fuck her. Yes, he would screw her. Yes, until he could no longer hear the echo of Headley's voice taunting him, until he could no longer remember the bafflement of the women at his father's wake. *Not his wife. Not any other woman, either.* Yes, until there was no more echo left in his head, until the promise Thomas Appleton had collected from his father had been returned in kind. Yes, he would use her.

Cedric was gritting his teeth with his determination to stick to his resolve, when Rosa entered the bedroom. He smelled the incense before he saw her. It wafted on the breeze sucked through the window when she opened the door, and he remembered that falling was not all he had done the night before when he came home from the hospital. He remembered the dark smoke from the censer, the flickering light from the candles, the statue of Our Lady, her hands clasped in prayer beneath her chin. He remembered the smug smile on Rosa's lips. It had set his head on fire and he raised his arms and smashed her altar to the ground.

He asked her for Ena immediately. She was gone, Rosa told him.

"Gone?"

"I told her to leave."

"Gone?" He repeated the question.

"When they took you to the hospital."

"You? You told her?"

"I didn't think you would need her anymore. I thought after you got well in the hospital, there would be no need."

"Get her!" he shouted.

Rosa flinched but she stayed where she was. "She's in church," she said.

He didn't believe her. "Get her, now!"

"It's Sunday," she said.

He called her a liar. He had returned from the hospital on Friday, he told her. Last night. Today was *Saturday.* He was almost whining when he said Saturday.

"Yesterday was Saturday. You slept all day," she said. "All night, too."

He lost his voice. When he found it again it was to order her again to get Ena, to bring her back now, even if she had to drag her from the church.

And perhaps Rosa could have stood her ground and not done as he had ordered her to do, because, in fact, he had no way of forcing her. She could see from the contortions on his face that his pain had returned. He was imprisoned on his bed, and all his shouting would not be threat enough. But he had a weapon she had not thought he had, and when he aimed it at her, she became a manicou scampering away from the hunter's gun.

"You're worse than the man you called Father," he had said, and then added, unaware of the true explosive nature of his attack, "if ever he had it in him to be your father."

When Cedric told her that and the words that followed, he was thinking, of course, of his own father and of his conviction that Rosa's father had extorted from him one humiliating night in the cane fields, for a giddy ascension from cane cutter to bottler, to supervisor, and had done so with such finesse and with such decorum that his father could place blame on no one but himself. Then all he wanted was a place to be safe, a place to find himself again. He got up one morning and swam to India.

It was a conviction that, perversely, gave Cedric solace. For it provided him with motive for the days and nights he had pursued Rosa, the days and nights he had made love to her. It silenced, too, the question she had asked him: *Why did you marry me?* And it answered the more pernicious one he had asked himself: Why, when she had willingly given herself to him, had he honored their fucking with marriage? So when he struck out at Rosa again, he believed he was doing so to avenge his father's death—the part Thomas Appleton played in taking his father to such desperation that one day he stripped himself naked and walked into the sea. Cedric did not know, not only because no one wanted to tell him, but because everyone knew he did not want to be told, that Thomas Appleton was not Rosa's father.

"Not even the man who fathered you was man enough to be a man," Cedric shouted and polished off the insult he had hurled at Rosa.

But Mary Christophe had already told Rosa that Thomas Appleton was not her father. The terror she felt when she bolted out of the room was that Cedric knew it too, and that the punishment he would inflict on her for tricking him into marrying a woman he thought was white (to the extent that white women in Trinidad were white) would be greater than the revenge he would exact from her for his conviction that she had poisoned him with pork. Because about this, Mary Christophe was right: She was the poison eating him alive, the poison he had freely swallowed because of his hatred for her people and also his insatiable need for their approval. If he had found out that most of the people whose blood ran through her veins had none of the power he venerated, though he credited them for his misfortunes, there would be nothing to stop him. Not fear of her name or of her color. He would come after her with murder in his eyes. She had made him drink a potion that was not poison at all. He would make her pay for his anguish, waiting for it to destroy him. Now she had to cool his rage. She had to bring Ena to him. Yet little did she know when she ran in search of Ena, that Cedric was at that moment more afraid of her than she of him, for the phantoms that tortured him were not the ones she imagined. Cedric was not thinking about his plans to destroy her; rather, he was consumed by fear of what she could have done to him in those long hours between his sleeping and his waking, between Friday night and Sunday morning, when he had lain unconscious at her mercy without Ena to protect him.

Now desperate to convince himself that Rosa had not harmed him, he found consolation in the truth—he had felt the pains in his stomach *before* he ate the pork she fed him. The sharp points of the steel daggers had pierced the lining of his intestines before he shouted *stinking* and drew her the picture of the body of a white woman rotting on a beach while her husband sipped rum punch at The Pelican. No, it could not have been poison. Poison would not have lingered so long. Weeks before, he had felt a gnawing pain he had tried to ignore. At first it lasted seconds, then minutes, until, by chance with Rosa, long enough and intense enough that he blacked out in the dining room in front of her.

So great was his need to believe that Rosa had no power over him when he lay powerless within her grasp that, barely conscious of what he was doing, he was beginning slowly and surely to slide down that slope toward acceding validity to the diagnosis the doctors had given him. But the moment that thought grazed his mind, that they were right when they said he had cancer, an old anger arrested him: a rancor about a father brought down lower than a cane cutter in spite of his ascension to supervisor; a resentment of a class system that gave the doctors the right to pin him on that rung of a ladder to which his birth had assigned him.

He wet his lips and swallowed to slake the sudden dryness in his mouth, and in swallowing he was aware for the first time of a gritty sensation in the back of his throat. He swallowed again and felt it again. Then he remembered the rest. After the fall, he had gagged. After the fall, something had slid down his throat; water had spilled on his chest.

Rosa came back just as he was still trying to connect this memory to the discomfort he was feeling in his throat. She stood at the doorway biting her lip nervously. "She will come tomorrow. First thing in the morning," she said.

But Ena was not foremost on Cedric's mind. Was it a liquid she had fed him? Was it a solid? He couldn't remember which. The pain in his stomach surfaced again and he wrapped his arms around his waist to push it back. It was a reflexive action but it brought him the peace of mind he had been desperate for, because as Rosa reached for the bottle of pills on the dresser, he remembered that the chief surgeon had given him a bottle of pills.

"You brought these from the hospital," Rosa said. "I gave you some."

"How many? How often?"

"Do you want one now?"

"You gave me one every time the pain woke me up?" Like a man trying to forestall the inevitable, he fed her the response he wanted back.

"Yes," she said. "Every time. I thought that was what you would have wanted me to do."

His relief was palpable. *It was the chief surgeon's pill he had felt sliding down his throat.* "Well," he said, "I'll take it myself the next time. I want to feel the pain. I want to know."

But at noon that day when his body was drenched in sweat from the knowing, he opened his mouth and let her push the pills down his throat. Still, he did not trust her, so after he woke again, he endured the pain as long as he could and ate only the crackers he watched her take from the box and drank only the water he saw her pour from the faucet. In the morning when Ena arrived he said, "Last time." No one but Ena would give him his pills. No one but Ena would cook for him. Then he counted the pills left in the bottle and matched them to the days of the week. There were enough to last him until Friday. He would rest, recuperate. On Friday he would go for a second opinion, this time to a private doctor in the white man's nursing home.

∗≪ Chapter 14 ≫∗

*R*osa, too, counted the days. It was the fifth day of the nine-day novena she had begun to Our Lady, the fourth day since Cedric had come home from the hospital, and the first day that she had not given him Mary Christophe's medicine.

It had been easy for her to get him to take it the first time. When he fell to the floor, his mouth was already open, though not for her—for the pills he was trying to pull out from the breast pocket. Yet she did not anticipate his reaction. The gagging, perhaps. She clamped his lips shut until he swallowed it all down—the pills and Mary Christophe's medicine she had pushed down his throat. But when he fell to his side and she could not wake him, she became afraid.

She could see from the rise and fall of his chest that he was still breathing. She put her ear to his chest and could hear his heart beating, but she could not get him to stir no matter how hard she shook him. It was only her faith in Our Lady that prevented her from panicking. Our Lady had not led her to Zuela, and from Zuela to Mary Christophe, so she could harm him. No, she told herself, Our Lady could never have had such evil intentions. Reasoning this way, she made herself calm. And four hours later, the joint in Rosa's thumb sore from rolling over the hard surface of more than two thousand rosary beads, Our Lady answered her prayers. For when Cedric opened his eyes, she knew what she had to do. She gave him Mary Christophe's medicine again before he recovered full consciousness, because she understood that it was only in that state that he would take it from her, because Our Lady had revealed to her that, as a consequence, he would be healed; that, as a result, he would no longer think she was trying to poison him.

Each time Cedric woke up, Rosa fed him the medicine, and each time he swallowed it, he fell into a deep sleep. But after the fifth time, thirty hours since she had gotten him to crawl to his bed, since she had kept him in a coma-like state, she became wary of the potency of the cure Mary Christophe had given her. She did not want to kill him. When dawn broke on Sunday, she snuffed out the candles, covered the censer and dismantled the altar, and when Cedric stirred, she allowed him to awaken. Monday, the fifth day of her novena, the day Cedric said *last time* and vowed to take his pills only from Ena, she worried about how to get him to take Mary Christophe's medicine again.

"Mix it in the water when you give him the pills," she told Ena.

But Ena refused. "Is because Mr. Cedric trust me. Is because of that, I don't let him down."

On the sixth day Cedric almost strangled himself with his pillow stifling his screams, and Ena became so frightened of the bulging blue veins pulsating on his temples that she surrendered to Rosa.

"Anything, Miss. I do anything you say. And God protect the two of us."

After drinking the potion Ena had given him, Cedric slept for eighteen hours without waking. Rosa had put three spoonfuls of Mary Christophe's medicine in water, instead of one, to make up for the time he had gone without it, and it took him to a sleep deeper than the one the night before. He was still sleeping when Ena came to work the next morning, and when she saw him, nothing Rosa said could sway her from her conviction that he had fallen prey to obeah magic. If he woke up again (for his returning to consciousness was in the realm of *if,* for her, not *when)* she swore whatever it was that Miss Rosa had given her and she had given to Mister Cedric because her heart was good and she felt pity for him, she would give him no more. Because as God was her witness, that stuff she saw Miss Rosa put in the water had the hand of the devil in it.

"I don't practice obeah no more," she said. "I am a church-going, God-fearing Christian woman."

So Rosa returned to Zuela. The ninth day of her novena was approaching, and while she believed in the power of Our Lady (she had made a miracle for her in Laventille), Rosa believed, too, in the medicine Mary Christophe had given her, whether it was obeah magic or not.

"Why you didn't go direct?" Those were the first words Zuela said to her when she heard the fear in her voice. "She would tell you how to make him drink it."

Then Rosa had to explain to Zuela that Mary Christophe had shamed her. The next time she went to her home, she said, it would be to see her for her own sake, not to beg for her help.

"So what you want me to do?" Zuela asked her.

"Tell me how you think I could make Cedric take it. Ena won't give it to him again and Cedric won't take it from me."

"Why you want him to live so bad for?" Zuela eyed her carefully.

"You told me when the pain stopped he would leave me alone."

"I also tell you, Careful what you pray for. And I know in your heart you pray for him to dead."

"I prayed for him to live."

"To dead."

"I prayed to Our Lady."

"You pray she answer your true, true prayers."

"No!"

"Don't have shame. If was me and I was in your place, I pray for him to dead, too."

It was one in the afternoon. They were sitting on the bed below the picture of the Virgin, in the room behind the shop. Zuela's two youngest children were sleeping in the bed opposite them. The other children were in school. The shop was quiet, yet Zuela knew the Chinaman would be listening to them. From the moment Rosa had entered the shop, Tong Lee had pulled him aside and whispered in his ear. Zuela did not know what he said to him, but whatever it was, the Chinaman had let her take

Rosa by the hand to the back of the shop. Now, from where they sat, she could see the Chinaman's back hunched over the shop counter. Tong Lee was standing next to him, still talking.

"No, I know you want him to dead," she said, turning to Rosa. "Like I wanted Chinaman to dead. Like I want God to do something so he free me from him. Only God not helping me. He helping you."

When she glanced into the shop again, the Chinaman was not there. She got up and walked to the doorway. Tong Lee met her. "He gone upstairs to sleep," he said. She pressed his hand. She knew it was because of him the Chinaman had left the shop.

"You begging Him to change His mind and still He helping you." She sat down next to Rosa.

"I don't want him to die," said Rosa.

"He listening to you even when you don't ask Him loud."

"I never asked Him."

"You lying, Rosa."

"I would never ask God to do that."

"You lying and I don't know why. Because you don't have to lie to me. I'm nobody." She balled her hand and struck her chest. "Look. Look where I living."

Rosa squeezed her cuffed fist. "It's the truth. I'm telling you the truth."

"I see the truth on your face that first time you come here. You frighten, but your face tell the truth. You frighten more because he live than because you think he sick."

Rosa removed her hand from Zuela's. "I didn't poison him," she said.

"I didn't say that."

"I asked you to help me."

"I know that."

"I asked you to show me how to stop him from thinking that that was how I was thinking."

"You feel bad?"

Rosa did not answer her.

"You feel bad because it happening like you want it to happen?"

"No!"

"So it happening. Let it happen. Why you come here asking me to tell you what to do? If you don't want it to happen, you go direct to the horse's mouth. You go to Mary Christophe. You ask her how to make Cedric take what she give you. You don't ask me."

"I thought . . ."

"You think nothing. You know I can't help you. If I could help you, you know I help you the first time you come. You know I don't send you to Mary Christophe."

Rosa began to cry.

"I not blaming you. You understand I not blaming you, Rosa. I only tell you to see the truth. You hope in your heart Cedric dead and now he sick. And now you want to pretend. You only come to me because you don't want responsibility. You don't want to think is you self make him dead. If that's what you want, I give it to you, Rosa. Okay? No, you didn't make him sick. You won't make him dead. You not responsible."

Zuela lowered her voice. "Only thing I wonder," she began slowly, "is why you pray to make it not happen. Why you do that, Rosa?"

Rosa stopped crying.

"Why, Rosa?"

"He married me."

"What?"

"When I needed to be married, he married me."

Zuela squinted her eyes. "Needed? You were having baby for him? I thought you say you never had children."

Rosa corrected herself. "Wanted," she said. "When I wanted to get married."

The wanted still bothered Zuela. "I never wanted to marry the Chinaman," she said.

"Cedric asked me," said Rosa.

"Chinaman never asked me." Zuela stood up. "Not direct." She crossed the room to the bed where her two daughters were sleeping. "Priest ask him." She brushed back the hair that had fallen over the baby's face. "Then Chinaman tell me."

Rosa looked away from her. "Cedric didn't have to marry me," she said.

"Neither did Chinaman," said Zuela. "It didn't make no difference to me. Married or not, I still making baby." She bent down and kissed her daughter's forehead.

"You don't understand," said Rosa.

"No. I don't understand." Zuela straightened up and turned to her. "I don't understand why you so grateful. You forget how you come in here saying he see you like Dalip Singh wife. Saying he see you in a bag with a rope round your neck, lying dead on the beach, gut out like a fish."

"I never said that."

"Same thing. Same thing as when you say because Dalip Singh wife dead, your husband think you trying to poison him."

Rosa leaned forward to get up.

"No, don't go." Zuela came toward her and pushed her back down gently. "I didn't mean it so." She kept her hand on Rosa's shoulder until she felt her sink deeper into the bed. "Is just that I don't understand why you so grateful, you pray he don't suffer. Why you praying for him to live."

Rosa pressed her lips together.

"No," said Zuela, letting go of her shoulder. "I don't understand it at all." She reached for a pile of clothes in the middle of the bed. Rosa moved to make room for her. "I don't understand why you say your mother shame to take you back home and save you from suffering." She gathered the pile to the edge of the bed. "Because I tell you, Rosa, I sure if my mother was alive, Chinaman have no power over me. I sure if she was alive, I could go back to her in Venezuela."

She separated the clothes, using her hand as an iron to smooth each piece before she folded it. "That kind of grateful you feel," she said, "that kind of shame you say your mother will have is something you could never explain to me." She shook the ruffles out of a skirt. "No, it never make sense to me why marriage so big for you people, so important, is a shame if it break. A shame even if you suffering, a shame to be by yourself and better to be with a man taking pain. No, I never understand that at all." She folded a pair of pants. "Because if I was your mother, I send my daughter to school. I make sure she could buy her own bread. In fact, I glad if she could buy her own bread by her ownself. Because when my daughters marry, they don't marry for bread. They marry for love."

"Love?" Rosa stared at her. "Love?"

"Love," said Zuela and looked up at her. "Love." For that Saturday she had used Boysie as an excuse again, and the Chinaman allowed Tong Lee to take her to five o'clock Mass. Then, when she was safe in his house, after he had poured her tea in a cup without handles, Tong Lee gave her her first glimpse of romantic love.

"Why no handles?" she asked him, because she had always wanted to know. And he took her hands and wrapped them around the sides of the cup.

"See," he said. "Feels warm. Feels good. Chinese like it so."

She smiled.

"But English," he said, "they like it hot. Then they don't only need handles, they need saucer, too."

Her smile widened.

"Because when tea hot, it blister their tongue. And when it blister their tongue, they do like this." He spat on the ground. "Then they need saucer to catch what fly out their mouth."

Tears were still rolling down her cheeks from her laughter when she noticed that Tong Lee was not laughing, too. Just staring at her. Just sitting still and looking at her, as he did that first time in his house when his eyes moved from the paintings on his wall to her and from her to them, and foolishly she had made him turn away.

"First time I see you laugh," he said. "First time I see it come from your heart."

First time. Zuela knew it was so.

"You know," she said to Rosa, sliding the folded clothes to the middle of the bed, "what we see behind the hibiscus that day was not how it suppose to be. It happen to me, but it not right. Not even for female iguanas. I see how it impress you. I remember how hard I have to try to pull you away." She sat down close to Rosa. "What was it you see so, I didn't see that day? What was it you see that make you shame to talk to me again?"

Rosa did not move.

"What?" Zuela asked again. "What?"

"The power."

Zuela did not hear her.

"The power the girl had over that man," Rosa whispered.

Yet even when she was asking the question, Zuela knew the answer. Only days ago she thought she had power like that. Only days ago she thought she could use it with Tong Lee to free her children. Now she squeezed Rosa's hand and stilled her trembling.

"You wrong, Rosa," she said. "You right to feel shame, but you wrong to think the way you thinking. That was no power." She knew better now. "Listen. Listen good to me. See that socket over there?" She pointed to the socket on the wall separating the bedroom from the kitchen. "See that lamp?" She got up and lifted the reading lamp off the bookshelf over the bed. "That socket have power. Electricity. But that kind of power no good till somebody use it." She went to the socket. "I plug in the lamp, the light go on. See?" She switched on the lamp. "I plug it out, the light go out. That power is only power for people to use. The power you think you see that girl have behind that hibiscus bush is only because she soft and smooth. Only because she pretty. Remember the lipstick? The pearls? But that man use her till he don't need her no more. She have no power to say yes or no. He use her when he want to use her. Like I use this socket."

Zuela put the lamp back on the bookshelf. "That is not the power I want for my daughters," she said. "I want them to have the power they can use, not the power man can take from them." She waved her arms in the direction of her daughters. "That's why it break my heart, but I give Agnes to the nuns. I give her to them so she have a chance. So they watch her for me and they teach her about books." Her voice was tender now. "She turn sixteen Saturday and already she have more power than I have at twenty-nine. Already she can make her way by herself if she have to. Already she know what only now I know—that when man love you, he don't take the power you have, even if you give him. Even if you want to

185

give him. Because man who love you, want you to keep your power. Then the power you have is the power both of you have." She sighed. "Chinaman not done using me yet, and never with him I feel the power you see behind that bush. Never in twenty-two years."

Still, Rosa asked her, "Didn't you ever want it?"

"The power? So I could get away from Chinaman, yes. When I was guessing and guessing what my mother will tell me if she was alive and witness how Chinaman box me in, I make mistake and want the power you see. But that kind of power tear you up, leave you with nothing inside. You worse off than before. You lose your pride. You lose yourself. You lose everything."

"And you never wanted the other thing?" Rosa's voice was hoarse.

"The other thing?"

"The other thing men want."

"Sex? Is sex you mean? You mean lying down and letting Chinaman cover me? *That* you mean?"

"It never felt good to you?"

Zuela grimaced.

"It never made you feel wanted?"

"Wanted?"

"That you were beautiful?"

"Not once."

"Not once with Chinaman?"

"Never."

"Before the Chinaman?"

Zuela looked away from her. "I was eleven years old with the Chinaman."

"It felt good to me," said Rosa.

"When you was eleven?" Zuela faced her.

Rosa could not meet her eyes. "No," she said, and crossed her hands on her lap.

"Then when you was already a woman?"

"At first that was how it made me feel. At first it made me feel I was beautiful."

"You didn't need Cedric to tell you you was beautiful, Rosa."

186

"My mother took my sisters to England. She never took me."

"I thought you didn't want to go."

"I said that to you and I said that to myself, but still it bothered me that she never asked. Deep down I thought it was because I wasn't pretty enough." *But now I know it was because I wasn't white enough.* But Rosa did not say those words to Zuela. "Then Cedric asked."

"Why you keep being so grateful, Rosa?"

"And I thought because he liked it so much, he thought I was beautiful."

"You talking about that little girl again, Rosa."

"I thought that because he liked it so much, he would be good to me forever."

"That man was not good to that little girl forever. He not good to her when we see what we see him do."

"Then he asked me to beg."

"Beg?"

"The same way that man asked that girl. He asked me to beg for what I thought he wanted."

Zuela clicked her tongue. "And you call that power? And you praying for him to live?"

But in the end, no matter how many times Zuela told Rosa that she was not responsible for Cedric's illness, that Cedric was a snake that bit her and she owed him nothing, Rosa still insisted on knowing how she could get Cedric to take Mary Christophe's medicine.

"Come with me to Tacarigua," she begged Zuela. "You can talk to Ena. You can get her to give it to Cedric."

But Zuela could not do that and would not do that, not only because the Chinaman would not let her, but also because Agnes was coming to visit her. "To spend the weekend," she told Rosa, her voice shaking with the anxiety of years of vigilance, years even before Agnes, too, turned eleven. "And I do nothing to make Chinaman spoil it for her."

Yet she offered Rosa a solution. A deceptively simple one.

"Leave Cedric without Mary Christophe medicine again. Then wait. You see not a long time pass before Ena beg you to give it to him."

≪ Chapter 15 ≫

*A*nd that was what happened, and much more. By the ninth day of her novena, Rosa had two miracles: Cedric got well again and her mother, whom she had not heard from since Paula Singh's decomposing body washed up on the sand on Freeman's Bay in Otahiti, became, in a perverse way, the catalyst that finally gave her the courage to choose the wanting over the needing; love, if only for herself, over lust; strength, if just enough to say to Cedric, "Never again."

The first miracle happened because Ena, as Zuela had predicted, had a complete change of heart. But not right away. When Cedric woke up, she was still praying to God for forgiveness for letting Rosa tempt her into getting involved with obeah. When he asked her for Rosa, she crossed herself first before answering that Miss Rosa had gone out, "And thank God."

Cedric frowned. "Thank God?"

"That you well, Mr. Cedric."

Cedric touched his stomach. "No pain," he said.

"It stay long enough. Is time it leave you."

The frown on Cedric's forehead deepened.

"What day is it?" he asked her.

"Tuesday," she said.

"Tuesday?"

"You sleep since Monday morning, Mr. Cedric."

His old fear returned. "And Miss Rosa, where was she?"

"Here, Mister Cedric."

"Here with me alone?"

"No, I here, too, Mr. Cedric."

"Last night, too?"

"I leave ten o'clock. I come back six o'clock this morning."

"And Miss Rosa? She was here with me while you were gone?"

"You mean here, in this room, Mr. Cedric? No, she downstairs in the study when I leave. I stay as long as I can. In case you wake up. Then I have to go home to feed my children."

Cedric swallowed hard. "Who gave me my medicine before I fell asleep?"

"Me, Mr. Cedric. Like you tell me to. I take it home with me, too."

"Home?"

"So I is the only one to give it to you. Like you say."

"The *only* one?" Cedric exhaled.

"Yes, Mr. Cedric."

He swung his legs over the side of the bed and got up. He had turned the corner, slept out his sickness, his poison, if that was what it was. The bedsheet was damp. He patted it. Yes, he had sweated out the poison in his sleep. He felt better now. Good as new. Better than before. He reached for his pants.

"Maybe you need some more rest." Ena approached him. He turned away from her and walked to the bathroom.

"Maybe you should give yourself more time."

He did not answer her.

"Maybe you should go to the doctor to make sure."

He came back into the room. "I feel better. I feel strong."

"Maybe . . . "

"No!" he shouted at her and then felt sorry he had done that. It was she who had protected him from Rosa. He lowered his voice. "I'll go on Friday," he said. "To make sure."

But by dinner the pain returned. Slowly. At first he felt only a slight irritation under his left rib, but little by little it spread to his right side until the pain was blinding. He swallowed to force an air bubble into his stomach, then belched. The pain went away. It was hunger, he told Ena, and asked her for dinner. Yet before he could finish the rice and peas she had cooked for him, he was writhing on the floor.

Ena met Rosa at the door when she returned home from Zuela's. She was ready to beg. "Anything. Anything you say, Miss Rosa. Mr. Cedric twisting on the ground like a snake."

Two pills with the rest of Mary Christophe's medicine stirred in a glass of water—Ena gave these to Cedric on Rosa's instructions. The pain was so devastating, Cedric did not notice the bitter aftertaste, nor was he lucid enough to get his tongue to say that the choking sensation he felt, before the water Ena had given him washed the pills down his throat, was more intense than any pain he had ever experienced. His muscles closed in on his windpipe and he thought he was dying.

Rosa kept vigil at Cedric's bedside all that night. Ena did, too, because before Cedric shut his eyes, he had warned her, "Stay!" She watched silently as Rosa rebuilt her altar to Our Lady, lit the candles, and filled the censer with incense. She did not help her, but when Rosa kneeled down to pray, she joined her. Mr. Cedric had not said, Don't pray, and Miss Rosa was not using obeah again.

Together, she and Rosa prayed through every mystery of the rosary: the Joyful, the Sorrowful, the Glorious. They said ten Hail Marys, one Our Father, one Glory Be, ten times for each of the mysteries. They sang "Ave Maria Salve Regina," "Stabat Mater." They recited the *Credo*, the *Gloria*, the Confiteor, which Rosa said in Latin, and Ena ended for her, because, as she said, she was a good Catholic, and though she had little schooling, she had gone to Mass every Sunday of her forty-two years, every feast day and some weekdays, too, that were not days of obligation, enough to know by heart the words the priest used to start up and end up his Latin prayers.

Seven hours later, after the third recitation of the Confiteor, Ena was moved to remorse by Rosa's praying. She struck her breast. *"Mea culpa, mea maxima culpa.* You really a good Catholic, Miss Rosa. Better than the convent nuns. I sorry I doubt you. I sorry I say anything about obeah. You a God-fearing, God-loving Christian woman. I make mistake. I sorry."

Cedric woke up at nine o'clock that morning—on the dot, Rosa would later point out to Ena—on the ninth day of the novena she had begun to Our Lady. He opened his eyes and said he had had a dream. A vision. He saw his pain leave him in a black cloud that grew lighter as it rose from his stomach.

He said this addressing Ena, but his eyes were on Rosa, following her movements as she dismantled the altar to Our Lady. He said that at first a white cloud entered his stomach, and when it came out again, it was black.

"Carrying the evil with it, Mr. Cedric," Ena said joyfully.

"Yes," he said, still watching Rosa. "Carrying all the evil with it."

"Well, you have the Blessed Mother to thank for your vision, Mr. Cedric. The Blessed Mother and your wife, Miss Rosa, that pray to her for you."

But Cedric had not attributed either the dream or his recovery to the statue of Our Lady, or to the tumblers of lighted candles and the perfumed incense curling out of the blackened holes of the brass censer, though now they did not fill him with the rage that had consumed him when he swept them away in that one forceful blow of his hand that had also pitched him to the floor. For he would attribute nothing to Rosa. Still, he recoiled from her simpering contrition that had sent the blood boiling to his head when he first saw her at her altar. She and her kind resorted to these whimperings to God when conscience dug its claws into them and they feared bleeding. Yet the altar brought him a sort of peace now. It was the symbol of hope, proof that while he slept those days and nights sunk into the stupor of Dr. MacIver's numbing drugs, she was totally distracted by prayers and remorse for what she had harbored in her heart. For if by chance she had poisoned him, if the pain he had felt that evening was caused by an evil that had entered his intestines through the poison in the pork she had given him, it had had time to weaken and finally to leave him in that dark cloud he had seen in his dream.

Ena confirmed it. "All night she praying for you, Mr. Cedric. All morning. Me, too."

Her words erased the lingering doubts.

"All morning, all night?"

"She pray for you, Mister Cedric. She pray real hard."

Rosa was extinguishing the candles at that moment. He watched her snuff out the flame between her fingers. Cold, cold. Not the slightest wince from the pain of her scorched flesh. "All night, and all morning too, Rosa?" Cold, cold, but he would stoke the fire between her legs that she could not put out.

She lowered her eyes.

"I didn't know you wanted me to live so bad. I didn't know you loved me so much."

Rosa hurried out of the room, but before she left he saw the old twitching, the old fluttering of her muscles along her temples that always gave her away, that always exposed her.

It was this trembling that emboldened Cedric, that restored the control he had felt slipping away from him the moment Rosa said Sunday and he thought it was Saturday; that erased the fear that had surfaced again when Ena said Tuesday and he thought it was Monday. He used this new confidence to convince himself that he was right when he had concluded that Rosa had not poisoned him. No, he thought; like a child she was guilty of recalcitrance, no more; of the same puerile disobedience that prompted her to rebuild the altar after he had knocked it down; to cook pork after he had explicitly forbidden her to buy it. Yes, he had contracted a virus. That was what it was. It was not poison; it was not cancer. It was an infection in his stomach that had caused the pain and the weight loss he had noticed the week before he was taken to the hospital.

He had had the same ailment when he was a boy. For days his mother had tried everything—cod liver oil, Epsom salts, long baths in Epsom salts; senna pod tea, shining bush tea, long baths in shining bush tea, but the pain persisted. Then four weeks later, just as his mother was at the point of despair from the thunder in his stomach and the pain that kept him awake all night, he suddenly recovered.

It was because she had put the obeahman's mojo bag under his mattress, his mother told him, but he did not believe her, no more than he credited his recovery now to the candles Rosa had burned to Our Lady. Not that he doubted the efficacy of either. He had never had that much courage that would tempt him to reject beliefs that had been fused into myths in his subconscious, and the subconscious of every man whose childhood was forged, like his, in those villages where the sea taught respect for the inexplicable, for the mystery of the movements of the currents, the disappearance of fish, the arbitrary cruelty of thunderstorms. Yet of this he was certain—Rosa had longed for his death. Not even her lowered eyelids, her tremulous temples, could mask the intensity of that flame burning in her heart for his destruction. She would pray for him now, he knew, but not for his recovery. She would pray that God's will be done, but she would hope God's will was her will. She would hope that God's will would be for him to suffer and die. Then she could claim her innocence.

He would start her debasement tonight. He would drain the power that she and her people thought they had over him; the power Thomas Appleton exercised over his father, forcing him into the watery darkness until it swallowed him. He knew from that first night when Rosa flinched from his touch, that her loathing was not enough to cool the fires between her legs. She would still rise for him when he entered her. She had always risen for him. She had risen for him after he called her *bitch*, after he brought Ena to cook for him. Perhaps like that white woman in Otahiti, she had wanted new blood. Perhaps she had dreamed of a new lover, but until then, in-between then, her lust, the siren call of that nymph within her would hold its grip on her, would make her lift her hips to him.

Near noon he felt such vitality in his legs, he told Ena he would come downstairs for lunch. She begged him to reconsider, but he would not take no for an answer.

"Then nothing solid," she said. "Drink the fish broth Miss Rosa make the morning."

He hesitated.

"She say is nine days since she start her novena for you. She know you get well now and she could cook for you."

Still, he hesitated.

"She pray for you, Mr. Cedric," she reminded him. "She want you to live."

Yes, it would be a good place to start, a good beginning to let Rosa know she had not toppled him with her hatred, her longing for his death. He would drink Miss Rosa's fish broth, he told Ena. "And tell her to have some with me, too, in the dining room."

They ate in silence, he and Rosa. Ena stayed in the kitchen. When he had swallowed the last spoonful of his broth, he blotted his mouth with his napkin, which he folded neatly and placed at the side of his plate. Before he spoke, he poked his fingers into his stomach, pressing hard on the upper right side where the x-rays showed that his cancer lay. His fingers sunk into soft flesh.

"Ena," he called out to her, "take the night off tonight. Come back in the morning."

"And what about dinner, Mr. Cedric?"

He looked across to Rosa. Her face was impassive, her eyes the same iced-tea brown. "Rosa's here," he said.

"What time you want me to leave, Mr. Cedric?"

Still with his eyes on Rosa, he answered, "After you clean the kitchen. After you wash the dishes."

Rosa had her second miracle that evening. It came when she most needed it. For at five that afternoon, after he had taken a nap, Cedric said to her that he felt more refreshed than ever, stronger than ever, and that she need not sleep on the cot in his study where she had been sleeping since he had come back from the hospital. "I don't think I'll be sick again tonight," he said. "Sleep in the bed." Then he went back to his room upstairs and left her crying into the onions she was chopping for dinner.

It was shortly after that, when she was sorting and unsorting love and lust, wanting and needing—the socket that gave power, the lamp that used it—that she heard the knock on the front door. She looked up and saw the silhouette of a woman behind the thin curtains on the window that faced the front porch, a silhouette she would know anywhere, even if she had not recognized her sister's face pressed into the glass pane.

"Rosa! Rosa!" It was her sister who called her, but she could not move, transfixed by the unlikelihood of substance in the mirage of the silhouette, refusing to believe that at the very moment, when more than at any other time she needed a savior, a protector, her mother would appear in front of her. Her sister had to call her name twice again before, finally, Rosa accepted the fact that Clara Appleton had come to see her.

Her sister Annabella was the first one to kiss her. Her mother kissed her, too, but as if duty or some unwritten law required her to do so. She did not press her lips to Rosa's cheeks but turned her head and offered her own cheek, so that in fact it was Rosa who kissed her and not she, Rosa. Then, even though the temperature had reached eighty-five degrees that evening, she shuddered, drew the sides of her cardigan around her body, walked past Rosa into the house, and collapsed into one of the Morris chairs.

In that single action, Rosa felt her mother's disdain for her, and she found herself sucked into the memory of nights when she rocked herself to sleep in the empty embrace of her own arms. It was as if the effort her mother had made to be in her presence, to be close enough to kiss her, had so drained her of energy, she was forced to sit down.

Rosa was trying to find her footing again when Annabella pulled her down with her to the couch. "People are talking, Rosa."

From the corner of her eyes Rosa saw her mother wipe the final traces of her daughter's lips from her cheek.

She was a slim woman, Clara Appleton, slim in the way Caribbean women of her age, past sixty, were slim. She had narrow hips and thighs, and a stomach that protruded high below her waist. Her breasts were small, but it was difficult to be certain if this was true, for they were always covered, as they were now, with a loose white cardigan, which she wore during rainy season or dry season, in the cool of the evening or the heat of the day.

Annabella Harrington resembled her mother not only in her looks, but also in her prejudices. It was she who had warned Rosa, the day before her marriage to Cedric, about the inherent insecurities of fisher-women's sons. She was in her early forties, but her face had already been etched by the same crow's talons that dug deep lines across her mother's forehead and cheeks. She had recently returned from a vacation at the beach and her skin was tanned bronze. That day the ravines that trickled down the sides of her mouth and fanned out on her lower jaw were lighter in shade than the rest of her body, and so they seemed deeper, and she older than her age.

"They are saying it was you who sent him to the hospital." Annabella held Rosa still. "I tried to warn you. I told you you couldn't handle him the same way as if he was one of us."

Her mother folded her hands on her lap and turned her head away from them, but Rosa could tell by the lines tightening into wires down the sides of her face that she was paying more attention to her than she had for years, that she was listening like a drama coach in the wings of a stage, ready with her cues if one sentence, one single word, swerved from the ones she had rehearsed with Annabella.

"They're saying," Annabella hissed in her ear, "that it was you who poisoned him. You! Can you imagine how this has hurt Mother and me? The whole family?"

Cedric's footsteps resounded down the staircase. Clara Appleton swung her head sharply toward Annabella and raised her finger to her lips. It was a commanding gesture that caused Annabella to lower her voice immediately, but it also gave Rosa her first clue, if indeed she needed one, that Clara Appleton had not come to visit her, but to visit Cedric. The mirage she had seen behind the curtain was not the silhouette of a savior, but the familiar shadow of the woman who had abandoned her since her childhood.

Her mother was already on her feet when Cedric reached the bottom of the staircase.

"I'm so sorry. I'm so sorry." She walked towards Cedric. "I didn't realize it was so serious."

Rosa watched her closely.

"I would have come before."

Cedric shook his head. "That was not necessary. Sit. Sit."

"No, I had to come." Her mother followed Cedric to the dining room.

"Rum punch?" he asked her.

"It's a little early," she said.

"Since when?" He laughed, and took a bottle of rum punch out of the cabinet. "Ice, Rosa."

It was an order for Rosa to fill the ice bucket, but Annabella put her hand on her thigh and held her down.

"I'll get it," said Clara Appleton.

Cedric glowered at Rosa. Her mother grabbed his hand. "Come with me." He threw Rosa one last angry look and followed Clara. They were both holding glasses filled with ice when they returned from the kitchen.

"No, when I heard you were in hospital . . . "

Rosa stiffened. Annabella pressed her hand down harder on her thigh. "She was already on her way out to the wharf," she whispered. "She couldn't just turn around. You know, George and I and the children were going to Tobago."

"I was just so relieved that it was just some pork you had eaten."

"Relieved? I thought you said she was hurt." Rosa shifted her body so that Annabella's hand fell away from her thigh to the cushion.

"Then I heard about your cancer."

"Cancer?" Rosa turned to Annabella.

"That's not certain," said Cedric, but he was addressing her mother, not her.

"And about the x-rays."

"They are not always correct." Cedric unscrewed the cap from the bottle of rum punch, filled her glass, and then his.

"That's what Dr. MacIver said." Her mother brought her glass to her lips.

"Cedric said nothing about cancer." Rosa looked at Annabella as if expecting an explanation.

"Mother found out last night at a cocktail party."

"He was wrong," said Cedric.

"He said the x-ray showed cancer," Clara Appleton was insisting.

"It was a mistake."

"It showed a tumor the size of an orange."

"It was the shadow of a bone."

Rosa slid to the edge of the couch. "Is that why you're here?"

Her mother pursed her lips, and ignoring Rosa, she shifted her eyes from Cedric to Annabella. She did not say a word, but the look she gave Annabella was enough for Rosa to know she wanted Annabella to silence her.

"Sit back." Annabella tugged Rosa's sleeves. "She couldn't come before now," she said.

"But she knew I was alone."

"Dr. MacIver said it had advanced." Her mother was speaking directly to Cedric.

"It was a virus," said Cedric. "I had it before. When I was a child."

Annabella put her mouth close to Rosa's ear. "You're lucky," she said.

"No, it was definitely not cancer," said Cedric. "It's all over. I am fine."

"Dr. MacIver said they wanted to operate."

Cedric refilled his glass with rum punch.

"He said he stopped them."

"Because it wasn't necessary," said Cedric.

"Dr. MacIver said it was because it was too late."

Cedric drained his glass. Her mother waited until he had swallowed the last drop. "Dr. MacIver said it was inoperable," she said.

Annabella pulled Rosa closer to her and breathed in her ear. "You should thank God tonight. You should get on your knees and pray."

"No," Cedric was saying, "it was because I did not need one. It was a virus."

Clara Appleton put down her glass. "He's a doctor," she said. She closed the top button of her cardigan. "English. Trained in London."

Annabella flattened her hand on Rosa's cheek and twisted her face toward her so that Rosa could see neither her mother nor Cedric. But Rosa did not need to see them. She did not need to see her mother to know that at that moment she was gathering the neck of her cardigan in a knot at her throat, and was holding it in front of Cedric like a talisman, as if she thought it would protect her from the same contamination from which she sought to insulate her white daughters, the ones she thought too valuable to leave in the care of Mary Christophe. She knew, without seeing her face, that her mother believed that the stark whiteness of the cardigan and the foreignness of its wooly fabric were symbols enough to remind Cedric of the superiority of her ancestors. Her people, she had often said, had a right to colonize the Caribbean. They had won the islands fairly and squarely in wars. *To the victor belong the spoils.*

No, Rosa did not need to see Cedric's face, either, to know he had understood her mother completely. *Trained in London.* She heard Cedric struggling to reassert himself.

"It's *my* body. I know what's in *my* body." But his voice had lost its strength. It had a pleading quality to it.

Annabella was now filling Rosa's ears with her breathless whispers. She wanted her to know that their mother had paid Father Kilgan a hundred dollars to offer next Sunday's Mass in the family's name to express their gratitude. She wanted her to know she was not saying that Cedric deserved cancer, but there was an immutable universal law, timeless as the beginning of eternal time, changeless as the end of earthly time, and no one, not Cedric, could escape it. "You reap what you sow," she said. "Cancer is hard punishment to take, but Cedric was bringing us down, dragging our name through the mud."

Rosa strained to hear her mother, to hear how Cedric would defend himself again against her cool self-assurance, but only bits and parts of what they both said, bouncing now off each other like rain upon stones, splashed through the rush of words Annabella was pouring down her ears. From her mother: *Technology. London. Science. England. Dr. Maclver said . . .* From Cedric: *Animal hospital. Stench. Enema. After I slept . . . After I sweated it out . . .*

"When?" Her mother's voice whipped through Annabella's liturgy on divine retribution. A bolt of lightning.

"Yesterday. I haven't felt any pain since yesterday morning."

Annabella released her cheek. "She's caught him. See, see. He's lying."

Rosa turned toward them. She saw the faint lines of a smile spreading out from the sides of her mother's mouth.

"It will return. The pain will come back again." Her mother raised her glass to her lips.

Cedric snatched it from her hand. Rum punch spilled down her white cardigan. It left a stain, the color of diluted blood, on her chest.

"God is always alert. Sinners always get what's coming to them," she shouted to Cedric. Annabella jumped up from the couch and rushed to her.

"Leave! Get out!" Cedric pointed to the door.

"Ruin us. That's what he wanted to do." And for the first time Clara Appleton looked directly at her daughter Rosa. "Ten generations and it would take a black man to pull us down."

Cedric dragged her by her elbow to the door.

Long after they left, Rosa still could not keep her hands from shaking. It was possible that Cedric had cancer and that cancer was the cause of the pain that made him strike out at her. It was probable, too, that her prayers to Our Lady and Mary Christophe's medicine had removed it, excised it in that dark cloud Cedric saw rising from his stomach. But Rosa was not thinking of Cedric now—not of his cruelty, not of his false accusations, not of the terror he had put in her mother's eyes. She was thinking of her infantile gullibility, her yawning hunger for affection, her fathomless need that had caused ten seconds to so mesmerize her that she had suspended all reason, believing her mother had come to rescue her, to spare her the degradation of Cedric's bed. Between the silhouette she had seen at the front door and the head turning to avoid its lips on her cheek, how had she allowed herself that momentary illusion? How could she have been so foolish?

For years her mother had separated herself from her with her interminable trips to England. She had known for days about the accusations of poisoning. She knew her daughter was alone in an area not likely to spare the progeny of an overseer of a sugar-cane estate (whether the people had guessed her secret or not), and yet, in spite of that knowledge, she had continued to pack her towels and her sundresses and her bathing suit, and to fill her wicker valise with her English tea biscuits and her bottled water and her netting for the mosquitoes, refusing to spoil her holiday by the sea to stop her car, even for a minute, on the way to the wharf.

No, Rosa thought, her mother had not come before because she had not cared before, had never cared until Dr. MacIver gave her hope of ending the gossip about poisoning that was ruining the family name. For if Cedric had cancer, it would stop the rumors she could not risk, rumors that could uncork other rumors. Then the people her mother tried so hard to impress would know the answer to the riddle—Why was no one suitable for her Rosa until her husband, Thomas Appleton, was six feet under the earth feeding the worms?

Cedric was also thinking about Clara Appleton when he lay on his bed waiting for Rosa to come out of the bathroom. How desperate he had been to convince her! How crucial it had been for him to make her think he was right, that he knew more about his own body than a doctor trained in London, even if he were English. He would not submit. They did not have the power to give him cancer. He would not submit to them or to Rosa.

Would they have said cancer before they knew Rosa was an Appleton? Would that doctor have probed his fingers into his stomach if he had not said DesVignes née Appleton? He had been ready to discharge him. He had no diarrhea, no nausea, no odor from his mouth, no whatever it was that doctor was searching for in the palms of his hand. But the doctor asked his question and he answered *poisoning*, and accused her, Rosa DesVignes née Appleton. No, even if his life depended on it, he would not have cancer for them.

He had not, he reminded himself, escaped the fishing boats in Cedros to surrender to their cancer. Perhaps he was not like them. He had no father to give him money to take a ship to England, none to allow him the luxury of seven years in a university, a medical degree in the end so he could title himself doctor. He had had to work his way through Teachers' Training College, tutoring the sons and daughters of the rich at night. But now he had passed his first examination for an external baccalaureate degree at the University of London. He was studying Latin and Greek. How many of them knew the languages of the Ancients? Yes, he was the son of Anna DesVignes, a fisherwoman, but he was still good enough for Clara Appleton to say yes when he asked for the hand of her youngest daughter, good enough, though she had traveled to England for husbands for the other two.

Each time she told him the doctor had proof, he defended himself. Each time she said the x-ray showed he had a tumor, he recoiled at their arrogance, their assumption that they could control his body and his mind. He was well. He felt strong. Now he turned the humiliation of the enema into the source of his recovery. He convinced himself that the pain had finally left him because of that enema and the pills Dr. MacIver had given him, which had caused him to sleep for hours, allowing the toxins to leave his body in the sweat that drenched his mattress. The pain would not recur, he was sure of that. He had had a virus. He had had it before.

But Clara Appleton had persisted in knowing when. *When* did the pain leave him? *When* did he last feel it? He knew she would laugh at him if he told her that the pain had ended only just that day, a mere eight hours before, so he had lied. Fortunately, Rosa did not hear him, and so could not contradict him, for at that very moment her sister was bending her ear with her righteousness.

"Since yesterday," he said to Clara Appleton. "Since I woke up yesterday morning." But she dismissed him. "The pain will come back again," she said.

After he had put her out of his house, he made up his mind that he would make her pay by humiliating her daughter that night—she and her dead Indian-loving overseer-husband. But an old fear resurfaced. What if Rosa had done more than just pray for him while he slept those long hours in her presence? He did not trust them, those generations of European outcasts who had nursed at the breasts of African women. They believed in obeah, finding in their religion, in their system of angels and saints and the icons they used to worship their God, a perfect match in an order of gods and lesser gods and intermediaries who walked the earth, and in rituals that closely paralleled their own. So they burned candles, wore their scapulars like mojo bags, licked the blood of the sacrificial cock, confessed to the obeahman. Perhaps he should wait one more day before he fucked Rosa. Perhaps he should wait until after he had gone to the doctor to confirm his conclusion that his old virus had flared up again.

He had made up his mind to wait, when Rosa entered the bedroom. But before he could say anything to her, she refused him.

"Not tonight, Cedric," she said. "Not tonight. I don't think you're strong enough."

Her words set him off churning again. *Not strong enough? Not tonight?*

"Another time, Cedric."

He leaped from the bed. "Now!"

Rosa raced for the door.

He grabbed her hair and twisted it until the strands stiffened into wires fanning from her hairline. Thin red lines streaked down her forehead and temples. "Now!"

He yanked her head to the back of her shoulders. She struggled to reach his wrist and loosen his grip, but he pulled harder, dragging her to the bed. "Now!" He straddled her. "Now! Zip down my pants. Take them off. Take them off like you used to do. Like you did when you came sniffing for me. You want it. You want it."

She was no match for him. He had her in a vise between the bolts of his knees. Yet because he was lost in the memory of her lust, reveling in her yawning greed that had driven her time and time again to rise for him in spite of her revulsion, she had managed to bring one thigh to the other and fuse them into a solid mass, a rod of steel to shield her. Except that when the rigidity that had begun in her face and had spread to her breasts at last had made metal of her thighs, he suspected her, and sensed that this time was not like the other times, and he took his knee and made a sledge hammer, rammed until he broke her apart.

The way dry and unyielding, bruised him, tore at the thin surface of his foreskin, blistering it each time he thrust, grating it raw each time he pushed against the cold, passive iron of her insides.

"Wet! Get wet, damn you!"

Sweat poured off his face and soaked her neck.

"Damn you!"

Sweat plastered her nightie to her breast.

"Damn you!"

And she did not move or get moist. And when he could do no

more, because he was outdone by the labor, because his shaft had stiffened beyond the limits of endurance, because the relentless plunging had
brought him not a sliver, not an iota of pleasure and release was what he
wanted and knew he would not have, he rolled himself off her. Then,
without looking at him, she said in a voice he could not remember: "Never.
Never again."

❰ Chapter 16 ❱

*I*t was Zuela who had given her courage, who had inspired her, Zuela who had no choice but to endure her suffering, yet fought the Chinaman with her dreams for her children, her plans for their escape. For even before Cedric reached for her hair, even when she was saying *Not tonight,* when she was promising *Another time,* Rosa knew that that time would be the last time, that that time she would say no, she would say *Never again* to Cedric. It was Zuela who had helped her face her complicity in her humiliation, who had shamed her into ending it, into realizing that the awe she had sought from Cedric had left her powerless; that the haven she had thought she had found was his briar patch; that she was the one who had made it easy for Cedric to head her there. Her cunning, her arrogance in her cunning, engendered by a terrible need, had backfired. Like the fox, she had found herself trapped in the prickly bush; she had snagged herself among its thorns.

Why had she permitted Cedric to abuse her for so many years? Why had she armed him with the knowledge that her need was so great that no matter how often he debased her, she would lift her hips to him, always? She was not eleven years old, as Zuela was when she lay still for the Chinaman. She was not a little girl still believing in fairy tales, in false-hoods about the harmlessness of the spikes on the backs of iguanas. She was a woman, already twenty-eight when she removed her bra and panties and waited for Cedric; already twenty-eight when she took him to her room in the shadow of the tall, wild grass and blew her hot breath on his neck until he cooled his fingers on the marble whiteness of her breasts; already twenty-eight when Cedric caught her scent and began weaving his lies that deluded her into thinking she had seduced him.

And why hadn't she known better? Why hadn't she known that she was the one caught in the snare, not he? Why, like Zuela, hadn't she seen the terror in the eyes of the girl behind the hibiscus bush, the prong in the belt buckle the man swung above her head? Was it because of her mother, because of the woman who called herself her mother?

Perhaps if Clara Appleton had loved her as a mother should love a daughter; perhaps if she had showered her with love as a mother should her infant, yes, even her adolescent girl, even her woman-daughter; showered her with love indiscriminately, without restraint, until she was drenched to the bone, drowning (only fools say too much love can spoil you; the wise know too much is not enough), she would not have needed to distort the photographs of that little girl and that man behind the hibiscus. She would not have been greedy for his perverted embrace. She would not have needed to twist that little girl's anguish, to blind herself to her pain until all she saw was that little girl's power (what she thought was that little girl's power), and she wanted it, desired it, envied it, was jealous of it.

If she had felt from Clara Appleton, even for a moment, the maternal affection she yearned for, she would not have craved the awe she had sought from Cedric, she would not have been enslaved, as she had been, by his embittered and loveless passion. If she had known her mother's admiration, even for the least significant aspect of herself—her hair, her eyes, her smile—she would have found something in herself to have made her feel worthy, to have made her feel deserving, to have made her wait for love. Then she would not have needed, in the way she needed air to pump her lungs, water to make her blood, the calculated attention Cedric gave her that fatal afternoon when he came, on her invitation, to her bedroom to tutor her. She would not have then, nor have now, been at his mercy. A name, even a saint's name, could not have contained enough magic to shape her destiny.

Yet couldn't she have salvaged her life in spite of Clara Appleton? Couldn't she have known better, done better? Hadn't Zuela? Zuela had lost her mother, had been abandoned by her father. She was made mistress to the Chinaman at eleven, wife to him at fourteen. She had conceived a daughter before she understood what it meant to be a daughter. If Zuela, why not she? And not knowing about Tong Lee, how his love had led Zuela to see her beauty, Rosa wondered why she couldn't have dreamed of love; known as Zuela seemed to know, that love was possible between a man and a woman, passion and friendship reconcilable in a marriage; that a man could desire a woman and treasure her, too. Value her.

There were times she could have learned, if not about romance, about love—if not about love, about making something of her life, taking control of her future, having power she could use, not power a man could take from her. She could have learned these on her aunt's cocoa estate in Toco, where her mother had sent her when she smelled danger in the call for Independence rising on the winds blowing from Port-of-Spain. She could have learned about planting, about growing, about harvesting, even about nurturing. Yes, even that she could have learned from her spinster aunt who gave of herself freely, who never asked for anything in return.

"In the towns they destroy you," her aunt said. "You begin to think in categories—you, them, the land. You separate yourself from them and the land. You think whenever you want, however you want, you can use them, you can use the land. But here you learn there are no categories. We are all the same. You, me, they, the land, the cocoa, we are all one—the expression of the Spirit."

She never said God. She didn't believe in God—not God of her people's god—but not because she did not think He was God, too, but, rather, because she saw her people place Him higher than the gods of the people they despised or thought inferior to them. So she said, Spirit, and told Rosa she put a capital "S" on it for she meant the Spirit that pervades everywhere—the intangible that flowed around her, here, in the forest in Toco and, there, in the cement lands in England and in the bushes of Africa.

Maybe she could have learned about nurturing from her, and so, about love. For that was the lesson she had tried to teach her, this aunt who was as white as her mother. She was part of a universal sisterhood, she said, a link in the chain of humanity that included all people, regardless of their color. Maybe if she had looked for love, not a place to quench her passion, when she *needed* a husband; maybe if she had looked for someone to care for, someone to cherish, someone who would care for her, protect her, safeguard her, she would not have chosen Cedric. Then when she had stopped him in the street and asked him to tutor her, she would have seen the vindictiveness in his eyes, in spite of his answer. She would have known he would try to destroy her.

And after Toco, there had been another time, between twenty-one and twenty-eight, when she could have learned about love. Once, when she had been idle, she was given the chance. A priest who had suffered through the seminaries in Ireland and had come back, not exalted by his calling, but, rather, chastened by an experience that made him humble, had petitioned the colonial government for a sanctuary for the destitute. He was a local man, who, though like everyone else had been taught from the cradle to bow to Mother England, had unlearned his indoctrination in the slums of Dublin. The vision he had was as miraculous as any Our Lady had wrought from her shrine in Laventille. There was no difference, he said, between the white child and the black child, none, except poverty—poverty of the body, poverty of the spirit. He wanted to feed, house, clothe, and, above all, teach the poor. Simple as it was, his vision was too radical for the colonial government. But some rich people contributed. Rosa's parents did, but only money, money that kept the devils at bay but demanded no sacrifice, no penance. But the priest wanted more; he wanted commitment.

Clara Appleton compared his request to that demanded of a pig to satisfy his master's appetite for bacon. No, she was no pig. She was a hen that would gladly give him some eggs for breakfast. No more. So he turned to Rosa.

Rosa always reminded herself it was her mother who had said no first and she had merely followed her example. But did it matter? she wondered now. Did it matter when she was twenty-three and had time on her hands, when she knew, if not how to recite Shakespeare, how to read the primers the priest had asked her to teach to the children? What was it? Indulgence in a luxury the priest had warned her was soon to pass? "Independence is coming," he said. "The rulers will change."

Or was she afraid that in the company of men not of her class or of her color, she would submit to the temptation to fulfill her longing for veneration? She had run from the gardener when he genuflected before her, offering his bouquet of bougainvillea. Had she wondered if she would have had the strength to do it again? But now thinking of Zuela, thinking of the snare she set for herself with Cedric, she knew she had not made more of her life because she was a coward, because she was selfish, because she was foolish. And she saw the waste.

What could she do now? Having confronted the why, she wanted to know the what. What would she do?

She would leave Cedric.

Where would she go?

She would go to the sanctuary. She would offer the priest her time and her knowledge, insufficient as these were. She would learn to choose love, as Zuela hoped her daughters would, not need; love, because she had empowered herself to love, because she *wanted* to be loved more than she *needed* to be loved.

How would she begin to find forgiveness?

She would begin with gratitude. She would thank Mary Christophe who was a mother to her when her own mother did not want her. She would thank Our Lady who knew her dark wishes for Cedric, but still answered her prayers, still allowed her choice, and yet pointed the way to Zuela. She would thank Zuela who made her see the horror, the tragedy behind the hibiscus bush. She would begin the road to healing that Saturday. She would go to see Zuela in the shop in Nelson Street. The next day, on Sunday, she would go to Laventille to thank Mary Christophe and Our Lady. On Monday she would offer her services to the priest.

Yet Rosa was to fulfill only two of those intentions—two, because Tong Lee was to overhear the cloaked whisperings of two men beneath the leafy shadows of the chataigne tree that grew in his backyard. What he would hear would change his plans for Zuela that Saturday, and, in that way, change Rosa's, thus affecting the most important part of what Rosa most wanted to do. For before the dawn that day, when Tong Lee opened the shop for Ho Sang, he had already decided he would take Zuela to Manzanilla on Saturday, not to Maracas on Sunday, as he had promised her he would. And he had decided to do that because he had overheard the men saying that the roads near Laventille would not be safe that day. The people were angry that an innocent man was apprehended for the murder of a woman chopped into fodder for pigs, when everyone knew that the man who had butchered her was the one who was seen with the Bentley purring at the bottom of the hill. Tong Lee wanted to protect the woman he loved, the woman he had adored for years, so that what was on his mind that morning, when Rosa was making her plans to visit Zuela, was how he could persuade the Chinaman to close his shop on Saturday so he could fulfil his promise to Zuela, and take her and her children to the beach for her daughter Agnes's birthday.

Cedric, too, had heard what Tong Lee now knew. He was told twice, the first time by the driver of the taxi who was taking him to the doctor, for he intended to confirm, once and for all, that he did not have cancer. But he was listening with only one ear, because the tape of Rosa's last words to him was blasting through his other ear: *Never again. Never again.* So he heard only part of what the driver said, the part that ended with a catalog of names that began with a name that should have caught his attention if he were not still sifting through the morass of motivations he was accumulating to explain to himself Rosa's sudden uncharacteristic defiance of him. Only when the driver reached Delilah, and only because when he reached there Cedric had arrived at a conclusion that fit exactly into the schema the driver was unfolding, did he hear what he was saying, that it was Helen's lechery that had brought down Troy; that it was Cleopatra's lust that had broken the back of the great Anthony, that it was Eve who had set the stage for man's destruction. Then Cedric said bitterly to the driver, because now he knew there could only be one reason, and one alone, why Rosa had refused him,

"They are bitches, harlots, whores, all. They don't know how to close their legs."

The woman the taxi driver had been talking about, the woman who had precipitated his long discourse on the infidelity of women and their lasciviousness, was the same woman who was the subject of the conversation Tong Lee overheard that morning. In fact, she was the same woman who was responsible for Cedric's illness, that is, if one believed that because two pigs had eaten the flesh of a woman, no pork was safe to eat. Had Cedric been more attentive to the driver and less to designing a snare to entrap Rosa, he would have learned how it came to be that the woman was fed to pigs. He would have found out about her deception, her infidelity to the one man who loved her; he would have found out that she had betrayed him with two brothers, but that was not all. She had sold herself to a man who owned a Bentley, and the night she was butchered, he was waiting for her at the bottom of the hill.

As it was, Cedric had been too consumed with rage and humiliation, but after the doctor he consulted at St. Anthony's Nursing Home had given him the results of the x-rays he had taken of his stomach that morning, and while he was waiting for him to compare it to the one that was taken at Colonial Hospital, he felt sufficiently avenged, enough to make his mind free and calm again so that when for the second time that day he happened upon a group of people talking about pigs that had vomited a ring from the finger of a woman, he listened, and so he heard about Melda's treachery, and about her deceit, and he felt justified, if indeed he needed more evidence to feel justified, in the new plot he was hatching for Rosa. Sisters of the same kind, he had told Rosa, when Paula Inge's body washed up on the beach in Otahiti, but now he knew she was sister, not only to her, but also to Melda.

When he wrote of Laventille that it was tempered in violence, the poet raised specters of the horrors of the middle passage and the cruelty of slavery, but he was mindful, too, that violence, like love, feeds on itself and breeds a progeny often worse, or, like its opposite, more perfect than itself. So at first when Laventille transferred its resentment of Melda toward two pigs they barricaded in a clearing behind Our Lady, and then pardoned two brothers accused of hacking her to death, people in the valley said it was predictable. They expected such behavior from a people who had experienced no better, a people for whom love and hate were sides of the same coin, who, blinded by self-hate, could not distinguish between the hand that fed them and the mouth that bit them. So they were not surprised that the hill people dismissed the confessions of the ring giver and turned their hatred inward to their women, or that the women did not protest. They expected Laventille to seethe when they arrested the ring giver. They anticipated Laventille would point its fingers at a man in the valley. *No, the man who killed Melda was not the man who gave her the ring. It was the other man, the man with the Bentley, the man with the buttoned-down shirt.* The accusation from Laventille was typical.

At the arraignment, the people in the valley had their defense. They explained why the ring giver had chosen his particular method of murdering Melda: "He was copying Boysie. He heard Boysie say, "No body, no crime. No crime, no execution."

Mimic men, the novelist had called the hill dwellers, but they had neither the intelligence nor the money to copy the masters exactly. European logic always eluded them. So Boysie, the worst of their kind, fed human hearts to racehorses because he had learned that God had created man after beast, and in that jumbled-up version of the European sense of man's relationship to beast that swirled in his brain, it followed to him that the one made last would be better, and thus could give strength to the other. It had not occurred to him that the opposite could be true, that it was in eating the heart of the horse that man became superior.

Boysie had probably heard of a case in England about a murderer who escaped his punishment because of the law of corpus delicti. The hill dwellers, imitating him, figured out that they, too, would invent ways to destroy the bodies of their victims. They would chop them up and feed them to pigs if they had to, or else gut them, tie them to rocks and sink them to the bottom of the sea. That was what the doctor-murderer had done. But his roots, the valley people reminded themselves, were planted in his tomato patch in the Caroni. Thus his failure was inevitable: the body he had tried to conceal resurfaced. For the valley people, like the novelist, believed they alone had perfected the art of imitation, so much so that except for the primordial tanning of their skins, there was little difference one could discern between them and a proper Englishman.

But this time they were prepared to be less assertive, less dogmatic, for they were still tottering from the aftershock of a humiliation: Scotland Yard had merely glanced at the body of the woman in Otahiti and fingered the murderer. A scalpel, not a knife. A doctor, not a butcher. Now they would do the right thing. They would conduct an investigation; they would hold a hearing. The two brothers had some cause, but, they had to concede, no damning motivation. A woman loose enough to have had them both (and during the investigation both brothers admitted they knew she had had the other) was hardly worthy of passion, even the passion to kill her. No, they had their man when the ring giver confessed he had given Melda a ring, she had sworn to be faithful, he had caught her in her lechery with the brothers.

But the hill dwellers had seen the Bentley that night and other nights before. They were unshakable in their conviction that the man in that car was the one who had butchered Melda and fed her to the pigs. Now the rage that had spilled over the boiling cauldron no longer cooled to a trickle. Now the fire roared and the boiling water rushed down toward the valley, hot and steaming.

Cedric heard it was coming and used it as a warning to Rosa that night when he returned from the nursing home with the results of the x-ray of his stomach.

"Nothing. Not a blur, not a mark, not a line," the doctor had said.

He was a black doctor, but still Cedric had confidence in him. A black doctor in the white man's nursing home had to be better than the best.

"Why did you think it was cancer?"

Cedric had told him everything—the degrading ride down the corridor of the hospital, which he insisted on calling an animal hospital. A hospital for baboons. "Horsepital," he said, mimicking the cadence of the people he called lower class. A hospital for horses. It stank worse than the gutters near the fish market, worse than the sewers, worse than the La Basse, worse than sugar-cane juice fermenting in Usine Ste. Madeline. And the indignity of newspapers instead of sheets! "Free, and they wouldn't even change them on the beds. Shit, blood everywhere. They didn't care." They wanted to strip his pride, he said, reduce him to an animal with the enema they gave him in front of everybody, in an open ward, where they had crammed in patients like sardines in a tin can. But they didn't break him. It takes more than them to break him, he said. More.

"And the nurse didn't draw the curtain?" the doctor asked.

"Curtain? What curtain? There was not one curtain around a single bed. I tell you it was an animal hospital."

The doctor was sympathetic. Yes, he said, his mother had had the same misfortune. That was before he returned to Trinidad from the university in England, qualified. Then everything was different for her after that, after he qualified.

Cedric felt a familiar twinge of resentment when the doctor said, "qualified." He had not been able to afford to go to England; he was still studying for an external baccalaureate degree from the University of London. But that old grievance was lost in the immense satisfaction and pleasure he was experiencing at that moment in the restoration of his dignity. His confidence soared.

"And before I said my wife was Rosa DesVignes née Appleton, they didn't think it was cancer either. It was *after*. *After* I said her name they took the x-rays."

To be fair to the doctor, he was not impressed by the Appleton name. In fact, his reaction was opposite to that of the doctor who had first examined Cedric. It was white people like the Appletons who had used his people like chattel to fatten their wallets, who had led his father to an early grave, who had made his mother suffer the indignities Cedric had described. No, he had no respect for them. No fear, either. But he had not known of the earlier x-rays. Cedric had told him that he had gone to the hospital, but he had not told him the doctors took x-rays. When he said, "They think it's cancer," he had presumed *they* to be the people in Cedric's town, his

214

neighbors, the ones he had complained to about his pain. He had never suspected doctors, his colleagues whose referrals he counted on for patients for the private practice he was starting. If he had known the doctors had taken x-rays, he would never have taken one, or if he had, he would have concealed the results.

To be absolutely certain, the doctor told Cedric he would compare the x-rays. He would give him the results the next day. But Cedric was willing to pay to have them read earlier. "Today," he said. "This afternoon." He wanted his vindication to be absolute. Total. The doctor, too, wanted to be sure.

It was then, while he was waiting for the doctor to return from Colonial Hospital, that Cedric learned about Melda, and, later, he fashioned her story into a new trap he planned to set for Rosa.

By two o'clock the doctor had his answer. He had not seen the doctors who had submitted the report to the chief surgeon but he had seen the x-ray. An orderly remembered Cedric DesVignes. He was the man who refused to talk, then talked at the wrong time, he said. He located the x-ray for him. Afterward the doctor wished he had not told Cedric, *Not a blur, not a line,* for he could not deny the evidence before him. On the x-ray the orderly had given him, there was a shadow the size of an orange; on his, there was nothing. There was no doubt, no question in his mind: The x-ray from the hospital showed that Cedric had a tumor in his stomach that most probably was malignant.

What would he say to Cedric? Should he say he had had a miracle? That in two weeks he had had a remission so absolute it defied every logical, scientific explanation culled from centuries of medical experience? Should he tell him that the other doctors, his colleagues, had made a mistake, perhaps a deliberate one? He did not believe the latter, not because he did not believe the doctors culpable of mendacity and treachery, but because he discovered that it was not they who had taken the x-ray. It was a nurse, a longtime friend of his and childhood classmate, whom he, nevertheless, had questioned carefully. No, he was satisfied that the first x-ray was accurate, authentic and incontestable.

He was left then with the only answer he refused to believe. For to believe it would be to negate the worth of years of study and sacrifice in a cold country he detested. To say that Cedric had experienced a miracle, a cure that could not be explained scientifically, was to accede to the chief surgeon's claim: He and his local colleagues had exchanged art for science. They had foolishly given up a gift, passed freely down to them by their people, to see, understand and appreciate the intangible. Now they no longer trusted the efficacy of the hands of the obeahman, nor the power of the spirit. They had given this up for a set of formulas—cold, hard, concrete—that could do no more than predict, that could change no more than what it had predicted. So the doctor told Cedric what he was certain was a lie.

"A mistake," he said. "They mixed up the x-rays. It probably was a virus, as you said. I've seen that before. The effects can be devastating. The stomach cramps, you sweat, you have diarrhea, you vomit. You're right. It is an animal hospital."

But Cedric had not vomited, and except for the enema, he had not had diarrhea.

≪ Chapter 17 ≫

*Y*et the absence of nausea was not enough to dampen Cedric's spirits. He gloated over his vindication: It was a virus, not Rosa's poison, that had brought him to his knees. But his moment of glory was to be short-lived, for at the very time he was plotting his revenge, Rosa was sorting out her things in readiness for Monday. For now she knew exactly what she would do and how she would do it.

First, she had to go to the bank, but she would not go there immediately. She would not take the chance that Cedric could return from the doctor and find her missing. Then there would be questions to answer. She would go to the bank on Monday, before she entered the sanctuary. She would withdraw the five thousand dollars Thomas Appleton had left for her, a third of the fifteen thousand dollars he had bequeathed to his daughters. No one had questioned her right to it; no one had said Thomas Appleton was not her father.

In the lawyer's office her mother had warned her, "Don't tell anyone your father left you money." But she had said the same thing to her other daughters. "There are some things you don't share with your husband. This money gives you a little protection. Just in case."

Yet six weeks after her marriage, Rosa came close to disregarding this advice. For it was six weeks after their marriage that Cedric began setting the stage for her final humiliation, certain then that he had already laid the foundation for her addiction. For she was addicted to having sex with him, she knew that now. Her desire had become greed; her greed had become a need that was never satisfied. She had said to Zuela that she *needed* to be married, not *wanted*, and Zuela had made her confront the difference.

First it was only a longing, a hunger she could control, then a desperation that made her willing to do anything to have Cedric enter her. They would have conversations before sex, all of them innocent. She did not suspect him then; she did not know he was beginning to stage her addiction. One day, stroking her cheek with a single finger, he said to her, "You will age like your mother—all wrinkles quickly."

She laughed. She was young. Her skin was firm.

Then, another time, during sex, he asked her, "Can't you do it better?"

Afterward, many times afterward, he compared her with black women. "They do it with more feeling," he said.

She tried harder.

Then came the abstinence. For days he would not touch her. He would say he was tired. He would say they had too much sex. She would beg him: "Then, just your arms around me." He would turn his back on her. A week later, she would do anything he asked.

Finally he said the words that took her to the brink of telling him that her father had left her the five thousands dollars: "Really, in the end that's all you Trinidad white people are. You are castoffs. White niggers. Your father sold your sisters to Englishmen. Look how he left you without out a penny when he died."

The humiliation. It was not that she was not conscious of it, but the addiction was already rooted. She needed his body on hers. *In hers.* So after he no longer waited for her to beg, but demanded she beg, she still rose for him.

She had said to him *Never again,* compiled her reasons for *Never again,* yet those nights of those twelve days when he was sick, those times when she lay alone in her bed, the addiction still gnawed at her. Even while Zuela's words were giving her the courage to say no, the muscles at the base of her stomach were tightening, her tension escalating to such a point that she felt a constant quivering under her skin that she could not stop.

How little sense she had had of how the need for sex would take hold of her, how it would become a habit, not a habit like chewing her nails, which she could overcome with practice by putting drops of bitter aloe on her finger so the taste would repel her, but a habit that was greater than that, a hundred times worse than that. Nothing could make sex repulsive to her. She would want it again and again. She would never have made love—not once—if she had known she would ache this way for it; if she had been warned that after she had let Cedric into her bed, there would be no turning back, no more possibility of cooling the burning between her legs without his body on hers, no way for her to reenter that Eden, flawed as it was with her adolescent craving, with the relief she had sought, rubbing her bare skin against her hard mattress. Afterward, it was too late and Cedric knew it. He played her like his instrument, dangled his carrot, withdrew it, offered it again, knowing that in spite of his taunts she would arch like a cat, knowing that she was his for his taking, that even after he said *Beg* and she refused him, that in time . . .

So she had said no last night. So she would say no forever. She would take the five thousand dollars from the bank and give it to the priest, and he would let her stay in the sanctuary.

She rearranged her closet and the drawers of her dresser so that the clothes she would take with her were gathered together. She put her suitcase under the bed. She would not pack now. She would not give Cedric the chance to suspect her, to foil her plans. Monday morning would be soon enough for her to leave him forever. When she heard Cedric's footsteps on the front porch she came downstairs to the kitchen. She would cook. She would pretend nothing had changed.

"It was a virus." Cedric had entered the kitchen. "It's a miracle I got out of that animal hospital alive."

She reached for a saucepan in the cupboard. She would betray nothing of her plans.

"A miracle. A goddamn miracle I'm well." He came close to her. "Even the doctor said so."

She filled the pan with water.

"A goddamn miracle," he said. He circled her. "A miracle."

But the fourth time he said it, she couldn't resist telling him the truth. "She made it happen for you," she said.

His brow darkened.

"She made the miracle for you."

"She?"

"Our Lady." She stepped away from him.

"Our Lady?" He kept the space between them.

"Our Lady of Fatima." She took the bag of rice from the shelf, measured a cupful and poured it in the pan of water.

"So you think it was you?"

She looked up. Even his eyes had grown dark. "No," she said.

"You think it was you and your sniveling prayers?"

"No." She felt his breath on her neck but it was an illusion, a figment of her imagination. He had not moved. Still, it took courage to continue. "But I said a novena to her when you were sick."

He leaned against the counter. She could tell he was bracing himself to stay in control, but when he spoke his voice vibrated with his anger. "You damn white people. You think it's always you. Everything happens because of you. *You* made me sick. *You* cured me. *You* made a miracle for me." The words strained through his teeth and he pressed his back deeper against the side of the counter top and curled his fingers around the ledge.

Her heart beat faster, but she would not let him see that he had frightened her. "Our Lady of Fatima," she said. "Not me. And Mary Christophe helped. She gave me medicine for you."

He made sounds with his tongue, but they were not words.

"She said it would help." She would wash the rice though she felt his eyes on her. She would concentrate on rubbing it clean between the palms of her hands. "I gave it to you."

The sounds out of his mouth made words now. "All the times I slept?"

"It made you calm so Our Lady could come to you."

"Obeah? You worked obeah on me?'

"No. Mary Christophe doesn't believe in obeah. I know her. She used to take care of me when I was a child. It wasn't obeah." She would not let him scare her. Monday, Monday she would have her freedom. She lit the stove. "You don't have to be afraid," she said.

"Afraid?" He let go of the counter top.

She had made a mistake. She saw it as clear as day before her. "No."

He stood upright, away from the edge of the counter that had kept him in check. "That's what you want now, white lady? That's what you want? You want me to be afraid? Afraid of you?"

"No."

"You want me to be afraid of you?"

"No. I gave you the medicine because I wanted to help you. After you took it, on the ninth day of my novena, you were better. You said so yourself."

"Well, I'm not afraid. I'm not afraid of you or your mother or that whole damn lot of white doctors. Watch me. I look afraid?"

"I don't want you to be afraid, Cedric."

"Watch me. Do you see my hands trembling?"

"No, Cedric. I don't want that, Cedric."

"Do I look as if you weakened my knees?"

"You don't *need . . .* "

"Need?"

"You don't need to be afraid, Cedric."

"What did you say, white lady?"

"It was not obeah. Our Lady . . . the prayers I said, we said, Ena and me . . . "

"No! Not you! It was not you."

"You're right, Cedric."

"Not your prayers."

"No, Cedric."

"Not your damn, sniveling, conniving prayers."

"No, Cedric."

"Not your . . ."

"No. I did nothing. I did . . . "

He sucked in his breath.

" . . . nothing to help you, Cedric."

His breathing grew calm.

"Nothing, Cedric."

He spat on the floor near her feet. "You're no different, no different from them."

A drop, an infinitesimal drop of spit grazed her bare leg. She felt it and it comforted her. Yes, she was no different, no different from the Mary Christophes, the black people he despised. Yes, maybe he knew that now. Maybe he was more certain of that now than he was when he said to her that Thomas Appleton was less than a man. Maybe he had resigned himself now to the fact that Thomas Appleton did not have it in him to be her father.

She was glad he thought she was no different, for she wanted to be no different. It was better to be like Mary Christophe and Zuela. It was better to be like them than to be like her mother. It was better to belong to their world than to the world of the Appletons, the world Cedric was straining to be part of, with his books in Latin and Greek. She was not afraid of his anger now. So he knew about Thomas Appleton, but she would leave him Monday.

"Yes, I'm like them," she said.

"Like the Meldas," he shouted at her.

She did not recognize the name. She had not heard it, as he had, twice that morning—once on the way to the doctor who vindicated him, the second time while waiting to know how great was the miracle that he had survived Colonial Hospital. She did not know Melda was the one who had caused him to forbid her to cook pork.

"Why do you think those men chopped her up? Why do you think they gave her to the pigs?"

She looked up at him.

"Because she was a pig like those pigs." The veins strained in his head. "A pig wallowing in her lust. A pig like you."

She folded her arms under her heart and squeezed back the fluttering in her chest.

"You think I don't know why you said *no* last night? Why you said *never again?* As if you think you could say *never again*. As if you think you have some right to say *never again*. You think you could say it even if you had the right? I rescued you, goddamn it. I rescued you!"

She would remain calm. She would remember that Zuela had not let the Chinaman destroy her.

"I saved you! I, Cedric DesVignes. All those trips to England, but your mother could not find a single Englishman who wanted you. She raked through the men here, too. Not a single one. Nobody."

She unfolded her arms and reached for the frying pain.

"Nobody! Because nobody wanted you."

She tried to strike a match to light the stove under the frying pan but she could not hold her fingers steady.

"You think I'm stupid? You think I don't know why you settled for me?"

She put down the matchbox.

"Nobody! You hear me? Nobody!" He grabbed her arm. "Twenty-eight years old and nobody had wanted you. Nobody!"

She made herself concentrate on Zuela. She made herself think about her aunt, about the sanctuary. Monday. After she saw Zuela on Saturday, Mary Christophe on Sunday, she would go to the sanctuary on Monday.

"I was the last black man alive who would take you. The last!"

Monday. After Zuela on Saturday, Mary Christophe on Sunday.

"The last!" He shoved her away from him. "And God knows you wanted to be taken."

Monday.

"You think I forgot how you took off your panties before you stopped me that day you asked me your hopeless question about tutoring? I know why you took off your bra. I know you plotted for me to grab your crotch. You would have fried from that fire between your legs if I didn't hose it down."

Her arm ached where he had squeezed her. She rubbed it. *Saturday, Zuela. Sunday, Mary Christophe and Our Lady. Monday, the sanctuary.*

"And you think I should be grateful? You think I should thank God for you? For a mistake some stupid doctors made? I say God punished me. I don't have anything to thank Him for on that score. Nothing to thank Him about you. He punished me with you. Yes, that's what it is. I'm working off my sins with you."

Saturday, Zuela. Rosa faced him. "I'm leaving you, Cedric. Not today. Monday. When you come home from work on Monday, I'll be gone."

"Yes, working off my sins with you. Not even children you could give me. You're worse than an empty calabash. A man could pump himself all day in you and still you'll spit out nothing."

Quietly, she repeated her words. Softly. "Monday. I'll be gone Monday."

"To your lover! To your *black* lover! Your *black* lover in Laventille. That's all who would want you. All you can get. And you know why? Because they are poor. Because they don't know better. Because your people reduced them so far down that when they look up, all they can see is you."

"Monday, Cedric, but not to a lover."

"Don't think when they look up, they look up for love. Don't think when they reach up to put their arms around you, they don't want to choke you. Don't think that man in Laventille will be as easy on you, as civilized with you, as that doctor was with that woman in Otahiti."

"I'm leaving, Cedric."

"Don't think they don't want to tear you to pieces, to throw you to the dogs."

"Monday," Rosa repeated.

"Dogs!"

"Monday, Cedric."

"No. No. You don't go anywhere. You stay here. You will stay right here. You will fuck me when I want to. You will fuck me when I want to be fucked."

"Monday." It had become a chant for Rosa now. A mantra. It blotted out all other reality. It blocked out all other possibilities. It sent everything to the darkness. Even Cedric's voice. Even Cedric's hatred. It made a light. Clear. Bright. Pristine. A flame burning blue, pure at the center of her soul. She was hardly aware when sound came from her tongue or when it came from that center where she alone could hear it, but the word made her strong. She was a woman of steel. She was Zuela—a woman of the Amazon. *Monday. Monday.*

"Monday." The word had sound this time.

"Why not today? Today! Make it today. But you won't make it today, Rosa. Not you. You know nobody wants you. Nobody. Not even a Laventille man."

Monday. The word resounded in her ears only.

"Go. Go today. They're breaking down the place since the police arrested that man who butchered Melda. Go. See the kind of people they are. See the kind of men that tear up women, that hack them into pieces for hogs. Go. Today. Go."

Monday. Her mantra kept her steady; it cemented her resolve.

"They're stoning down anybody who comes up the hill. Go to your lover. Does he know you're planning to come? I hope he knows, because he's going to have to meet you at the bottom of the hill. And even there they are cutting up people."

"Monday," said Rosa.

"Monday, Monday, Monday. You're going insane. You're going crazy. Monday, Monday, Monday. Is that all you can say?" He grabbed her wrist, made a manacle of his hand around it, locked it. "Now!" he commanded. "Now! I want to be fucked now, white lady."

She had not planned it. She was not in the emotional state to plan anything, even to comprehend the danger she was in—either to assess it, analyze it or to determine the best routes for escape, far less to have selected one, to have put one into effect. It was simply that his last two words had penetrated her defenses, stirring the blue flame of a mantra not even *Fucked now* had disturbed. The fluttering in her breast escalated to a gallop, tears broke loose from the dam she had made with her stoic determination to hide her feelings from him, to deny him the satisfaction of knowing how completely he had degraded her. But now *white lady* had fanned that blue flame red and she reached for the hand clamped on her wrist.

"White lady? White lady? You call me white lady, Cedric?" Rosa looked directly into his eyes. "My blood is as black as yours."

Cedric froze. He knew he had stripped her so bare that she had neither the time nor the presence of mind for artifice. The tears that rolled down her cheeks were not a sniveling cheap trick to pull her neck from out of his trap: She was not afraid of him. She had put her hand on his as if she had nothing to fear, as if she thought he had no power to harm her. His fingers grew limp and he loosened his grip on her wrist. She lifted his hand and made him set her free.

He watched her slide past him in the narrow passage between the refrigerator and the stove. She walked through the doorway with her shoulders held high. Tears were still rolling down her cheeks, but they were different tears, not the hysterical tears he had so often managed to reduce her to. They were cathartic tears. She was sobbing, but as if a huge boulder that had been crushing her had suddenly been removed, as if when he released her wrist, he had released her soul, too. Then sense merged with intuition and he understood at last the full meaning of her words. "As black as mine?" The knowledge terrified him.

She had already walked across the drawing room and was opening the door to his study. Before she shut it on him, she said, brushing away the tears that had drained to her mouth, "I thought you knew. I thought when you told me Thomas Appleton was a homosexual, you knew he was not my father. You knew my father was as black as you."

⋘ Chapter 18 ⋙

*R*osa planned to leave the house early next morning before
Cedric woke up. She did not want anything to prevent her from going to
Nelson Street to see Zuela that day. But as she tried to put the key in the
lock on the front door, it slipped from her hands and clattered on the
wood floor. Then afraid that Cedric had heard her and would try to stop
her, she unlocked the door quickly and ran down the steps.

The taxi driver she stopped was surprised she would be out alone
when it was still dark and he warned her about Laventille.

Hadn't she heard?

But she had not, for not once had Cedric's warning penetrated her
mantra, *Monday*, that kept the flame of her determination to leave him
burning bright in her heart. Not once had she allowed his taunts about
the dangers of Laventille to enter her mind. So she had heard nothing
Cedric had said about people stoning, or tearing or breaking down
Laventille.

"If I was you," said the driver, "I stay here till the sun come up."

She had no other choice. He had stopped his car in front of one of
the benches that circled the savannah, near the horse and cart of a coconut vendor who was still asleep under a brown burlap bag, and he refused
to take her any farther. "I don't want responsibility for you," he told her.

But the sun rose an hour later, shimmering its rainbow colors across the dew hanging off the spreading trees near the edges of the savannah, and when the bell in the archbishop's chapel rang for the six o'clock Mass, people began slowly trickling into the street. Then, Rosa felt it was bright enough and safe enough to stop another taxi to take her to the Chinaman's shop. But the Chinaman's shop was not open that Saturday, and when she reached there, there was a small group of people standing before a sign tacked on the front door: *Closed till Monday.*

The moment she read the sign she looked up to the attic. It was perhaps simply a matter of reflex that made her do that, an instinctive reaction to deflect the glare of eyes fastened on her—people, like the taxi driver, who were staring at her, surprised that she had dared to be in the street alone so early in the morning. And in that single glance upward she saw the pale fingers of the Chinaman's hand curving around one of the dark, weather-worn slats of the bare wood jalousies and his eyes and mouth glistening in the ghoulish light of a candle flame. A sudden wind blew the strands of her hair in her eyes and blinded her. When she looked up again the jalousie slats were closed.

She shuddered, thinking of Zuela, and then she remembered Zuela had told her that she was going to meet her daughter at the convent school that weekend. Relieved that Zuela was not in the shop, Rosa decided she would return on Monday before going to the sanctuary. Today she would visit Mary Christophe and Our Lady, and if Mary Christophe permitted her, she would spend the weekend with her. Then she would never have to return to Cedric. Buoyed by that possibility, she summoned up the courage to ignore the small cluster of people who were now looking malevolently at her and she asked one of the men to show her where she could find a taxi to take her to Laventille.

But Zuela was not at the convent where Rosa had imagined her to be. She was with Agnes, but she was also with Tong Lee in the front seat of an open truck where the wind tossed the hair of her ten children, blew across their laughter and whipped their clothes high in the air with each turn Tong Lee made around the bends, speeding toward the sea.

It had not been easy. While Rosa had been considering the why and how to leave Cedric, Tong Lee was choking on the what—what to tell the Chinaman so that he would not be tempted to put his fingers around the Chinaman's neck and strangle him. What to tell him so he could keep his promise to Zuela when Agnes came home.

"You never saw the sea?" He couldn't believe it when Zuela told him one day that she had never been to the sea.

"The docks, the harbor where the ships come in, but never to the sea people talk about when they say they went to the beach. Never sea with coconut trees and sea-almond trees."

"And not in Venezuela?"

"When Chinaman take me out of the Orinoco I see the big sea, not the one with beaches."

"And your children?"

"Chinaman never take them to the sea."

That was when Tong Lee decided to surprise her. "For Agnes's visit," he said. "Her birthday present."

He knew Agnes would be sixteen that Sunday. So he said it would be that Sunday. "Maracas, where the precipices fall so far down, you could see straight down to the sea and it feel like the waves crashing on the rocks could reach up and splash you."

"No beach?" she asked. The corners of her mouth drooped.

He smiled. "Yes. Maracas has plenty beach. The rocks are out in the sea. Plenty beach. You see."

But she didn't see. Not Maracas. For by dawn that Friday, Tong Lee heard two men whispering under the chataigne tree about Melda, and by the time he got to the Chinaman's shop he knew he had to go to another beach, on another day, if he wanted to escape the trouble that would surely come to Laventille that day.

"What you going to tell Chinaman?"

He still didn't know the what then, when she asked. He didn't know it either when he sat down next to the Chinaman. He thought only of keeping his fingers still, holding them steady in a clasp like a prayer above his chest.

"But Saturday is the busiest day," the Chinaman said when he told him he wanted to take Zuela and the children to the beach. "Everybody make business on Saturday. She have to work in the shop on Saturday."

"You can come, too."

Chinaman shook his head. "No. She can't go Saturday."

"Sea breeze good for your lungs." Tong Lee tried to persuade him.

Chinaman pressed his lips tightly together and said nothing.

"You don't cough so much when you by the sea."

"No, no, she stay here on Saturday."

"You feel better."

"No, she don't go."

"Zuela never see sea."

Chinaman became agitated. "She lie." His head swung from side to side. "She lie. She see sea. I take her on sea."

"You take me on sea, too, but still I didn't see sea when you take me." Suddenly, without warning, Tong Lee found himself slipping down to the bottom of a river, the watery grave where he had buried a memory of a boy drenched in his father's blood. "I remember that sea. I remember the time before you take me to that sea." The images broke loose now. "I remember the blood."

"Blood? Blood? What blood?"

"I remember when you say, 'What? And lose time?'"

"What blood?"

"I remember when the river turn red."

"Boat capsize if I don't throw out the body. Both of us drown."

But it was not only his father's blood Tong Lee was thinking of at that moment. It was also his mother's blood. He was thinking of the question and the answer that saved his life and cost his mother hers.

"You or her?" The people who had let loose the bloodtide in revenge for opium gave his father this choice.

"Me." But it was his mother's head that whirled in the wind. Afterward they took him and his father in a sampan down to the banks of the Yangtze.

"You or the boy?"

"Me."

Tong Lee heard his father's head hit the edge of the sampan before it bounced into the river. His father's body fell across his lap like the trunk of a tree.

The pain of that memory was so searing, he fought to suppress it with generalities. "Is not right what you did to me, Ho Sang. What you did to my family."

"No. Not that." The Chinaman lost his eyes. His pupils rolled under his eyelids. "Not that."

"If it had not been for you, for your father and your greed, all of us would have lived. The whole village."

"No. No." The Chinaman's head rocked on his neck.

"Your daughter and your wife, too. Because of you, because of your greed and your cowardice, they took their lives. Think I don't know what you let happen to them? Think I don't know why you take Zuela?" Tong Lee inhaled deeply, then let out his breath and with it the ghosts he had tried to forget. "The blood will never leave you, Ho Sang, until you ask for forgiveness. You will be covered in your wife's blood and your daughter's blood, and my father's blood. The blood of a village of men." The last wisp of the breath he had inhaled whistled through his lips. "My mother's blood will haunt you."

Zuela could not figure it out. She did not understand, but she didn't ask for understanding, only that God would let it last, whatever it was that had come over the Chinaman so that he said to her after he had eaten his lunch, "Tong Lee taking you and the children to Manzanilla in the morning. I close the shop till Monday."

Tong Lee did not want to think, either, about what he had to remember so that he finally terrified the Chinaman into allowing her to go. Happy to be with her on the beach under the wide-latticed fronds of the coconut trees, he put all sad thoughts out of his mind. "What you miss most from your country?" he asked her. He wanted her to be happy, too.

Her eyes were fixed on her children playing in the frothy white surf. They were dressed in the bright-colored bathing suits she had made for them within the week he had promised to take them to the sea. The older boys wore green shorts, the younger ones, red. "Sea clothes," she told them when they complained about the brilliance of the colors. "Like in American magazines. You don't have to wear them in the street." All the girls, except Agnes, had on bathing suits made from the red and white gingham tablecloths the parish priest had given her after a church bazaar, but Agnes wore a sundress. It was yellow and had little blue boats with white sails on it.

"I save the cloth years now since Chinaman bring it home when Achong shop catch fire. I wash it and keep it for a special day. Today."

Tong Lee followed her eyes to Agnes who was holding her baby sister akimbo on her hip. How much she resembled Zuela when she was her age! And yet at that age Zuela had already known, had already been made to know by the Chinaman, that life for her would never be what it had been before he came to her rainforest and took her away. Agnes had her mother's firm brown limbs, her tiny ankles and wrists, her smooth round face and her full sensuous lips. Yes, Tong Lee thought, it was those lips that had made the Chinaman take that apocalyptic leap from his wife to his daughter, from his daughter to his wife, from his daughter and his wife to Zuela.

He heard her sigh deeply and knew that her sigh came from the same comforting thought that crossed his mind—Agnes had escaped the life she had had. She would not have her future. It was not her daughter she rocked on her hips; it was her sister. Yet how much more Zuela wanted for her!

"The noise," Zuela said at last, answering Tong Lee's question about her home in Venezuela. "And the way I felt safe in the dark."

He would ask her about the dark later that night. Now he wanted to know about the noise.

"I love this, too," she said. "I like the noise the waves make when they break up on the sand. I like the sound of the coconuts when they fall."

They were sitting on a deserted section of the beach where the coconut trees fanned out in a wide arc as far as the eye could see. It was a surrealistic dream: tall, thin tree trunks, ringed brown-gray, like the legs of giant prehistoric ibis, rising steadily in the somnolent shadow of green palm fronds glittering in the sun. There were so many trees stretching out for so many miles that even if the pickers picked a hundred trees clean a day, it would take more than a month to notice that coconuts were missing.

"I like the bup, bup sound the coconuts make when they fall on the ground," she said.

Tong Lee could hardly contain his happiness. "Tell me about the other sounds," he said. And she told him about the monkeys that chattered between the trees; about the birds that had such distinct sweet whistles she could name them from their songs; about the graceful white herons near the river that walked without sound; about the vibrations of animal feet before a thunderstorm and the crash of branches to the underbrush breaking the silence afterward.

"We had a parrot that hiccuped," she said. "Then my mother notice one day that it wasn't just hiccuping, it was saying my name. *Hija.*" She laughed and closed her eyes. "I could tell you about the colors, too," she said. "The trees from my home are greener than any green you can imagine in Trinidad. They green like emerald."

Tong Lee let her dream and when the sun was halfway in its descent to the edge of the sea and she was laughing easily, crinkling her eyes above her sunburned cheeks, he broke a vow he had made the day he first compared her to a painting on his drawing room wall and she said she could see why he didn't want a woman. It was the beginning of the end of the last vow he was yet to break.

"You could have been Chinese," he said.

She asked him, "How?"

"Your eyes. Your face fold up when you laugh and then your eyes get narrow, narrow like Chinese eyes."

At about the same time that Zuela was basking in the tenderness of Tong Lee's love for her, Rosa was climbing the Laventille hill on her way to the shrine of Our Lady. She had just left Mary Christophe, promising she would return. She would stay the night with her, all day Sunday and Sunday night, too. Hours before, while Tong Lee was driving Zuela and her children to the sea, she was clutching Mary Christophe's hand, allowing her to drag her through the trees, up the slope to her house. They could not take the path. Seven boys in torn undershirts that ballooned

233

behind them had blocked it. Their fathers stood at their sides, guarding them.

"I thought I warn you last time. Why you take the chance coming here? You didn't hear what going on? You didn't hear about the arrest?"

Inside the house Mary Christophe questioned her again. "Didn't nobody tell you? Didn't nobody warn you not to come? Didn't you hear about the lawyer?"

But a mantra had closed off Rosa's ears to everything but *Monday.*

"Not always things black and white. Police arrest that poor man and everybody know he didn't do it. Black as that lawyer is, he's still one of them. He *think* like one of them. Everybody see him coming every night for Melda." She bolted the front door. "Not that I blame her. She have to feed her children. Still, she should know she couldn't cross him. It's the civilized ones you have to frighten for." She locked the back door. "Like that doctor, how cold, cold so, he take his knife and open his wife belly. How cold, cold so, he stitch her up. Not a tear he shed. Nothing hurt his heart. Same as this lawyer, black as he is. He give Melda money so he think he own her. I warn her many times, but she love the man who give her the ring. She love him too bad, she tell me. So every night when she leave the lawyer, she go back to the man who give her the ring. She was pretty."

Her eyes swept over Rosa—her skin that the sun had burnished gold, not freckled as the sun made the English; her light brown hair, cut to the shoulders, framing eyes the color of warm brewed tea (iced tea, Cedric said); her high cheekbones and lips more generous than her sisters' could ever be. "Pretty like you," she said. "The hair and skin different, but pretty like you."

"He was the one who chopped her up?"

"And feed her to the pigs. They do that when they lose their soul."

"Cedric said I was coming here to meet my lover."

Mary Christophe pointed to a chair. "Sit." She pulled the rocking chair and sat down next to her. "He's another one who lose his soul," she said.

"You think he would do that?" Rosa locked her fingers under her knees.

"He read books. He worship the brain."

"But he wouldn't do that?" Her voice was strained.

"All he do is brainwork."

"He never hit me."

"No." Mary Christophe rocked slowly. "No. Man like Cedric don't hit on the outside." She closed her eyes. "No, man like Cedric make your flower bloom inside."

"My flower?"

"Your blows." She opened her eyes and looked directly at Rosa. "Woman here, their flower be on their arms and legs. But your Mister Man, he know better. He know it hurt more when you take your blows on the inside." She pressed Rosa's clasped hands. "Stay here tonight."

Rosa told her of her plans for Monday.

"Stay Sunday, too."

She would come back later, Rosa told her, but first she had to go to Our Lady.

"Why? What you want to go to her for? You not safe here, you know, Rosa. Don't think because they don't lose their soul here, you safe. Police wear them down about this man they arrest. They tired and they angry. Don't find yourself in their way."

Rosa said she wanted to thank Our Lady.

"What for? What she do?"

"Cedric," said Rosa. "All the pain left him."

"And the cancer, too," said Mary Christophe. It was not a question.

Rosa looked at her in amazement.

"I tell you already I'm no obeahwoman. Don't start looking at me as if I'm a obeahwoman. People talk. Even hospital people. A man that work in Colonial Hospital live here. He tell everybody Cedric cancer disappear. I listen."

"You think it was the medicine you gave me?"

Mary Christophe shrugged.

"The novena I said to Our Lady?"

"Why you pray for him so?"

It was the same question Zuela had asked her and she had no answer to give her. "Because you feel bad?" Zuela had asked her.

"Because I feel guilty," she said to Mary Christophe. Her hands fell to her sides.

"Guilty? Guilty about what? Guilty for wanting man?"

Blood rose dark and red beneath Rosa's cheeks.

"Don't have shame before me. I raise you from the cradle. I know. I name you and that I sorry for. But still I don't make you so. I only give you the name for what already was meant to be in you. Think I never see you on the bed in your bedroom?" She reached over and held Rosa's hand. "Don't blame yourself. Is Nature make you so. Sometimes Nature make some woman need to love man bad, bad, bad. Some woman, it don't matter if they never make love. Man is a problem for them. They could live without what man and woman do in the night. Not you, Rosa. But that don't mean is wrong for you to be so. You hearing me, Rosa? Woman like you not wrong."

"Then why am I poison? You told me it was I who was killing Cedric."

Mary Christophe squeezed her hand. "No! No! I don't say so. You not poison. Not you yourself. Is he who *see* you like poison. Remember I tell you about that doctor wife? She not poison either, but the doctor *see* her as poison for him, so he want to get rid of her. Look how she end up. No, you and she was sisters all right, but not how your Mr. Cedric say. You not bad. You not crazy. I know you, Rosa. You are a loving kind of woman. You just make mistake to give your love to the wrong man. The right man don't see you like poison."

"It's too late for the right man."

"It's never too late to find happiness."

"I'm never going back to him, Mary Christophe."

"I know that. I know that. Don't feel bad for that."

"No. I know that is what I should do, but still I feel guilty for what I wished had happened to him."

Mary Christophe held on to her hand. "Let me tell you, Rosa, I love you like the daughter I never had and I tell you now is normal what you wish for. Is normal to want what's bad to leave you and make it pay for hurting you." She touched the bark on her own face. "The wolf's mark," she said. "That's what they call it. I try to kill it, to kill the wolf

236

that mark me so. One night he squeeze my face and all my joints so hard, I tried to kill him. I had knife in my hand that I sharpened already. I was one inch—one inch from stabbing him here." She stuck her finger on her brow between her eyes. "One inch, and my hand pulled back. I fall down on my knees and ask God to forgive me after that. I tell God I have no right to take a life I couldn't make. Even if it's my own life. I pray and I pray and I pray until little by little I begin to realize is God who put the wolf mark on me. Is God who called the wolf. I praying for help from the very same God who responsible for giving this to me." She smiled, a bitter smile. "I not vex. I not saying that God wrong. God, or whoever you call God. He make me. He design me. He could put on me whatever He want. I have no say and I know I have no say. But that don't mean I have to like it and I don't have to wish I could throw it away. I don't have to wish I could kill it."

"I thought it was a butterfly," said Rosa.

"The wolf's claw." Mary Christophe let go of her hand.

"When I was little I used to think a butterfly came from the cane fields and landed across your nose. He loved you so much he wanted to stay."

Mary Christophe sucked her teeth. "And he stay till he frighten you so much, you run for your life."

Rosa lowered her head.

"It don't matter." Mary Christophe leaned back in her chair. "I forget. I forget all of that already."

"I'm glad you didn't kill yourself. I'm glad God held back your hand."

"You hearing me, child, but you still don't hear me. Maybe He cares. Maybe He looking down on you right now like He look down every day to see what you doing, but I don't get my satisfaction from that. Love. I get my satisfaction from loving other people and from learning to love myself. Even with the wolf's mark."

Again the word *love*. Rosa asked her, "Love?"

"Yes, love." Mary Christophe sat up. "If you love yourself, it's natural to want him to leave you."

"But not natural to cause him to die."

"Nobody can take you when your time not come. You think is me or you or Our Lady that save Cedric? Is Cedric himself. Cedric time not come."

"But I know the medicine you gave me helped him. That's why I came here. I wanted to thank you for giving it to me."

"Don't thank me. I give it to you because you want it, not because I think it could work with the man you married. Sometimes I see people drink twice the amount I give you and still they die. Sometimes they wear mojo bags around their necks like scapulars and pray harder than you, and they end up six feet under."

Rosa found her words impossible to bear. "How could you live without God, Mary Christophe? How could you live without prayer?"

"I never said I lived without God. Just not the God you believe in. You want control. You want things to be just so as you arrange them. And when they not so, you pray to God to arrange them back for you. But life is not so, Rosa. You can't always say when and how. Sometimes things happen just for happening sake. Like this thing on my face. I don't make my god follow my orders. He order me around when and how He want. Is not prayers alone help you, Rosa. Most times is you yourself have to change what you don't like. And I think that's how He plan it to be."

But Rosa wanted to thank Our Lady and went to the shrine in spite of Mary Christophe's warnings that Laventille was dangerous, that until the police released the man who had put the ring on Melda's finger, the hill was safe for no one, not even for the women living there. For Rosa believed, if not God, Our Lady had cured Cedric of his cancer and would save her, too, from any danger that could come to her on her way to her shrine. She believed, too, with all her heart, that her salvation had to begin with her repentance. For regardless of what Mary Christophe and Zuela had told her, she knew in the depths of her soul that she had not merely wished that Cedric would die, but she had willed it. Willed it as if her mind had power to consummate what her body lacked courage to do. No beginning could start without her remorse for that sin. Monday could not begin until she confessed to Our Lady that from the day Cedric put his finger to his lips and warned her to be careful, to be careful that what had happened to Paula Inge could happen to her, she had laid his body on that same beach in Otahiti, between the same bamboo and the same sea reeds. She had gutted him like a fish. She had thrown his entrails on the sand for the vultures. She had left his rotting carcass for the tide. She had waited for the sharks to rip him to pieces and devour him. And when the currents swept away what had remained of him far into the sea, she had felt a pleasure so thrilling, so exhilarating, so absolute that only praying for him eased the guilt of it afterward.

❦ Chapter 19 ❧

*A*nd so Rosa walked up the hill to the shrine of Our Lady, refusing Mary Christophe's final pleas that, at the very least, she should accompany her. But Rosa did not go there alone. Others were following her: others who had been tracking her long before she left Mary Christophe's house; others who had seen her get out of a taxi at the Chinaman's shop; who had noticed her white pearls and her batiste blouse embroidered with red and yellow flowers and green leaves around a neckline that could have dropped to her breasts but didn't—didn't because she had pulled the red drawstring and tied it in a bow at the center, just below her collar bone, so that the top of the blouse fell above the pearls. Nevertheless they had seen her bare arms, golden brown below the white cap sleeves of the batiste blouse. They had seen the outline of her thighs when the folds of her skirt dropped in that gully in her lap before she lifted her legs to get out of the taxi. Then, minutes later, when she stood on her toes to read the sign the Chinaman's friend had nailed to the shop door, they had seen more—the slope of her backside that filled out and dipped when a sudden wind blew and plastered her thin cotton skirt against her legs; and the whiteness of the part it gutted on the back of her head when the gust flung her hair forward and glued the thick strands to the sides of her face.

She had asked one of the men to tell her where could she find a taxi, but they knew she would not remember which one she had asked, nor would she remember he had a smirk on his face when he said to her that she had no business being on Nelson Street so early in the morning and without her man. Not a woman pretty like you, he said.

She needed a taxi, she told him. He said he would call Battoo's and get one for her. But she said, "No. Not a private taxi. I don't want a limousine with a chauffeur." She was just going to Laventille, she said. "To see my friend Mary Christophe."

The cluster of people around the Chinaman's shop mimicked her words in their minds. *Just going to Laventille.* They knew women like her didn't think they needed a chauffeur to go to Laventille. They were the wives and daughters of the colonial owners of Trinidad. They believed they could go wherever they wanted and no one would dare harm them.

One of the men broke away from the group. He knew Mary Christophe, he said. "Last time I see how she walk you down the hill. I see how she guard you."

Rosa smiled. "She wasn't *guarding* me," she said. "She was waiting with me till a taxi came."

The man clenched his fists, but the people knew she did not know why he did that. She did not care that she had made him feel like an empty calabash, like a schoolboy, like one of those painted devils at Carnival time that frightened no one with his fire-red pitch fork.

"Yet calabash make you jump," he lashed out at her.

Still, the people believed she would not remember his face. She would not remember that he was the one who pointed at her bare leg when she raised her skirt to step into the back seat of the taxi; the one who whispered in the driver's ear something she could not hear. They knew she would not remember the face of the taxi driver, either, though he tried to warn her: "This is not a place, not at this time leastways, for a white lady, and one as pretty as you, to be taking a taxi by herself up Laventille."

And the taxi driver knew, after he stopped his car to let her out near Mary Christophe's house, that she had not noticed that he did not drive back down the hill, but parked his car next to the gru-gru boeuf tree at a bend in the road. But neither had she paid attention to the other car that had been following them up the hill and that had pulled up behind him when he stopped. For the taxi driver believed that women like her did not notice people like him, at least not in the daytime.

But he was wrong. Rosa had noticed them all: the one who wore his cap low on his brow, the one whose mustache grew down the sides of his mouth to his chin, the one whose nostrils flared, the one who bit the toothpick between his clenched teeth, the one who had a scar across his right cheek, the one who limped, the one who laughed the loudest when she clutched the collar of her dress and tightened it around her neck. She had forgotten the face of the one who said he saw her when breadfruit made her jump, but afterward, when he reminded her, she remembered him. He was the one with the bushy eyebrows.

But she was not afraid of them. The black-and-white wall of bodies and tattered undershirts that blocked the path to Mary Christophe's did not scare her, though she was forced to stand at the side of the road until Mary Christophe came to rescue her. The hatred in the eyes of the seven boys troubled her (they were too young to have lost their innocence), but the resentment that hardened the faces of the men was familiar to her. She had seen that age-old anger in the faces of the people who worked in the sugar factories and the rum distilleries for men like her father (or the man she had thought was her father). And although she did not doubt that what Mary Christophe had told her would one day come to pass, that, without warning, without announcement, without apparent motive, resentment would turn hearts to stone, would explode from chests like gunfire, she did not think it would be aimed at her. For having discovered she was not a pure white woman, she was certain they knew it, too. She believed they recognized her black blood in her cheekbones that rose high on her face, in her fluid glide that began at her hip, and in her backside, which caused Cedric to declare, surrendering one day to a moment of nostalgia that could have redeemed him, "If I had not known better, I would say it was throwback from Africa."

No, she had not feared them, for no matter how they pretended to frighten her with their stone faces, she was convinced they knew better. And even if some were uncertain, Mary Christophe, the woman they feared but respected, was proof enough that she was one of them. She would not have protected her like a daughter, held her hand and brought her to the safety of her house if it were otherwise. So when Rosa heard the footsteps behind her on her way to the shrine, she was concerned but not afraid; troubled, but not worried. They kept a good distance behind her and nobody spoke. Once, when she turned around, she thought she recognized the taxi driver. Her heart froze, but her fears vanished in an instant when he smiled and waved at her. When she turned back again soon afterward, he was laughing with two men. So she believed what seemed logical to her then—it was a long ride to Laventille, so he had stayed to visit his friends before going back to the city.

Yet Rosa was glad when she reached the top of the hill to see other women at the shrine of Our Lady, though none were as light skinned as she. She noticed that difference immediately and became slightly apprehensive, though not sufficiently to believe she was in danger. True, usually on Saturdays there were people from the valley at the shrine who came to make their devotions to Our Lady, and true the chapel was usually open, but she accepted the explanation one of the women gave her: "Everybody gone to the Cathedral in Port-of-Spain. Archbishop saying a special Mass, so trouble stop in Trinidad."

She should have remembered. The special Masses had started ever since the body of Paula Inge washed up on the beach in Otahiti, though weeks before, two hearts, assumed to be female, had been found among the garbage. But that was in the La Basse where the poor people lived. Now, just days ago, two more hearts were discovered in the early dawn, luminescent with pink beads of dew. They had been carefully placed under the red anthurium lilies in the elegant Botanical Gardens across the savannah in the valley. "Is white woman heart Boysie using now to rub on his racehorse. Now they lock him up for sure." Ena had tried to console her that the danger would pass soon.

Rosa kneeled before the shrine of Our Lady and clasped her hands under her chin. There was nothing unusual about the Archbishop saying Mass to put an end to the slaughter. There was nothing unusual about the priest closing the chapel to join his parishioners in the Cathedral. She closed her eyes and thanked Our Lady for saving her from total damnation. She had not thought of poisoning Cedric, but perhaps one day she would have. She thanked her, too, for the miracle she had wrought for

Cedric. For in spite of Cedric's arrogance, Rosa believed that the first x-ray that was taken of Cedric's stomach was as valid as the second. So she thanked Our Lady that Cedric was alive and well, but not because she wanted Cedric to be alive and well, but because she was glad she had spared her the responsibility and guilt for his death.

She was so deep in prayer in the rosary she had begun to Our Lady that she did not hear when the first stone hit the ground. Her eyes were shut so tightly that she did not see when the first woman rose from her knees. She did not feel the absence of the others, either, though the wind now blew freely around her, making sails of the skirt she had anchored tightly under her knees.

She did not hear when the first man said, "Melda," but she had felt his hot breath on her throat and she knew when he pulled the red draw-string of her batiste blouse and broke it.

"For Melda," he said again. "For the innocent man you have locked up in the jail. For the guilty man you let roam free."

She did not see them. But they had not covered her eyes. One of the men grabbed her from behind her neck and pulled her down to the ground. Another man looped his arms under her armpits, and though she had eyes to see him and them, she found it was better to look up at the grieving sky draped purple with the embers of the dying sun, and at the pitying gaze of Our Lady, who, nevertheless, did not turn her head when they dragged her through the dirt and into the slime in that clearing behind her. And it was better there to block out all sound except the squeals of the pigs; to fuse the obscenities they hailed on her into one long scream, even though blood poured out of the side of her mouth when they struck her. Better after that, after they silenced her, to lock her eyes into the eyes of the man who held her down, to make herself feel nothing, hear nothing but the patter of sweat falling from his forehead onto hers. It was better to see his eyes and the eyes of the man who replaced him and the eyes of the other man and of the other man, and to make believe it was one man, one pair of eyes she had locked into hers, and that the sweat that fell on her face was the drizzle of raindrops that had soothed her that one morning when her father slapped her and stopped her from crying after Mary Christophe left: "She was just a servant, Goddamnit. We don't cry for a servant."

And so she saw only one pair of eyes and felt only raindrops on her face and the dull pressure of rods ramming back and forth between her legs, but no pain, no pain until the mouth above hers shaped a word, *beg*: "Beg. Say you want it. Beg. Say you want it or I beat you."

Then the pain was excruciating. Then the memory was blinding.

"Mother." The word slipped to her tongue from among the many that bombarded her brain: *Where was that little girl's mother? Where was she when her daughter put red lipstick on her mouth, a string of pearls around her neck?*

A blow to her head absorbed the pain. Her rosary fell from her fingers into the soft mud around her, the tiny white beads twinkling like stars as they sank. Purple turned to black in the sky above her. Then all was dark in that clearing a priest had blessed, in that enclosure meant to protect humans from two pigs no longer beasts, but not humans, though they had eaten the flesh of a woman a human had slaughtered.

Mary Christophe was cradling her in her arms when she woke, rocking her like a baby, saying over and over again, "I tell you not to come up here. Not always Our Lady save you. I tell you that, Rosa. Remember I tell you that?" The butterfly on her face fluttered its wings and then closed them. Its body disappeared in the folds on her cheeks. "I tell you but you don't listen. Not always she save you. Not always."

Rosa laid her quivering body against the hardness of her chest and Mary Christophe let her stay like that until her quivering stopped. Then she placed Rosa's limp arms around the bend of her waist, and holding her up with an arm grown too strong from holding too many women like her, Mary Christophe lifted her to her feet and wrapped her in a blanket a woman had given her. She was a woman who had come out of the tenebrous stillness of the falling dusk, whispering a prayer, "I'm sorry. We're sorry." Then she disappeared into the line of silent women that had formed along the sides of the street in that town of tears—a corridor of women sobbing so quietly they could not be heard. Ten of them wore flowers on their arms.

In the house Rosa said in a voice Mary Christophe remembered from another time of promise and hope: "When I was a little girl, before

I saw that man through the hibiscus, I believed in fairy tales. I had such fantasies! I thought one day, when I grew up, a man would come on a beautiful white horse and he would ask for me, 'Rosa? Rosa?' I would answer, 'Yes. I am Rosa.' And he would take me to live with him in his tiny blue house with a white picket fence, where red, red roses climbed through the pretty white trellises. And, oh, they would smell so sweet."

Then Mary Christophe went outside for the buckets of rainwater she had collected in her backyard so she could wash away the stink of the animal sweat, so she could cleanse the smear of the animal thighs that had hammered the last nails in the coffin of a pubescent dream that never was realized.

First she wiped the dried blood from Rosa's mouth and then she bent her legs in the crook of her arm and lowered her body into the tub of rainwater and shining bush leaves. She soaped and rinsed her hair and her neck and her arms and her breasts. Then she helped her to her feet again, and washed her belly and her buttocks and her thighs and her legs and her feet. And when she was finished, she whispered in her ear that she loved her. She had always loved her. She had loved her from the moment the midwife had put her in her arms. Still whispering this to her, and about the times they had spent together, she washed her in her secret place, in the place where the men had violated her. And after she had dried and powdered her and dressed her in one of her own nighties, she put her in her bed and spread a mattress on the floor for herself, leaving a space between it and the bed for Rosa to walk to the rocking chair, in case she got up and remembered, and so preferred sitting there than lying on her back.

But Mary Christophe need not have done that, for Rosa would sleep for hours. She had been soothed by the bath and the restorative power of forgetting that allows us humans to erase that which we cannot allow ourselves to remember, and so nothing would wake Rosa in that bed, or wake Mary Christophe, though once she stirred in her sleep, but not to consciousness. For the thud that disturbed her sleep ended with a swish so soft and alluring that she drifted to dreaming, pulled to the false serenity of that other world by the deceptive calm of the evening tide caressing the sand to surrender, rolling it inexorably out to the open sea.

✑ Chapter 20 ✑

*N*ot far away, in a tiny blue house bordered with ornate white frets and pink and orange bougainvillea—a house not unlike the one Rosa had dreamed of when she was a little girl—Zuela was asking Tong Lee to paint her.

"You think you can do it so it look exactly like I look?"

And Tong Lee who had studied her face for hours all that day on the beach at Manzanilla ran to his bedroom for his drawing book and watercolors.

Moments before, they had arrived at Tong Lee's house, after returning the truck Tong Lee had borrowed from a friend. It was Agnes's idea that they go to his house, for in all her sixteen years she had never seen her mother so happy, so peaceful.

"Your present to me, Ma, for my birthday. He can walk you back home."

Perhaps she should have known better, but Zuela could not remember one time in her life when she had been happier—except those days when her mother was alive, and the day Tong Lee said she had laughed from her heart. But her happiness during those times paled when compared with her contentment now. She felt like a young girl on her first date. She bit her lips to bring color to them and fussed with her hair in the mirror of the truck, smoothing her long black plait down her back and pushing back the strands that had fallen across her face.

"You look beautiful," Agnes said in her ear before she slipped out of the seat next to her with the baby in her arms. "Don't worry. I'll look out for them."

Perhaps she should have thought, as she had never had time to think about herself, that Agnes was too young to be given the responsibility of taking care of a two-year-old baby and eight other children. She was too young to be left alone with the Chinaman having nightmares in the attic above them. But that night, the end of a day she had wished were endless, was not a night to think such thoughts. It was not a night to consider such dark realities. It was a night for dreaming, for holding on to the hope that was ignited in her heart when the Chinaman said Yes, she could go to the beach. Yes, Tong Lee could take her to Manzanilla. So Zuela let herself be swayed by Agnes's confidence that in the year while she lived with the nuns in the convent she had not forgotten how to heat pelau, how to wash dishes, how to bathe children, how to put them to bed. Alan said he would help.

Now seated in the bamboo armchair where Tong Lee said he would paint her, Zuela felt a youthfulness she had all but forgotten.

"What you look for, Tong Lee, when you look at me like that and move my face? You trying to find the best way to draw me?"

But Tong Lee could have drawn her with his eyes shut tight.

"Yes," he said, and he turned her face from side to side and shifted her body this way and that. Yet he did those things only so he could touch her, only so he could feel her nearness to him. He put his hand on her cheeks and on her shoulders and on her arms as if he were positioning her for her portrait, but he did so because he was afraid, because he did not trust the trembling in his heart that urged him to hold her, to clasp her to his bosom.

"Then tell me what you see when you look at me."

"The Orinoco, the jungle trees."

She laughed. "No, tell me, really."

"A yellow and red macaw. A scarlet ibis."

"That's what I tell you about today, on the beach."

"Not about the macaw or the ibis."

"Yes, but I tell you something like that. I tell you about the herons and the parrots. You tell me what *you* see."

"A woman."

"What kind of a woman?"

"I draw you now," he said.

"Tell me. What kind of a woman you see in me?"

Tong Lee looked down to his paint box and stirred the watercolors.

"Tell me."

He couldn't tell her without giving himself away.

"Tell me."

"A beautiful woman," he said. "A woman more beautiful . . . " His voice faltered. He cleared his throat. "A woman more beautiful . . . " He could not continue. He put down his paintbrush. "It's late."

"A woman more beautiful than what?"

He shut his drawing book.

"More beautiful than what?"

"I draw you another day."

"Than what?"

"Ho Sang might wake up."

Her face aged before him in that single second. Now hating himself for the habit he had made of not permitting himself to love, he reached for her hand to still his and hers.

How easily he had lied! How quickly he had tried to rescue himself from falling down the chasm that petrified him. He knew that, even now, the opium he had seen Ho Sang light would keep him numb, would make him useless until the next morning. For before he left to go to the beach with Zuela and the children, he had made one more trip to that attic. Afraid of what the day with Zuela would do to his heart? Yes, he was afraid. So he needed to steel himself against the futility of hoping; he needed to remember that she could never be his, that no matter how hateful he was, Ho Sang was her husband.

Ho Sang was striking a match to the hardened resin when he entered the candle-lit room. He thought to say, his conscience urged him to say, *Not now, not so early in the morning*, but his tongue was struck dumb as if a leaden weight had been put on it.

"Lin me, Lin fa," the Chinaman was singing.

Against his will Tong Lee moved closer to him.

The Chinaman grabbed his shirt and pulled him toward him. "Chinese wife. Chinese daughter: Lin me, Lin fa."

After he broke away from him, Tong Lee convinced himself that it was a good sign Ho Sang had said their names. A breakthrough. And perhaps on a different day, at a different time, before he had broken the bindings he had wrapped around his eyes, he would have sat with him and helped him remember more. He would have helped him go back to the time before the blood, so he would know that it was Zuela, not Lin me, who was now his wife. He would have helped him go back to the time afterward when he crawled on his belly like a snake, so he would know it was through Zuela he had to get forgiveness from them. But not that day. Tong Lee would not spoil that day he would spend with Zuela.

He glanced back at Ho Sang from the entrance of the attic and felt no compulsion to help him, no pity for him when he saw him beat his head with his cuffed fists and he heard the coming of the storm: "Lin me, Lin fa. Lin me, Lin fa." For he no longer had his schoolboy gratitude to Ho Sang that kept him watchful, if not caring, of the land mines that would destroy him. Now it did not matter to him whether Ho Sang lived or died, whether he remembered or forgot, only that he remembered two things—that Lin me and Lin fa were dead; that Zuela was alive. So, satisfied that Ho Sang had begun finally to drive a wedge between Zuela and the ghosts that haunted him, he told himself it was better to leave him alone, better for the ghosts to torment him, for they could, for it was possible that they could, force him to set her free.

"No," he said, tightening his grasp on Zuela's hand. "He won't wake up."

"Then why you lie?"

"Because I was afraid."

"Afraid? Afraid of what?"

He had always admired her beauty. Now he admired her soul. In spite of the desert the Chinaman had created for her, her spirit had bloomed. She had none of the frivolity left in women from the headiness of their youth (the Chinaman had made certain she would not), but she

250

had dignity, a quiet self-assurance that came from measuring everything: the time to sleep, the time to cook, the time to clean, the time to work in the shop with the Chinaman, the time to love her children. And she had strength, a determination that came from calculating everything: the time it would take for them to grow, for them to learn, for her to prepare them to leave the shop, for them to be free.

She had squandered nothing, always planning, always watching, always counting. Except now. Except for this one day, more than fourteen hours since they first left the Chinaman's shop, when time did not seem to matter to her, when she let it move on and swallow her, and not once did she notice its passing, not once did she say, "I think we should go back."

It was he who had taken note of the movement of the sun. It was he who said, "It's late," and tried to put an end to the day. Now he felt unworthy of her.

"There is nothing to be afraid of," she said. "At least, not of me."

Panic made him think of bringing up the old ache, the difference between their ages, but that lie was too obvious even for one who was tottering on the brink of a chasm. She was, as he had already known, older than her years. He was, as she had told him, younger than the Chinaman. But only in years.

"What you so 'fraid of? Tell me." She brought his hand to her lips and kissed his fingers.

He shut his eyes and looked down into the chasm. Before they sliced off his father's head, they gave his father two chances to save his life: *You or her?*

Me.

His mother's headless body fell with a thud to the ground.

You or the boy?

Me.

They could not bear the intensity of that love.

"Good friends," Tong Lee told Zuela. "That is what we will be till death do us part." He, too, was afraid of the dizzying depths of his father's love. He, too, was terrified by the joy his father relished in martyrdom.

Zuela's eyes grew misty. "Friends? That's all?"

"You are married," he said. But he knew he was lying again. It did not matter to him that she was married. He removed his hand from hers and made a desperate attempt to justify his contemplation of suicide: his soul would die if he could not have her. "Is wrong," he said. "You are Ho Sang's wife."

Tears rolled down her eyes and she wept as if her world had ended. Once before, he had seen those tears. They had made his body tremble. Then the ring slipped from his hand and fell to the terrazzo floor in the back of the church where she was to be married.

He reached for her. "I do anything. I do anything for you."

"Then love me," she said. "Love me like I was a woman."

He touched her breasts and plunged down to his salvation. Because ultimately he had not forgotten the joys of love, because ultimately he had been given love, had been showered with it, washed with it until it had penetrated every pore of his being. That mother whose eyes shone with gratitude when the blade moved from her husband's neck to hers; that father who dropped his head for him the moment they asked their question, both had shown him love, both had taught him about love. He knew, therefore, how to receive it, how to give it. He had only to release it from behind the trapdoor he had secured with passion that contained no affection, carnal pleasure that neither gave nor required caring, and they fused—sex and love; desire and adoration.

He felt the muscles of her body grow limp when he put his mouth on the nipples of her breasts. Slowly, but finally, the armor she, too, wore to protect a love she had known and was taken away, loosened and dissolved. For she, too, had a mother who loved her, and when she died, she lost a love that was never replaced.

"Tell me my real name."

As much as he wanted to give her everything—her memories before the Chinaman, the time when she had known happiness in her home in Venezuela—he had no answer to give her.

"Chinaman call me Zuela, but only because he find me in Venezuela. Then my father call me Hija and only because I was his daughter. My mother, she listen to my father. So tell me, what is my real name?"

He did not know it. Ho Sang never told him. Zuela Simona—that was the only name he knew. He could only press her to his heart.

"Then what name you call me?"

This time he had the answer. He did not hesitate. "The name you want to call yourself," he said.

She smiled. "I think about that. I think about that." She shut her eyes. "Maybe a bird name. Maybe I choose that. Maybe a bird that could fly where it want to and could sing when it want, because it want to."

He brushed his hand over her hair and she, thinking of iguanas, murmured, "And do that down my back, too." And when he did it, the hair on her neck remained soft and still, and her pores stayed closed. "Do it, more," she said. "More."

He wanted to know how else he could please her, and though she should not have known what to tell him, because in twenty-one years with the Chinaman she had not known, she had not found one touch from him that had pleased her, not once, not in that eternity she had spent with him, she took Tong Lee's hand and guided it to places that gave her such rapture, she screamed out loud with the joy of it. Afterward she confessed, her eyes wide with the wonder of her new knowledge, that once she had asked Rosa: "How could I ever want *that?*"

So Tong Lee asked her now about the dark. "You said you felt safe in the dark in Venezuela. You feel safe in the dark now?" His voice was reassuring—a promise of a net to catch her if she fell.

"Second time," she said. "First time when I was small and I knew, no matter what, my mother would protect me."

Still, he wanted to give her more. He needed to repay her for her generosity, to thank her for saving his life. For when he held her, when he sank into her softness, he felt the crust around his heart crack, split open. He felt renewed, reborn. Human.

"How I make your life easier?" he asked her.

"It easier when Chinaman die," she answered him. "But it easier, one way, harder the other."

So he told her what he had wanted to tell her that first day in his house when he saw her body crumple like the folds on an accordion, after she understood the full truth of the Chinaman's threat to her.

"Chinaman keep his money in the wood box where he put his pipes. A lot of money," he said. "Don't care if he dead and Luck Chow take the shop, you still have the money."

For half an hour Zuela snuggled against Tong Lee, savoring her choices—to leave the Chinaman or to stay with the Chinaman. To leave, take the money and begin life again with her children but risk the chance that the Chinaman would go hunting for her. Or to stay. Stay and count the days, the hours when the Chinaman's coughing would finally kill him. Stay and still have Tong Lee.

"Whichever," Tong Lee said. "I'll be here for you no matter what."

But what would happen in those thirty minutes between the time she basked in those choices and the time she returned to the Chinaman's shop in Nelson Street would change her life forever, though she would not know that until she awoke the next morning and saw her daughter counting the tips of her fingers as she had once taught her to do; saw on her face the same dreaded gaze, the same vacant stare that had ended her own girlhood. Then the world would stop for her and leave her one option. *One,* and it was not even an option; it was not a choice. It was a decision that would be no decision, for it was as ineluctable as the tides, as bound to the laws of the universe as the illusion of a falling sun, and as inevitable as the phantasm of a rising moon.

Ho Sang had lit the brown resin but he did not smoke it. Even after he could no longer hear the roar of the truck taking Zuela, Tong Lee and his children to Manzanilla, he had remained where Tong Lee had left him, his fists raised, though no longer pounding his head, but still fending the ghosts that swirled around him.

He had not blown out the candle. Its yellow flame guarded him, insulated him, protected him from their fury. As long as there was light, the ghosts would not enter him. Then a wind—quiet, deceptive, stalking the ground like a hungry cat—stole past the empty garbage cans, past the border of refuse left in the wake of the street cleaners' brooms, eased about the legs of the people huddled around the sign on the door of the shop, pounced, blasted against the back of one, a woman, rose and blew through the spaces of his window shutters. The candle flame flickered and dimmed, and in the infinitesimal moment before it glowed again, the swirling ghosts saw their advantage.

Ho Sang grasped a slat on the jalousie to steady himself from the force of their entry. Before they enveloped him and brought him to the Land of the Dead, he saw the woman, Zuela's friend, standing in front of his shop, looking up at him.

Boysie had pointed her out to him years ago. "Her name is Rosa. She play with your woman when we went down the Bocas."

The ghosts saw her, too, and remembered. Rosa and Zuela. They used to play together in the cane fields on the Orange Grove estate.

"Play? Play like a child play?" The Chinaman couldn't believe that was possible. "She too old to play."

But now the ghosts came to Zuela's defense.

Because she was a child.

Ho Sang let go of the slat and squeezed his eyes tight.

Because you killed a child.

Ho Sang opened his eyes. The flame had gone out. There was no light to break the darkness, no light to chase the ghosts away.

And you killed a woman.

He pressed his hands against his ears.

You killed a woman and a child.

No!

But the ghosts would not leave him or give him rest. They held his hands when he reached for his pipe to suck in the memory-killing fumes.

A wife and child.

No!

A wife and daughter.

Not them. Not a wife and a daughter. It was not he. It was the People. It was they who killed them. They had wanted his head, too. They said they would mount his head in the middle of the village to warn the others.

But they slaughtered us.

He had shown them where the sacks of silver were hidden. He thought the silver was enough, that it would pay for his life and for theirs.

But you ran away.

Because he knew they would still want revenge. But he did not

255

think they would take revenge on his wife and daughter. They had done nothing. They were innocent.

You should have come for us. You should have taken us with you.

He thought they were safe.

Liar!

He came back for them.

When it was too late and you thought you were safe.

No!

Our blood is on your hands. Theirs, too. Three hundred men.

Not theirs.

Theirs!

He had done nothing. His fault was in loving his father. His fault was in wanting to be like his father, to be as rich as he, as powerful as he. Any boy would want to be like his father.

Three hundred men.

Didn't they choose to follow his father, too? Didn't the opium give them money to feed their families, silver to buy boats and build houses? The greed was not his father's alone. They knew the risks. The Commissioner was at war with the British. It was treachery to defy him. Yet no one would have guessed it would be the People who would unleash the bloodbath, or that they would be so vindictive. No one would have guessed the innocent would have perished.

So many of them.

The ghosts yanked him down. He fell into a bottomless hole. The dark penetrated him. A multitude of spirits reached for him. A father. Tong Lee's father.

He fought him off. He had not even known him when he was alive. How could he be held responsible for his death?

A wife. A mother of a little boy.

He fell deeper into the hole. Fire licked his heels.

Was he to burn for her, too? When he took pity on Tong Lee (pity was what he called it), the boy said that none of the women and children had been massacred. How was he to have known he was lying? How was he to have guessed his mother had been caught on the razor edge of the People's swords?

Three mothers.

The fire scorched his thighs. It reached past his waist. Somewhere in his brain he heard Tong Lee's voice. "The blood will never leave you till you ask for forgiveness." But he could find no reason for contrition. What had he done that required repentance?

Three mothers: the mother of Tong Lee, the mother of Lin fa, the mother of Agnes and nine other children.

Hadn't he saved Tong Lee twice? Hadn't he come back for Lin me? Hadn't he married Zuela?

Now the flames engulfed him; the fire ravaged him, but not for long. The late morning sun burned through the lingering shadows of the dawn. Light poured through the spaces in the slats of the window jalousies. In minutes the spirits were gone.

Smoldering, ashen gray on the outside, bubbling red in the inside, Ho Sang groped for his pipe on the wooden box, relit it, inhaled, and sunk into the welcoming arms of Death-still-Living.

But when night came again hours later, the demons from below the Land of the Dead came looking for him. Then his torment was unbearable and he begged the spirits of the dead to return and rescue him.

"Lin me! Lin fa!"

Agnes heard him call out their names, and though she did not know who they were or what his calling them meant, she feared for her mother. She would go to him, she said to Alan. "If nobody goes, he will notice Ma is not here."

"I'll go."

"You're a boy. He'll sooner think I'm Ma."

They could not have imagined, they could not have conceived the nightmares that made the Chinaman call out again: "Lin me! Lin fa!"

Less than an hour before, Agnes had fed the children and put them to bed. She and Alan had been talking in the tunneled light of the reading lamp, remembering the sea, remembering the laughter.

"You think she and Tong Lee?" Agnes had dared to dream.

"No, he helps him out in the shop." *Him.* They never named him; they never called him Father. "Tong Lee is a friend," he said. "No more."

Twice the Chinaman called out for Lin me and Lin fa, the third time for their mother. Agnes told Alan he could not go. In the dark, the Chinaman would mistake her for her mother. He would know Alan was a boy, even if he did not speak. The fourth time the Chinaman called out the names of two women that ended with Zuela's, Agnes did not have to convince him. The Chinaman's scream was bloodcurdling.

Agnes lowered her head at the entrance of the attic, as she remembered she used to do. She was just four, too short for the beams to strike her, but like all little girls, she loved imitating her mother.

It was desperation that had made Zuela take her to the attic that first time. Agnes had held on to her dress and refused to let her go. Fearing she would awaken her baby brothers and cause the Chinaman to hurl curses on them, Zuela took her with her when the Chinaman called.

"Shut your eyes and don't open them until you reach five hundred," Zuela told her. "Five hundred, not before."

Three times Zuela took her there, and only one time did Agnes disobey her. She had passed counting to five hundred and Zuela had not returned, so she spread her fingers wide across her face and peeked.

Afterward, her mother explained, "Female iguanas do that, too." But Zuela never took her to the attic again, only her baby brothers, and only until Agnes was old enough to watch them for her, which was when she was five.

Alan said the Chinaman would want to smoke the ganja leaves. They were in a small tin can on the box, near to his bed. "Spread the ganja on the square paper under the tin can." He showed her how. "Roll the paper, light it, inhale and blow the smoke in his face. That's what Ma does."

She said she would do it exactly that way—the way her mother would.

"Nothing else," Alan warned. "If he wants anything else, call me."

"Wants?"

"Call me."

The moment she entered the attic, the Chinaman sensed her presence. He had reached *Zuela,* in his chant of *Lin me, Lin fa, Zuela* when he saw the shadow of a woman opening and then closing the door. His hand grew still against the side of the bed. He craned his head forward and peered into the darkness.

"Lin me?"

The roundness of the face was the same; the curve of the back when she bent her head to the wooden box beside his bed, the same—the same as it was before he found her bleeding from her neck at the root of the sapling.

"Lin me? Lin fa?"

Against the blackness of the tin can, pale fingers glowed—pure as a baby's fingers.

"Lin me, Lin fa."

Against the whiteness of the thin paper, a pink tongue glistened—pure as a baby's tongue.

"Lin me! Lin fa! Zuela!"

The demons rose. He fought them. He propped his body on the crutches of his elbows.

"Lin me! Lin fa! Zuela?"

A plait of hair fell across one shoulder.

"Zuela?"

She had already inhaled, filled her mouth like a blowfish.

"Zuela?"

She bent over him. Low. Inches above his face.

"Zuela?" His bony hand reached out for her.

"Zuela?" His bony hand found the back of her head and pulled her to him. "Zuela."

Thin lips fastened themselves to her mouth. "Zuela." Viper's teeth dug into her flesh and pried her lips apart. "Zuela."

Fingers worked their way down the neck of her blouse. Ragged claws scuttled across the bolts of her spine. "Zuela."

Down, down, the claws scratched her smooth flesh. Down, down, they scraped her naked buttocks.

"Zuela."

She struggled to escape.

"Zuela."

She reached for his neck.

"Lin me. Lin fa."
She dug her fingernails into his flesh.
He pinned her down.
"Zuela."

Zuela! Zuela! Zuela!
Zuela woke with a start.
Zuela! Zuela!
Next to her on the bed, Agnes was counting: seven hundred and one, seven hundred and two, seven hundred and three . . .
Zuela!
Next to her on the bed, Agnes was murmuring: seven hundred and four, seven hundred and five, seven hundred and six . . .
Zuela!
She had taught her daughter to count only to five hundred: Seven hundred and seven, seven hundred and eight, seven hundred and nine . . .
Her tiny body was curled into a tight ball like a fetus. Her eyes were glazed. Seven hundred and ten, seven hundred and eleven, seven hundred and twelve . . .
For thirty minutes longer with Tong Lee, she had allowed herself to believe that Agnes was safe, that the Chinaman could not harm her.
"No worse than for a female iguana." Agnes tried to soothe her.
But now Zuela was no longer a woman or a human. She was not a mother, either. She was a meteor responding to the pull of gravity.
Zuela! The ghosts shrieked her name again. *Zuela!* Their outrage pierced time, pierced consciousness. *Zuela!*
She would go down in flames if she had to.

At first the Chinaman thought he recognized her.
"Smoke," he whimpered when she stood over him. "Smoke." He beat the side of his bed and beckoned her. "Smoke."
She came closer to him.
Then he saw she was not the woman he had named after a country.

260

She was not Lin me or Lin fa, or what he had made of Lin me or Lin fa in the creation of Zuela. She was a woman he had never seen, a woman he had never known.

"Smoke." Fear relieved itself through habit. He said it again. "Smoke."

But the ghost of the woman from China, and the ghost of the daughter she conceived by a man who resurrected her in a woman he made his wife and his daughter, would not let him escape her. They would not let him take *smoke* and make a fog in his brain to elude her. They cleared a space in his mind and forced him to face her.

"Zuela!" His body crumpled against the wall. His nightmare had been made incarnate: It was she who stood before him, but she was also Lin me; she was also Lin fa. He twisted his head to avoid her, but the ghosts held him down. He shut his eyes, but they lifted his eyelids and fastened them to his brow.

He would look at her. They would force him to look at her.

She sprinkled the ganja on the milk-white paper, she flicked her pink tongue over the edges of the milk-white paper, she inhaled, she filled her cheeks with smoke like a blowfish.

He could not move.

She blew.

The women: the ghosts of the wife and the daughter tied up his hands.

She blew.

The women: the ghosts of the wife and the daughter closed off his nostrils.

She blew.

The women: the ghosts of the wife and the daughter pried open his mouth.

She blew.

Smoke can kill you.

She blew.

Smoke can kill you.

She blew.

Smoke can kill the Chinaman.

≪ Chapter 21 ≫

𝒯hat morning when Rosa left her house in Tacarigua for the last time, Cedric was not asleep as she thought he was. In that long torturous night that began when she said to him, *My father was as black as you,* not once had he shut his eyes. He had lain awake, tormented by the waste, by the futility of the years he had spent pursuing the restoration of his father's name. *She was not an Appleton; she was not even a white woman.* Then when the rising sun streaked a silver line along the edge of the horizon and he heard her muffled movements in the room below him, he began to fight his way through the darkness that had enshrouded him, the utter despair that had immobilized him, buoyed by the victory he seized out of his conviction that she was trying to conceal her departure from him. When the floorboards creaked, he was certain she was walking on tiptoes; when the front door key fell from her hand, he was sure it was nervousness that had made her drop it; when he heard the rapid patter of her feet down the front steps, he said it was fear of him that made her run. Yes, he told himself, she was afraid of him. And thinking that, he made himself believe the illusion that she was still one of Thomas Appleton's lily-white daughters, that he had cowed her, that he had terrified her.

He was in good spirits, therefore, when he woke up that morning, elated by his triumph over her. The waste would have been total if she had not pretended she was one of Thomas Appleton's daughters; if she had not been a willing participant in Thomas Appleton's sham, in his Judas bargain with his wife: *My silence for your silence.* The years he had spent tracking her would have been for nought if Thomas Appleton had not been a knowing accomplice in his wife's adultery: *She is my daughter if you say nothing of my nights in the cane fields.*

Nothing would have been worth it—not his escape from Cedros, not the hours he had spent learning Greek and Latin, not the baccalaureate degree he would get from London—if Rosa had not pretended she was a white woman. No, he was grateful she had let him think she was white. He was glad that though many times he had called her white lady, thrown those words in her face like a piece of raw fish, she had never set him right. Not once.

She had let him plot and plan her debasement. She cowered for him. She let him strip off her panties on the dining-room floor and demand that she beg. She let him have sex with her where he wanted, when he wanted, even when he said, *Now! I want to be fucked now!* She let him spread her soiled panties on the bed and send her foraging for more in the dirty clothes hamper. And when he pointed to the purple marks on her arms and legs and intimated she had been unfaithful (though he knew she knew he had made them during his rough sex with her), she allowed him to say: "No, no. Don't tell me how you got them." But later, when he sharpened his claws and pounced, when he was ready to finish her off, she let him know she was white. "No," she said to him the day her mother had humiliated him. "No. Never again."

So Cedric found solace that morning in her deception, in the memory of that time when she claimed her superiority as if she had gotten it legitimately. For though he told her no one would want her, he needed to believe that everyone would. Though he accused her of having a black lover, he needed to believe she would take on none. Though he did everything to force her to be submissive to him, to make her contrite for a sin she never committed except in his thoughts, he needed to know she would spurn him, that in the end she would stop him. So now, even after she told him she was not Thomas Appleton's daughter, Cedric was able to glean a victory that was no less satisfying, no less gratifying. She and her kind had used their skin color to declare themselves God's chosen, a people anointed by Him to rule the world, but he had made one of them bow to him—one who acted as if she were one of them. Appearance is all, he reminded himself. He had avenged a father by ruining a daughter.

And while there was light, the illusion of this victory sustained him. But night came and Rosa did not return. Then, surrounded by the darkness outside, his failure became visible again: the days he had squandered in her wasteland believing she was Thomas Appleton's daughter; the months and years he had lost plotting vengeance on a man already dead when he made his Pyrrhic crossing to the other side of the street on the Orange Grove estate and into Rosa's bed. Only one thought brought him relief from the overwhelming sense of futility that crushed him now. She would be back tonight. Monday, she had said. Monday, she would leave. He still had time, if not to redeem his father's name, at least to restore his dignity.

He bolted the inside lock on the front door so she could not open it with her key. He turned off all the lights. He would wait for her in the dark. He would sit still when she tried to use her key, when she knocked on the door, when she called out his name. Soon she would become desperate. *Then* he would tell her to beg. *Then* he would make her say never again would she say, *Never again.* Or, *Monday.*

But if Cedric could have foretold the future, he would not have waited for Rosa to return. He would have gone to Laventille to find her and bring her back home. For his very life depended on his willingness to lay down his vengeance now, to remember the timeless lessons of his youth: Hate can be its own destroyer. Luck smiles on few men more than twice. For even if he were not grateful, Dr. MacIver had rescued him from the operating table; for even if he did not believe, there were those who were certain Our Lady had given him a miracle.

But Cedric was obsessed with vengeance. Indeed, so intense was his thirst for it that when he heard a knock on the front door, not the futile turning of the lock that he had been waiting for, he managed to convince himself that Rosa had forgotten her key or had lost it. So he waited, calculating the minutes to her desperation. But after the third knock, he heard her footsteps retreating from the door. He slid to the window to see what she would do next, and then he knew it was not she. It was not Rosa. And afterward, he discovered that no matter how long he would have waited that night listening for sounds he hoped would escalate to points of desperation—to beg—he would hear nothing. For Rosa did not return. Not that night when thoughts of the unimaginable kept him awake: she had a lover. Not that morning when he heard another knock on the door at the precise moment when he was devastated by what he now believed was the truth—she had spent the night with her lover in Laventille.

He was still reeling under the starkness of those images when the woman with the wolf's mark pushed past him through the door he had opened for her.

"Where is she?"

He had never seen her before but he lied. He lied because only lying steadied his head. "Upstairs," he said. "In bed."

He saw the crust on her cheeks soften, her eyes lose the anxiety that was there when she entered the house, but in that tumult in his brain there was no space to consider why, only to notice that when he answered her, she breathed in slowly and lowered her body deep into an armchair. It was sufficient to unnerve him. He demanded that she tell him who she was.

She did not give him an answer. "Why you cut her up so?" she asked.

His temples throbbed with his anger at her insolence. He ordered her to leave.

She persisted. "Why you tear her to pieces?"

He said he did not know her.

"Why you can't love her?"

He said he would call the police.

"I frighten you so?"

He walked toward the telephone.

She laughed.

Her laughter confused him, intensified the throbbing in his head.

He put down the telephone receiver, reached deep in his throat and regained his composure. Did Rosa know her?

She smiled.

"What do you want? Why did you come here?"

Her face darkened. "Why you frighten her so?"

He asked her how did she know Rosa was afraid of him.

"She tell me."

"When?"

"She tell me when she come to see me."

"Mary Christophe?" *Rosa had gone to her for medicine for him.*

"Same one. I mind her from a baby. She tell me you have no heart."

He wouldn't let her frighten him. Rosa said it was Our Lady who made the miracle for him. It was not obeah. "When did she come to see you?" he asked her.

"She tell me you hard, hard as stone."

"When did she come?"

"She come."

"Yesterday? Last night?" Rosa had gone to her again, but not for cures to ease her conscience. For potions for her lover. He would not lose focus.

"Yesterday and last night," she said.

He kept his voice deep. "When did she leave?"

"I thought you tell me she sleeping upstairs."

"Yes. Yes."

"Then you know when she come home. She leave me just before that."

"When?" He would remember: *Nympho, Nymphomaniac, Nympha, Rosa.*

"She spend all day with me."

"When did she leave you?"

"She tell me about you and your hard heart."

"She has nothing to tell you."

"Why you can't love her?"

He would keep his mind on the facts: *Nympho. Nymphomaniac. Nympha. Rosa. A black lover in Laventille.*

"Answer me. When did she leave you?"

But even if she wanted to, the woman with the wolf's mark could not tell him. She had heard only the thud and the swish, and only in her dreams.

"Where did she go after that, after she left you?"

"You tell me she sleeping upstairs. Ask her."

"What did she tell you?"

"Call her. She tell you all you want to know."

"She needs to sleep. She came home late. After eleven."

"That's when she leave me. She leave me close to eleven."

"You're lying."

"It was dark. I don't always check the clock."

"When?" he asked again. "When did she leave you?"

She answered with a question. "When did she come back?"

The throbbing in his head was blinding him. "Get out!"

"She stay a long, long time with me. Past eight o'clock."

"You're lying." The drums beat faster in his head.

"Maybe past nine o'clock."

"You're trying to protect her."

"Protect her from what?"

"I know."

"You know?"

"I know about her black lover in Laventille."

"You hard."

"Yes."

"Like stone."

"Harder."

"What she do that make you so hard?"

He answered her before the drums could warn him. "It's what her father did."

The bark shifted on her face.

"It's what he did to my father."

"Bossman do something to all man father here."

"I said *my* father." He could not stop the whine that rose in his throat—the pathetic wailing of a boy, pleading. "I'm talking about *my* father."

"You making excuse."

"My father." The boy was insisting, begging her to understand. "Just because her father had power over him. Just because he gave him a job and a house."

The boy had tried, but no matter how many books he had memorized, no matter how long he had stared at the sky, he had not been able to shut out the question born months before the fire; born long before the women whispered maliciously: *Not any other woman either.* He had witnessed his father's humiliation. He had seen his father rush down the front steps when the dirt from Thomas Appleton's galloping horse rose above the incline on the road.

"He thought my father should be grateful. Should do anything for him."

"Yes, yes. I know why you hard on her." The bark on her face settled and spread across her cheeks.

He was conscious of what she was doing. He knew she was taking advantage of his whimper to claim the right to speak to him like a mother, but he could not quiet the boy, though the man was chewing the insides of his lip with his anger. "Made him feel like nothing. Made him feel like nobody until he wanted to die. Yes, it was her father that made my father drown."

"I understand."

"Her father."

"I feel sorry for you. Every day I see cockfighter like you on the hill . . . "

The pity in her voice gnawed at the man. He came closer to her. "Shut up!"

" . . . preening, preening."

"Tell me her lover's name or leave." The muscles on his temples twitched. He loomed over her but the boy was listening.

"Looking for prize cock only so you could knock him down. Flexing your muscles, but it don't matter."

The man fought to keep the boy from resurfacing. "His name!" he shouted.

"Is only when your cock knock down his cock you think you somebody. Only then you think you worthy. Yes, for that you could blame her father. Bossman treat man like mule, make all you feel inferior."

Even the boy saw the danger in the route she was taking him. It frightened him, so he let the man shout louder to her to keep his body from trembling. "His name!"

"Yes, all of you. Bossman beat you like mule and make you do what he want you to do. Make all of you feel inferior."

"Her lover's name!"

She looked up at him. "But you, particular man like you, you need something bigger to think you superior. You need woman like my Rosa, and you need to think woman like my Rosa have a lover even though you hoping with your life she don't have one."

The twitching on his temples had descended to his hands. He shoved them into his pocket.

"Because that way you know what you have is something good. Because is something somebody want."

The boy's whimper returned and trilled the strings of the man's vocal cords. He had to bite his lips to press the sound back.

"You need to think she have man so you have excuse to destroy her. Because man like you need to destroy woman like Rosa. Woman they think better than them. Worth more than them."

The man broke through the stranglehold on his throat. "I'm warning you."

"Is not only her white skin. Is whatever she have that make you think she superior."

"I'll call the police. I'm warning you."

"Man like you go looking for woman like my Rosa. That way when you break her up, you think you bigger, you stronger, you better."

He grabbed her arm to stop himself from falling, to stop her from pushing him down the abyss.

"Feeling bad afterward because you lose what you think make everybody think you a powerful man."

He tightened his grip.

"But is not enough for particular man like you to take woman like

Rosa for your pleasure. You have to marry her. You have to *own* her. You have to let everybody know law say is yours."

"Shut up!"

"You want to kill her if she give somebody what you think you own. What you think you pay for."

With all his strength he pulled her out of the chair.

"Don't worry, I leaving now. I say my say." She shook his hand off her arm. "But I tell you, if my head wasn't so full with worry for Rosa I could find it in my heart to feel sorry for you."

He couldn't help himself. Her pity disarmed him. It reached to the center of his vulnerability where he had given flesh to the specters that were haunting him. His head exploded.

"You feel sorry for me? Feel sorry for the man she spent the night with. Feel sorry for the man she screwed all night and all morning."

And when Cedric said that, the woman with the bark on her cheeks gasped and threw her hands over her face, but he did not know why. He thought it was because he had caught her, cornered her with the lies she had told to protect Rosa. He did not know of the thud and the swish. He did not know of the receding tide that had caused her to flinch in her sleep, turn on her side but not awaken until it was too late, too late to discover that Rosa was not in her bed, that she was not in the room. So when she sank into the armchair, he did not know that it was despair and grief that bent her knees and pushed her back down. He did not know that his threats were so insignificant to her now, that if he called the police, as he shouted to her again he would do if she did not get up, that it would not have mattered to her if they came at that moment. And later, when the police did come, though not for her, he could not have guessed that she would have thought that their arrival was not retribution enough for the thud and the swish that, to her sense of justice, he had caused to happen.

⋘ Chapter 22 ⋙

But Cedric had not caused the thud and the swish. Not directly. And the man who had, had little reason to cause it. That is, he had no score to settle with Rosa, except, perhaps, that his father, like Cedric's father, had been made a mule, as had the father who fathered his father. But there was nothing that Rosa or Thomas Appleton had done to him. Nothing personal that would have linked him to her. In fact, he hardly knew her. Until his friend pointed her out to him, he had not known she existed, though in the pigsty behind the shrine of Our Lady she had opened her eyes and looked at him as if she had seen him before.

"She was the one that come last time," his friend had said. "See, see, she come back again."

Even then he had not thought of harming her. Other matches had lit the fire raging in his head that morning. He had spent the night before with his brother, the ring giver. Sat with him as long as the guards would let him. Talked to him for hours in his damp limestone cell in Royal Gaol trying to convince him to tell what he knew about the lawyer in the Bentley. But nothing he said changed the ring giver's mind. He was determined to take the blame for Melda. He loved her, he said. He would die for her. Since she was gone, his life was worth nothing. He'd rather swing from the hangman's noose than keep on living.

He tried to use the point about Melda's children to turn the ring giver against her.

They were not his, the ring giver conceded, but still he loved them as if he were their father. "Somebody will watch them for me," he said. "People in Laventille always look out for children."

He told the ring giver that Melda was not worthy of him. She was a lecherous woman, a whore who sold her body to anyone who could pay. She bred babies like a stray bitch, he said.

The guards had to pry the ring giver off him. He almost strangled him with his iron chains. "Brother or no brother," he said. "No one calls her that."

He said the lawyer would get off scot-free if the ring giver insisted on his silence.

The ring giver laughed. "They always do," he said. "They know how to lie. See how Boysie cutting out hearts and his lawyer lying through his teeth to let him cut out more." His cynicism deepened. "Boysie is money in the bank for them. They make a killing when his horses win."

He said it wasn't right. The lawyer was the one who cut her up.

"He cut her up just because he wanted to hide her." The police had taught the ring giver about corpus delicti. *No body, no crime. No crime, no execution.* "They take their learning and use it against us. But he didn't have to do it so bad. He didn't have to chop her up in so many pieces. He didn't have to feed her to the pigs." His lips quivered. He was close to tears. "How she go resurrect on Judgment Day?"

The man said he couldn't just do nothing and see them execute his brother for no reason at all. He didn't say for Melda, though that was what he thought. He said, "It's not right for you just to waste your life like that when is not you who kill her. I can't just sit back and see them do that."

So while the man who said *Beg* in that pigsty behind the shrine of Our Lady, and the one Rosa remembered she had seen behind the hibiscus bush, quite possibly could have been one and the same man, it was equally possible that this man, the ring giver's brother, was not that man at all. For this man was too dazed by the grief for his brother to notice when the taxi stopped or when Rosa got out of it. Until his friend's resentment pricked his own, he was barely aware that Rosa was there. "See, see, she come back again," his friend said. "Last time we warn her not to come back."

It was only then that he noticed her, and when he did, the fire burning in his head consumed him. She was standing in front of a line of seven boys in tattered white undershirts, their fathers guarding them with eyes like bullets, and yet she was calm, self-assured, just like that lawyer was when he told his lies to the police: Yes, he had seen Melda before. He had clients in Laventille. He had seen her many times with the ring giver. Yes, since he had time to think about it, he was certain it was the ring giver he had seen her with.

Rosa, too, was not afraid of them. Did she think her white skin would protect her from them? They had warned her that Laventille was not safe for white people.

His friend stoked his anger. The word was out everywhere, he said, even in *The Guardian*. He showed him the clipping: *In summary, it is unlikely that Laventille will sit quiet and let an innocent man rot in jail, waiting for the moment when the ground will be swept from under him, while a man in a pinstripe suit wears the barrister's gray wig and feels himself safe in the halls of justice.*

Everybody knew Laventille was dangerous now for white people and rich people like that lawyer.

When the other men followed Rosa to the shrine, this man went with them. But he was not one of the ones who dragged her from her knees to the clearing where the priest had put the pigs. He was the patient one—the one who had waited, who had let them shove her deep into the mud with each thrust they made into her body, and when they were done, he was the one who took his turn last. Then she opened her eyes.

With no one else had she looked. With no one else had she let her eyes rove. With no one else had she bared the agony in her soul. With no one else had she uttered a sound.

"Mother." When he told her to beg, he thought that that was what she said.

His rage flared. "Mo-the-fuc-ker! I said beg for it!"

He struck her. Her rosary beads curled down her fingers and into the mud.

Afterward, he was not sure what made him come back for her. Was it because the woman with the wolf's mark cradled her in her arms as if Rosa were her daughter? Was it because when he saw the woman with the wolf's mark do that, he remembered his own mother? How many mornings had she left him and his brothers alone at home, though they cried bitterly for her, begging her to stay? But the babies in the valley were crying, too. She would get paid to cradle them.

Or did he come back for her because the men taunted him? "She didn't beg. She didn't beg."

Or did he return because when he struck her, her head rolled back on her neck and she lost all consciousness before he could spill his seed in her? His presence mattered. *He mattered.* He wanted her awake so she knew he mattered.

He did not leave with the other men. He hid behind the statue of Our Lady. He watched quietly when a woman gave a blanket to the woman with the wolf's mark. He saw that line of tears—the other women crying for her.

When they went down the hill, he followed them. When they stopped at the she-wolf's house, he waited. It took more than an hour for the men to pull the women away—they did not want to leave—but he stayed there waiting, watching the she-wolf. He saw her when she went to the backyard to pick the shining bush leaves. He saw her when she climbed the ladder to the top of the barrel to dip out the buckets of rainwater. He dug his fingernails into his hands to control his anger when she stumbled under the weight of the bucket she carried on her head and the other two she held in each hand. The old she-wolf was willing to be a beast of burden, a donkey for that white woman!

He crept to the window. She was washing her now, touching her gently as if she were a little china doll, a precious, helpless thing. Would she have kissed her, as she was doing now, if Rosa were one of the countless women who had been defiled on that hill, defiled not by the men on the hill, but by the men below the hill? Melda, whore though she was, had been chopped into tiny bits and fed to pigs. Did the she-wolf cry for her?

His outrage fanned the fire burning in his head and forced him to his knees. When the flames died down, he hoisted himself to the window again. This time the woman with the wolf's mark was stretched out on the floor next to the bed where the white woman lay. *Like a dog, an old faithful dog!* His fire roared. He made a plan for revenge—not a plan with a middle and an end, but a plan, nevertheless, though he only knew the beginning. He would salvage the she-wolf's pride for her, the pride of the innumerable black women who for two hundred years had been forced to sleep at the feet of their white masters.

He went back down the hill and borrowed his friend's car. He drove first to the pharmacy for a bottle of chloroform. That was for the white woman. For the she-wolf, too, if she woke up. Then he drove back to the she-wolf's house. There were no curtains on the bedroom window; he could see the two women were sound asleep in the room. He broke the lock on the front door. They did not stir when he entered the room. Still, he soaked a rag with chloroform and clamped it over the white woman's nose. Then he had to do the same thing to the she-wolf, because when the body of the white woman hit the floor with a thud, the she-wolf turned on her side, and when the white woman's nightgown made that swishing sound as he dragged her across the polished floor, the she-wolf's eyelids fluttered, and he had to shut them still to keep them from opening.

Minutes later in the car, the chloroform wore out and the white woman spoke. "Where are you taking me?"

He had not thought of where. The ravenous fire that was devouring his soul had demanded nothing else, only what he had already done. He had tied her hands in front of her waist and laid her down on the back seat of his car. "Shut up!" he shouted at her, but he didn't look back.

Still, she asked the question again. "Where?"

This time his answer silenced her. "Shut up! If you want to see tomorrow, shut the hell up."

Yet her question irritated him, made him feel foolish. Where? What next? What would he do now that he had the white woman in his car? His anger was toward her people and toward black men like that murdering lawyer who worshiped her people. The rage he had carried most of his life was directed toward the ones who lived one to five rooms and forced his people to live five to one. They were the ones he despised, the ones who kept their heels forever pressed into his back. What would he do now that he had one of them in his power? What could he do now that his mere thought could cause *her* destruction?

He drove past the La Basse where vultures slept, crouched low on heaps of garbage, their black feathers chiseled out in the diaphanous darkness. He raced past the stinking rum distilleries and fermenting mangrove swamps, past the sea of sugar cane fields that flowed on for miles. Still without a plan, he sped through towns and villages, heading south. Where was he going? What would he do when he got there? When he saw the lines of smoke, blacker than the night, belching from the metal stacks on top of the petroleum refineries, he panicked. He was approaching the end of the island. Just a few more towns and the road would end. Just a few more villages, and on this island no longer than an evening, he would come to the sea.

"How much farther?"

He felt her shadow on his back. Until now she had stayed down low on the back seat, lying the way he had placed her, her head below the door handles, her legs folded to her chest.

"Where are we going?"

He swung out his arm and struck her. His car careened across the road. He turned the steering wheel and brought it straight again. When he looked back, she was lying still, her eyes closed.

Thirty minutes passed. He let himself forget her in the silence of the night, in the mesmerizing perfume of the nocturnal flowers. The salt scent of the sea blowing onshore from the east filled his car. He found himself thinking again of his brother, remembering the happy times they had spent by the sea. They used to dive for copper coins tourists threw from their boats. They were the best. One day they made more than their father had earned in a week. "Monkeys on a string for white people." His father's voice echoed in his ears. He squeezed his eyes shut. She was crying now, whimpering like a child.

He shouted: "Enough!"

But she began to cry louder.

"Enough!" He turned and faced her for the first time.

She gasped. And then he saw it again—the same look in her eyes; the same shock of recognition, as if she had seen him before, not just that one time in the sty behind the shrine of Our Lady, but years before.

"You, you."

He wanted to put out her eyes, to shut her up. *Mother,* she had whispered, when he told her to beg. *Beg, say you want it now.* But she said *Mother* again and he had to crash his fist into her temple to quiet her.

Mo-the-fuck-er!

He twisted the steering wheel. The car skidded on a mat of wet leaves, ploughed into a line of coconut trees and came to a stop where the sea stretched out silky, silvery, serene, at the edge of a bamboo-strewn beach.

"The sea." She lurched forward and clutched the back of his seat. Her fingernails dug thin lines down the vinyl covering.

Mo-the-fucker! The end, the end, he had come to the end.

"Otahiti." Her voice broke before the tears.

He spun around to silence her but the raw terror in her eyes arrested him.

"Otahiti!" She was pointing to the beach in front of them. "Otahiti!" Her outstretched arm was trembling uncontrollably.

He did not understand.

"Freeman's Bay!"

Suddenly he saw in his mind's eye the image that terrified her. Suddenly, on the sand, between the bamboo reeds, imperceptible to the naked eye, he saw the brown burlap bag. He saw the human head protruding through the stranglehold of the cord tied at the top. It was the head of a white woman. Fish had gouged out her eyes, her lips and tongue.

Mo-the-fucker! Before he could conceive it, she had known the middle and end of his plan.

Mo-the-fucker! Before he could grasp it, she had led him to the diabolical perfection of his plan, to the dreadful symmetry between its beginning and its end.

"Mo-the-fucker!" He would have seen it eventually. He would have realized that it was no accident that he had first felt the full force of his anger when he visited his brother in his cell in Royal Gaol. It was no mere

277

coincidence that he had conceived the beginning of his plan when he noticed that the other man on Death Row was the Indian doctor who had slaughtered his white wife.

Mo-the-fucker! Always they demanded his awe.

No one in the Chinaman's shop paid much attention to the van from the mortuary when it stopped in Nelson Street. They saw when the men in white coats bearing an empty stretcher followed Zuela and her children to the backroom, but they were distracted that morning by the news they had heard about another murder at Freeman's Bay in Otahiti. True, there were some people who had paused briefly to shake Luck Chow's hand (he was already taking inventory, now the Chinaman was dead and the shop belonged to him), and there were others who were curious to know whether Luck Chow would put Zuela and her ten children out on the street or allow them to stay in the shop, but most of the people were listening to a man who seemed to know more than anyone else did about the murder in Otahiti.

Not so Tong Lee. He was waiting at the foot of the ladder for the men to lower the Chinaman's body from the attic. Early that morning Zuela had come to his house to tell him that the Chinaman was dead. He had asked her to blow smoke in his mouth, she said, but after she did that, he couldn't blow it out. Tong Lee went immediately with her back to the attic to get the box where the Chinaman had hidden his money. "I keep it in a safe in my house for you," he said. He knew that within hours Luck Chow would be there to claim his property.

Later, when he came back, he saw Zuela rocking Agnes back and forth in her arms. She was murmuring something about iguanas that he did not understand. She said she should have told her about the spikes on their backs, and about their eyes. "They have snake eyes," she said. "They look like lizard, but is snake eyes they have."

Alan said he knew that one day smoke would kill the Chinaman. He was smiling when he said that, but then in seconds his face fell. What was going to happen to them now that Luck Chow owned the shop? he asked Zuela. Tong Lee answered for her.

"You live in my house until your mother buy one for herself." He had counted the money the Chinaman had stashed away in his box. He knew there was enough.

How she do that? Alan wanted to know. So Tong Lee told him about his inheritance.

"I live with a friend until your mother buy a house. I don't interfere."

Tong Lee stayed with Zuela and her children until the men from the mortuary put the Chinaman's body in the van and clanged the door shut. But minutes after he left, the men returned, drawn back to the shop by the scent of rum and the clamor of voices they had heard earlier, speculating on the murder in Otahiti.

It was a copycat murder, a very officious-looking man, a retired magistrate, told them. He had lost his audience once he had given them his verdict, but like the Ancient Mariner, he needed to explain his conclusion again. The body washed up on the same beach—Freeman's Bay in Otahiti. She was the same kind of woman—a white woman, though not a true, true white woman. It was the same kind of murder—death before drowning. But this murderer was not as smart as the other one. He was no doctor who knew how to use a scalpel, disembowel a woman and stitch her up tight. He was not as cunning. He didn't walk into police headquarters the next morning to plant the seed of a defense of honor, like that doctor did with his talk about his wife going by herself to a conference in St. Vincent. This was a headmaster, a teacher, a man who knew the world only through books, not through real life. This was a man with no common sense, a man foolish enough to identify his wife in Colonial Hospital *after* he had accused her of poisoning him. "DesVignes née Appleton," he told the doctors.

His defense was that he had been in his study all night waiting for his wife to return home. "But he lied," the magistrate said. "A woman had come forward to say that she had knocked on his door around nine o'clock that night and no one answered. She wanted to tell him what had happened to his wife at the shrine at Laventille, but he was not home. Her husband corroborated her story. He said his wife knocked on the headmaster's front door three times. If he was home, he would have heard her."

The magistrate then told them that when Cedric saw he was trapped, he came up with a bogus story about his wife having a lover in Laventille. "He was trying one more time to copy the doctor, but it was too late for that. Scotland Yard figured him out."

The next day *The Guardian* reported that the police sergeant in charge of the case concluded that before the headmaster dumped his wife's body in the sea, he had twisted a rope around her neck and strangled her. The rope had cut so deep into her flesh that when her body was discovered among the bamboo reeds on the beach the next morning, there were huge black and blue marks on her neck where her blood had broken through her veins and clotted under her skin.

"It made a pattern on her neck like the petals on a flower," he said. "Like the petals of a hibiscus bruised blue."

≈ Chapter 23 ≈

Six months later, a woman with a butterfly on her face stood on the other side of the street across from a pretty blue house where red roses climbed a white trellis a few feet behind a white picket fence. The woman was not standing there because she was admiring the roses, though they were what had confirmed for her that she had come to the right place. Even from a distance of half a block, the bright red of the rose bushes shone through the greenery of fruit trees, dispersing the gloominess of the zinc-wrought chain fences wrapped around the tiny homes near Nelson Street. She had stopped in front of the house because she knew that that was where she would find Zuela. She had heard that the Chinese man who loved flowers had given her his house—loaned it to her while he was building her another. He had dug up the orange and pink bougainvillea that used to grow next to the picket fence and replaced them with rose bushes because Rosa was the first name of Zuela's best friend, and Zuela was the woman he adored.

For five minutes the woman with the butterfly on her face stood across the street breathing in the scent of the roses and warming her heart with the picture she had prayed to find. In the front yard, a balding Chinese man was sitting on his heels in the garden, flanked by two small children who clearly adored him. Each time the man dug a shallow hole with his shovel, one of the children placed a small plant in it and the other covered it with dirt. Each time they did that, the man patted them on their backs. From where the woman stood, the children's smiles were blinding.

Veiled by the sheer white curtains that covered the front windows, Zuela, too, had been looking at Tong Lee and her children, thanking God for her good luck, not just that morning, but the months before when Tong Lee opened his house to her and promised her marriage if she wanted it.

Tong Lee was planting a red hibiscus bush in the corner of the garden, near the chataigne tree. She had not had to explain to him why hibiscus. Why red. The minute she asked, he seemed to know. Like the constable, he had seen the red petals, turned blue, on Rosa's neck.

"Even flowers grieve for her," he said.

Hibiscus around the chataigne tree was the right memorial for Rosa. It was a hibiscus bush that had pulled them apart, a hibiscus bush that in the end had brought them together.

When Tong Lee had dug his last hole, he stood up and waved to Zuela. Then it was that she saw, beyond his hand, the woman in the stark white dress, her gnarled fingers pressed against her mouth.

After almost twenty years, still she recognized her. She could not forget the wings across her cheeks that had terrified Rosa's father; the lines he called the wolf's mark until Rosa thought so, too, though she cried her heart out when she was gone.

They embraced at the front gate. Zuela had wrapped her arms so tightly around her neck that Mary Christophe had to pry them off. "I not leaving, Daughter. I stay a while. I not leaving."

Tong Lee clutched the children's hands. "I have to go buy a spade in the store," he said to Zuela. "I take the children and come back soon."

Inside the house Zuela could not hold back the tears that fell down her cheeks.

"I remember Rosa all over again when I see you."

The butterfly on Mary Christophe's face spread its wings. "No tears. I come here to see you because they say you happy. I want to see with my two eyes. I want to make sure. I want to glory in your happiness."

"She ask me to let her stay with me. I don't let her." Zuela wiped her cheeks, but the tears still flowed.

"Is not your fault."

"She tell me he plan to kill her."

"Is not he who kill her."

"She tell me one day he do it for sure."

"He didn't kill her."

"She tell me . . . "

They were standing next to the dining-room table that had once so dazzled Zuela that she foolishly said to Tong Lee she could see why he did not need a woman. Mary Christophe trailed her fingers across its polished surface. "Beautiful," she murmured. She turned to the paintings on the wall: the portraits of a Chinese fisherman, one with his wife and son, and recent watercolors of Zuela alone and with her children. "Beautiful," she repeated.

"He paint me and the children," Zuela said. She was no longer crying.

"He paint you nice. He catch the happiness I see in your face. In your eyes."

"He's good to the children, too. He do everything to make them and me happy. He don't live here with us but he come every day to help. He fix the garden for me and he teach the children to grow flowers like he do. He make me happy."

"And the other children besides the two I see outside with him?"

"They in school, but they live here with me, too. Tong Lee let all of us live here till the house his friends building for us finish. Sit. Sit." She led Mary Christophe to an armchair in the living room. "Tell me about Rosa."

"I tell you one thing for sure—her husband did not kill her." Mary Christophe lowered her body slowly in the chair.

Zuela sat down opposite to her. "The police say he kill her."

"No. It's not he who kill her."

"But he's in jail."

"Yes."

"But you say . . . "

"No, is not he who kill her, but he deserve jail."

Zuela closed her eyes and leaned back on her chair. Yes, yes, it was possible. She was there among the crowd that day when they arrested Cedric. She saw the bewilderment on his face, heard the desperation in his voice when he pleaded innocence. How many times had she seen that same look, heard those same words? *Not me. Not me. I was not there. I was nowhere around.* Still the Chinaman punished one of her sons, one of her daughters for stealing the shilling or farthing he said was missing from his money box when he added up the sales for the day. And if she did not have doubt then of Cedric's guilt, she did when she spat on his face, and, without wiping off the spittle that rolled down his cheeks, he looked at her directly and said, "But it *wasn't* me."

No man who had murdered a woman could have faced the anger and hatred in her eyes and not burn with guilt. No such man could have held her eyes if he were not telling the truth.

"They say he sit every day in his cell just reading a book. They say he memorizing it. He read a little bit, then he look up at the ceiling and he start saying it by heart."

By heart. By heart. Zuela fought against the flood of pity rising in her.

"Like only his body in jail," said Mary Christophe. "His mind, like it far away."

"Far away?" She and Rosa were lying in a canal in the cane fields when they saw the boy sitting on the front steps of his house talking to the sky.

"Like he don't care." Mary Christophe shook her head. "Like he finish living. It don't matter to him if they hang him or not."

"No, it don't matter. He never was living anyhow."

"Maybe so, but he was living enough to try to break Rosa."

"Long time he dead inside," said Zuela. The memory was vivid now. The boy had kept his eyes on his book though his father had called out to him and waved. It was as if he did not want to see when his father mounted the horse, as if he knew his father would hug the Englishman's waist and the Englishman would stroke his hand with such tenderness, the movement of his fingers would seem like a kiss.

"He was not so dead he didn't try to take the life from Rosa."

"No," said Zuela. "He was not so dead."

"Yes, he tried to take his vengeance out on her."

Zuela was not sure what she meant, but she knew that for years she had plotted to make the Chinaman pay for stealing her childhood.

"He was not so dead that he didn't make life hell for her," said Mary Christophe.

She had not made life hell for the Chinaman. No matter what, she had not harmed him. Not until he forgot Agnes was his daughter.

"And she didn't do him nothing."

Zuela reached for her hand. "She loved you," she said.

Tears welled in the corners of Mary Christophe's eyes.

"She said when her mother went to England, you was a mother to her."

Mary Christophe's lips shaped a smile. "In the end he had no power over her. She had left him already. She had come to tell me so."

"You was a better mother to her than her mother was."

"Yes, in the end she free herself. His blows on her inside couldn't hurt her no more."

"She learn from you how to free herself."

Mary Christophe removed her hand from under Zuela's and covered it with her own. "Daughter," she said.

And though Zuela was aware that Mary Christophe was merely calling her by the name by which she had known her, her heart raced with happiness.

"Daughter," Mary Christophe repeated.

Her face glowed. It was the right name. In spite of what she had said to Tong Lee, it was the name she wanted, the name that named her rightly, the name her mother had chosen for her because she loved her. Its meaning got lost when the Chinaman translated it from Hija. It became obscene when he planted the seed of her daughter in her.

"I like how you call me," she said to Mary Christophe. "I like it better than Zuela."

The butterfly fluttered its wings on Mary Christophe's face. It seemed it would fly. "I see the purpose now," she said. "I see why I come here. Is to get back my Rosa. To finish being a mother to her by being a mother to you."

"Sister," Zuela whispered. Yes, that was what she had called Rosa in those days when they played in the cane fields, when they wore each other's dresses.

"Yes, you was sisters," said Mary Christophe. "I, the mother."

A large lizard scuttled up the trunk of the chataigne tree. Like in a dream, Zuela stopped it in its tracks with her eyes. It turned and looked at her. She stared back. Transfixed it. Unable to move, it blinked its heavy eyelids over its bulging eyes. An iguana. The spikes on its back collapsed on each other like a stack of cards. *A mother. A mother who could teach her that even the spikes on the back of an iguana could not hurt her if she owned herself.*

"Daughter." Mary Christophe squeezed her hand, and claimed her.

Yes, Daughter. Zuela sighed. She was a daughter again. She had found a mother. She loved a man who loved her. Her children were free of the Chinaman's prison. Soon she would have a house that was hers. She breathed in deeply and slowly let the air out of her lungs.

Author's Notes

All the events and characters in this novel are fictitious with the following exceptions:

On April 7, 1954, Dr. Dalip Singh, a Trinidadian physician, strangled his German wife, Paula Inge, removed her intestines, sutured her abdomen, ferried her body in a pirogue to the middle of the Gulf of Paria and dumped it there. The next morning her body floated up on the beach at Freeman's Bay in Otahiti. Dr. Singh's defense at his trial rested largely on his allegations that his wife had been having an affair. He was eventually hanged for her murder on July 28, 1955.

During the 1950s in Trinidad, Boysie Singh, a notorious gangster, reputedly cut out the hearts of young women to rub on the hooves of his racehorses in the belief that that would make them run faster. Though he was accused of several murders, he always managed to get acquitted until 1957, when he was hanged for the murder of his mistress, Thelma Haynes.

In the 1960s, two Trinidadian brothers in love with the same woman murdered her after a quarrel. They then hacked her body to bits and mixed it in the food they fed to their pigs. The brothers served time in jail and are currently on parole.

Finally, the events in Laventille described in this novel are loosely connected to the 1977 Black Power revolution in Trinidad, which pitted the working class against the middle- and upper-classes, and, inevitably, Trinidad's black population against its brown and white people.

About the Author

Elizabeth Nunez is the author of two previous novels, *When Rocks Dance* and *Beyond the Limbo Silence,* which won the Independent Press Award for Multicultural Fiction, as well as the co-editor of *Defining Ourselves: Black Writers in the 90s.* Her writing has appeared in the *New York Times Book Review, Essence,* the *Philadelphia Inquirer* and *Black Scholar,* among others. She is a professor of English and the director of the Black Writers Institute at Medgar Evers College, the City University of New York. Born in Trinidad, she now lives in Amityville, New York.

Selected Literature from Seal Press

Angel by Merle Collins. $12.95, 1-58005-014-X. A richly evocative and memorable novel, *Angel* centers on three generations of women during the Grenadian struggle to achieve political autonomy.

Another America by Barbara Kingsolver. $12.00, 1-58005-004-2. In a luminous book of poetry, Barbara Kingsolver offers a strong and clear vision of the complex strata of American life.

Beyond the Limbo Silence by Elizabeth Nunez. $12.95, 1-58005-013-1. A spellbinding novel tracing a young woman's journey from her Caribbean home to the United States during the civil rights struggle.

Blessed by Thunder: Memoir of a Cuban Girlhood, by Flor Fernandez Barrios. $22.95, 1-58005-021-2. In this compelling memoir, the author tells the story of her childhood during the Cuban revolution and the irrevocable changes it brings to her family.

If You Had a Family by Barbara Wilson. $12.00, 1-878067-82-6. This novel traces Cory Winter's journey as she comes to terms with the memories of her Christian Science childhood and experiences a transformative new relationship.

Nervous Conditions by Tsitsi Dangarembga. $12.00, 1-878067-77-X. Set in colonial Rhodesia in the 1960s, this is an evocative story of a girl's coming of age and a compelling portrayal of the devastating human loss involved in the colonization of one culture by another.

Nowle's Passing by Edith Forbes. $12.00, 1-878067-99-0. Rooted in the austere beauty of northern New England and masterfully portraying the subtlety and stoicism of its people, *Nowle's Passing* is the story of a woman who faces her exacting family legacy to discover her own life.

A Week Like Any Other: Novellas and Stories by Natalya Baranskaya, translated by Pieta Monks. With candor and satirical wit, Baranskaya captures perfectly the everyday realities of family and society in the former Soviet Union.

Where the Oceans Meet by Bhargavi C. Mandava. $12.00, 1-58005-000-X. A magical story that captures the lives of Indian and Indian-American women and girls, whose paths vividly intersect and gracefully glance off one another.

Seal Press publishes many books of fiction and nonfiction by women writers. If you are unable to obtain a Seal Press title from a bookstore or would like a free catalog of our books, please order from us directly by calling 800-754-0271. Visit our website at www.sealpress.com.